I0593134

Built for Sin

Kerrie Maxon

Built For Sin

Copyright © 2023 by Kerrie Maxon

Edited by Word Emporium – www.wordemporium.co.uk

First edition 2023

BUILT FOR SIN

Dedication

To Karma for giving me the push, literally, and lots of free time to get started on this journey.

ACKNOWLEDGMENTS

MY HUSBAND FOR HIS patience and putting up with an 'absent' wife while I am busy writing and for taking care of the housework and other chores so I don't have to. His love and support mean the world to me.

My daughters for listening to me prattle on for months, for your advice regarding aspects of the story, and for your faith in me. I am forever thankful that I have been blessed with you both as my gorgeous girls.

To my family and dear friends who I have confided in along this journey, thank you for your support and for enriching my life. To my dearest friend Rae, my soul sister, for pointing me in the direction of TL Swan's books and Facebook group, and for being an unwavering loving amazing friend.

To my beta readers Shani, Nicola, Patricia, Kirstie, Brandy and Stephanie for your constructive criticism in the early stages of writing.

To Sarah from Word Emporium for being my saviour, turning an awkward draft into a meaningful cohesive story. Thank you for your patience, wisdom and editing mastery. Without you, I wouldn't have gotten this far. www.wordemporium.co.uk

And to TL Swan, for your inspiration, generosity, guidance and mentorship via your Cygnets groups and video tutorials. And for keeping it real. Words can't describe my gratitude to you for providing the tools and encouragement and your Cygnet Inkers and Swan Squad networks that have allowed me to embark on this journey. **To my fellow Cygnet and Swan Squad colleagues** for your never ending support, advice and patience.

KERRIE MAXON

Without you all, this book wouldn't exist. Thank you for your support, advice and patience and everything else.

Contents

CHAPTER 1 - Gina

THE TALL, ATTRACTIVE MAN watches me race toward the hospital's elevator doors, as I focus on maneuvering my large suitcase. He holds the doors open for me as I trudge inside, puffing, dragging my luggage behind me.

"What floor?" His well-modulated voice is on the deep side, with just a hint of impatience as he stands with two coffees in his hand and a laptop bag slung over his shoulder.

"Oh, sorry. Five, please." Staring directly into his beautifully warm green eyes, I muster a bright smile, and thank him as the doors close. I hate that I seem dithery, but I had very little sleep on my flight, and my brain is not firing as well as normal.

"Same as me. Who are you visiting?" he asked, pressing the button.

"My grandfather. You?"

"My brother."

"Nothing too serious, I hope." I juggle my laptop bag, which is heavy on my shoulder, while checking my watch again. *Ouch*, my long hair catches under the strap. Sighing, I shift my head to release it.

He shakes his head but remains silent. Mid-thirties, in a smart light gray business suit that hugs his fit-looking body and speaks of expert tailoring. His tie is missing, and the top button of his shirt is open. He exudes an air of confidence. Sensing me watching him, he throws me a polite smile and nods before turning back to stare at the elevator doors. *Damn.* I feel myself blush, embarrassed at getting caught checking him out.

Thankfully, the elevator sounds as we reach our destination, and I sigh with relief that I don't have to continue the small talk.

He holds back, waiting for me to tote my cumbersome luggage out of the way.

"Thank you." I edge my mouth up in a half smile as I pass him. *Ooh, he smells good. I wonder if he is single.* I push the random thought aside and glance up and down the corridor, while he walks decisively to the right. Dismissing him from my mind, I seek out the nurse's station for directions to Grandfather's ward, then make my way to a nearby restroom to freshen up.

I am weary and sore from a long international flight, and impatient to see Grandfather who had only days ago undergone emergency surgery after a sudden heart attack. I have frantically crammed eight days of business into three once I learned of Grandfather's illness, and the flight home has been tedious and cramped, wedged between the window and a large, loud, smelly couple. Adding to my irritation, the taxi ride from the airport crawled through peak hour traffic.

Feeling more presentable after wiping my face and neck with a damp paper towel, I head toward Grandfather's ward, pausing in the doorway, noticing that the two beds in the small room are both empty. *Do I have the right room?* I step into the corridor to check again. *Yep, right room. Ok, maybe he is in the bathroom,* I consider, deciding to sit and wait.

Pulling my luggage over to the window side of the bed with Grandfather's name clearly written above it, I plop into a vinyl armchair. As I become aware of the sound of running water from the bathroom, I take a better look around the room while I wait.

The sheets on the other bed are rumpled, and the name Drakos is written above it. Two takeaway coffee cups are sitting on the hospital's overbed table, next to a laptop. *Mmm, the coffee smells good. I should have got some when I was downstairs.*

I turn my head to look at the view of a bustling car park from the window, then stand to straighten the sheets on Grandfather's bed. I notice his cell phone on the bedside table, and remember my own nearly flat phone battery. Retrieving it and the charger from my bag, I reach over to plug it into the wall socket and then sit to check it for messages.

"What do you think you're doing?" A deep, assertive male voice barks. Startled, I nearly drop the phone and manage to knock Grandfather's one onto the floor with my elbow. I quickly bend to pick it up, hoping I haven't broken it.

"What?" Gasping, I turn my puzzled wide eyed gaze toward the voice and am met with an ill-tempered-looking man who would be beautiful if his face wasn't scrunched in a stern scowl and covered in a three-day growth. With his almost black hair, wet and neatly brushed off his face, and piercing blue eyes, he gives off a bad-boy vibe that makes my skin prickle. His loose shorts and fitted t-shirt highlight his broad, sculpted upper body and strong muscular legs, but my eyes are drawn to his lower right leg, which is in a cast and bent up off the

3

ground. Supported on crutches and holding a toiletry bag at the handgrip, he glares at me.

"I asked what you are doing?" he demands, his words clipped. His hooded, assessing eyes are icy as they glower in my direction like I am a recalcitrant child caught with her hand in a cookie jar.

"Um, I'm charging my phone," I scoff and arch my eyebrows as I throw him a sideways mocking stare.

He hobbles the short distance to his bed as I am speaking, then turns and perches on the edge, while he drops the toiletry bag on the bedside table and rests the crutches against it.

"How dare you come in here to steal from others." He spits the words as he hoists his body further onto the bed and props his broken leg on some pillows. His surliness imitates the annoyance of a powerful animal confined in a cage.

"Whoa! Whoa! What do you mean?" I choke out the words, perplexed, shaking my head in shock, and barely able to contain my anger. "Hang on a minute. This is my grandfather's phone, the one you made me fucking drop on the floor," I stand and snarl, waving the phone in the air for him to see. "And this is MY fucking phone that I have just put on charge." I pick it up and wave it as well.

His eyes narrow, seemingly unimpressed by my explanation, then he spots my suitcase.

"What's with the case? Is that so you can transport all your stolen possessions?" His voice drips with condemnation.

"Oh, fuck off, you jerk," I hiss and plonk back onto the chair, focusing my attention back on Grandfather's phone..

"Ha! He affects me the same way most days." I jump at the voice I recognize from earlier as Elevator Man casually strolls

4

into the room and picks up a coffee cup. He moves to the window side of the bed and passes the other cup to the man in the bed who, I assume, is his brother.

"You piss me off every day," Mr. Scowly Face replies, deadpan, although his lips twitch at the corners when he glances at his brother, then takes a swig of coffee.

I look from one man to the other and notice Elevator Man's friendlier, more laid-back air. "This is your brother? I feel sorry for you."

Seeing the two of them together, I realize Mr. Scowly Face is more attractive than his brother, but seems a few years older. They are vaguely similar in appearance, their cheekbones, noses, and mouths underlining their familial relationship. However, the swarthy complexion and dark brown hair of the surly bedridden brother indicate he could be of Mediterranean descent, while the visiting brother is fairer in skin tone with light brown hair.

"Hoh. Epic burn, man," Elevator Man laughs at his brother. Neither man notices the hint of a smile that I quickly hide by dropping my head.

"Fuck off," Mr. Scowly Face utters before drinking more of his coffee. He glares at me before turning to Elevator Man and asking, obviously irritated, "Where the hell have you been, anyway?"

"Arranging a date with the cute nurse," he shares, grinning and winking. "What did you do to piss off the lady?" He nods his head in my direction.

"Ginnie! So good to see you, my love," my beloved grandfather beams as he is wheeled into the room. His eyes well up with delight, and I fondly smile at his nickname for me. With my attention solely on him, joy fills me to see how well he looks, so I am only vaguely aware that the other men have paused their conversation.

"Grandfather." I let out a sigh of relief, hugging him tightly as he stands to climb into his bed. I step back and take a good look at him; he has good color on his cheeks, but I also notice a slight air of frailty that I haven't seen before in this charming, proud, strong patriarch.

"Where have you been? Tell me how you are feeling." I hold his hand, relieved to finally be with him, his presence calming my anger with his fellow patient.

"I'm fine, child. Nothing to worry about. My operation fixed the blockage that caused my heart attack, and I'm already feeling so much better than I have for a while." Pausing, he pats my hand as he continues, "I had to have some scans done to ensure everything is working as it should."

Flicking his eyes past me to look at the men on the other side of the room, Grandfather comments loud enough for them to hear, "I see you have met Xander and Ethan." Both men halt their conversation, which must have restarted while I was focusing on Grandfather.

"Yes." A twinge of anger laces my voice as I try to ignore them. "I'd much rather talk about you, Grandfather." Then the sound of a deep chuckle coming from the other side of the room riles me some more.

I refuse to turn my head to look at them and, with determined interest, ask Grandfather about his operation, opening up about how much his heart attack had scared the family and I. Meals arrive as I update him on general details of my business trip, and during gaps in our conversation I hear the men opposite discussing a building project that is hitting obstacles. However, my focus remains on keeping Grandfather comfortable.

Suddenly my phone rings, interrupting us, so I unplug it and excuse myself, walking down the corridor back toward the elevators to answer the call from my brother.

"Hi Luke, what's happening?"

"Sis, I'm working on a job in the city, and need your expert opinion on the landscape aspect of the build. Have you got a minute?"

"Sure, but I can't chat for long because I am visiting Grandfather in hospital."

I listen intently as Luke quickly outlines his problem and proposed solution, querying whether it is the most viable option.

"Yep, that's the best way to approach that issue, Luke," then I remind him of a couple of potential problem areas and update him on Grandfather's progress before we say our goodbyes, promising to catch up soon.

I pause and stare at my phone, smiling, reflecting on how much I love my job, and that I have a personal network of experts to bounce ideas off because most of my close-knit family are involved in the building industry in one way or another. Grandfather, who was a master builder, grew and expanded a very successful business, with his sons and their children joining him, diversifying into luxury homes as well as commercial development and construction that is well-respected in the international market.

Meals are finished and cleared away by the time I get back to the room, and the men are engaged in animated conversation. I pause in the doorway, watching Grandfather, who is enthusiastically discussing aspects of a construction technique with Mr. Scowly Face and Elevator Man, both of whom seem genuinely interested in his point of view.

Surprised by their apparent camaraderie, I scan from Grandfather's side of the room to the previously snarly and reluctant conversationalist on the other side, then back again. Scowly Face now looks surprisingly less like a tiger about to pounce and devour its prey and more like one confidently roaming his territory.

This man reeks of successful businessman. I should know. I have met a lot of them in the course of my work. They usually wear expensive clothes and jewelry without flaunting it. They radiate self-assurance and calmness, are quick thinkers and decision makers who actively seek input from others. Just like Scowly Face. And Grandfather. At the sound of laughter, my head spins toward the brothers.

Oh, my goodness.

I almost melt at the rich, honeyed sound, and my stomach recovers quickly from its flip-flop reaction to that delicious laugh, but I am left confused as to why my body behaved in such a way. As my gaze darts between them, I am not even sure which brother it came from.

"Ah, there you are Ginnie," Grandfather enthuses, noticing me in the doorway. "We were just wondering where you had got to."

"We've been discussing some difficulties Xander and Ethan are having with a luxury hotel redevelopment. As you've been doing a lot of work in that area lately, I thought you might have something to contribute."

I inwardly smirk at Grandfather's insistence on my involvement, just as he often does in business meetings with his clients. I don't want to help Scowly Face with anything after accusing me of stealing but I know there is no way I am getting out of Grandfather's veiled demand, so I grit my teeth and plaster on a fake smile, then gather as much of my remaining professional demeanor as I can muster in my tired state, and turn toward the brothers.

"Xander. Ethan. It's nice to officially meet you both." I acknowledge them coolly (and with fake sincerity directed toward one of them) as I walk over and shake their hands, giving each a business card. Surprised by the tingling in my hand when it's clasped by the elder brother, I note absently that neither man looks at my card. Still not quite sure who is who, I hope I looked at the right brother when saying his name. "How can I help?"

"Firstly, I owe you an apology," Mr. Scowly Face states, his face unreadable and his tone indifferent. My anger toward him has subsided, but his earlier words still sting, and the lack of sincerity in his apology annoys me because it feels like he is apologizing just to get information out of me.

With difficulty, I decide to be the better person and nod, giving him a tight smile. "Accepted."

Elevator Man (whom I assume is Ethan because the name seems warmer and easygoing like his personality) picks up the lead and explains their difficulty, showing me some concept drawings on his laptop, while his brother sits tight-lipped, eyes cool and assessing as he watches me. *Scowly Face suits him so well.*

"Anything you would like to add, Xander?" Ethan asks, confirming that I had correctly guessed their identities. Xander shakes his head. He has his noncommittal business face on and seems to expect me to falter under his cold demeanor.

"Not yet. I'll wait to hear what Ginnie has to say first."

Ha. Little did he know. I have dealt with his type many times and I bristle at the tinge of condescension in his tone, as if he is skeptical of my experience.

You don't intimidate me, Mr. Scowly Face. So, taking a deep breath, I set out to prove to him that I know exactly what I am talking about.

My voice is calm, strong, and confident and I suggest subtle modifications to their concept, providing pros and cons and answering a couple of Ethan's questions, all while Xander silently scrutinizes my every move and expression. I can see by their looks that they are mulling over my ideas, and while Ethan seems impressed, Xander is much harder to read.

As I turn to walk back to Grandfather, Xander's deep-clipped voice sounds out. "If you're not an architect, what exactly are your credentials?"

I halt mid-stride, irked by his question. Fuming, I bite my tongue so I don't spit out the words I am thinking. *Really? Do you need a breakdown of my qualifications? Lots of people before you have tried to pigeonhole me without any success. So good luck with that, buddy.*

I look him squarely in the eyes, flattening my tone with an edge of boredom and reply, rote-fashion, trying not to sound pompous. "I'm a Landscape Architect. However, the role has many overlaps with other fields, and surprisingly, requires an understanding of architecture, building construction, lighting, color, furniture, and landscape design. Having worked with, and for, many architectural and landscaping firms, engineers, and other specialists across large and small projects, I can provide you with many referees if you need them." I raise my eyebrows and ask saccharine sweetly, "I hope they are sufficient credentials for you."

I note the flash of humor that quickly lights Xander's eyes before disappearing, as if he is pleased that his goad hit its mark. As I continue staring unblinkingly at him, I hear his brother snicker at my comeback and shoot him a shrewd glance before spinning on my heels, marching back to Grandfather, chiding myself for rising to his bait.

Grandfather's wink and look of pride, as well as the smile he is trying to hide, make me blush. He has seen me stand my ground before, usually with more vehemence than I have just displayed, and has been on the receiving end of it as well, so he is fully aware of my internal battle between self-assertion and professionalism. I love this man so much and give him a huge, beaming smile.

Out of nowhere, a wave of fatigue hits me hard, so I make my excuses, kiss Grandfather on the cheek, gather up my bags, and after bidding a brief cursory goodbye to the brothers, make my way home, pleased to be leaving Mr. Scowly Face behind.

During the cab ride, I reflect on the two men. Ethan seems likable enough, but certainly not a walkover. He seems to have a heart behind his strong, no-nonsense business façade. Xander, though, is steel through and through, and I get the impression that very few would ever know what he is thinking or feeling.

His preposterous allegations when we first met hit me like an incendiary bomb, prejudicing me against any niceties he may have, but aside from that, his smugness irritated me.

Even his apology had been superficial, I seethe at the recollection.

I have met many who bear similar superior attitudes, particularly in this last week, but none has irked me quite so much as he does. Something about him just gets under my skin, and I allowed my snarky remarks to slip through my normally polite, friendly persona.

Now, I am mentally and physically drained and feel like I could sleep for days. Finally, the cab pulls up outside my home. Relief fills me as I trudge indoors with my luggage. I send up a silent 'thank you' that my flat mates are out, and fall into bed without even changing or unpacking.

CHAPTER 2 - Gina

IN THE LAST FEW days, I have managed to catch up on sleep and feel relatively normal again. Usually, I would drive my van, but as all my work appointments are in the center of the city and very close timewise, I decide it will be far easier to Uber in and walk between meetings instead.

I take care in dressing this morning, not wanting to appear a disheveled, jetlagged, and exhausted mess like a few nights ago when I visited Grandfather. Choosing a figure-hugging black turtleneck, I team it with a black calf-length pencil skirt and knee-high black boots that complement my figure; I am pleased that I look neat and respectable. I grab a blazer that accentuates my hair's copper highlights as I run out the door to meet my Uber driver.

Staring out the window as I am driven through the bustling traffic to my first appointment, I am lost in thought. Despite my busy workload over the last few days, I have phoned Grandfather several times to see how he is, and am pleased that he seems stronger and brighter every day. But the calls also prompted thoughts of Xander and Ethan.

It wasn't just their redevelopment project and its possibilities that kept playing on my mind, but the sexiness of both men. *I might not like Xander very much, but he is a stunning male specimen. One who, for some reason, stirs up my normally calm emotions and rouses my body.*

Each has the looks and magnetism that draws the eye, but Xander oozes power and a 'don't mess with me' air. Ethan seems like he would be formidable, but be more approachable and a bit softer; more human, and real somehow. *Maybe it was his warm green eyes.*

Whilst traveling, I question why I felt I needed to look my best today. *It's not as if I am trying to impress the very hot Xander or anything. Yeah right! Mr. Scowly Face certainly didn't register any sort of interest in me last time, so why would he now?* my cynical side reminds me.

Although I resented his initial assumptions of me, I still can't quite understand why I feel drawn to him, but know myself well enough to acknowledge that I have dressed to impress him—hoping to see him at the hospital later—which is unusual. *Is it his air of domineering untouchability that attracts me like a moth to a flame? Or is it simply that I haven't felt such an immediate attraction to a man for several years? In fact, since I met my ex-fiance?* Realizing we are at my destination, my introspection stops as I ready myself for my meeting.

After a hectic day, the hospital room is an oasis of secluded calm, but I am stung by disappointment at seeing a freshly made bed with no sign of Xander. I give Grandfather a huge warm hug as I drop my bag on the chair next to his bed.

"No roommate anymore?"

"No, he had his surgery the day before yesterday and was out of here this morning," Grandfather responds with a wry smile, acknowledging my quickly masked disappointment.

Not much gets past him, and he is still as sharp as a tack despite his age.

"What have you been up to today? Any word yet on when you can come home?" I deliberately push the brothers out of my mind.

"Yes, tomorrow."

Grandfather seems as happy with that news as I am, and we chat idly as I outline some new plans I have and ask his opinion on a couple of points. Soon visiting hours are over and I wearily make my way downstairs to get a taxi home.

Relief floods through me as I walk in to see my social butterfly flat mate Hayden has cooked and is having a quiet night in with his boyfriend, Kurt, making me thankful that he isn't hosting one of his spur of the moment get togethers.

Hayden, who's a chef, could whip up a simple, yet amazing, meal in no time, many times with plenty of leftovers for late-comers. *My cooking abilities had certainly improved under his guidance.* I chuckle as I quickly change into track pants and a t-shirt, while the teriyaki chicken with zucchini noodles is heating.

After eating and washing up, I reluctantly tackle the several hours of notes I had to write up. Fortunately, my office is adjacent to home, so I can also head there if I need a bit of quiet. The converted warehouse I live in is on a corner plot, where my office at the rear of the building is accessible to my staff and clients from one street, while my apartment and undercover parking are accessible from the adjoining street.

Living close to the city suits me, as it provides easy access to corporate offices in the business district, development projects around the city, and I am close to family members, who are all about half an hour's drive away in various directions.

Grrr. That damn alarm. Grumbling, I roll over and hit it hard to turn it off, realizing it has interrupted a dream I was having. *What a strange dream.* I had been staring into the warm green eyes of a noble Great Dane; proud, trustworthy, loyal but not to be messed with, which morphed into the cold piercing blue stare of a black wolf; unpredictable, predatory, and ready to attack. Feeling unsettled, I shake my head to clear the images, and get on with yet another hectic day.

CHAPTER 3 - Gina

A FEW WEEKS LATER, Tash, my PA, interrupts me. "Sorry Georgie, I know you hate being interrupted when you're in creative mode, but Robert Mitchell from MJA Architects insists on talking with you about a project he is working on."

Really? The head of one of the biggest, most prestigious international architect companies is insisting on talking with me?

"Thanks, Tash. Put him through, please."

Sucking in a deep breath to calm my apprehension, I pick up the phone on my desk. "Hi, Mr. Mitchell. This is Georgie Colby. How can I help you?"

As I listen intently, he explains that his firm was contracted to design and project manage a major commercial redevelopment.

"My client has asked for your company to submit some concept drawings after hearing some good things about your work," he clarifies, his tone eloquent.

"I'd be very happy to, Mr. Mitchell." My mind is scrambling trying to decide which plans to send to him. "Can I ask the name of the client who referred me?"

He declines telling me the client's name, so I gather a few more specifics about the project and then arrange a briefing meeting in a few days.

How strange was that? My pointer finger plays with my bottom lip, and I ponder the entire exchange as I hang up the phone. *Oh, well. Business comes from strange places sometimes.* I shake my head and make a few notes and reminders in my diary, then phone Grandfather to check in on him. I also ring my brother to get some insight on Robert Mitchell's architecture firm so I know who I might be working with.

Several days later, I am sitting in a café preparing for my meeting with Robert Mitchell. My long, shiny, light chestnut hair is tied neatly in a bun, and my makeup is light and natural. My navy pants and a matching blazer, teamed with a lightweight patterned shirt in yellow and teal, add to my confidence. I always like to dress for the occasion and today I feel poised and prepared. Aware of admiring glances from several men as they pass my table, I choose to focus on my notes rather than pay them any attention.

Armed with the positive information my brother has provided about Mr. Mitchell's firm, I feel ready to tackle anything he may throw at me. I finish my mediocre coffee and close my laptop, mentally checking off all the collateral I have if needed, before heading across the street to a very swish, modern building.

The light airiness of the office strikes me as I step out of the elevator and pause to study the pleasing décor with interest. The space is beautiful and very contemporary; the partitions are glass, partially frosted for privacy, and there is lots of greenery, brightly colored furniture and feature panels are scattered throughout to complement and contrast the space.

Hmm, nice. It has a good vibe. Functional but modern and aesthetically pleasing.

"Hi. Georgie Colby to see Robert Mitchell, please," I greet the receptionist.

The smartly dressed woman smiles politely and leads me to a conference room not far down the hall, then knocks on the door, opening it and poking her head around the door to announce my arrival. Rich, deep tones of laughter emanate from the room and send a tingle through me, pooling in my core, as I wait to be let in.

Whoa. That laugh would surely get many women into bed. Why does it feel vaguely familiar, though?

Blinking quickly to compose myself as the receptionist steps aside, I smile politely as the door opens wider, and I am greeted by a tall, stocky, smartly dressed, older man with white-gray hair. His physical size blocks my view of the room, and his warm, welcoming smile reminds me of my father. *I wonder if he is a big marshmallow like Dad too.*

"Oh hello. Robert Mitchell." He introduces himself, his blue eyes friendly but obviously surprised. "I wasn't sure whether to expect Georgie or George," he queried. I was used to this look. All my new clients and prospects usually had it at the first meeting, made all the more confusing by my business card. I make a mental note to replace the old cards in my purse with my new ones.

With a warm smile, I shake his extended hand. "Yes, that's me. George E Colby, but please call me Georgie," deliberately pausing between George and E but running the syllables to-gether for Georgie. With a quick nod of his head and a slight twitch of his lips, he steps aside to allow me to move to the table, but my steps falter when met with two sets of eyes that had been in my dreams recently.

"Georgie, I believe you have already met Xander Drakos and Ethan Wiggins from Drake Enterprises." Both men stand as they are introduced but stay behind the table as I move toward them and shake their hands.

"Yes. Ethan, Xander. Nice to see you both again." I nod and give them a polite smile, while wondering about why they had different surnames when they are brothers. Their tailored gray suits, expensive and stylish, fit them both like a glove. Xander's suit is darker than Ethan's and both are wearing crisp white shirts and coordinated ties. *Wow.* My stomach lurches, my heart rate races, and my mouth drops, gaping, as I openly stare at these gorgeous men. They are truly stunning, and I momentarily lose my focus. Hoping to mask my reaction, I blink quickly and take a deep breath.

"Xander, how is your leg now?"

"Not as far advanced as I would like." Leaning against the table while he stands, Xander responds politely, sounding almost evasive, as I settle my belongings on the table.

"Why so many variations of your name, Georgie?" Xander probes as he sits back down, his gaze watchful and assessing, as if he is looking for some sort of chink in my armor.

I give him a lopsided grin and look him directly in the eyes.

"Hmph. I get asked that a lot, as you can imagine. My name is officially Georgina, but my family calls me Gina, or Ginnie, while friends and colleagues call me Georgie or George and sometimes Gina. When I started my own business, I wanted to pay homage to my grandfather, George Colby, and came up with the marketing strategy of separating the E sound in my name." Pausing briefly, and to soften my lengthy explanation, and in a self-derisive manner, I add, "The downside of that is, of course, that people expect me to be a man."

With a swift glance at Ethan, I see him nodding slightly and hiding a twitch of his lips behind his professional facade, although his eyes sparkle with amusement. Xander merely raises an eyebrow, as if questioning my business sense.

"Okay then. Let's get underway. Please help yourselves to the refreshments over there if you wish." Robert points in the direction of a table against the nearby wall with beverages and pastries, then continues, "Georgie, for your benefit, our previously appointed landscape architect died unexpectedly, and my team is not able to carry out the work due to other commitments. So, when Xander and Ethan heard your ideas in the hospital, they wanted to see how you might be able to adapt the previous plans. We need to discuss some scoping, approaches, and concept ideas for the redevelopment, as well as your availability."

The men field lots of questions that I answer with ease, offering practical solutions as they pore over the existing designs. I elaborate further on points we discussed in the hospital and provide counterarguments for some of Robert's ideas. I also present photos of my work on similar projects and how I see the built environment and the landscaping working seamlessly together.

Several times, Ethan stands to pour a cup of strong black coffee for Xander and himself. I follow his lead at one point and pour myself a cup while the men discuss a point that doesn't relate to my work. *Hmm, it's odd that Xander only calls me Georgina, pronouncing it as if it is a caress while the other men refer to me as Georgie. Also very odd that it makes my tummy flutter because it sounds so good.* While it should

21

irritate me, I enjoy the sound of my name on his lips but I make a deliberate effort to not react when he next calls me Georgina because I don't want to give him the satisfaction of seeing the effect he has on me.

An hour and a half later, Robert finally concludes the meeting. As we all stand and gather our belongings, Xander is cautious as he moves. *I wonder if his leg still hurts.*

I know I am good at my job, but sometimes it is hard going in a male-dominated environment, so I am feeling proud that the meeting appears to have gone so well as I shake hands with each of them.

When I take Xander's hand, our touch seems to linger longer than it has with the others, and the look of respect from him makes me stand taller. I feel my cheeks warm and ask myself why his opinion of me matters so much.

Reluctantly releasing his hand, which surprisingly still tingles from his touch, I slip on my blazer, pick up my laptop bag and move toward the door with Robert as he mentions they will be in touch. Turning back to say a final thank you and goodbye, surprise strikes me as I see Xander walking with crutches under his arms and his laptop bag slung over his suit jacket, while Ethan walks beside him. *Wow, that injury must have been worse than I realized. It's been several weeks since I last saw him, so no wonder he said it isn't progressing as well as he would like. A man as dynamic and fit as Xander would be very frustrated with his mobility limitations.* I feel sympathetic for his situation, having seen my brother go through a similar scenario.

"Would you like me to hold the lift for you?" I am trying to hide my unusually topsy turvy emotions over Xander and be polite, but Xander's lips tighten slightly at my question.

"No thanks," Xander clips back.

"Yes, thank you." Ethan gives his brother a side glance, and continues, "We will meet you there in a minute."

I nod in acknowledgment and smile at Robert as I stride confidently, hips swaying, out of the conference room toward the elevator.

The elevator doors open before Xander and Ethan are out of the meeting room, so I stand against the opening, holding the doors, mentally preparing my to-do list and checking my watch as I wait. Hearing their voices, I turn and watch Xander as he moves far better and faster on crutches than I expected, but from the little I know of the man, I suspect he would excel at everything he did. *Hmm, I wonder what else he might excel at? If his media saturated playboy image is to be believed, he would be exceptionally skilled at lovemaking.* An embarrassing, wayward image of his hands on my body suddenly pops into my head and warmth spreads over me.

I clear my throat and try to pull myself together as they finally step into the elevator, pressing the button for the ground floor.

"How much longer before you're weight-bearing, Xander?"

Being this close to both men is nerve-wracking, making me short of breath, so I evade eye contact as we descend. At least there was a table between us in the meeting, but I am finding that so much time in their dominating presence is making me want to escape and regroup.

"Another week before I switch to a boot, then physio for about six weeks while my leg gets used to walking again," Xander answers disinterestedly, as if bored by the question.

"Hmm, that's no good. My brother was in a similar situation a while back, so I fully understand your frustration. How are you managing at home?" I stare at the elevator doors as I try to ignore his tone.

"Are you offering your assistance, Georgina?" his voice purrs seductively, as is his expression.

My head spins, my gaze locking on his, surprised by the tongue-in-cheek comment. As I look wide-eyed at him, startled, I catch a glint in his eyes and a smirk on his lips. My body pools with heat as I stand open mouthed, staring at him, speechless. His hypnotic charm is mesmerizing, and I am rattled that just one small question makes my body dissolve. *Geez, I'd be a goner if ever he decides to apply the full force of it.* Glancing at Ethan is no better, as he is wearing a similar expression. He clears his throat as if to stop himself chuckling.

"No, not at all." I stammer breathlessly, blushing, as I try to recover my composure by staring at the elevator doors again, willing them to open. "I just know from my brother's experience how hard things were without help and, even though he's as stubborn as a mule, even he had to ask for help from his flat mates."

Thankfully, the elevator doors open, and I stand back to hold them as the men exit, but I am confused by the quizzical look Xander gives me as he passes.

"So true," Xander acknowledges. "Fortunately, Ethan and my sister are helping a lot." He continues, sounding almost warm and friendly, "How is your grandfather, Georgina?"

I'm sure he's deliberately using my full first name just to rile me. Irritated, I pull a long breath in and hold it for a moment as we continue walking toward the street. I give him an obligatory smile and control my voice in a conciliatory tone.

"He's doing well, thanks. Happy to be home, but not resting as much as we would like." Ethan and Xander pause on the sidewalk to wait for their driver, so I put an end to our small talk.

"Well, gentlemen, it was nice to meet you again. You have my contact details if you have any further questions." Xander, balancing on his crutches, and Ethan extend their hands, which I shake before turning, strutting in the opposite direction, and disappearing, feeling both sets of eyes on me as I leave.

Once out of their sight, I slow my gait and hail a taxi, unable to stop thinking about how intense my interactions with Xander and Ethan were. My heart is racing, and I feel exhausted from the impact of those powerful brothers, unsure as to why they have such a physical effect on me. Individually, they are impressive and dynamic, but together they are mind-blowing. It took everything I had to keep my wits about me, to remain cool, calm, professional, and outwardly unaffected by them. Right now, I am a melting pot of emotions, proud that I have earned their respect, but equally irritated by my schoolgirl-like reaction to Xander's sexual innuendo, and annoyed at the resulting desire building between my legs.

***

"Well, how did it go?" Tash asks eagerly as I step back into the reception area of my office a short while later.

"I'll make us both a coffee and tell you all about it." Calmly, I place my laptop on my office desk and move to the kitchenette. Tash is sitting impatiently at the small, round meeting table in the corner of my office when I return.

"Well? Spill. I want all the gory details."

I chuckle at Tash's insistence. We have been friends for a long time, have weathered many a personal storm together, and frequently vent to each other over life's conundrums. Tash's forthrightness and candor both frustrate and amuse me, but I couldn't get through life without her.

"Well, you remember the two brothers I told you about that I met when Grandfather was in the hospital?" I pass Tash her coffee, then take a seat behind my desk.

"The really hot ones?" Tash questions.

"Yes..."

"No way!" Tash gushes in disbelief.

"Yes. They are the clients that Robert Mitchell wanted me to meet with."

"Both of them? Together? Whoa!" Shock widens Tash's amber eyes as she stares at me.

I grin and nod. "Robert is very nice. He reminded me a bit of my grandfather. You should see his offices. So light, airy, and modern."

"And?" Tash exclaims, raising her brows and stretching out her hands, palms upturned. I laugh and roll my eyes at Tash's impatience.

"Well, if you stop interrupting me, Tash, I'll tell you." I deliberately pause to tease her, then share the information I'd learned about the brothers in the meeting. "You've heard of Drake Enterprises? Xander Drakos, the one with the broken leg, is the CEO, and his brother, Ethan, is the Chief Property Manager." I sip my coffee while Tash waits eagerly for more

BUILT FOR SIN

information. "Both seem to be smart, personable, intelligent and charming, but neither are walk-overs. "

"So, what happened?" Tash interrupts excitedly.

I take another sip of coffee before answering, laughing at Tash's eagerness. "We discussed the previous designs. Sadly, the designer passed away, so they are considering other designers to take over. It was more of a brainstorming session to determine our scope and availability, really. Their vision for the project is amazing, Tash."

Excited about the prospect of being involved in the project, I stand and pace. "They seem impressed with the images from similar projects that we've done, but this will be on a *much* larger scale. They really like the idea of the indoor waterfall in the foyer that uses recycled water from the garden beds. All I need to do now is adapt the original concept plans and incorporate aspects we discussed today. So, I'm hopeful we'll win the contract."

"Great. Is that it? You seem excited about a new project, but what aren't you telling me? What about the brothers?"

Silently cursing Tash for seeing through me and needing to know every detail, I shrug and turn my attention to my coffee. "I am excited at the possibility of potentially working on this project, Tash, but there isn't much point getting carried away until we know it is ours. How many times have we seen that happen before?"

Pausing, I let my mind run back to the brothers. "I'm just not sure how I feel about Xander. He asked me about the variations of my name, then continued to call me Georgina after I specifically asked them to call me Georgie. He grilled me on several occasions, which even Ethan seemed surprised about. I know he was just trying to unsettle me and see how

I reacted, but it was a struggle at times to bite my tongue and stay professional."

I let out a sigh and perch on the edge of my desk, watching Tash's enthralled face.

"Xander's leg is still in a cast, and he is getting around on crutches, so I mentioned Ryan's broken leg, and asked how he was managing at home. Guess what he said?" I sit back down at the round table and lean towards Tash, who raises her eyebrows and shrugs.

"He asked if I was offering my assistance and he had this smirk on his face." My cheeks flush with the memory. "The annoying thing is, I'm not sure if he was flirting or trying to rattle me, Tash, but I know that it flustered me, and he knew it."

Tash lifts her coffee mug to her lips, obviously trying to hide a smile that I chose to ignore.

"And Ethan was also smirking, but I think that was more at the exchange between the Xander and I." I pause and tuck my hair behind my ear. "Then, as we were walking out of the building, he asked about how Grandfather was, like he wanted to keep the conversation going."

My brow creases and, with elbows on the table, I wrap both hands around my cup and hold it in front of me. "I don't know, Tash. I am so confused. I know he was playing mind games, but there's something about Xander that unsettles me."

"What about Ethan? Do you feel the same around him?" Tash queries, and her brow furrows.

I pause in reflection, then admit my feelings. "I quite like Ethan. He is witty, not afraid to poke fun at his brother, and you would always know where you stood with him. Whereas Xander is an enigma and seems to like keeping everyone on their toes. Even Robert Mitchell seemed to defer to Xander, despite them appearing to be good friends."

"Hmm, interesting," Tash comments, thoughtfully. "So, what next?"

Finishing my coffee and pausing again in reflection, I slip back into work mode. "Well, not much point worrying about it until we know if we get the contract. And if we do, then hopefully we will be dealing predominantly with Ethan."

***

The day flew past and before I knew it, an alarm on my phone reminds me it is time to get ready for dinner with my youngest brother at Hayden's restaurant. Quickly locking up the office and running across the courtyard, I have just enough time to change before my Uber driver arrives. Usually, I would take either my motorbike or work van, but parking was abysmal near the restaurant, even for a motorcycle. Besides, it was difficult to look dressy and lug all the bike gear around.

Hayden is having another busy night, and the restaurant is packed. It is proving to be a popular hang-out because the food is amazing and the atmosphere warm and lively. Several well-known faces are dining in tonight, which is becoming common.

"Hi, Tony. How are you going? Wow, busy night." I know the older, good-looking maître d' well through my relationship with Hayden, and we usually have a bit of a chat. "I have a table booked for two. Is my brother here yet?" I look around the crowded room for him, to no avail.

"Georgie, great to see you again. Yes, another busy night. I haven't seen your brother yet, but Monica will take you to your table and take your drinks order while you wait," he responds with a warm smile, hurrying me along as a large group arrives behind me.

"Ok, thanks. I'll catch you later."

While I sit at the table keeping an eye on the entrance for my brother, I watch the eclectic mix of people with interest; some casually dressed, others dressed up in smart suits and fancy frocks.

My drink arrives just as my brother does, and I notice as he walks into the restaurant that the limp from his previously broken leg is almost non-existent now. I stand, providing Ryan with a loving smile and a huge, warm hug, pressing a kiss to his cheek, realizing it has been way too long since we last saw each other.

"Hey, sis, what have you been up to? Has anybody been giving you a hard time?" Ryan offers his standard greeting, and I roll my eyes at him. He, and our brothers Luke, Tyler, and Zack, have always kept an eye out for me, being the only daughter, and are annoyingly overprotective.

Taller than me, Ryan curls his lean body into the chair as I sit down across from him. Ryan is his usual laid back self, and we spend the next couple of hours laughing and teasing each other, catching up with what has been happening in our lives and work.

As we finish our meal, I am chuckling at a predicament Ryan has narrowly managed to escape when I glance up and see Xander approaching our table, followed by an extremely attractive, petite brunette. His flirty remark from earlier in the day pops into my head, and I feel like hiding under the table, so I whisper a silent prayer that he keeps walking past but, of course, he doesn't. *Just like him to deliberately irritate me.*

"Georgina. Lovely to see you again," Xander greets me good-naturedly, his eyes scanning me appreciatively, before giving me a warm smile and glancing toward my brother, assessing him shrewdly. The cool businessman I am used to seeing seems more affable somehow, but I still detect a glint of challenge in his eyes.

Tonight, he is dressed in dark gray trousers, and a black long-sleeved shirt, with the cuffs rolled up showing his tanned, corded forearms and expensive looking watch. The shirt, hugging his broad defined torso, is unbuttoned at the top, exposing glimpses of his smooth chest. I feel my tummy flutter, my mouth salivate, and my eyes drink him in, as my tongue makes a subtle swipe across my lips. *Whoa, he was hot!* Looking equally as impressive as he did this morning in his full business suit, this more casually dressed Xander exudes a magnetism that yells 'player'. Alarm bells began clamoring in my head, warning me off this man. If only my traitorous body would listen, because it is tingling from the air of sexiness that surrounds him.

"Hello, Xander. Fancy seeing you here." I fervently hope he hasn't noticed the blush I am sure is spreading across my cheeks. "This is my brother, Ryan. Ryan, meet Xander. And..." I smile toward the attractive, dark-haired lady standing next to Xander, curious as the woman's eyes run appreciatively over Ryan. As I glance between them, I hear the other woman sharply inhale and notice Ryan's eyes flare with attraction as he stares at her with a wolfish grin. Xander also seems to be assessing Ryan closely, his eyes narrowing and lips tightening, as if trying to work out our relationship, or maybe giving Ryan an unspoken warning to stay away from his date.

"My apologies," Xander eventually replies with a smirk as he nods his head slightly. "This is my sister, Louisa. We won't keep you, though. We are just leaving." Xander glares at Ryan one last time before they turn and make their way to the exit. Ryan swivels in his seat, watching Louisa, who turns her head to smile back at him, as she walks gracefully alongside her brother.

"Whoa, who was that?" Ryan queries, his eyes still firmly fixed on Louisa. I know he has had a raft of girlfriends over the years, but I have never seen him so smitten before and he'd never reacted quite so openly.

"Impressive, huh? Settle down there, Tiger. I can see Louisa rings your bells, Ryan, but it is not like you to openly drool," I tease, trying to hold back a chuckle. "Xander is the potential client I told you I met today."

He tilts his brow. "Huh, you should talk, sis. I saw you blushing like a school kid as soon as you laid eyes on him. And he was giving me the warning look about you. Do you reckon we should double date?" he laughs, delighting in teasing me. My family give as good as they get when ribbing each other and the banter when they are all together is hilarious.

"Idiot. I thought he was warning you to stay away from his sister." As we stand and pay, I can't help but think about Ryan's comment. *Had Xander really been focusing intently on me? Why?* I push the thought to the back of my mind, as I hug Ryan goodbye.

CHAPTER 4 – Gina

AT THE END OF the following week, Robert calls to let me know that I am successful in securing the work and we promptly sign contracts. I am thrilled and take my whole team and a few of my regular contractors out for a good night of celebration and catch-up.

After numerous emails, phone calls, and concept plan amendments between myself and Robert, I am finally able to arrange a site visit with him so I can get a visual of how both the built form and landscape aspects of the project fit together. Work had already commenced on the refurbishment of the hotel's exterior, so my team need to start the foundation work for the landscaping as soon as possible.

"Tash, I'm heading off to the hotel's site visit and will be gone most of the day. Call me if you need anything," I call out as I head to the back of the office to make my way across the courtyard. Quickly, I braid my long ponytail and don my motorcycle helmet, jacket, and gloves before driving out onto the street for my appointment. I have deliberately dressed practically today in a long-sleeved work shirt, trousers, and boots for my ride, and the conditions at the worksite.

It is a beautiful sunny day, and while I make my way through the city, I wish I could take the bike for a long ride in the country where I could open it up and the experience the adrenaline rush I knew would follow.

Instead, I am caught up in the city traffic, which is bedlam, but marginally easier on a bike. I find the site easily, and expertly maneuver around moving cars, work trucks, and parked vehicles, whilst trying to locate a spot to park. A gap appears and I quickly stop, pushing the bike back against the curb while astride it.

Stepping off with ease, I glance around, searching for the café where I am meeting Robert, while I remove my gloves and helmet. I place them, along with my folded leather jacket, in the top box at the back of my bike, before locking it. Adjusting my sunglasses, I straighten my shoulder bag and walk up the road to the busy café, situated next to a small, shaded park.

I walk into the café and look, unsuccessfully, for Robert, before finally heading back outside where I hear my name being called from the park. Swinging around, I find Robert sitting at a small table. With Xander. *Damn!*

"Hi." I greet both men, plastering on a professional smile and shaking their hands, although my hand lingers on Xander's for a heartbeat too long, and sends tingles along my fingers from the warmth of his touch. "I didn't expect to see you here, Xander." He seems to always have the same effect on me, whether it is his touch, look, or proximity; lustful pangs and an acute awareness of my body. *And it drives me mad.*

Looking me up and down, Xander's dark eyes glint. His cool professional mask is in place, but then he arches an eyebrow suggestively, letting me catch a glimpse of the man behind the mask. "And I didn't expect to see you riding a motorcycle, Georgina." Pausing briefly, he quickly continues, "Ethan will be here shortly with one of his project managers to accompany Robert and you over the site. I'd go with you, but I can't walk for long periods yet." I then realize that he doesn't have crutches with him, but instead, a walking stick leans against the table.

"Oh, of course." *Thank goodness for that*. I am still rattled from the tingling reaction to shaking Xander's hand. "Do I have time to grab a coffee while we wait?" I missed my morning coffee this morning, so am pleased when they both nod. "Can I get you both one as well?"

"No thanks," they answered in unison.

Hurrying away, I need to escape Xander and compose myself. Knowing his presence would distract me too much to do my job, I whisper a grateful thank you that he wasn't accompanying us on-site.

When I return with my coffee, Ethan and his colleague Miguel have already arrived and are in deep conversation with Robert and Xander. Ethan, like his brother, raises an eyebrow, presumably at my outfit, but he says nothing other than hello and introduces Miguel.

We make our way the short distance across the road to the hotel. Putting on our high visibility vests and hard hats, Xander surprises us when he does the same, apparently having changed his mind. Then we begin our tour with the site manager. *Damn*, I curse the man as I bolster my professional persona and concentrate on the discussion rather than Xander.

Stepping into the large lobby, it is clear that it is in the early stages of redesign. Everything is still very raw, but the bones of the layout are obvious. Robert points out where the indoor water wall is going to be, between the lobby and restaurant entrance. I can already imagine it to be an impressive color-changing water feature and will provide some acoustic white noise to diminish the sound reverberation from the other hard surfaces.

"That looks impressive, Robert. The water will recirculate up and down the water wall, won't it?" He nods in response, and my enthusiasm gets the better of me as I share the ideas I have been working on. "If we were to recycle it through the planned external water gardens, it should eliminate the need for chlorine and other chemicals, making it more sustainable and cost-effective." I look between the men and notice Ethan taking notes. "I know it isn't part of the original concept, but I have a vision of the water flowing across the lobby floor, like a river, via a glass-covered, in-floor channel, then splitting into two rivulets before continuing either side of the entrance into the porte-cochere pavement." I turn and point, my hands flowing and following my words. "It would then dip under the entry roadway and resurface as a water wall and water garden on the other side of the porte-cochere."

Despite my enthusiastic description, the men remain silent, much to my surprise. Xander and Ethan are tight lipped, although their faces look thoughtful, while Robert appears noncommittal, making me panic that they are too polite to shoot down my ideas. From what I know of Xander and Ethan, though, neither would hesitate to shoot down an idea if he didn't like it. *Or maybe they are regretting hiring me?*

"I fully understand if you don't like the idea, but this is what I was thinking." I flip through a few pages of the large notebook I always carry with me at site visits for sketching ideas, and taking down measurements and notes. I find the page I am looking for that I sketched yesterday. Turning the notebook to show them, I lean forward, hoping the visual will make them more enthusiastic than they've been so far.

"It provides impact and symmetry between indoors and outdoors, tying the two together, but also provides better efficiencies in water purification and sustainability."

"Is this doable? What about the cost?" Xander questions, as if he likes my idea.

"Yes, it's doable, but will be an expensive addition and possibly blow out the projected completion date." Robert twists his lips into a half-smile, placatingly, but I don't miss his almost cynical eye roll.

"Initially, yes, it will extend your build costs," I clarify, confident in the benefits my idea will bring to the project. "However, there will be long-term savings operationally because the pumps to drive the water will run off the solar electricity system you are having installed. The groundwork hasn't started on the porte-cochere or the floor of the lobby, so trenches for the power and watercourse can be dug at the same time. The structural grade glass covers for the watercourses will be your only real additional outlay."

They all remain silent. *Have I overstepped the mark?*

"Robert, I'm not trying to override your design, just trying to value add and create synergies. Is that not why you hired me?" I pause, looking directly at Robert, then glancing at the other men. "It is just a suggestion that is easier to implement at this stage of work rather than retrofitting later."

"Thank you, Georgina. We'll consider your suggestion. Robert, I'll come with you around the building for as long as I can. However, as time is of the essence, let's continue with the site inspection." Xander lifts his chin dismissively. Mr. Scowly Face, CEO, is back in place, and in charge. This surly side of him irritates me, but I acknowledge that it is his job to intervene and move them on. The other men accept his comments without question; however I feel like I have been put in my place and press my sketch book against my chest.

"Certainly." I straighten, nodding stiffly, and take his hint to drop the matter, deciding that I will only offer suggestions when they ask for them from now on.

We continue around the building, Xander's lips noticeably whitening around the edges and pursing together, as his pain becomes apparent. My heart softens at his discomfort, and I suggest a few times that he should sit, but his pride refuses. Eventually, he makes his excuses and leaves before we continue around the grounds. I push thoughts of Xander aside and ask questions about plumbing and power line locations and make copious notes about access, slope, and projected timelines that I will need to consider for the landscaping.

Ethan asks me a couple of times if I have any ideas or suggestions, which I answer, but I make a deliberate effort to downplay my enthusiasm, deciding not to show the sketches I have made. Despite seeming to like my ideas, Ethan seems to notice my diluted replies and seems somewhat disappointed. However, Robert appears much happier now that I'm not altering his plans or blowing his budget.

A while later, we all return to the site office and part ways. Parched and headachy after standing in the sun for a couple of hours, I call into the café. It is just about to close, and while I sit in the shade guzzling my cold water and munching on a dry muffin, I reflect on how disappointed I am with the site visit.

Usually, the clients don't want to meet with the designers and contractors, happy to leave it up to the project manager, so getting ideas to the client is sometimes difficult. *Maybe the problem is that I raised my ideas in front of the client before running them past Robert first. He is the project manager, after all. However, I needed to see the site to determine if they were viable.* Although, it is up to Xander and Ethan now and there is nothing else I can do but wait for their decision.

Feeling more refreshed, I walk back to my bike and make the frustratingly slow ride in peak hour traffic to my office. All my staff have left by the time I park my bike in the garage and cross the courtyard to the office. Deciding to follow their lead, I turn around and go back home, shower, and climb into my track pants and singlet top for a relaxing night in.

The delicious aroma of Hayden's cooking has been teasing me since getting home. We haven't seen much of each other over the last week, so I grab a glass of wine and sit chatting with him about my day while he prepares dinner.

"Wow, that water wall river sounds like an amazing idea, sweety. I can't understand why they didn't all jump at the idea." His praise warms me. "You never cease to amaze me with your creativity and the beauty of your creations," Hayden continues lovingly, while speedily dicing carrots. This man always has my back, as I have his. We have a mutual admiration society going on, which includes our other flat mate, Simone, who is currently working away for a few days.

"And you never cease to amaze me how you still have all your fingers." I laugh, admiring his skill and speed with a knife. I get up, kiss his cheek in thanks, and pour us both another glass of wine before setting the table. "I was surprised at the lack of response when I suggested it, but when Xander cut the conversation short, it felt like a smackdown, that I was being put in my place. I haven't had such a lack of reaction in a long while and it is certainly not a feeling I like. Maybe I've become pompous after all the business's successes recently," I voice my earlier musings.

Hayden chortles, spraying his mouthful of wine over the bench. "You? Pompous? Pfft. Get real, girl! You are one of the most down-to-earth people I know. How can you be part of your family and not be a realist?"

"Ha. True that," I acknowledge as I get up to answer the front doorbell and squeal in excitement to see my best friend Allie and her husband Jack standing on the doorstep with a bottle of wine and a bowl of salad.

"I didn't know you were coming over. The night just got so much better." I spread my arms wide and give them both a warm hug and kiss before they make their way to the kitchen.

I met Allie at college. Now a forensic accountant, I love how people always underestimate her, thrown by her quiet nature, dry-cutting wit, and huge, warm heart, they are always shocked when she outwits them. Allie and Jack had met on campus too, and despite their rocky start are perfect together.

"How's it going, bro? Smells fantastic, as always." Jack shakes Hayden's hand and they pull each other in for a manly hug. "It's been too long." Hayden and Jack have been best mates for a long while, but as Hayden works most nights, it is always difficult for him to get to their catchups.

We talk and laugh the night away, enjoying the good food, too much wine and our good-natured teasing.

It is after midnight when Allie and Jack say their goodbyes. As I close the front door on my friends, I wish I could find someone, like Jack, who let me be my own person but would support and love me unconditionally; someone who would look at me as adoringly as Allie and Jack look at each other. *Oh, and someone who was a great lover*, I chuckle.

Despite being happy with my life and friends, I haven't felt that special connection with anyone for a long time. I always feel like the zing is missing but can't define what that *zing* is. I know this is why I look for the *zing* in other places like the adrenaline-charged activities I love, but that rush always fades too soon, leaving me with just a fun memory and a hollow feeling inside.

Shaking off my maudlin thoughts and blaming the amount of wine I've drunk during the night, I help Hayden clean up before going upstairs to bed, where I fall into a deep sleep.

Groaning at the amount of light streaming into my bedroom, I squint through bleary eyes to see what time it was. "Shit." I leap out of bed. It is already 8.45 am and I could see lights on in my office across the courtyard, which meant Tash or Raj are already in. I am rarely ever this late to work. Most days I am in the office by 8.30 am, sometimes earlier, but normally not more than five minutes after Tash arrives at 8.30 am.

I had been tossing and turning all night from a crazy dream where a man with an obscured face was smashing my newly built gardens to pieces with a mallet, causing me to sleep through my alarm. *That'll teach me to drink so much on a weeknight.*

Showering quickly, I am disappointed when it doesn't clear my foggy head. I am just finishing applying my mascara when my phone rings.

"Hi, Tash." I sigh heavily, my voice croaky.

"Georgie, are you okay? You're never late in." Tash sounds flustered.

"Yes, I'm fine. I had a heavy night with Allie, Jack, and Hayden, and slept in. Just on my way over now." It is odd that Tash called me, but I appreciate that she is checking on me.

"Good, because you have someone here wanting to see you, and he says he's in a hurry."

"Really? Who? I didn't have any appointments this morning." Puzzled, I mentally scan through my day to check I'd not forgotten.

"Xander Drakos," Tash's breathy, whispered response tells me that he is within earshot, but the note of urgency in her tone also speaks of Xander's impatience.

"Great." Sarcasm oozes from my voice, and I rub my forehead in frustration. "Just what I need this morning! Put the coffee machine on, please Tash. I'm going to need a strong one." I sigh heavily before swallowing down some painkillers.

Two minutes later, I walk into the reception area to see Xander standing, hands behind his back, staring out the front window as if watching for my arrival. As I do every morning, I crossed the courtyard and entered my office through the back door, cutting through my own office into the lobby.

"Good morning, Xander." The corners of my lips twitch ever so slightly at the sight of him spinning around in surprise, although he quickly masks it. I step forward to shake his hand, surprised yet again at the strength and warmth of his hand and how small my hand feels in his.

"Georgina." He nods, his eyes narrowing slightly as he stands unnervingly close to me. My skin prickles as his upper arm brushes against me and I stiffen my spine, trying to ignore the sensations.

Quickly, I take the coffee cup Tash hands me and then I step back with one arm extended toward my office in invitation. "Please come in." My calm voice belies the flip-flops in me at the scent of his musky aftershave and the touch of his hand against mine, making me wonder, yet again, why my body reacts this way to him, despite how much I have disliked him since our first meeting.

I silently direct him to the round meeting table in the corner of my office. "Would you like a coffee?" At the shake of his head, I close the door, taking a seat opposite him. "To what do I owe this unexpected pleasure, Xander?"

He sits back in the chair, with legs crossed, positioning his walking stick next to him, and his hands are clasped loosely in his lap. His eyes glint in humor, and his lips twitch into a half-smile, acknowledging my veiled sarcasm.

"I'm heading to the airport and just thought I would call in on my way past to discuss a couple of things with you." He pauses. "Firstly, I want to say how much I loved your water wall river idea and sketches. Ethan mentioned that you also have some other excellent ideas that you mentioned after I left. I am hoping you can elaborate on those for me, and if you have any sketches of your ideas, like you had with the water wall..." The timbre of his voice is smooth and matter-of-fact as his eyes remain fixed on me, looking and sounding every bit like the CEO he was.

My chin lifts in pride at his interest in my ideas, although I hope he isn't just playing me as some cruel joke. "Certainly, and I have sketches for all of the ideas I raised yesterday. Were there specific suggestions you had in mind?"

"I would like to know more about the water gardens and proposed minimization of mosquitoes, as well as the oasis in the city aspect, and the green terraces."

Nodding, I stand and retrieve my sketchbook, placing it on the table in front of him. Leaning down, I enthusiastically outline my ideas in detail, showing him my sketches and pointing out points of interest as I speak.

He listens intently, glancing from me to the sketches as I outline each one. I can't help noticing his blue eyes as they change from icy and stern to a sparkling sapphire color, just like an ocean. I feel like I am drowning as I gaze into their enticing depths and wonder if the color change reflects his enthusiasm for my work or a reaction to me. I can feel his body heat seeping into me as he momentarily leans in closer to scrutinize one of my drawings, and my stomach lurches with desire.

His proximity overwhelms my senses and my body reacts needily; my nipples tingle, heat builds and pulses between my legs. Startled by the intensity of my response, the hand I am resting on one of the sketches jerks, bumping into his, which feels like an electric shock jumps between us. My eyes widened in surprise as I jerk my hand away.

Xander must have felt it too, because his eyes flash with what looks like desire for a split second before it is quickly replaced with his mask of professionalism. Checking his watch, he stands quickly, ending our conversation.

"Thank you, Georgina. That has been most helpful. If you could email me the sketches and your cost estimates, please?"

"Certainly, but I must ask that the designs remain confidential between the project management team and yourself and Ethan," I repeat the standard request as I walk with him to the external door.

"I am well aware of the confidentiality legalities around these, Georgina," he snaps at me disdainfully. "I'll be in touch." His lips press tightly together, his eyes narrow, and he walks quickly to his waiting car.

"Grrrr." Sighing, I am exasperated at the way he'd just shut me down and left so abruptly. I turn, shake my head and roll my eyes at Tash, then go back to my office.

My brow furrows in confusion as I try to work out why he'd shown up unannounced this morning. *Surely he could have got the information he was after with a phone call or an email. And then there was my body's reaction to him... Was it his brilliant mind which caused my senses to go haywire? Or his powerful physique and attractiveness? Or his delectable cologne?* The lingering scent alone has left me feeling light-headed and fluttery in my chest and stomach, and damp between my legs. I have to squeeze my thighs together to curb the ache there. *Oh damn! I need to find a distraction.*

Maybe I should call Mark.

It has been a while since we hooked up. Hopefully, he is in town. Getting laid might douse this flame of lust before it gets out of hand and I do something stupid, like mix business and pleasure with Xander.

CHAPTER 5 – Xander

As I relax back in the large leather chair, I stare out of the window of my private jet on a five-hour flight across the country to the West Coast, a trip I only do when I need visual updates on my property developments. I'm also looking to add to my company's property portfolio, so several meetings are set up to scope out possibilities.

I've spent part of the flight reviewing the original landscape plans for the hotel refurb, along with Georgina's suggestions, and emailing Ethan my thoughts.

They are good. Very good. Somehow, Georgina has managed to capture exactly the look and feel I had envisioned, that I'd always felt had been missing in the original plans. Robert had been satisfied with the earlier landscaping plans, as had I, but I always felt they didn't quite hit my high expectations for next-level luxury and for future-proofing our investment. I can't put my finger on what had been lacking, but as soon as I saw Georgina's amendments, I know that they are the missing pieces of the puzzle.

I rub my tired eyes and reflect that right from our first meeting in the hospital, when I was as cantankerous as a bear from pain, discomfort, and frustration, my eyes had immediately been drawn to Georgina's lithe figure and long, rich, chestnut hair which had been tied in a ponytail and flowed down her back, swaying from side to side as she moved.

She had not been intimidated by my surliness and accusations and responded with rightful anger at my allegations, then bored indifference when discussing plans, that I only rarely experienced from my brother and sister when my haughtiness needed bringing down a peg or three.

Her snarky remarks and swearing had irritated me. *Didn't she realize who I was? No. How could she possibly know?* If she had been aware of me from frequent paparazzi coverage, then seeing me in casual shorts and a shirt with a cast on my leg could well have disguised my fame. Very few people could or would stand toe to toe with me when I exerted my dominance, which was frequently, but she seemed unphased and almost appeared to revel in the challenge. Despite my irritation at the time, my loins had tingled in reaction, my body's betrayal infuriating me further.

Regardless of my annoyance at the time, I give credit where it was due and she certainly was skilled at cutting through the rubbish and getting to the heart of the matter, quickly summing up our concerns and providing solutions, something I don't see often. And after getting to know her grandfather, I could see where her tenacity and sharp business acumen came from.

The meeting in Robert's office had only reinforced my positive opinion. I had pushed her hard, challenging her time and again and she hadn't lost her cool. Although she had seemed annoyed with my intense scrutiny a couple of times; she had taken a quick, calming breath before continuing. I also noted a very subtle pinching of her lips every time I called her Georgina, her frustration amusing me. Initially, it had just been to rankle her, but the more I used the full name, the more I believed it fitted her multi-dimensional personality. I felt more invigorated in that meeting than I had for a long time. And, once again, my groin reacted, despite having tended to my urges in the shower that morning as the cast on my leg was playing havoc with my love life.

At the time, I had thought that my sexual response to her in the hospital was simply the lack of attention my cock had received while laid up, but my similar reaction in the meeting with Robert not only surprised but irritated me. Thank goodness I had been seated so the table hid my bulge, but I needed to readjust once or twice. Seeing her dressed in business trousers and a blazer with her hair neatly tied up in a bun and the occasional glimpse of her well-hidden, ample cleavage only accented my desire to discover what made her lose her cool. So, when Ethan accepted her offer to hold the elevator for us, I decided to change tack by applying my usually fool-proof charm by cheekily asking if she was offering her assistance at home. But it backfired. Her blush at my flirty teasing sent shivers through my body, making my cock swell. Again. *What is it about this woman that has me reacting like a school kid with his first crush?* However, I felt smug that I found a chink in her defenses when she strutted hastily away from us.

Then, when I was dining with Louisa, I'd seen Georgina across the restaurant with a man, offering him her genuine smile and laughter that crinkled her bright shiny eyes.

Georgina had looked beautiful, the auburn highlights in her light chestnut hair glimmering when she moved her head. Even from a distance, I had been tempted to run my hand through it and had to grip my crutches firmly to resist the urge.

A flash of annoyance had shot through me, which I couldn't explain or understand, but I know seeing them together made me angry and I needed to find out more about the mystery man. Despite finding out this man was her brother, I still felt jealous that he got to spend time with Georgina and that she offered him a side of herself that she'd kept hidden from me and I couldn't help glaring at Ryan as we said our goodbyes.

My mind went back to watching as Georgina got off her motorbike, striding toward our meeting in her tradies' work-wear. The trousers had hugged her firm, well-shaped butt, the buttons on her shirt pulling tightly over her generous bust. *Who knew tradies' gear could ever look so good?* Her luscious, long hair, that she wore pulled back in a braid, made me visualize it wrapped around my hand while I fucked her from behind. I'd thought about that morning a lot and my dick instantly stiffened every time I remembered that enticing sight. In fact, I realized I felt like I was permanently walking around with a semi-hard-on since Georgina had walked into my life.

As well as being attracted to her physically and intrigued by her no-nonsense attitude, I am equally drawn to her passion and imagination, which I've seen with the water wall. Her face had lit up, eyes sparkling, and her speech sped up as her hands gestured to demonstrate her ideas about how the water would flow under the floor. I'd played devil's advocate by cutting her off, as I rarely show my hand on which way my decision will go, but knew that I was leaning towards her idea.

My arousal hits overdrive as I imagine how she might use that passion and imagination... and those excitable hands in the bedroom. I am seriously tempted to break my golden rule of never mixing business and pleasure.

Get a grip, man, I chide myself, running my hands through my hair, then checking my watch quickly, pleased when I realize I had enough time to do just that. I need to extinguish this ache in my loins so I can focus on my upcoming meetings. Annoyed that I have to resort to tugging myself off more frequently than I am getting laid lately, I adjust myself, stand, and casually make my way toward the plane's bathroom. Once inside, I lock the door, unzip my trousers, and release my swollen shaft. With one forearm leaning against the wall, I caress my balls, squeezing gently. *Mmmm.* I close my eyes and inhale deeply as a familiar sensation rockets to my lower abdomen, making my cock jerk. I shift my hand, gripping my long, thick, hard cock firmly, wiping precum across the cockhead with my thumb. I stroke myself slowly at first, spreading the precum further down my shaft, but it isn't long before my hand moves harder and faster. My eyes close, as I return to my earlier fantasy of Georgina in her work gear with her long braid running down her back, imagining what it would be like to undress her, touching her body as I sink inside her, fucking her hard as she moans my name. *Ohhh.* Breathing heavily and moaning quietly as my pleasure skyrockets, my knees buckle as my climax peaks, jerkily spewing cum into the toilet.

"Fuuuuck," I utter, resting my head on my outstretched arm while I recover from the intensity of my orgasm. "Oh, God." Moaning, I sigh deeply, tugging my length and squeezing my balls, wringing out the last of my release. "Mmmm. Oh fuuuck."

I lean against the wall for a few minutes, while my senses and breathing gradually return to normal. *Geez, that was the hardest I've come in a long time. Man, I needed that!* My head falls backward and I let out a huge sigh of relief. Smiling wryly, feeling lighter and more relaxed, I clean myself up, tucking my package away and splashing water on my face before straightening my tie and smoothing my hair.

As I casually walk up the aisle to the stewardess and request a water, then return to my seat to focus on the paperwork for my upcoming meetings, thoughts of Georgina are firmly pushed to the back of my mind now that my lust has been sated.

After landing, I promise myself that I will get laid while on this trip as I limp across the tarmac toward my waiting car. Normally I don't have any difficulty in that area, as my good looks (so I've been told) have women throwing themselves at me. But while they were always physically enjoyable, after two or three dalliances with a woman, I become bored and move on.

Over recent years, the longest I have been with the same woman was a month. They all knew the score because I make sure to tell them that I am only interested in a good time, not a long time, and they usually only want to bed me for bragging rights, or my parting gifts. However, since my accident, the few encounters I've had left me unfulfilled. The sex has been good, but it is as if something is missing, almost like I am yearning for something more substantial. I couldn't figure out if it was just my body's reaction to the healing process or some emotional trauma from my car accident that injured my leg but haven't delved too deeply into the reason. *Maybe a change of scenery and a different pool of available women, together with my now healing leg, will make all the difference*, I ponder and smile in anticipation as the car whisks me away to my first meeting.

***

After three days spent in meetings with my nights catching up on paperwork or hitting the gym or pool, I decide some relaxation is in order, so I make my way to the nightclub attached to the hotel.

It is plush, decorated with dark carpet and wood paneling, violet-colored, studded suede inset in the lower walls of the bar, with caramel-flecked marble bar tops. The bar, which overlooks the nightclub and dance floor on one side and the lounge on the other, isn't very busy, and I presume it is because it is relatively early for nightclubbers, but there is still a sizable after-dinner crowd.

Taking a seat at the bar where I can see onto the dancefloor, I order a beer and watch the crowd. It isn't long before a group of four attractive women claim a table, laughing as they settle in. The tall blonde in a tight-fitting, body-shaping black dress approaches the bar, ordering a bottle of champagne and four glasses. She turns, giving me a seductive smile, then she wets her lips invitingly. Throwing her one of my charming smiles, I eye her appreciatively before one of her friends comes to help with the champagne and also gives me a wide smile, deliberately putting her phone down the front of her dress, exposing more of her ample cleavage. I raise my glass to both women. *This might turn out to be a good night after all.*

I sit quietly, watching the dancers and, whenever I glance back at the ladies' table, the blonde gives me another enticing look.

Normally, I would be semi-hard by now with the suggestion of a hot and heavy night with these beautiful women and I would take advantage of their obvious invitation, but tonight I'm not feeling my usual excitement of the chase. Realizing how lackluster I am feeling and surprised by my lack of arousal, I finish my drink, stand, and make my way to the casino without looking back at my admirers. *Damn, that's never happened before.*

CHAPTER 6 – Gina

SEVERAL WEEKS LATER, I spent the day at the hotel redevelopment site with my landscaper, Jamie, marking out where various features are to be installed and areas of dirt that have to be removed. We have worked together for several years and have become good friends who trust each other's judgment implicitly.

As is often the case, issues frequently occur once we start moving dirt and, regardless of all the planning and utility diagrams, we did not expect this site to be any different. We have been using an electromagnetic pipe detector and aerosol paint to mark out the location of water, sewer, power, and telecommunications pipes. That way, we can plan a workaround if needed.

It has been a beautifully warm day, but after working in the sun in long sleeves and trousers for protection, I am sweaty, sticky, and dirty. The thought of stepping into a shower to let the cool, refreshing water run over my head and back makes me long to get home. Finally, we are packing up our equipment and having a much-needed drink of water while discussing how best to tackle a problem area tomorrow.

"Well, we can narrow that water garden channel and incorporate a grass viewing area over the pipework, but that will cause further issues downstream," Jamie suggests as I nod, contemplating his idea. He brushes his curly, sun-streaked brown hair off his face, takes a huge swig of water, and then undoes his shirt to cool off. He is good-looking and well-built, if you are into the surfer type. He is also as strong and as reliable as a rock, and a very happily married man with two young children.

"Hmmm. Let me sleep on the idea." We are standing alongside each other with our backs leaning against the side of the red tray-back truck. I tap my top lip thoughtfully while staring off into the distance toward the troublesome area. "We will need to work it out in the bed like we usually do," I comment and smile warmly at him. Jamie nods and grunts in agreement.

"Am I interrupting plans for a heavy night?" a deep, rich, cynical voice that I instantly recognize jeers from behind us. The often clipped but sexy-as-hell tone has been haunting my dreams over the last few weeks, much to my chagrin.

Startled, I spin around. Xander, in all his captivating glory, is leaning on the other side of the truck, his hands clenched and hanging casually over the upright side panel. Inviting blue eyes glint and hold me captive as they rake over me before he offers me a tight-lipped smile, and raises an eyebrow in response to my gaping at him. He is dressed in a pale blue business shirt, tie removed and top button open, which provides a peek at the tanned column of his neck and taut upper chest. He looks fresh and cool as if he has just stepped out of somewhere air-conditioned; divine and as tempting as an oasis in a desert.

A flush of heat runs down my already overheated body and my knees tremble. A low, pleasant hum fills my body at the sight and sound of him. *Traitorous damn body! How can it react this way when he annoys the shit out of me?*

"Certainly not," I snap, indignant, glowering at him. "And it would be none of your business, even if we were, Xander." My eyes flash and meet his unrelenting stare, knowing he is trying to annoy me. I am annoyed, but also embarrassed at my body's reaction to him. As I stare, the slight twitch of his lips tells me that he is well aware of my arousal.

To maintain some semblance of professionalism, I take a calming breath and turn to Jamie, who is looking Xander up and down as if he was a total jerk. His tight-lipped mouth and furrowed brow tell me he issn't impressed with Xander's comments, either. My eyes glint, and I feel the corners of my mouth twitch as I recognize Jamie's irritation, loving how he is siding with me without me having to say a word.

"Jamie, this is our client, Xander Drakos from Drake Enterprises. Xander, this is Jamie Eklund, my landscaper. We were just mapping out the underground pipework to see where we might have to amend our plans." Pausing, I push the loose tendrils of hair from my heated face before continuing, "Can I help you with something?"

"I'd be interested to see what you have found." Xander straightens and walks around to our side of the truck, looking at me as if he expects me to immediately show him. As if I have nothing better to do.

Sighing heavily and giving him a reluctant nod, I turn to Jamie. "Why don't you head home? I'll handle this. See you in the morning, Jamie."

"You sure?" Jamie doesn't look comfortable leaving me alone with Xander but I nod, leaving him to pack up the truck.

"Xander, we don't have a lot of light left, so I'll show you our biggest problem area." Tired and achy from the day's work, I push myself to stride up the slight incline, leading Xander halfway across the site. When he falls into step with me, I notice by his confident stride that he no longer needs a walking stick, but I remain silent.

Rolling my eyes, I huff out a breath, needing to fill the silence with conversation. "How was your business trip? Ethan mentioned you were in Perth. Were you away for long?"

"Hmm, did he now?" he queries, then adds, "Did you miss me?" A mischievous look flashes across his face, then quickly disappears into the cool, unreadable mask he mostly wears. And I wonder whether he is flirting with me.

"The trip was fruitful in some ways, although it didn't fulfill some of the outcomes I had hoped for." His non-committal response makes me sneak a furtive glance at him, and I notice that he seems distracted, so I decide to hurry things along a bit.

"Well, this is the problem area. You can see where we have marked different colored lines for the different underground services. Here we have gas, sewer, and telecommunications lines, none of which we want to damage. This also happens to be the location of one of our larger garden beds, which can't be positioned over any of these services. So, we need to come up with an alternative," I elaborate, my tone matter of fact.

"What ideas do you have so far, Georgina?"

"None so far. I will sleep on it tonight. Although, sometimes inspiration comes when we are digging. It's almost like Mother Earth provides the answers," I offer, smiling at what some would consider a whimsical notion, but I feel very in touch with Mother Earth in my line of work.

He eyes me quizzically, before taking his now ringing telephone out of his trouser pocket. "Thank you. Sorry, I must take this," he adds dismissively before turning and walking away to answer the call.

While I stand, I stare at the ground for a few minutes, a mental picture of the garden plans running through my head for the umpteenth time today, hoping to be struck with inspiration.

Suddenly I realize I can't hear Xander anymore, and, as I spin around, I spot him almost back at the site office. Huffing, I stomp back to where the truck had been when Xander interrupted Jamie and me earlier. Collecting my hat and drink bottle from where they sit on the ground, I mumble to myself about what a waste of time that had been when I could have been in the shower or soaking in the bath with a nice glass of wine by now.

When I looked for Xander again, he is nowhere to be seen. Jamie always drives me off site to my vehicle and waits till I drive away, so an edge of uneasiness prickles my senses. Cursing Xander's lack of consideration for leaving me on a near-deserted building site in approaching darkness, I march toward the site office. Although, after many years of tousling with my brothers, I know I can protect myself if a situation arose.

Rounding the corner while glancing at the time on my phone, I collide with a hard immovable, but warm, object. "Oomph." My phone flies out of my hands as I stumble unsteadily on my feet, but strong hands grab my waist, keeping me upright.

Xander.

My eyes widen in surprise, my brain fries, and my body electrifies from his unexpected touch.

"Well, well. I was just coming to look for you and here you are, delivered into my arms," he says with a note of sarcasm, his breath tickling my ear, as he pulls me in closer.

The heat from his hands scorches my skin and instant desire burns a hot spot in the pit of my belly.

"Let me go, Xander." I wriggle in his arms, but my attempt to escape is futile. His powerful hold keeps me pressed hard against his firm, muscular body. He rests his chin on my head and he inhales deeply, before he tightens his hold even more, pressing my thighs against his, and my lower belly firmly against his rigid manhood. My mouth dries up and falls open, a yearning spreading through me.

Oh, My God. He is big... and hard.

"Stop wriggling, Georgina." His smoky, husky voice sends shivers through me. His hand tugs gently on the single braid that hangs down my back, tilting my head back to get a better look at me. His pupils dilate, eyes ablaze with hunger, while his tongue licks his bottom lip before he lowers his head, his mouth hovering over mine in anticipation of my taste. My eyes are glued to his, gaping. My heart pounds hard, my body thrums with anticipation, and my skin erupts in goosebumps as the heat between us becomes an inferno.

"Xander." Moaning, my voice is a bare whisper as our breath mingles. I have no hope of holding back the floodgates as need overwhelms me.

The sharp sound of a nearby horn blaring snaps us out of our carnal fog, both jerking at the sound. Xander's arms relax and drop. His head straightens, and he blinks several times as my palms push against his chest, trying to put some distance between us. I shake my head, trying to clear the thoughts spinning in my mind. When my senses return, I register that my palms lay pressed against his sinfully well shaped chest before I quickly drop them to my side. Stepping back with reluctance, my mind and body are in a quandary.

My emotions are all over the place as well. *How can I continue to be annoyed with him when he said he was about to look for me? How can I walk away from such a delectable male when everything in my body is screaming at me to get down and dirty with him?*

I have never had such an intense sexual response as this with any other man, so I am confused as to why I react so wantonly with Xander, a man I barely know. And that he is as rock hard for me, causes me both elation and self-doubt. *He has been with lots of women. Will I live up to his expectations?* I also promised myself a long time ago that I will not mix business and pleasure, but I need to quell this persistent ache for him, because it is distracting me from my work and ruining my sleep.

Putting my hands on my hips, I look him in the eyes, trying to mask my confusing, mixed-up thoughts, while he stares back as if trying to gauge my next move.

"What do you want, Xander?" I query, hoping he wouldn't notice my soft and tremulous voice.

"I think you know what I want, Georgina." He speaks in a low, husky voice seemingly struggling to regain his usual firm self-control but with a slight shake of his head, he runs one hand through his hair, blinks a couple of times, and his normal cool demeanor snaps back into place.

"I'm sorry I kept you so late. How are you getting home, Georgina? I can drop you if you'd like?" His tone is not quite authoritative, and not quite apologetic.

"Thank you for the offer, but my bike is outside the gates, so I'll ride home." I don't want to spend any more time in his overwhelming company until I can rationalize my emotions. Stepping around him, I continue in what I hope is a professional voice, "I just need to sign out first." *Hopefully he will take the hint and leave.*

Xander nods as I turn and make my way into the site office. The signing-out process should have only taken a minute or two, but I string it out for as long as I can by chatting with the Site Manager, hoping Xander would have left by the time I come out.

No such luck. I spot him near the gate, my fists tightening in frustration. Taking a deep breath, and stiffening my back, I gather my professionalism around me like a cloak and stride toward the gates.

"Thank you for waiting, Xander, but I'll be right from here."

"Maybe so, Georgina, but I will accompany you to your bike." He raises an eyebrow at my attempt to dismiss him. Huffing and rolling my eyes, I remember how my brothers have also refused to listen to me in similar circumstances.

We walk in silence the short distance to my motorcycle, each not sure of what to say about our moment earlier and how unprofessional it was. Darkness has settled while I was in the office, and the street is silent, so I am secretly pleased that I am not alone.

"You forgot your phone," he states casually, as he passes it to me.

"Oh. Thank you." I take it out of his hands carefully, trying to avoid his touch because it is more than I can take in my wound-up state.

I busy myself getting my motorcycle gear and helmet out of the bike tail bag. Then I put on my jacket, ensuring my phone is tucked into an inside pocket, before zipping it up.

As I pull on my gloves, Xander announces, "Let me know your ideas for resolving the issue with the pipes."

"Really?" I queried, lifting my chin, my brow scrunching in confusion. "I was intending to talk to Robert and Ethan about it."

His gaze sharpens into a commanding glare, his lips tightening as he insists, "Let me know as well."

I catch the note of hardness in his voice, recognizing it as an order. Tsking and nodding, I put on my helmet and straddle my bike. Gripping the handlebars, I am about to start the bike when he taps my hand and leans in to speak.

"Text me when you get home." His words demanding, yet again.

"Why? You're not my keeper, Xander," I spit back.

"Just text me, Georgina." His infuriated voice matches the hardness of his gaze and scowling expression.

"Whatever," I snap, my voice cold and dismissive. I start the engine, revving it angrily, before dropping the bike into gear and darting away faster than I normally would. The bike's front wheel almost lifts before I throttle back to a normal speed. I know how to handle my bike confidently from years of trail bike riding with my competitive brothers, but it isn't like me to be so reckless. The sight of Xander's angry face in my rearview mirror shows me that I'm not the only person to notice how remiss I've been.

As I navigate the light traffic on my way home, I reflect that I haven't seen that scowling side of Xander for a while and am beginning to recognize it as his look of frustration.

Why has he come over so possessive? Was it because we nearly kissed? The zinging chemistry and arousal from being in his arms still lingered, unsettling me. Needing to focus on riding my bike safely, I push thoughts of Xander from my mind, noticing how hard it is to stop thinking about him.

After a quick bite to eat, I run a bath, adding some relaxing bath salts to help ease my tired limbs. Slipping under the deliciously hot water, I rest my head back and exhale deeply. My body welcomes the soothing water while my turbulent mind takes a lot longer to unwind. I ponder the problem with the site some more and then decide to put it aside until tomorrow when no obvious solution springs to mind.

As I soap myself, my breasts tingle, my nipples harden and my core surges with heat, as the sensation of my touch reignites the latent hunger from Xander's embrace.

I don't know him very well at all, but my body craves him. Desperately. Normally I need to know a man well before I feel any desire for him and am not one to jump into bed with just anyone. But what I feel for Xander is primal and blinds my better judgment.

I remember how aroused Xander had been, and feel thrilled that he'd reacted to me like that, but then my thoughts begin to spiral again. *Was he like that with all women, or just me? Maybe my hunger is so intense because I haven't had sex for a while. When I arranged a hook up with Mark recently, I was half undressed when I realized I didn't feel aroused in any way, so I left. Even Mark had commented our hook ups had lost their heat recently. Was that because my body was begging for Xander?*

I need to ease this insane craving for this man and hopefully restore some sanity. As I have to work with him, I don't want to be incoherent and flustered because I yearn for him. Deciding that I need to ease the burning need in my belly, and thinking about Xander's long steel-like hard-on pressed against me earlier and the way his luscious lips had almost connected with mine, I flick my fingers over my peaked nipples, moaning softly as pleasure shoots between my legs, my womanhood pulsing with each flick. I run my hand down my stomach and between my legs, dipping into the cleft, tantalizing and teasing, making me sigh with pleasure.

The sudden ring of my phone startles me. Water splashes over the side of the bath as I hurriedly sit up and stretch to grab it, groaning as Xander's name lights up the screen. *Damn the man. Why can't he leave me alone? Have I conjured him with my thoughts?*

Breathlessly, almost guiltily, I answer, "Hello?"

"Are you home?" his deep voice seethes, each word clipped.

"Yes. Why?" My voice is emotionless, his apparent anger bewildering.

"Why didn't you text me that you were home like I asked?"

"Just because you bark an order at me doesn't mean I will comply. I had a lot running through my mind and forgot. Why does it matter, Xander?" I retaliate.

He is quiet for a moment before answering, as if drawing a calming breath. Leaning back, I swoosh water over my shoulders, and my fingers brush against my nipple. I sigh softly as pleasure ripples in my lower belly, so I circle my nipple again and again. Although it softens slightly, the sharpness of his

65

voice when he speaks again tells me that he is still annoyed. "I was concerned for your safety, Georgina. You took off like a demon, and I was worried about you." Xander pauses and qualifies his apparent concern. "I need you around to finish this project."

"Gee, thanks. I think." I am miffed that he seems more concerned about the project than me. Or is he covering the fact that he has some feelings for me? "Was there anything else, Xander? I'd like to finish my bath."

"Bath?" The timbre of his voice changes, becoming almost hypnotically alluring. I guess from that one-word question that he is reliving the heat of our earlier embrace, and I can't help wonder if his mind has conjured up all sorts of fantasies, just like I'd been doing. *You shouldn't be having fantasies about a man you are working for,* I chide myself futilely. *Keep it professional, Gina.* Although I know that is easier said than done.

"Yes," I shoot back, realizing that if I elaborate further, I would be getting into dangerous territory. "Goodnight, Xander." I hang up before either of us could say anything more.

Sighing, I glance wistfully at the cooling water and contemplate staying longer to finish pleasuring myself, but my mood has cooled like the water, and my practical side takes over. *I must clean up the water that I splashed getting my phone.* After doing that, I quickly dress in some comfy pajamas and head downstairs for a warm cuppa.

The house is quiet tonight, fortunately, so I grab my sketchbook, turn on some soft music, and firmly push Xander to the back of my mind as I begin working on some ideas for the garden layout problem.

After several hours, yawning and satisfied that I have a couple of options to discuss with Jamie, I go to bed. Sleep eludes me for a while because, now that my brain isn't concentrating on work, I am haunted by the fantasies and sensations of my stolen moment with Xander. So many unanswered questions flood my mind. *Is he interested in me, or just grabbing an unexpected opportunity that arose? If he was just an opportunist, it didn't account for the chemistry that seemed to exist for both of us well before tonight, though. Is he only interested in me as a quickie to satisfy an itch, or is it more?* Suspecting him to be a player from the multitude of social media photos I've seen of him with different women, I expect him to be incapable of anything long-term, which is the complete opposite of what I am looking for.

Sick and tired of the what-ifs, I manage to shut my brain down enough to sleep. Although it isn't restful, because I am tormented with an erotic dream of Xander tugging my braid and kissing down my neck, scraping his teeth over my sensitive skin before moving down to my erect nipples, laving, and sucking them, before finding my mouth and plundering my lips until I am breathless, repeating the ecstatic torment again and again.

I hit my alarm so hard it falls to the floor. I am hot and sweaty, my body is humming with unsated need, and the bed looks like an orgy has been writhing in it. *Shit, this is going to be a great day,* I snort with derision as I tidy up and get dressed.

CHAPTER 7 - Gina

"GEE, IT'S BUSY HERE tonight. I'm glad we booked a table," Allie throws over her shoulder matter-of-factly, and the others murmur in agreement as they look around the restaurant while we are escorted to our table.

Allie, Tash, Emily, Simone, and I are friends who have known each other for a long time. Despite our differences, we are besties who stick together, no matter what. I love these girls. We laugh together, cry together, and get drunk together. They supported me through a broken engagement and provided me with dating, business, and family advice over the years, as I have done for them.

Tash was the only one who hadn't shared a flat with us back in our university days. However, when I employed her and invited her along to our regular catchups, she fit in easily with our group. The girls have become so entwined over the years that Allie eventually married Tash's twin, Jack.

Tonight, we are celebrating Emily's birthday, and she needs some cheering up. She's had a dreadful breakup a few months back and is only now feeling up to socializing again. I know all too well the angst and loss of confidence that follows a breakup.

After the initial flurry of ordering drinks and food, our conversation turns to what has been happening with each of them.

"Your turn Georgie. Tell us what's been happening in your world," Emily asks enthusiastically, diverting attention away from herself.

"Why are we skipping you?" I tease my friend, just as reluctant to talk about the last couple of months as Emily seems to be. "Nice pass, though. We all see what you're doing, Em, and we will come back to you," I laugh.

"Yeah, you're not getting off that easy, Em." Allie chuckles and nudges her as the others chimed in, agreeing.

Emily bats her eyelids playfully, pulls a cute innocent face with her hands under her chin, and cheekily parries, "Birthday girl prerogative," before poking her tongue out. "Let's have it, Georgie."

I contemplate what to tell them and decide to keep it brief and factual because my true feelings about Xander are so muddled that I wouldn't know how to define them. I feel a bit foolish admitting to my friends my reactions to him, so decide not to divulge too many details, not wanting someone to overhear me talking about him. Staring into my nearly empty glass, my hands wrap around it, I hesitate, then take a deep breath and dive right in.

"Well, my grandfather was in hospital after a mild heart attack a little while ago." I pause as they chorus, "Oh, that's no good," watching me with keen interest as they all know how close I am to my family and that I idolize my grandfather, then I continue, relief showing in my smile.

"He has made an amazing recovery and you wouldn't even suspect he had been unwell. While he was in hospital though,

I met two brothers. The first was in the elevator, and the other was a patient with a broken leg. Elevator Man seemed charming and very good-looking and polite. And he smelled so good." I smile dreamily as I recollect. "The brother he was visiting was also very good-looking but accused me of stealing my grandfather's phone and then scowled the whole time they discussed a development project they were working on. Anyway, while I was out of the room, my grandfather convinced them that I might be able to offer them some advice. I gave them a few suggestions, but Mr. Scowly Face didn't seem too enthused and even asked me about my qualifications." My friends chortle, knowing me well enough to know that I would rather be recognized by my work than by a title or piece of paper, then bristled in unison on my behalf, commenting, "Scumbag." "Rude pig." "How dare he." and "What? Let me at him."

Chuckling at my amazing friends' loyalty, knowing full well that each of them would stand toe to toe with men like Xander if they or a friend was slighted, I reply, "Oh, don't worry, I dialed up the contempt and told him exactly what my qualifications and experience are. Anyway, after numerous conversations and meetings with them both, I ended up getting the contract for their hotel redevelopment."

"Mr. Scowly Face is hot, hot, hot. The air sizzles around him. You can almost feel the power, confidence, and magnetism dripping off him," Tash pipes up, elaborating on my sparse description, following my lead on not naming Xander.

"What? When did you meet him?" Simone demands, a touch surprised.

"He's come into the office recently," Tash answers. "And I tell you, his eyes follow Georgie everywhere."

"Ooh," they again chorus, looking directly at me as I blush.

"Tell us all the details, Georgie," Emily persists and claps her hands in excitement because they all knew that it has been a long time since I have been seriously interested in anyone.

"Nothing much to tell." I wish I hadn't raised the subject now, and try to downplay my feelings to avoid any more teasing, but then I remembered that these women are my closest confidantes and advisors. *Why shouldn't I share my innermost thoughts about Xander with them?*

"Ok then," I begin reluctantly, staring at the table. "I've had coffee a few times with Elevator Man. He is beautiful inside and out, but there is no spark. He reminds me of my brothers, so we have decided to enjoy being friends. But there is a definite chemistry between Mr. Scowly Face and I. He looks and smells so good; I tingle whenever our hands bump together. He makes me hot and horny, and I've dreamed about him... a lot. But he also drives me mad. He's usually either scowling or domineering, and we have barely said anything personal to each other." I look up at my friends, who are watching me intently, hanging on my every quietly spoken word.

"Hot and horny is great," Simone interjects with a roguish grin.

"Oh yeah," Tash agreed, almost drooling, while the others laugh.

"When Jamie and I were working on-site earlier this week, we were about to head home when we were surprised by Mr. Scowly Face, who insisted on seeing what we had been doing. To be fair, he did seem genuinely interested in our progress. Anyway, he walked away to take a phone call, and I was left standing around. As it was nearly dark and there was no sign of him, I trudged back to the site office and collided with him.

He caught me before I could fall flat on my backside, then held me for a while. He was hard. He didn't try to hide it. And let me tell you, his erection was huge." I know I am babbling, but it feels like a dam has been cracked open. "He was just about to kiss me when a car horn shattered the moment. After that, he walked me to my bike and insisted I text him when I got home, which I forgot to do because my brain was so lust fogged. So, he rang me, obviously pissed that I hadn't texted, and then he said he only wanted to ensure I was safe so I could finish the project."

I let out a long sigh.

"For weeks now, every time we've met for business, I've been aroused in one way or another but after the other day, it ramped up to a level of horniness that I can't shake," I admit.

"Whoa," Allie drawls. "You're in deep," she comments sympathetically, the rest nodding in agreement.

"You need to get laid, girl." Simone always gets straight to the point.

"Yeah, I know," I sigh. "I called Mark a few weeks back to hook up and douse the fire, but I didn't feel the spark anymore with him. Hadn't for a while. So, we went our separate ways before anything happened," I confide, shrugging before closing the scrutiny of my love life. "Enough about me. Emily, it's your turn."

After Emily finishes regaling us with escapades of her students on a recent excursion, which has the group laughing so much we complain our cheeks hurt, we stand and make our way out of the restaurant.

Simone links arms with Emily and I as we cross the road toward the nightclub and confidently predicts, "We, ladies, are going to find a hookup for both of you tonight." We all giggle, although I'm not into one-night stands, so doubt I will follow through even if I find someone interesting.

"Woohoo. This place is jumping," Simone shouts as she throws her arms in the air, gyrating her hips to the thumping dance music playing as we enter the nightclub. "Let's find a table so we can get partying," she announces, her eyes scanning the dimly lit room. The rest of us laugh, knowing that Simone is the die-hard party girl who usually dances all night with whoever she can find.

"There's one, right over in the back corner," Tash exclaims excitedly, pointing toward the free table. She hurriedly makes a beeline for it, plopping herself down on one of the stools as the other girls and I catch up and do the same.

"Well done, Tash. Great spot. We can check out the dance floor as well as the new arrivals," Simone yells across the table so we can hear her over the loud music.

She is a tall shapely brunette who looks like she could just as easily walk a fashion runway as well as she does an aircraft aisle as a flight attendant. She is always on the lookout for a new conquest, her strong-willed, self-assured personality requiring a good-looking male who has all the moves.

Allie and I make our way through the crowded tables to the bar and order our cocktails, which are delivered to the table. We grab a couple of bottles of water as well and laugh, shaking our heads when we spot Simone already on the dance floor.

The deep rhythmic beat pulses through our bodies like a life source, enlivening our senses. We bounce from foot to foot where we stand at the table, squealing and hooting, chanting the words of the songs the DJ plays. I look at my friends, who are wearing wide grins that match mine.

It isn't long before several men approach our table, chatting idly, getting a feel for who is keen to party a bit harder, inviting a couple of our group to dance.

"Let's go," Emily and Tash respond, strutting onto the floor, waving their arms as they move.

I am pleased to see Emily a bit more outgoing than her usual self, probably because of the alcohol we have all consumed, but also hopefully because her birthday is a cause for celebration. Maybe it even has something to do with Simone's plan for finding a man for her tonight.

I had finished my second cocktail and have been dancing on the crowded floor with my friends, and some keen men, for a couple of songs. Tired and thirsty, I make my way back to the table with Tash, just as Allie arrives with some more bottles of water, which we all guzzle furiously.

Sitting, fanning ourselves to cool down, we watch the fashionable crowd gyrate and sway to the heavy rhythmic beat, pointing out one or two who are more outrageous than the others. Most of the women are scantily dressed and the men are mostly wearing snug-fitting clothing that shows off their assets.

Simone returns to the table from the bar, excitedly commenting about the gorgeous hunks who have just come in, pointing them out as they move through the crowd to a small table on the other side of the room. My friends and I turn to check out whoever has Simone salivating.

My mouth drops, rendering me speechless as I catch sight of Xander and Ethan with another man I don't recognize. Xander looks just as scorching hot in his black dress trousers and a dark, open-necked, short-sleeved shirt. *Surely his clothes have to be tailored because they always shape his body perfectly*, I muse to myself, feeling heat creep over my body as the sight of him leaves me breathless. His thick, dark hair looks like it has been recently cut and is brushed back from his face. As he takes a swig of beer, he perches on a stool with a nonchalant air and casts an interested gaze around the crowd.

"Oh, my God," Tash screeches, grabbing my arm. "It's them!"

"What?" The girls spin their heads back to Tash and me in bewilderment, noticing the mortified look on my face, as I stare at the table, trying to make myself invisible, while Tash is wide-eyed and open-mouthed with excitement and surprise, then they return their gaping stares to the stunning alpha males across the room.

"Who are *they*?" Simone drawls, extending the last word in a long, sultry, breathy purr.

"They're the men Georgie was telling you about earlier. Xander and Ethan." After a subtle jab to the ribs from me, she corrects herself, "I mean Mr. Scowly Face and Elevator Man."

"Oh, no way!" Emily exclaims.

"You're kidding?" gushes Allie. "Which is which?"

"What the fuck?" comes from Simone.

Incredulous, their mouths remain open, and their heads on rotate. Simone looks like her intended marks have been ripped out from beneath her because she won't go after someone her friends are interested in.

Tash clarifies, "Xander is in the dark shirt, Ethan is in the blue shirt, and I don't know who the other one is."

"Don't worry, Georgie. We've got your back," Tash declares as she turns to place her hand on my shoulder.

"What are you going to do, Georgie?" Emily queries, concerned for me.

"I'm going for another drink. Does anyone want another one?" When they all shake their heads, I glance toward the men's table as I finish my drink and go to the bar.

Well, with a bit of luck, he won't see me and if he does, I'll just have to deal with it, I rationalize as I pull myself together, lifting my chin resiliently. *Damn it, I have nothing to hide. I am a free agent, and him being here isn't going to dampen my enjoyment,* I resolve as I skirt the crowd to the bar. By the time I have returned to the table, my usual self-reliance is back in place. I will ignore him and let my hair down for the night. Of course, the liquid courage helps.

Not long after, Simone comes off the dance floor, swaying to the music, her head bobbing and arms moving in front of her to the rhythm. She grabs me by the arm and drags me laughing out to our gyrating group on the floor. A couple of men are dancing near our group, circling like wolves after their prey. I turn a few times toward a blond man in the group who seems to be creeping into my personal space and give him a deadly stare to back off. Throwing myself into the dance, I make a concerted effort to not look toward Xander's table, even though I am sure he has spotted me by now. My spine prickles as if his eyes are raking over me.

It isn't long before I spy Ethan and his friend joining the throng on the dance floor. Despite every female, and some male, heads turning toward the two tantalizingly handsome men, neither Ethan nor his companion have a body zinging effect on me like Xander does.

Ethan looks directly at me, smiles good-naturedly, and raises his hand in acknowledgment, snapping me out of my introspection, so I return his greeting with a friendly smile and a quick wave.

Emily leans in close to me and shouts above the din, "Is he the one you've got the hots for?"

"No, his brother over at their table is," I divulge, tipping my head in that direction without looking over.

"Good, 'cause this one is *very* impressive," Emily slurs, seemingly captivated by Ethan. Her eyes gleam in fascination as she dreamily watches him dance.

And his gaze is holding hers, surveying her intently, as he slowly makes his way closer. *Hmm, this is interesting.* I contemplate his interest in Emily, and also notice that Ethan's friend appears to have found someone he is interested in on the other side of the dance floor.

When Ethan gets close enough, he mouths hello to me, and leans in closer to Emily to introduce himself. Her cheeks flush, and she smiles flirtatiously as they try to chat above the music.

It is great to see Emily genuinely interested in someone again. I make my excuses and go back to the table, not wanting to interfere with their getting acquainted. My feet are killing me, and I am also feeling quite tipsy and need more water.

Usually, when we girls are out in a place like this, we will take turns in holding the table and as a deterrent to would-be drink spikers, so Simone is pleased to see me return so she can get back out to dance, and the man who has been chatting her up follows like a puppy. *Simone will eat him alive.* I silently chuckle to myself as I sit down.

While I stare out into the crowd once more, I gulp some water and take a few deep breaths to calm the pounding in my chest.

Most of the tables are empty now as everyone seems to be on the dance floor or at the bar and Xander's is no different. I crane my neck, trying to see his tall dark head above the crowd. Nope, I can't see him. Disappointed, I huff, resting my head on my upturned hand, and look for my friends in the crowd, thinking about going home soon.

"Are you looking for me?" The deep, seductive voice close to my ear startles me, but I recognize it and whip my head around. My eyes blink, my lips part, and I chuckle warmly.

"Of course I am, Xander. Is that the best pickup line you've got?" I husk his name, batter my eyelashes, and smile flirtatiously, the alcohol providing a mischievousness I wouldn't normally display so openly to someone I know so little about.

His pupils dilate, and he licks his lips as I tuck a long strand of hair behind my ear. He looks me up and down, his nostrils flaring as he breathes deeply, dragging a stool closer to me before taking a seat. The air between us sizzles. I feel that familiar flood of desire as I watch him; my skin prickles in goosebumps, and my brain turns to mush.

"Well, now that you've found me, what did you want to do to me?" he asks, his eyebrows raised and eyes sparkling in appreciative roaming scrutiny. His voice is smooth as honey; playful and inviting. *Wow. I am a goner.*

When he turns on this blinding charm, it is hypnotic; I have no space for rational thinking left. I blink several times, trying to get my brain to come up with an answer. I feel like I am melting into a pool of lust and hormones at his feet.

"I could ask you the same thing, Xander." As I speak, my voice purring and playful, and in a move imitating the movies, I curl my hand, hovering it over his forearm which is resting on the table, and provocatively walk two fingers up to his elbow, my gaze following their path. He grabs my hand, halting its progress, then brings it to his mouth, pressing a soft kiss to my knuckles. A soft sigh escapes me and my eyes drop to where his lips touched me. He opens my fingers and presses another soft kiss to my warm, soft palm, then encloses my hand in both of his as if to stop the kiss from escaping. My heart flips. The warmth from his lips as they touch my hand runs up my arm and spreads across my chest, filling my body, causing a redness to cover my neck. Our eyes lock, and my chin lifts slightly, exposing my neck, as a moan sighs from my lips. His touch makes my nipples harden and my panties flood with my arousal.

Xander runs his lust-filled eyes over me, pausing at my plump cleavage and jutting nipples, continuing down over my accentuated figure in a neatly fitting dress, and my bare, tanned, toned legs before returning to look directly into my eyes.

"That's a conversation for another place, Georgina," Xander drags his eyes away, lets go of my hand, and moves his body back slightly as if suddenly remembering we are in a public place, that I am very tipsy and he needs to distance himself from the inferno between us.

"Who was the blond fellow on the dance floor?" he quizzes, turning his attention to the heaving throng, his voice deceptively indifferent.

"I don't know. We never introduced ourselves." I giggle, shrugging my shoulders as my words slur.

CHAPTER 8 - Gina

LAUGHING, ALLIE AND TASH return to the table and realize I am somewhere between tipsy but not yet plastered when I stand, stumble, and give them both a hug. They suggest it is time to head home, and I nod, giggling again, telling them what great friends they are.

"Good idea," Xander comments to Allie, briefly turning his attention to their efforts to get me home.

"We'll get Simone to take you home, Georgie, because we all live in the opposite direction," Allie remarks.

"Nope. That's not going to work," Tash declares as she watches Simone wave to them as she walks out the front door with a man who has been all over her on the dance floor. "Simone just left, Allie. If you grab Emily off the dance floor, I will arrange a rideshare for all of us."

"No need for you to go out of your way," Xander interjects. "I'll take Georgina home." Allie and Tash give Xander a suspicious look, not wanting to put me in any danger.

"I'm fine. I can get myself home," I argue, although no one seems to be listening to me.

"No, it's fine, Xander. We can all get a lift together. Thank you anyway," Tash argues.

Xander nods, shrugs his shoulders, and moves back toward his table, obviously intending to catch up with Ethan and their friend, as if recognizing there is no point in pushing the matter further. He doesn't seem particularly happy that I have drank so much, but seems pleased that my friends have my back when it comes to my safety.

A little while later, we are further down the path from the club entrance, waiting when our rideshare car arrives and Tash discusses with the driver the arrangement for dropping us all home. I hear them negotiating with the driver, who seems reluctant to backtrack on himself to take me home. Additionally, and probably very annoyingly, I keep piping up that I am fine to get home by myself and am obstinately refusing to get in the car.

"Can I help, ladies?" Xander casually asks, as he approaches us. I caught a glimpse of him outside the club waiting for his driver, so he must have overheard the girls arguing about our ride. They vent their frustration to him, annoyed with our driver and me for creating such a drama.

"Ladies, seriously. I will take Georgina home. I promise you all that I will make sure she gets inside, then I will leave. Taking advantage of inebriated women is not my thing at all."

As they still look skeptical, Xander continues, "Do you have one of those apps that tracks your friends to make sure they are safe?" When they nod, he continues, "Then you can track Georgina to ensure she gets home. Besides, from what I understand of her family, if anything untoward were to happen to her, I would have her burly, irate brothers out for my blood."

"You better believe it, mister," I chime in, swaying slightly, waving a pointed finger at him in a pseudo-authoritative manner.

"So true Xander. Well, if you are sure?" Allie queries reluctantly but also looking relieved that they could finally get in the car and on their way. "But we will be tracking her, just like you suggested," she warns.

"More than happy to help. And I would expect nothing less from Georgina's friends. I know you just want to ensure she's safe."

"Come on, Georgina. Let's get you home. Tash, what's her address?"

"It's just around the corner from her office. Easy to find," Tash comments as she scrambles into the waiting vehicle.

"I can direct you," I pipe up cheerily.

I watch, bleary-eyed, as Xander gives Allie and Tash a business card so they can contact him if needed, then he directs me to the large black SUV that has just pulled up next to the curb, his arm hovering behind me without touching, escorting me as I wobble a bit on my high heels. Because the fresh air seems to make my head spin and my legs wobbly, Xander stands next to the door as I bump my head and then clamber in, giggling as I slide along the seat to the other side. He quickly follows me into the vehicle with a heavy sigh. I rest my head against the plush headrest, admiring the sumptuousness of the vehicle with its leather interior, wood grain features, and tinted windows.

"Wow, this is a pretty impressive car, Xander," I observe, looking at him. He is sitting, with some distance between us, casually staring out the window, looking as if he is dealing with a petulant child.

"Thank you," Xander replies, then directs his attention to his driver. "Ramone, head towards George E Colby Landscape Architecture offices where you took me recently, please. I believe Georgina's home is just around the corner from there, and she can direct us."

Nodding in acknowledgment, Ramone steers the large vehicle into the late-night traffic. We haven't traveled far when a thought occurs to me.

I lift my foggy head and ask, louder than necessary in the quiet confines of the car as my ears are still ringing from the deafening music, "Why are you taking me home, Xander? I could easily have gone home with my friends."

Looking at me critically, his eyes narrow, and lips tighten, his voice and tone are carefully controlled, as he responds, "Their driver was causing some problems for them because your home is in the opposite direction. And I want to make sure you get home safely. Too many intoxicated women are taken advantage of by rideshare and cab drivers in one way or another."

"Oh, okay." My foggy brain can't come up with anything else to say, as a wave of tiredness hits me, so I rest my head back on the headrest and close my eyes.

Waking with a start, a strong hand grips my forearm, shaking me, as a deep irritated voice calls my name. "What? Huh?" My bleary eyes blink and eventually focus, allowing me to look around and get my bearings. "Where am I?"

"We are outside your office, Georgina. I believe you live nearby?" Xander questions impatiently.

Looking out the window to confirm our location, I reply with a thick voice and equally thick head. "Oh, okay. Thanks for the lift," I drawl as I open the door and get out of my side of the car unsteadily.

"Bloody hell," I hear Xander grumble, instructing Ramone to follow us as he hurriedly gets out of the car too, watching me as I walk crookedly. "What the hell do you think you're doing, Georgina?" Xander bellows, his long strides quickly catching up with me.

"I'm walking home, Xander. It's just around the corner." He slows his stride to fall in alongside me. I stop at the corner and turn to face him, putting my hand on his warm, strong chest. The heat on my palm surprises me, and I instinctively move my fingers across his firmly shaped pecs, my eyes following the movement, mesmerized, enjoying the feel of him under my hand.

"You don't need to walk me to my door. I can get there by myself," I comment huskily, speaking slowly to articulate my words. My eyes blink several times, trying to focus as I look directly into his.

His dark eyes flash with desire from my touch as they sweep up and down my body, and settle directly on me. Inhaling deeply, he says, in a deliberate voice, "I need to know you get home safely. This way, I can ensure that you do." His fingers wrap around my wrist gently, removing my hand from his chest, then he holds it upturned before placing a tender kiss in the center.

My throat suddenly goes dry, my eyes widen, dazed, and whatever remaining thinking ability I had quickly disappears. I have no words, so I turn and walk the short distance to my door, looking in my bag for my door key. I can feel his eyes boring into my back as he follows closely behind. Quickly turning into the narrow alcove of a gray-painted brick façade two-story warehouse-style building, I take three steps up to my door, which is set between a large glass panel window and a roller door, fumble in unlocking and opening it, and then turn to Xander who remains at the bottom of the steps.

"Thank you for getting me home, Xander. Would you like to come in?"

Xander appears to be debating whether to follow me in or not, as he hesitates. He quickly turns to Ramone, who has stopped the car at the curb and holds up his hand to signal five minutes.

"You live here?" he asks incredulously as he follows me indoors. I stop just inside the door, nodding in response, then remove the stilettos that are killing my feet before closing the door behind us.

The long, narrow, open-plan layout is dimly lit, but he can still make out the eclectic, yet tasteful décor.

"Yep. My dad bought the property. I designed the layout and bought it from him so I could have my business and my home close together," I comment proudly, my words slightly slurred.

"It looks like a great space. You have done a great job with it," Xander praises. His mouth curves into a smile as he peers around, but he is interrupted by a light suddenly coming on at the back of the building and a male voice speaking with familiarity.

"Ahh, you're home, sweety. I thought I heard a noise down here," Hayden says, as he rounds the stairs in only his boxers, and heads into the kitchen.

Xander's warm expression instantly turns cold. His back stiffens and his fists clench. He glares at me and snarls, "You could have told me you live with your boyfriend, Georgina."

"What?" My befuddled brain takes a moment to register his words, but he turns and walks to the front door. "Xander, wait."

Too late. The front door slams shut.

"What the fuck?" I utter. I stand, staring at it, shaking my head, perplexed, when Hayden sticks his head around the corner.

"Has he gone already?" he asks, bemused. At my nod, he trills, "Who was that delectable man?"

"I'll tell you tomorrow, Haydz. I'm going to bed." Shaking my head wearily, I stagger upstairs, puzzling over what just happened. Xander was as nice as pie one minute, the next he was as cold as ice. *Had I imagined, in my tipsy state, the warmth and praise he had given me before he left, or his interest in me?* Despite my confusion, I fall asleep as soon as my head hits the pillow.

CHAPTER 9 - Gina

THE AROMA OF FRESHLY brewed coffee wafts into my bedroom, waking me from a sound sleep. I groan as I roll over. My head thumps and my mouth feels like I have swallowed an ashtray. My stomach is jumping all over the place too, unsure whether it wants food or to expel its contents.

It has been a very long time since I drank as much as I did last night, but as practically a non-drinker, the four or five drinks throughout the night hadn't seemed excessive. *Those damn cocktails were potent though, and had been my undoing.*

Memories from last night come flooding back as I step under the shower, and Xander storming out still had me confused.

Should I ignore his dummy spit or clarify for him that Hayden is not my boyfriend? I ponder as I wash my hair. Just when I think we are making small steps toward really getting to know one another, something happens that takes us back to a wall of ice between us.

Toast and coffee settle my stomach, together with some painkillers for my headache, enough for me to head over to my office and get started with my day, but the quandary over last night isn't far away, and Tash's observations compound my uncertainty.

"So, what was with Xander dropping you home last night? What happened?" Tash interrogates me as soon as she sees me in the office. "You know we were tracking you to make sure you got home okay, don't you?"

"No, I didn't know that, but thank you. I have no idea why he wanted to do that, other than to save you all the hassle with your driver, but I appreciated that he was looking out for my safety. And nothing happened. He followed me inside and then Hayden came downstairs. In his boxers. Xander stormed off, mumbling something along the lines of that I should have told him about my boyfriend."

"Seriously? That man was eagle-eyeing you all night, so he sure seemed interested. What are you going to do?"

I want to explore these feelings I have for Xander, even though it means I will be breaking my self-inflicted rule of not mixing business and pleasure, and I have the impression he wants the same.

"I'm not sure yet." Quickly changing the subject, unanswered questions filter back to me. "What happened between Emily and Ethan? And where did Simone get to? Have you heard from her?" I query, concerned about my friends.

"Ethan got Emily's number and said he would call, but who knows if he was just playing with her? I certainly hope not. She seemed smitten with him, and I'd hate for her heart to be broken again." Tash pauses and shakes her head as she contemplates that notion. "But I haven't heard from Simone, although that's not unusual when she goes off with a bloke, as you know. We have tracked her, too, and left several messages for her to call us. I'll try her again later on." Tash finishes making us both a coffee, smiles, then comments, "It was a great night out."

"Yes, it was," I agree distractedly, making my way back to my office, thoughts of what to do about Xander at the front of my mind again. Regardless of who he is, good manners dictate I should thank him for the ride home. I justify to myself that I would do the same for anyone else, as it was the way I had been raised. Even if he ignores me, I will know I have at least tried. I quickly get out my phone before losing my nerve and text Xander.

> **Gina:** Thanks for the lift last night. I appreciate you going out of your way to see me home. And for the record, Hayden is my flat mate, not my boyfriend. Never has been, never will be.

I press *Send* before I could think twice about it. I'm not going to let his unjust assumptions go unanswered. Smirking to myself, I can imagine my brothers attesting to that because they often call me argumentative when I correct their mis-judgments.

Within five minutes, my phone rings. Glancing at the caller ID I take a deep steadying breath before answering.

"Hello, Xander," I greet, in my best business tone.

"How are you feeling this morning, Georgina?" His voice is courteous and businesslike, not giving anything about his feelings away. However, the sultriness of his voice plays havoc with my already churning stomach.

I catch my breath and close my eyes, savoring the sound, imagining his eyes darkened with lust to deep sea blue, undressing me like he had last night in my dream. I sigh, then shake my head.

"Average at best. Those cocktails have a potent punch. Last night was an anomaly, I can assure you," I reply, clarifying my out of character behavior. "Thank you again for the lift home." My voice softens with a touch of bashfulness.

"My pleasure. Glad I could help. I'd like to think that someone would do the same for my sister in similar circumstances." His voice has become more matter-of-fact, as if someone has walked in on his conversation.

"Yes, I would hope so too," I respond noncommittally, unsure of what else to say. "I'd like to repay your generosity last night by taking you to drinks or dinner, Xander," I ask him quietly, surprising myself, uncertain where that suggestion had come from, but feeling like it is the right thing to do. Although I don't normally invite men out to dinner, I am a modern woman who goes after what I want. And I want Xander, I realize suddenly. No doubt about it. I need to see where this attraction leads and if there is any future in it. Even if it is a passing fling, I need to satisfy the crazy continual burning of lust that seems to have overtaken my body.

"You don't need to repay me, Georgina. As I said, I just wanted to see you home safely. However, I would like to accept your dinner invitation, totally obligation-free, of course." I can hear the smile in his voice. *Was he laughing at her?* "I have a bit on for the next couple of evenings. I am free Saturday night, though. When were you thinking?"

"Let's see." I quickly check my calendar. "Yes, I can do Saturday night. What time and where?"

"I have to head into a meeting now, but I will text you the details. Until then." Xander's voice is friendly but business-like before he hung up.

I hold my head in my hands, suddenly questioning my sanity, my emotions tumultuous. I feel like I will be walking into a lion's den, dining with Xander alone. Yet, I also need to clear the air to get back onto an even keel like I was before I met him. *Really, Gina?* my adventurous side castigates. *That existence was predictable and boring, where work provided the only challenge and pleasure. Let your hair down and live a little, girl.*

Never one to back down from a challenge, I gulp the last of my lukewarm coffee, take a deep, bolstering breath, and plunge into my work, pushing the matter to the back of my mind.

I have been so preoccupied with what I was doing that I haven't heard the text message come in and only notice it later in the afternoon when I take a break to eat. Seeing it is from Xander, I respond quickly about where to meet and then briefly fill Tash in on my earlier conversation with him. Afterward, I realize that, if I think of it as a business dinner, then I can calmly hold my inner turmoil at bay.

CHAPTER 10 – Gina

AIMING FOR THE FINE line between business and date attire, I dress carefully for my dinner with Xander, choosing a body-shaping, red, knee-length dress with short sleeves, a cowl neck, and a cutaway back. It is comfortable and flattering, providing just a hint of sexiness. I team it with red stilettos that accent my tanned, long legs and gold drop earrings, a necklace, and gold clutch purse to add a touch of class.

I have defined my eyes with some subtle, smoky shadowing and apply three layers of mascara to my lashes so they appear longer, before I accent my curved lips with light rose-colored lipstick. My long, shiny, chestnut-colored hair is pinned behind my ears and hangs neatly down my back, reaching my shoulder blades.

My phone beeps, letting me know that the rideshare driver is outside, so I check that I have everything I need in my clutch purse before putting on a white blazer-style jacket and going downstairs. Xander explained that he will be tied up during the afternoon, so he will meet me at the restaurant, which suits me, as it gives me time to calm my nerves on the ride over, without the need for inane small talk.

***

As I get out of the car, I look around at the well-dressed crowd and am pleased that I have added the extra glam factor when getting dressed. I always like to be a bit early, so, checking my watch, I decide to make my way into the foyer of the Casino to find the restaurant.

I haven't been here before, so am surprised by the brightly lit façade in blues and mauves, the three, wide, multi-level flights of stairs, and the twin glowing escalators that lead into the entry. *Hmm, maybe they are supposed to represent a stairway to heaven*, I laugh to myself as I hop on one of the escalators.

The cavernous foyer has my mouth dropping open as I look around in awe, stopping and turning on the spot to take it all in. There is marble everywhere, subtle lighting, sheer white waterfall-like curtaining and undulating sound-deadening panels hanging from the roof, as well as more escalators to the upper level. There is also a colorful indoor garden and massive walls that dwarf the doorways and people. *Wow, impressive place.* I feel like a kid in a toy shop and am just starting to wonder how I will find Xander when his soft voice startles me.

"You seem to like what you see, Georgina." His voice is smoky and sexy, firing up my libido.

Turning, I give him a stunning smile, cheekily, openly surveying his strong, alpha male physique clothed in a perfectly fitting royal blue suit and crisp white shirt opened at the top two buttons, providing a glimpse of his tanned chest.

"How could one not, Xander?" I quip impishly, matching his tone and innuendo.

He cocks an eyebrow and throws me a lopsided grin before lightly taking my elbow. "Our table is this way," he comments huskily as he leads me up the escalators to a very fancy-looking restaurant. I feel nervous as we walk in silence, not knowing what to say. His strong, warm hand resting lightly on the contour of my back sends shivers up my spine, compounding my nervousness and stirring desire in my belly.

The maitre'd greets Xander by name, and we are escorted to our table next to a large plate-glass window overlooking a brightly lit promenade and an expansive harbor shimmering with the reflection of city lights. Xander graciously pulls out my chair, facing the inky water, before taking his seat at right angles to me, where he has a better view of the promenade.

"Very impressive, Xander. Do you come here often?" I quiz, tongue in cheek, eyebrows raised, eyes wide and sparkling at my deliberate use of the hackneyed pick-up line. Deciding to tease him as if he is one of my brothers, I hope it will break down the barrier between us.

Xander chuckles warmly, a deep mellow hypnotic sound, his eyes flashing with humor. *I can watch this captivating side of Xander all day*. "Occasionally, but mostly for business dinners," he drawls, just as the waiter arrives, and pours some water for us.

"I'll have a scotch on the rocks, please, and for the lady..." Xander pauses.

"A Moscato, please." The waiter nods, then turns back to Xander.

"Which scotch would you prefer, sir? Glenmorangie, Johnnie Walker Blue Label, Glenlivet, or Chivas Regal?

"The Blue Label, please." The waiter nods again and repeats our order, then moves away.

His choice of scotch confirms my impression that Xander enjoys the finer things in life, from his clothing to his cars and his drink choices. I must confess his presence in these surroundings affects me even more than normal.

"Xander, I just want to be clear at the outset that I'd like to pick up the tab tonight to repay you for taking me home the other night," My tone is matter of fact, as I remind myself to treat this like a dinner with a close business associate.

"Please don't insult me, Georgina. I appreciate your offer, but you know I was just looking out for your safety." Xander's smile slips. His expression becomes closed, and he gives me a piercing stare. After a moment he continues, his features softening, his lady-killer eyes flashing with heat as he gazes at me, his mouth curving into a charming smile. "Your presence tonight is repayment enough."

Smooth, very smooth. I raise an eyebrow, and my lips quirk at his comment. "Please, at least let me go halves with you."

He raises his eyebrows and looks down his nose at me as he shakes his head. "The matter is closed, Georgina," he commands.

"Okay." Nodding begrudgingly, I concede, then pick up the menu and scrutinize it.

I can feel Xander's eyes watching me as if expecting me to challenge him further. I peer at him over the top of the menu, blushing as our eyes lock.

"You look stunning tonight," he husks, his tone deliciously sexy. His blue eyes smolder and his pupils enlarge.

"Thank you. You look particularly delicious yourself." I smile invitingly at him, and my cheeks warm under his continued appraising gaze. The air sizzles between us, arousal stirring and rippling through my lower belly.

The waiter interrupts before either of us could say anything further. I take my glass and sip it, trying to quell my intense desire and maintain a semblance of calmness, reminding myself to view this as 'dinner with a friend' rather than a date. I am determined to know him on a more personal level before my lust runs roughshod over my commonsense.

Unable to decide what to order, I lift my enquiring gaze to his and ask, "This all looks so amazing. Do you have any recommendations?"

"Hmmm, I can think of a couple of options," he murmurs, dragging his eyes to the menu. "The salmon, or the scotch fillet. The lobster spaghetti is also very nice."

I mull over the decision for a moment or two, then turn to the waiter who has appeared next to us with a polite smile.

"I'll have the salmon, please."

"Make that two," Xander orders, then the waiter leaves.

Trying to make polite conversation while we wait for our meals, I ask Xander questions about the Casino and hotel complex, admiring the location and the beauty of our surroundings.

"Tell me about your family, Georgina," Xander asks as he relaxes back into his chair. I quiver as Xander's knee brushes against mine when he stretches his legs under the table, sending a pulse of pleasure between my legs and igniting the embers I thought I had under control. As I glimpse a twitch of his lips and a devilish twinkle in his eyes, I realize his touch has been deliberate.

Inhaling deeply, I catch his alluring, warm, woodsy scent and gulp my wine. When I replace my glass, the back of my hand brushes against his, which is casually resting on the table, sending another wave of tingles through my body. Before I can open my mouth to say anything else, the waiter arrives with our meals and we start eating.

"Mmm, this is good," I murmur, trying to appear unaffected as I savor my first mouthful, then finally respond to his question. "My family. Well, you've already met my grandfather. There's also Mum and Dad, and I have four brothers."

I acknowledge his raised questioning eyebrows with a chuckle and a nod. "Yes, four. Luke and Tyler are older than me, and Zack and Ryan are younger. You met Ryan a while back when you saw us in a restaurant. He's the one who broke his leg." I put a forkful of salmon into my mouth, chewing slowly and swallowing before resuming. "My brothers are very competitive, so I learned early on that I have to give as good as I get. Like all siblings, we have the occasional spats, but we are all very protective of each other, though." I pause and sip some water. "Dad has two brothers who have a couple of kids each, so there are lots of cousins as well. It's crazy enough when my family gets together, but with uncles, aunts, nieces, and nephews thrown in, it's usually pretty chaotic." The love and admiration I feel for my family must have shone through in my light, happy expression, as Xander's eyes twinkle.

"Hmm. I can imagine." Xander's brows crease together while he eats as if visualizing the cacophony of so many people together bothers him. "You mentioned a while ago that your brothers are also in the building industry, if I remember correctly?" Xander queries after a moment, coaxing me for more details, as if genuinely interested. It surprises me he remembered.

"Yes, that's correct. Luke is a commercial builder like Dad. Tyler is an electrician, Zack is a plumber, and Ryan is an architect." I chuckle   to myself and roll my eyes as I continue. "So, you can imagine what family dinners are like. It's all talk about work in one form or another and lots of good-natured ribbing." As I speak, Xander watches my animated face intently, a small smile curving his lips, the pink tip of his tongue peeking out to roll over his rosy lower lip before disappearing again. I blink under his intense scrutiny as heat creeps up my neck. My nipples harden and my pussy tingles and throbs as an image of his tongue tip flicking across my sensitive nipples or being buried between my thighs flashes through my mind.

I grab my glass of wine and gulp it, hoping to restrain my lustful thoughts. *Settle down, girl. This is no way to conduct dinner with a friend,* I chide myself.

"What about your family, Xander?" I quickly deflect. "I know you have a younger sister, Louisa, and Ethan. Any other siblings?" I have to concentrate on the conversation because I don't want to think about the heat flushing my body or the moisture pooling between my legs as his knee continues to brush against my leg intermittently, and his eyes remain hungrily focused on mine.

After a moment's hesitation, as if dragging his lustful thoughts back to my question, he clears his throat and replies, "No other siblings here, but I have two half-brothers in Greece. My father has been married and divorced several times." While Xander pauses to sip his scotch, I wonder about the edge of disdain I detect in his voice when mentioning his father while taking another mouthful of salmon. "I spent a lot of time at boarding school after my parents divorced, and holidays were split between my mum in England and father in Greece. Then, fortunately, I moved in with my mother and stepfather and their kids, Ethan and Louisa, when I left school. My father and I are not always on the best of terms, but I try to check in on my younger brothers regularly to make sure they are doing okay; they are only twenty and eighteen."

"Why are you not on good terms with your father?" I probe, my heart aching for the boy who had been sent to boarding school when he needed his parents the most.

"It's complicated, but mostly because he never wanted me around. He was more interested in running his business empire. The time I spent on holidays with my mum and step-dad made me realize what being a family was all about. I was pleased that I was able to call England home for a long while after boarding school. My mum's family welcomed me with loving arms, and I think of them as my blood relatives."

"Oh, that's a shame about your father, Xander, but great that you got to experience true family life." I hesitate, reflecting on his difficult childhood while I eat more of my meal before continuing, "How did you get to where you are today?"

"I'd learned a thing or two during my time with my father, because he insisted I work during the holidays in one of his companies, so I saved the small allowance he gave me and worked hard in construction and real estate jobs in England. Then branched out with my own business fixing up houses and re-selling them. It just grew from there."

Surmising Xander is downplaying his climb to the top, I know how hard he must have worked to get where he is. I recognize a similar drive and determination in my own family. Each is a role model in one way or another.

Our conversation, injected with a little humor, remains on neutral ground as we discuss family and memories, relatives spread across the globe, and boarding school while we finish our meals.

After a while, silence falls between us, and Xander calls over a waiter, settling the bill. A pang of disappointment stabs me as I recognize that our evening seems to be coming to an end so early, so I am pleasantly surprised when he clasps my hand between his. My eyes widen as they land on his desire-filled eyes; the color of a stormy sea as they look straight back at me. I feel like I am battling hard to keep my head above water as my full lips part slightly and I suck in a quick breath and brush hair from my face.

"Would you like to take a walk along the harbor?" Xander offers, his deep voice seductive and hypnotic as he drawls the words.

His eyes study my long, delicate fingers, running his thumb over the back of my hand before turning it over and doing the same to my palm. His touch electrifies me, turning my mind to mush. My mouth goes dry, and my face flushes with heat.

Nodding, because I can't get the words out, my eyes follow, mesmerized, as he lifts my hand, and his sinful lips press a feather-soft kiss against it. An electrified zap shoots to my lower belly as it spasms and drips moisture onto my panties.

"Come, then." His eyes darken, full of passion, running appreciatively over my body when I straighten my dress as we stand. Once again, his hand rests lightly on the small of my back, sending shivers up and down my spine as he leads me back downstairs and into the pleasant night air.

It is a balmy evening with the occasional breeze wafting off the sparkling, mirror-like water. Our arms brush as we walk to a railing at the water's edge, both leaning on it and peering out. I can feel the heat emanating from his body and his deliciously heady masculine scent mixes with the sea air invading my senses and I inhale deeply, savoring the aroma.

"Oh, what an amazing view," I exclaim, with a grin of pure delight, my eyes crinkling in the corners, as I survey the small bay lined on one side with moored motor yachts and glass-fronted office buildings and converted warehouses on the other side.

"Yes, it is." Xander's quiet voice makes me turn and glance at him. Surprisingly, his eyes are fixed intently on me and not the view. He lazily turns his firmly built body to face me and lifts a hand to brush some windswept strands from my face where it lingers, cupping my cheek, while his other hand holds my shoulder. His touch is as gentle as the night breeze, but every hair on my scalp stands to attention and every skin cell tingles. I am breathless and can't move, not that I want to.

Xander leans down, his lips brush just below my ear, raising goose bumps along my skin. Groaning, my body floods with desire.

"I've wanted to do this since our embrace at the site office," he whispers, his warm breath tickling my ear. His head moves slightly to gaze briefly into my engrossed eyes while his thumb gently strokes my cheek, making me lick my dry lips with the tip of my tongue. "I've dreamt of you and your delectable body for a long time, and it has been driving me crazy. I need you, Georgina." His mouth hovers so close to mine that I inhale his breath.

"Xander," I barely breathe his name, unable to formulate any other words before his luscious lips descend agonizingly slowly to land gently on mine. Our hunger for each other is palpable, our passion igniting like an inferno, as our lips mesh hard and hungrily.

Xander's hand tightens on my neck and shoulder, pulling me against him so his demanding lips can savor my mouth. My hands grip his strong broad shoulders as I fiercely kiss him, consumed by the lust that explodes within me. Xander presses me against his rock-hard erection and runs his hands down my back, skimming the top of my buttocks. We both groan blissfully.

After a few moments, I reluctantly pull my mouth away, taking a deep breath. My dazed eyes peer into his sultry, liquid blue eyes. He watches me closely, as if trying to gauge my next move.

"I need you too, Xander. Desperately." Achingly, barely above a whisper, I utter the words I know to be the truth.

He rests his forehead against mine, his large hand caressing my back as he gathers his scattered thoughts. "Your place or mine?" he finally asks, his voice a smoky drawl.

"My flat mates are all home tonight, so there won't be much privacy. It will have to be your place," I murmur, an apologetic smile on my lips.

He nods and slowly smiles, buttoning his jacket to hide his bulging erection. "My place it is then." He hugs me tightly and places a soft kiss on my forehead before releasing me, repositioning his arm around my shoulders, and steering me back inside the casino complex.

"How many flat mates do you have, Georgina?" Xander queries casually as we stroll through the foyer.

"Officially two. Hayden, you know about, and Simone, the tall redhead from the nightclub the other night, but she is not home a lot. And Hayden's boyfriend, Kurt, stays over a lot as well. So, there are lots of comings and goings all the time," I respond casually, feeling less nervous while discussing my friends.

Instead of heading out the casino's front doors to get a cab as I'd expected, Xander maneuvers me down a long passage-way lined with expensive looking shops into a hotel lobby.

"Are you sure this is what you want, Georgina? I will understand if you have second thoughts." Xander drops his arm, turning me to face him, holding my hand as he gently brushes his big hand up and down my arm, keeping me close, but giving me freedom to move away if I choose.

Pausing, I look him directly in the eyes and ponder his question. "Do you live here in the hotel?" I ask, suddenly confused about where we are. I hadn't really considered where Xander might live but hadn't expected it to be a hotel.

"No, I don't. My parents are in town and staying at my place, so like you, there will be no privacy for us there. I booked a room in the hotel in case we needed it," he answers matter-of-factly, watching me closely, but it raises another question.

"Were you so sure of getting me into bed with you tonight?" My voice bristles and my words are clipped, while my brows snap together in a frown, annoyed that he thought me such an easy mark.

"Not at all, Georgina." His voice is calm and placating, as if dealing with a temperamental child. "I was hopeful and had sensed that you were feeling the same heat between us that I had, but I have never considered you a 'sure thing'." Xander pauses, his eyes sincere as he gazes at me, and then continues, "If you want to go home now, I won't stop you. If you wish to wait a bit longer, that is fine too. However, I can promise you a night of pleasure if you choose to come upstairs with me. What happens next is entirely your choice."

CHAPTER 11 - Gina

I watch Xander closely as I consider his words. Grateful that he is giving me a choice, I briefly contemplate going home but realize that he is the only one who can douse the burning desire tearing through me.

I've tried to put out the fire by myself, but it was to no avail. The deep-seated yearning for Xander returns in full force every time I think of him or a scent reminds me of him. The only way I am going to get beyond the edginess that has taken up residence inside me is to face it head-on. *I need Xander to fuck me. And now is as good a time as any.*

After a small subtle nod, I raise my head, shoot him a sexy smile, batter my lashes mischievously, and, in an impish and sensuously husky voice, respond, "Let's do this, Big Boy."

Xander tilts his chin and chuckles, thrilled I have agreed and amused at my nickname for him, while his eyes scorch me with their heat.

Nodding, he murmurs softly, "Come with me, then." His arm snakes around my shoulders, holding me close to his body. I can feel his powerful thighs move against mine and the steel of his ribcage against my upper arm as we walk to the elevator. His heat and scent fan the simmering fire within me, flushing my skin a faint pink. When Xander's large palm drops again to the curve of my lower back, my legs became wobbly as his fingers brush against the top of my buttocks as he ushers me into the elevator.

Taking my hand in his and turning it over while the doors shut, he caresses my palm, making circles with the forefinger of his other hand, watching as goosebumps erupt over my arm. Mesmerized, my eyes follow the path his finger is making, while my free hand runs up and down his coated forearm. Neither of us can keep our hands off the other and his gentle circling movements stoke the inferno ablaze in my belly. I fight desperately against the urge to undress him right there and then.

"I want to kiss you so badly right now, but if I start, I won't stop," he murmurs into my ear.

Moaning, I nearly fall against him as my knees buckle, but the elevator dinging startles me out of my aroused fog. Xander clasps my hand firmly and tugs me into the hallway, reaching into his coat pocket for the key card as he strides toward his door. I keep pace, my craving matching his. Dropping my hand, he swings the door open and holds it, turning on the lights, and standing aside as I follow him in.

As the door closes behind me, Xander spins to face me, grabbing me and crushing me against the closed door. His hands cup my face, his warm fingers tuck beneath my hair while his thumbs run over my cheeks, and my hands grip his sides, scrunching his shirt. His darkened, stormy eyes hold my gaze for a moment before dropping to rake over my plump, kiss-ravaged lips, then my body, lingering on my ample breasts. My lips part in breathy anticipation as I watch his mouth lower to mine, my warm breath lightly fanning his lips as they hover.

"Last chance to back out, Georgina," he breathes into my open mouth, holding himself rigidly.

Moaning, my eyes lock with his, as I run my fingers up his chest, until my hands wrap around his neck, tangling my fingers in his silky hair and pulling his mouth onto mine, giving him my answer.

Xander groans and drops one hand to my lower back, thrusting my abdomen against his rock-hard bulge. He takes hungry possession of my mouth, devouring it with deep sweeping strokes of his sinful tongue, while my lips crush against his. My tongue plunges into his mouth, reveling in its heat, probing, and circling in its discovery of his carnal depth.

Lip-locked, we frenziedly tug off each other's jackets, letting them drop to the floor. Xander's hands return to my shoulders, then slide down my silky arms to hold my elbows as he steps backward into the room, guiding me along with him, pressed against him so that there was barely any space between us. He reaches behind me, his hands slipping under my long hair to stroke my back, groaning with surprise when his fingers find the open-cut back of my dress and my exposed skin. His hand repeatedly strokes my naked back, dropping to skim over my firm, rounded butt cheeks encased in the sleek figure-hugging fabric of my dress, as if he delights in the tactile contrast between them.

Roaming over his soft cotton shirt, my hands explore the muscle definition of his body beneath, tingling with every caress as they slide down to his trousers, desperate to get him undressed.

Bringing his hands to my face again, Xander softens our kiss, slowly pulling away, drawing in a much-needed deep breath. His large, warm hand lightly touches my shoulder and gently spins me around. Twisting my head, I watch over my shoulder, enthralled, as his fingers blaze an electrified trail down my bare spine, sending sparks shooting through my body and wet heat pooling between my legs, soaking my skimpy knickers.

"Oh fuck," he utters, his voice raw and primal, his hungry eyes raking my lithe, toned back and buttocks, which are defined beautifully by the clingy fabric. He undoes the small zip, causing the material over my bottom to gape, showing off my red lacy panties.

"Mmm," he whispers. Scooping up my hair, he lets it fall forward, over my shoulder, then his long fingers slowly glide down my back again, under the material of my dress and land on my lace-covered backside, gently squeezing the toned cheeks before running his fingers through the indented crease.

I groan, arching my neck, my knees almost giving out on me before he tightens an arm around my waist, pulling me against his rock-hard dick which is raring to escape the confines of his trousers, and positioning it to rest in the crease between my sexily covered cheeks.

"Fuck, Georgina, your ass is spectacular," he murmurs against my neck, kissing a trail to my ear while his free hand slips under the front of my dress, causing it to slip off my shoulders and pool at my waist. His hand pauses on the softness of my unsupported breast before skimming my flat stomach to my heated crotch, pressing against it, making me moan and twitch. My pussy clenches at his smoky drawl and the feathering of his hands, turning my mind into a buzzing mess of static. I reach behind him, running my hands over the soft fabric of his trousers and stroke his thighs, my fingers stretching to touch his ass, causing his cock to twitch against me, making my body clench again. I am a molten mess and need to taste him and feel him inside me now. Driven by my raging need, my hand slips between our bodies to cup his balls through his pants, relishing the heat emanating through them, thrilling at the involuntary jerk of his hips against my hand.

"Vixen," he growls, then nips my neck before stepping away. Xander turns me to face him. My dress drops to the floor and, stepping out of it, I peer at his face, which is captivated by my slender, toned, and tanned body snugly sheathed in lacy red skimpy panties. Hungrily gazing at my well sized breasts, cupping them, he then lifts them slightly, feeling their weight and moaning as he squeezes them.

Impatiently, I unbutton his shirt, spreading it wide over his shoulders and letting it rest on his bulging biceps. My hands trail over his bronzed, sculpted chest, my eyes ogling the broad and powerful man before me. A smattering of short, dark, curly hair lay between his protruding pecs and continues down the cleft between his sharply defined six-pack, disappearing beneath his trousers, making me want to follow where it leads.

Unable to stop myself from kissing him, I caress his mouth while my fingers run around his firm, pink nipples. At his sharp inhalation, I pull away, my eyes shooting to his darkened glazed stare focused on my face. I smile devilishly, realizing how sensitive his nipples are.

"Fuuck," Xander groans, blinks, and gives me a sexy smile.

"You like?" I purr teasingly, circling his nipples again as I watch his pupils dilate further and his tongue flicks across his bottom lip. Xander's groan sounds more like a growl as he pulls me tightly against his body once more and devours my mouth, while I frantically tug his shirt tails out of his trouser waistband. Stepping back slightly as he lets go of me, he frantically undoes his belt buckle while I let his shirt drop to the floor. His hands cup my breasts again, thumbs swiping over my pebbled nipples. Moaning in delight, my head drops backward, and my hands fumble with his trouser button and zip, unable to undo them as my brain has turned to mush.

Xander drops his hands to his trousers instead, deftly undoing his fly, before his head lowers to pull my nipple into his warm, wet mouth. Loudly I moan from his touch as I bury my fingers in his hair. I feel him kick off his shoes and step out of his trousers. Wrapping his arms around me, cupping my ass, he expertly lifts me, encouraging my legs around his waist as he does. I cross my feet behind his back and drape my arms around his neck to hold on, and he readjusts an arm, placing it around my waist, pressing my soft, round breasts against his chest. He strides past the sofa into a separate bedroom, carrying me confidently in his strong arms.

The tip of his rigid erection rubs against my lace-covered folds with each step. Excitement pulses through me each time, my arousal soaking my panties, making me desperate to feel his thick length inside me as soon as possible.

"Xander," I beg.

"Mmm, I know, Georgina. Soon," he promises as he sets me gently down on the bed, with my feet dangling over the edge. I drink in his buff, well defined body, my eyes pausing at his trunk-style cotton underpants. They fit snugly around his waist and thighs but are stretched tightly over his large erect dick. My eyes widen, my nostrils flare, and I lick my lips as I stare hungrily, fascinated by his length and the thick girth of his erection through his underwear.

He gives me a cheeky grin while he loops his thumbs under the waistband of his jocks, stepping out of them quickly and kicking them aside. My eyes blaze with need as they sweep over his neatly manscaped groin, down to his long, thick shaft, captivated by it as it juts horizontally from his belly, tilting slightly upwards, making me wonder if it would ever fit inside me.

Reaching out a hand to caress the vein that runs the length of his shaft, my touch causes a drop of precum to spill from his slit, glistening on his crown. Xander grabs my hand before I can touch him again. His face strains as he shakes his head slightly.

"I'm barely holding on here, Georgina," he murmurs, sounding almost pained. "Play with it as much as you like later."

"You can count on it." I gasp as he eases me back onto the bed.

Chuckling, he kneels, straddling my body, interlocking our fingers and positioning our hands above my head, while his face hovers over mine.

He kisses me hungrily, releasing his hold on me so he can trail his fingers down my arms and shoulders. My senses tingle in their wake while his hands slide further to cup my breasts, molding and squeezing them, his fingers circling the stiff peaks with satisfaction. Squirming and moaning beneath him, I arch my back, rolling my hips and pressing my pussy against his hard cock, silently begging for more. The combined moans of our arousal echoes into the room around us.

Releasing my breasts and pushing up off the bed, Xander stands between my legs. Skimming his hands sensuously down my midsection, my skin quivering in their wake, he loops his fingers into the sides of my panties and pulls them down my legs, letting them drop to the floor.

He pauses momentarily, taking in the neat, narrow line of hair like an aircraft runway leading to its destination. His eyes gleam in anticipation, peering at me like I am the most beautiful woman he has ever seen. That look steals my breath and makes my heart flip in anticipation of what is about to happen.

His large skilled hands skim sensuously from my knees to the top of my thighs and back down again, where he spreads my legs wide. Holding me open, he stands staring longingly at my wet pussy.

"Beautiful," he murmurs, his voice thick, like his jutting cock. His wicked eyes float to mine, holding my gaze for a moment before returning to my slick sex. He runs his hands over my smooth thighs, skimming the soft flesh near my apex and over my mound. His thumb slips into my folds, landing on my clit, pressing, and circling the swollen nub. I buck my hips and sigh ecstatically. He slips two fingers into my tight dripping entrance, making me buck again.

"Ahhh," I cry, rolling my hips against his hand. His eyes flit to my face, and my glazed eyes lock with his, vaguely registering his smug expression in the passion-fueled haze in my head, and that he is enjoying driving me crazy. He shoots me a cheeky grin as he removes his fingers and quickly thrusts three fingers back into my slickness several times, moaning as he does.

"Ahhhh," I cry out again. "Xander, I need you. Now!"

"Patience, Little One," he cajoles. Xander removes his hands and leans to the side of me, reaching for his trousers and taking out a foil packet that he rips open with his teeth before he rolls the condom onto his cock. The bed dips slightly as he straddles my hips, my legs falling wide in anticipation. His body perches over mine, the tip of his erection touching my navel, whilst his chest barely touches my nipples as he rests on his forearms. His hands hold my head, and his face is so close that his breath feathers against my lips. Finally, his warm, luscious lips caress mine, softly at first, then meshing with hunger. Our tongues fervently explore and savor each other.

Xander breaks the kiss abruptly, breathing heavily, as he slides further down my legs and repositions himself between them. I watch his tight facial features as he strains to hold himself back.

Grabbing his shaft with one hand, and rubbing the tip through my slick folds, the velvet-smooth head of his rigid cock presses against my entrance. He is motionless as he relishes my wet heat.

"Mmm, definitely ready for me," Xander utters as if to himself, his voice husky. "I'll try to take it slowly, so your body can adjust to accommodate me."

I nod, begging, "Now, Xander. Now." The feeling of him at my opening sends me into a frenzy, desperate for him to be inside me. He watches my face intently as he pushes slowly inward, then pauses, and I groan as I am stretched by his girth.

"Oh, Yesss!" I exhale, tilting my head back in pleasure at the tightness, the fullness of him. He pushes forward again, burying himself inside of me, filling me. "Yes. Yes. Ohhh, so good." Inhaling deeply, I raise my hips to allow him deeper.

"Geez-uz," Xander growls. "Fuck, you are so tight," he grunts, the usual hint of his accent more obvious now. Sliding out, he pushes in again, impaling me in one steady motion. He momentarily pauses, scanning my face to ensure I am not in pain. I reach down and gently tug on his thighs, as my eyes implore him to continue. I am in heaven, deliriously lost in the sensation of intense arousal and fulfillment.

Needing more, Xander pulls out and stands, grabbing me behind the knees and dragging me to the edge of the bed before wrapping my long, tanned legs around his waist.

He thrusts into me without warning, taking me hard and deep, again and again, his control unleashed with an animalistic drive that matches mine. I push against him with each thrust, short moans escaping my mouth as I gasp for breath. My face flushes with a feverish heat that consumes me, my heart pounding in my chest, my vision and hearing muffled and my mind buzzing with white noise as the crescendo of my release nears its peak.

"Xannnder," I plead, stretching out his name hoarsely, my mouth parched. My back arches as he hammers into me, then my core convulses and spasms around him. A silent moan flows from my open mouth as my entire body clenches. My orgasm is all-consuming, shattering me into pieces whilst my juices gush and leak from me as he slams in and out.

Xander groans loudly and his pelvis pistons as his climax peaks. With one final hard thrust, he grips my hips tightly, holding himself deep inside me as he explodes. "Gina!" He drags out my name with a guttural moan as his head flies back, thrusting one last time before letting my hips drop to the bed and sagging on top of me.

We lay there for a few moments, drawing in ragged breaths, sated, waiting for vision and sanity to return. After a while, Xander stands and walks to the bathroom to dispose of the condom, and my eyes follow him. My stomach flips at the wide grin he flings at me as he makes his way back to the bed. I lay exactly as he left me, with my arms flung over my head, legs still spread wide, my body exhausted. He is physically a beautiful man that I could drool over all day, every day. As good as he looks in a business suit, I will never unsee the magnificence of his nakedness. *He was built for sin,* I muse. *Hmm, that will be a hell of a distraction in our next business meeting.*

Xander stands between my legs and trails his fingers around my nipples, then down to my navel, continuing to my drenched pussy. He throws me a self-satisfied grin as he holds out his arms.

"You look very pleased with yourself." My eyes crinkle as I grin at him, and place my hands in his outstretched ones. Then he pulls me to my feet.

"I am. Very pleased that I could make you come in such a spectacular way."

Wrapping his strong arms around me, holding me tight against his body and kissing the top of my head, my sensitive breasts squish against his shapely pecs, and my hips push against his now-softened cock. Coiling my arms around his waist, my forearms sit over his shoulder blades, and I rest my cheek against his firm shoulder. His warm, musky scent fills my nostrils as I snuggle closer.

"I didn't hurt you, did I?" Xander queries softly, his breath fans my forehead as he looks down at me.

Tilting my head back, I take in the sight of his relaxed features and catch a glimpse of emotion that flickers through his twinkling eyes before he masks it again like he's done so often since I met him. Shaking my head while I hold his gaze, I respond, "No, definitely not."

Touching his cheek with the palm of my hand, I stand on tiptoe and kiss him lightly on the lips. I don't recognize this warm, relaxed, and considerate man as the stern, take-no-prisoners, scowling man I had first met. Maybe it was post-coital euphoria, but I trust and feel a real affection for this version of Xander.

"Good," he laughs. "Because I haven't had enough of you yet."

"Really, Big Boy? What did you have in mind?" I chuckle flirtatiously.

Suddenly, he scoops me up in his arms and carries me into the bathroom, where he returns me to my feet. With one arm still around my waist, Xander turns on the water, testing its heat before dragging me into the oversize shower with him.

I gaze at his enthralled face as his hands run over my buttocks, slick with water, then travel up and over my shoulders. Then, putting a slight distance between us, his eyes focus on my ample, rounded breasts while his hands massage them, softly, expertly.

I adore his body, even though I have only just begun exploring it. He seems to feel the same about mine as well, bending his head to suckle and lave my nipples. I smile in pleasure, moving away slightly, but not far enough to break contact with his tongue. Then soaping my hands as he straightens, I trail them from his shoulders over his toned chest and down over his ripped six-pack, skirting around to his buttocks, soaping and squeezing them. Soaping my hands again, he watches as I run them over his abdomen again, and down into the v-shape of his groin, circling the base of his shaft. I lather again and cup his clean-shaven ball sac as I gently tug and roll them. He inhales sharply, lifting his head to look at me.

As I chuckle, Xander grabs my hand and slides it onto his soft shaft, gliding it back and forth before moving it back to his well-defined pecs. "More of that later, Georgina." He grabs the soap and skims his foamy hands over my breasts again, this time circling and squeezing my nipples before slipping down my flat stomach and sliding between my legs to cup my sex. One long finger dips into my slit, and I circle my hips against it. I tilt my head back as he withdraws and inserts his finger a few more times before removing his hand entirely. With one arm around my waist, he twirls me, facing away from him, then pulls me against him. My back rests snugly against his torso, while his semi-hard cock lay against the crack of my butt cheeks, as if enticing me to allow his entry later. His hands cup my breasts, and he bends his head to lay small soft kisses up my neck and behind my ear.

"Mmm, you have a delicious body, Georgina. One that I would like to spend a lot more time in. Can you stay a while longer?"

"Only if you promise to fuck my brains out, Big Boy." Cheekily, I press my ass against his cock. Surprised by my brazen and forward behavior with Xander, because I haven't been that way with other men, I briefly wonder why he brings out a different side in me, but I push the thought aside for now.

"I thought you would never ask," he chuckles, then turns off the water, grabs a towel, and gently dries my body. Covering myself in the towel, I step out of the shower and wrap another towel around my wet hair, as Xander quickly dries himself and wraps his towel around his waist. He turns me to face him, then picks me up, holding me close to his body. Giggling, I wrap my arms around his neck and my legs around his narrow waist, interlocking my feet behind him. As he walks us back into the bedroom, he claims my lips again in soft, lingering kisses.

When he approaches the bed, he bends down to pull back the sheets, then deposits me gently on the cool fabric. He quickly disappears into the lounge before dropping his towel on his return and places more condoms on the bedside table. Clambering in next to me, he covers us both with the soft, crisp linen then we turn to face each other. Propping himself up on one elbow, his dick rests against my thigh. His warm hand skims my cheek, resting on my chin as one finger traces the outline of my full lips, then runs across the seam. I flick my tongue out, licking his fingertip before he pushes it inside my willing mouth. Closing my lips around his finger, I suck and lick it like a lollipop.

Xander groans, his eyes flashing with desire, as he moves his finger in, out, in an erotic dance, as I run my hands over his broad back. I can feel his taut muscles twitch and ripple under my fingers while he shifts his hand down my neck to skim my shoulders and chest, before circling and squeezing my breasts.

He continues, laying a trail of tingles across my belly, and skimming over my mound, before returning to capture a breast with his hand and mouth. He licks and suckles one nipple, then pays the same attention to the other, continuing to alternate between them.

I sigh as my arousal builds again, arching my back slightly to push my nipples further into his mouth. I love what he is doing to me and want to hear him call out my name again.

"Xander, why did you call me Gina earlier?" I husk, suddenly remembering him changing my name when he came.

Engrossed in my nipples, he pauses and lifts his head, puzzled by my question. "What? What are you talking about?"

"Earlier, when you came, you called me Gina. Why?"

CHAPTER 12 –
Gina

"Did I? I wasn't aware of it." Xander dismisses the question and goes back to focusing on my nipples, giving each a sharp pinch before he repositions himself, straddling me, devouring my lips.

I forget my question as his hot, ardent kisses and touch reignite my arousal. I love the way he touches me and, driven by the rising hunger for him, my hands roam his body again, letting him know how much I enjoy what he is doing. I skim my hands up and down his legs. One hand circles his shaft, slowly sliding from base to tip while the other cups his balls, squeezing gently. Xander moans, and his dick flexes. I run my hands up over his chest and his shoulders and back, finishing at his shaft, repeatedly running the same course over his body. He breaks the kiss, his eyes dark and horny as they peer into mine.

He grabs one of my hands, places it near my head, then does the same with the other, interlocking our fingers. Dipping his head, his tongue torments my body as it runs over my sensitive nipples and down my stomach, his hands following the moist trail as he crawls down my body until he steps off the bed to kneel at the end of it. Spreading my legs wide, he pulls me down to the edge of the bed until my pussy meets his mouth, and lifts my legs over his shoulders. Entwining his arms under my thighs and over my hips, his fingers play tantalizingly around my outer lips, making me squirm.

I can feel the breath from his deep chuckle and shudder, so he softly blows on the sensitive area again. At my gasp, he lifts his head to watch my blissful face before his thumbs open my outer lips and his tongue flicks at my clit. Squealing in pleasure, I push my hips higher and spread my legs wider, allowing him more access to my sex.

He flicks again and again before sinking his mouth against me, sucking and licking, tormenting me. I moan and writhe against his mouth and talented tongue, an achy fullness amassing within me from his touch. Xander lifts his head and places his thumb over my sensitive clitoral nub, sliding his tongue down my slit, burying it deep inside me. I yelp and thrust against his hot, thick tongue. His moan vibrates against me as he fucks me with it. Each time, I thrust against him as my internal muscles tighten, my fire intensifying.

"Ahhh, don't stop," I pant as Xander moves his mouth and laps at my flowing juices. The way he touches me makes me melt.

"You are so wet, agapi mou." Lifting my head as he speaks, I find his head raised, smiling down, almost proudly, at my wetness, before he meets my adoring gaze. "Absolutely beautiful."

His fingers reach up to tweak a nipple, while his other hand cups my sex briefly before running a finger up and down my slit. One finger is thrust in and out of my opening, then two. My nipple is pinched every time he thrusts and I am moaning and writhing against his hand. He plays my body as a skilled musician plays their instrument, with finesse. Then his mouth descends on my clit again, sucking and flicking the nub. I am an incoherent mass of sensation. The inferno within me has swiftly become a white-hot wildfire, consuming me.

Under the continued onslaught of his mouth and fingers, my powerful orgasm lifts my hips off the bed, breaking the contact with his mouth, as my muscles clench around his fingers. A high-pitched, strangled keening sound escapes me, and my vision fades to stars.

Vaguely, I hear Xander softly murmur "That's it. Come for me, baby," while he holds still as my contractions grip his fingers. When I drop to the bed, gasping for air and my body listless, he removes his hand and crawls up next to me, laying on his side facing me with his head propped on his hand. Gently, he brushes some hair out of my eyes, watching them as they slowly refocus.

"Are you okay?" he asks tenderly, with a satisfied smile as if riveted at the delectable sight of me coming.

"Ooh. Am I ever." I manage to get the words past my parched throat, my chest heaving as I take a deep breath. "Whoa, that was intense and magnificent." I throw my arms over my forehead and sigh in contentment.

He chuckles. "You looked like you were having a good time."

Nodding, I turn my head to look at him. "I hope you were too."

"Very much so. You taste like a fine wine that I just want to keep drinking," he murmurs as he bends down and places a featherlight kiss on my forehead. "I want more of you, Gina, but only when you are ready."

My gaze scans down his body, stopping at his swollen shaft, then I raise an eyebrow and give him a sly smile and a devilish wink. "Insatiable, Xander. Just give me a few minutes to get my breath back."

"Okay." He smiles at me as he gently kisses my lips. "Would you like something to drink?" His breath feels warm against my damp face.

As I roll over to face him, I return his kiss and run my hand down his cheek, enjoying the feel of his chiseled features. "Yes, just a water please."

"At your service, milady," he teases, flipping himself off the bed and to his feet in one supple, athletic move. The almost unnoticeable buckling of one knee reminds me that his injured ankle is still occasionally causing some issues for him. I drool at the delectable sight of his perfectly toned ass cheeks as he confidently strides into the lounge area and raids the mini bar, returning with two bottles of water. This lighthearted side of Xander is a delight, and I suspect is rarely something he displays, so I savor the moment.

On his return, he slides back between the sheets, sitting with his back against the bedhead. Xander passes me a bottle, which I take as I also move to sit next to him, pulling the sheets up over my chest. Being naked with a man while having sex is necessary, but sitting naked while talking between make-out sessions is not something I am comfortable with. Taking a couple of sips from the bottle, I watch him do the same, my eyes following the bobbing motion of his Adam's apple as he swallows, almost finishing the bottle.

"I haven't heard you speak Greek before, Xander. Do you speak it often?" I query as I re-cap my bottle and place it on the side table.

"It is my native language, but I don't speak it much here. Usually only when I catch up with my father, which is rare. Do you speak any other languages?"

"No, other than the usual hello, goodbyes, thank you, etc. in French and Italian, but I have always wanted to be fluent in another language. Just never had people around to learn and chat with."

"I could teach you if you like. I speak Italian, French, and Spanish as well."

"Wow. Impressive." I smile at him with admiration. "I bet you could teach me a lot of things, Big Boy," I tease, as I move to my knees and lean over him, running my hand down his chest to his groin and back again. I then push the sheets aside and straddle his thick, defined thighs. It is my turn to start a wildfire within him.

Xander raises his eyebrows and throws me a crooked grin. "You don't seem to need much instruction," he mocks as his eyes glint.

Chuckling softly, I sit upright on my knees with my arms extended in front of me, my fingers circling his nipples. Xander's eyes blaze as they roam over my exposed breasts. His chest twitches, and he breathes in sharply as I scrape my nails across the pebbled tips. With his raw, hungry eyes devouring me, Xander makes a low, deep noise in his throat, relishing in my touch. I lean in and lash his hardened peaks with my tongue, then circle them with my lips and suck vigorously, the lingering scent of soap tingling my nostrils and reigniting the pulsing in my pussy.

He moans again, throwing his head back, savoring the sensations while he rubs my shoulders tenderly. Loving the feeling of being in control, I trail my tongue, followed by my fingers, down the hollow between his six-pack, flicking into his navel and stopping at his groin.

As I wiggle myself further down his long legs, I place my hands on his inner thighs, feeling their heat emanating as I spread him wide, kneeling between them with my butt resting on my heels.

His hands drop to the bed as if bracing himself. A quick, furtive glance from under my eyelashes spies Xander's eyes focusing on me, almost black as he anticipates my next move. Teasingly, I smile and slide my hands over his inner thighs and circle, without touching, his dick and balls.

Delighting in tormenting him, I note his inner thighs as they twitch and repeat the movements for several moments, thrilled when his cock becomes ramrod stiff again. *Hmm, hands or mouth*, I ponder, knowing by his scorching hot look and held breath that he is wondering the same thing. Holding his gaze, I move one hand to gently cup his balls, while the other wraps around his shaft, giving both a slight squeeze.

"Fuck! Oh yeah." His hips buck, and he sighs heavily.

His reaction and the feel of his hot stiff shaft and soft balls in my hands has my stomach contracting, and a rush of heat floods my body. I lick my lips and squeeze him again, hunching over, catching his tip with my mouth as he bucks.

"Oh, Fuck." He pushes his now rigid dick in further. I lick his length, swirling my tongue around his tip, and suck him in till he bumps the back of my throat, savoring his velvety iron hardness. Gliding my hand up and down his shaft, I move my mouth around him, his hips pushing in sync with me, making him moan loudly.

His raging inferno ignites mine. I want him inside me. Badly. Urgently.

Breaking contact, I reach for a condom, but before I can get to it, Xander grabs one and rips the packet open with his teeth. Speedily, he rolls it on, driven by the same intense need.

As he shimmies down the bed to lay on his back, he gives me a cheeky wink then grabs my hips so I am straddling him, then he holds his eager, steel-like shaft at the entrance to my hole, while my hands brace his chest. I can feel his heat and my slickness as I slowly slide down his erection, taking him inch by inch. Twisting my hips slightly, I shut my eyes and sigh, reveling in the feeling of fullness as he bottoms out inside me.

"God, you're killing me here, Gina," Xander gasps, his voice raspy from holding back. His thumbs swirl softly over my clit, spiking my desire.

"What's the rush, Big Boy?" I tease, watching his eyes glaze as I move up and down, sinking down onto him again and again. I can feel the rumble of his deep growl beneath me, the sound of it exciting me and making my body throb feverishly, increasing the speed of my hips bucking against him.

"Ahh." I pant with every down stroke, grinding myself against him shamelessly, chasing my release.

"Can't. Wait. Much. Longer." Xander moans loudly, desperately, as he grabs my hips, and flips us over in one swift move, so I am now on my back. With my legs wrapped around him, he continues to thrust like a piston in a speeding race car. His teeth grit and jaw clenches, as he holds back, waiting for me to come.

As he hammers into me, his deep thrusts drive me wild, flinging me into the abyss of a blinding orgasm.

I shriek. My back arches, my legs lock around him, my pussy clenches, flooding my body with a rosy pink glow.

Feeling my climax, Xander thrusts twice more, throws his head back, and groans loudly.

"Fuuuck. Ohhhh Fuck. Geeenaaah!" He explodes inside me, gripping my hips tightly as aftershocks from my orgasm pulse on his cock.

Heavy breathing fills the room, along with the tangy scent of sex, as we slowly regain our senses. Xander pulls out and collapses face down on the bed, and then he turns his face toward me. With my arms flopping listlessly above my head, my body is covered in a fine translucent layer of sweat and a feeling of euphoria engulfs me, which must show on my face. Feeling his eyes on me, I turn my head to look into his sultry eyes. He wears the grin of a sated man. I gift him with a look of adoration and see a flicker of surprise cross his face before he masks it. My brain feels as thick as porridge, but my senses sing with joy at how he has made me feel tonight.

Propping himself on his elbows, he kisses me lightly on the forehead and casts his eyes over my body as if it is delectable.

"Are you ok, Gina?" he asks, his voice husky.

Nodding, I beam. "I'm in heaven, Xander. I've never had so many orgasms in the same session before." At his questioning look, I continue, "I'm serious. You really fucked me over." I chuckle to myself.

"That surprises me, Georgina. You are such a sexy, beautiful, giving woman. I can't imagine a man not enjoying every opportunity with you." He stands as he speaks, his words seeming sincere and moves to dispose of his condom. When he returns, he brushes my hair off my face and kisses me lightly on the lips. "Come under the covers before you get cold."

Filled with lethargy, I shuffle under the sheets Xander has pulled back. He climbs in after me, snuggling in behind me, and pulls me back against him, spooning me as he wraps his strong arms around me. We lay in silence for a while, enjoying each other's warmth and the way we fit together.

"Have you had many lovers, Georgina?" he murmurs against my ear, his warm breath tickling it. I hesitate before answering. Not that I am ashamed by how few men I have slept with, I just don't think it is any of Xander's business. But then I realize we have just shared far more intimate moments, so decide honesty is the best policy after all.

"You are the fifth, Xander. A couple of one-night stands, my ex-fiancé, and a friend with benefits. What about you? Have you lost count of the women you have slept with?"

"Don't believe everything you read in the press." He nips my ear in a gentle reprimand. "I am not with a different woman every night, but there have been quite a few. I don't keep count because it achieves nothing." After a short pause, he continues, "Tell me about your ex-fiancé."

"Not much to tell. I broke it off a couple of years ago when I found out he was cheating on me." Despite playing it cool, there is a bitter tinge to my voice. I had been devastated at the time, loving someone so desperately, only to find out they didn't love me anymore, but now the bitterness stems from my failure to acknowledge what had been going on for so long.

"He didn't deserve you, so you are well rid of him," he dismisses. "What about the friend with benefits?"

I roll over and place my hand on his cheek, peering into his clear blue eyes, detecting a guardedness in them. *Is he jealous?*

KERRIE MAXON

"Don't worry, Xander, I am only ever with one person at a time." I want him to see the sincerity in my eyes. "I finished with him a few months ago because I wasn't getting anything out of it anymore. We are still friends, but there won't be any more benefits."

"Good," is all he says, in a non-committal tone, but there is an edge to his voice.

Although he seems relieved, I can't understand why a man like Xander would feel even the smallest amount of jealousy. Or why he hadn't been snapped up by now? *Is he jealous or just possessive, like a kid with a new toy?*

"What about you, Xander? Have you had any long-term relationships?" I query, intrigued.

"No." His tone is abrupt, and his eyes flash. *Is that anger*, I muse? *Or just irritation because he has been asked that question many times?* His tone softens, and he continues, although there is a coldness to his words.

"After seeing my father go through so many relationships, all supposedly for love, and each one ending after a while, I learned to be skeptical of a relationship's staying power. For some people, like my mother, love is enduring. But I believe I am more like my father in that regard." He pauses, his tone solemn as he continues, "So, my relationships are short and physical and end when I get bored. Also, the time I need to devote to business is very limiting to a relationship."

You've just been put on notice, Gina, I reflect, hurt that he only seems to see me as a temporary bed partner, as I ponder the emotional toll growing up in such an environment has had on him. *Or is he remaining detached so he can avoid getting hurt and stay in control?* With a flash of perception, as I scrutinize his face, I realize his business persona is so much of whom he believes himself to be, but while we've been together tonight, I have caught glimpses of the warm, caring man he really is. The one he keeps buried from himself and the world; the little boy who has been hurt by his parents' divorce and the division between households.

"Surely that depends on the people in the relationship, Xander."

Instantly I see the cool, impersonal businessman mask Xander wears so well, overtake the warm, sensitive man I am lying next to, so before he could respond, I roll away and get out of bed.

"Look at the time. I must get home, as I have an early start in the morning."

Xander's face flickers with surprise, relief, and disappointment. He blinks at the rapid change in my demeanor, as I also don my business persona. He watches me closely as I gather up and throw on my clothes, then he jumps out of bed and does the same.

Neither of us speaks as we dress, but as I turn to say goodbye, he declares, "I'll take you home, Georgina."

"There's no need, Xander. Thank you for an amazing evening." My smile is polite and matches his impersonal façade. I just need to get out of here. Now. While my haywire emotions are only slightly bruised.

"That isn't a request, Georgina." His words are clipped, typical Mr. Scowly Face clearly annoyed at my dismissal.

Checking that we have all our belongings, we leave the room and have a silent trip in the elevator to the foyer. Xander hails a waiting cab, and we clamber in as if we have just finished a business meeting, rather than having spent hours wrapped in each other's bodies. Each stares out our windows, deep in our thoughts, as the cab drives through the light traffic.

"Georgina, we're here. Wake up."

Jumping at the sound of Xander's voice in my ear, I am startled to realize my head has been on his shoulder. *Really? How could I have fallen asleep on his shoulder?* Multiple orgasms, a lot of expended energy, and emotional upheaval have obviously exhausted me. *So much for playing it cool, Gina!*

"Oh. Sorry." Flustered, I blush and bolt upright, casting embarrassed eyes toward him. His smile is warm and genuinely caring, which confuses me.

As he gets out of the cab, he stands and waits for me to clamber out, holding his extended hand to steady myself. The warmth of his touch shoots tingles up my arm, jolting me into quickly removing my hand from his.

"Thank you again for an amazing night, Xander," I state coolly, my voice husky from sleep. Hesitating, I am not sure what else to say. *Hope to see you again. Till next time? Hope it was as good for you as it was for me.* So, I rummage in my handbag for my keys instead.

When I am finished, he bends his head and kisses me on the cheek. "It was my pleasure, Georgina," he murmurs. "Goodnight." *Wow, that is a very standoffish farewell*, I huff to myself.

"Goodnight Xander." With my head held high, I walk up the stairs and unlock my door. *Two can play at that game, Mister*, I brood and note as I turn in the doorway that Xander is already in the cab, and it is pulling away from the curb.

Shutting the door behind me and leaning against it, I can't help feeling a sense of finality in his goodnight kiss. So, he's had his way with me, slaked his thirst, and is prepared to move on to the next conquest. *Is that how it is? Or am I misreading the situation?* Annoyed at his casual dismissal of me, and myself for expecting there would be more than one amazing night, I stomp upstairs as questions assail me. *He has a reputation for loving and leaving them and has admitted that himself. So why did I think I would be any different?*

Get a grip, Gina, I chide myself. *If that is how he is, you are better off without him. Better that he say goodbye now before you get emotionally involved. Mark it up as an amazing experience.* The sex had been the best of my life and at least I know now that this was all tonight was. Deflated, I head to bed and hope to get some sleep.

137

CHAPTER 13 - Xander

I BATTLE SLEEP ON the cab ride back to my apartment. No point in going back to the hotel. It had only been somewhere to take Georgina, so I will finalize the account in the morning. Besides, my mom and stepfather, Jonathon, will most likely be in bed asleep by now, so I can let myself in and get to bed without any need for conversation. As much as I love catching up with them both, which I have been able to do over the last few days, I also really like my bachelor lifestyle, and the freedom of coming and going as I like, with whomever I like. And I am very pleased that my family wasn't exposed to the animalistic noises of my night with Georgina.

As I stare out the cab window, a video replay of my night with Georgina runs through my mind. What a hot, sexy woman she is. As well as being a generous lover, she is able to get me to heights I haven't felt in a long time. My recent hook-ups have left me feeling shallow and incomplete. I have enjoyed the sex but felt like I have been on autopilot, not wholly present, despite my attentiveness to their needs.

But Georgina is different. The searing kiss we had shared on the development site had left me in a constant state of horniness, my balls buzzing till I had to jerk off to relieve some of the tension. Something I haven't had to do with the other women. I haven't been previously tempted to break my 'no mixing business with pleasure' rule, either.

But there is something about Georgina that fires my blood. It isn't just her scorching kisses or how she openly gives of herself. It isn't just about her beauty or confidence, or that she is a smart ass happy to challenge me. It is all those things and more. She is a complete package: intriguing, sensible, daring, adventurous, intelligent, and perceptive. I feel that she sees me as an ordinary man, not a rich playboy, and her down-to-earth attitude and teasing are refreshing, particularly as tonight is the first time we have been on a personal level. And she is able to surprise me, not only with her conversation but with her sexy lingerie and bedroom antics.

Just remembering her stunning lithe body swathed in that figure-hugging, red dress, with her long hair draping down her back, stirs my balls again. Fantasies of that long hair wrapped around my fist only stoke the fire more. I have cum twice tonight, more than I have in any session of late, and my cock is raring to go again at just the thought of Georgina. Flashes of her red, skimpy panties hugging her well-proportioned contours have my cock straining against my trousers. Again. Taking a deep breath to clear the visions in my head, I readjust myself, so I am more comfortable.

No matter how hard I try, my thoughts drift back to Georgina. There is her delicious mouth. I was thrilled at the feel of her tongue and the taste of her sensuous, full lips sliding across mine. I hadn't meant for our kissing by the harbor to get so frantic, but she drove me wild, to the point where common sense deserted me. I would have taken her then and there if a shred of sanity hadn't crept in. It took a lot of willpower to break that kiss, but the possible media headlines were enough of an incentive to ensure I took her back to the room. Thank goodness I'd had the forethought to book the hotel room. But her mouth was worth the temptation.

My name on her lips made my balls tingle, and my dick wanted nothing more than to push inside her the minute we stepped into the hotel room. And when I saw and felt those luscious lips wrapped around my cock, it took everything I had to not blow in her mouth. *Damn, I have to stop thinking about her.* I need to readjust my trousers again. *Surely, we must be nearly at my apartment by now.* I desperately need a cold shower. With great effort, I switch my thinking to my business agenda for the next day, but I am still too distracted to do it any justice.

Not long after, I let myself into my apartment. I can hear snoring coming from the spare room down the hall and am thankful that Mom and Jonathon are indeed asleep. Hastily, I undress and step into the shower, shivering under the cold water until my body adjusts to the temperature. It has the desired effect of cooling the fire in my balls, my dick deflating and pointing to the ground again. That's it. I just have to stop thinking about Gina, although that is easier said than done.

Gina? Why had I called her Gina? Hadn't she asked me the same question? I normally call her Georgina, so why had I abbreviated her name? I hadn't even been aware that I had done it until she questioned me about it. Is it just that in the throes of passion, Gina is easier to say? I think deeply about that as I dry myself, my hand loitering over my groin, enjoying the now familiar tingling sensation that comes with thoughts of her. Georgina seemed to fit her business persona. Efficient, confident, assertive, talented, and intelligent. Georgie, as her friends call her, doesn't sit well on my tongue, nor match the elegance of the woman. So, Georgina, it is. But Georgina is too formal and serious for the hot, sexy, imaginative, fun-loving woman I bedded tonight. She is soft-hearted but giving and generous, someone I could spend a lot of time with, not just in bed. The softened shorter version of her name suits this warmer, earthier persona. Had my subconscious recognized the different aspects of her, and when my defenses were over-come with passion, softened her name to suit her passionate nature that appealed to me so much? *Wow, that was deep. You idiot, it is probably just because Gina was easier to say.* I scold myself, but her different personas ring true for me, so I can't dismiss the thought entirely.

Another thought crosses my mind as I clamber into bed. *Why had she dismissed me so quickly?* We had been discussing how long-term relationships aren't my thing. Is that why she suddenly decided to go home? I was only stating the facts, as I had with all my previous women. There is no point in getting their hopes up for something I can't give them. That must be what had got to Gina. *Had she been hurt by my comment? Had she been angling for me to be her next fiancé? Nope, not going to happen.* Marriage isn't for me. Unless it is marriage as a business arrangement, where we enjoy each other's company and bodies, but are devoid of emotions. *Yep, best to just stick with emotionless relationships.* That thought chills me, despite my brain thinking it is the better option.

"What? Holy crap." I wake, having just cum all over a pil-low I have been humping, and find myself lying in a pool of sticky mess. What is going on? I haven't done something like this since I was a teenager in boarding school. Although the dream I had been having was very realistic. About Gina. She permeated my dreams all night long, and I had her in so many ways. I wish I'd had the time to do some of them in real life. And she kept screaming my name, clenching around me with every orgasm, as she had done last night. Rattled that my dreams had been so intense and lifelike, I quickly strip the bed, dumping the soiled sheets in the laundry basket, before I go for a shower. One thing is certain. I need her again, as many times as it takes to get her out of my system.

Sharing breakfast with my parents and making plans for a family dinner that evening keeps my mind away from Georgina, and my body is almost back to normal. Ramone, my driver, is to drop me at the office and then return to take my parents shopping, so I am able to feel less guilty about spending little time with them during their stay.

"How was your dinner last night, Mr. Drake?" Ramone queries as we pull out of the garage.

"The food was great and the company amazing," I respond briefly, wanting to keep my date's identity private for a while longer. I trust Ramone with my life, literally, but my relationship with Georgina is too new to divulge details about. Besides, after the way she suddenly walked out on me last night, I wasn't too sure she would want to see me again, particularly if she felt hurt by my words.

I ponder the best course of action where Georgina is concerned. Usually, I would leave it a day or two before contacting a date again, but I am worried about my suspicion that I have hurt Georgina. *Oh, fuck off, you idiot. You have never felt this way about a woman before, so why change things now?* My ego berates me, reminding me that I would be bored within a week or two, like all the others. *Okay, so treat her like all the others then.* I can handle that easily. Decision made, I push her out of my mind and focus on work for the rest of the trip to the office.

Ethan barges into my office mid-morning, his usual jovial self. I can tell from the smirk on his face that he is about to gloat over something.

"What do you want?" I grouch and slam my phone on my desk. Annoyed with myself at how many times I have checked the damn thing this morning, waiting for a message from Georgina. I have been snarly all morning and feel edgy but put it down to my restless night. Ethan isn't deterred though and sits in the chair opposite my desk, silently smirking at me.

"Get your gloating over and done with, then get out. I'm busy," I huff and continue typing. Ethan chuckles, quite used to my ill temper, and, like any loving brother, takes great delight in irritating the shit out of me when I am already annoyed. I don't mean anything by my grumpiness though, and Ethan knows that our brotherly love-hate relationship includes taunts and rude remarks. Ethan gives as good as he gets as well.

"I went to dinner last night," Ethan responds, deliberately being vague and pointless and seems to be enjoying the perplexed look on my face.

"So, fucking, what?" I bark, not in the frame of mind to listen to Ethan prattle on about whomever he picked up. The guy is almost as much of a player as I am, and I'd heard it all before.

"You'll never guess who and what I saw." Ethan pauses for maximum effect while I shake my head disinterestedly. "At the

Casino," he continues, chuckling as I swing my head to glare at him.

"Do tell," snapping sarcastically. I am on guard now, guessing where this is leading.

"I saw this couple making out by the harbor. They were so into it that I'm surprised they didn't undress right there. It was smoking hot," Ethan continues drolly, deliberate in his bland tone as if he is talking about a TV show.

"And your point is?" I challenge, my eyes narrowing, and my jaw clenching, as I feel heat spreading up my neck.

"Just when I thought they should get a room, they unclenched and made their way into the hotel, apparently with the same thought. How is Georgie, by the way?" Ethan's eyes glint with mirth, watching me squirm, reveling in catching me out for once.

"Fuck off, E! I'm not discussing last night with you."

"In all seriousness, Xander, if I recognized you, then a lot of other people would have, as well. From a business perspective, maybe you should consider some damage control for social media." Ethan has reverted to his serious business persona. "Although, as your brother, I am very pleased to see you with someone as wonderfully down-to-earth as Georgie."

"Have you finished?" At Ethan's smirking nod, I continue, "Good, then get out." Distracted from my work now, my eyes throw daggers at Ethan's back as I watch him walk out, chuckling.

I stand and stare out the window, frowning, with my hands in my pockets, unease quivering in my stomach. *Damn, Ethan is right.* I don't want to publicize my liaison with Georgina, but I need to put some sort of damage control out there. Not for my sake, but for hers. I am used to my love life drawing endless focus from the media. But I feel certain that Georgina would not welcome it at all.

Should I contact her and warn her? Maybe. But how would I approach it? Have I done that for any of my other women? No. So why should Georgina be any different?

Just as I decide to get the media department to draft up a generic response in case it is needed, my phone vibrates on my desk. Swooping on it, I am surprised to see it is a call from my father's latest wife in Greece. Although my stepmother is nearly the same age as me, I consider her more of a friend and she occasionally calls to complain about my father's antics or business spending. *Damn, I'm not in the frame of mind to listen to her now.*

"Hello, Mariella," I answer in a resigned voice, knowing I can't ignore her call.

"Oh, Xander. It's your father. He has had a heart attack," she sniffles. I am instantly attentive, and sit, shocked, while noting how her Swedish accent is more pronounced than normal, indicating her worry.

"What happened? How is he, Mariella?" My genuine concern over my father's health situation surprises me. I don't like him much, and always feel duty-bound to keep in touch. Despite the need for civility between us, I know I still harbor resentment toward him from my childhood. But I never expected the gut punch that this news gives me, always expecting my strong, proud father to be a thorn in my side for many more years.

"Nikolas is in hospital, Xander, about to have an operation. It is very serious and the doctors don't know if he will make it. Oh, please come, Xander," Mariella begs, in tears now.

My heart lurches hearing her sob, wishing the tyranny of distance wasn't such a barrier at times like this. "Don't worry, Mariella. Nikolas is a strong, old bull, and I am sure he will pull through. I will be on the first available flight but, at best, won't be there much before tomorrow evening. In the meantime, who is at the hospital with you? "

"I hope you are right, Xander. I can't bear to lose him." She sobs again and continues as if she had pulled herself together for the moment. "I am here by myself now, but Stavros is on his way."

"Good. I'll be there soon, Mariella. Just hang in there for now."

We said our goodbyes and, with mixed emotions, I walk out of my office to my assistant as I hang up the phone.

"Paula, please book me on the first available flight to Athens, even if I have to use a private jet. My father has had a heart attack, so I don't know how long I will be gone for. Please cancel my appointments this afternoon. Also, re-arrange my schedule and flick as much as you can to Ethan and Mario. I will let them both know the situation. I'm heading home to pack and will call Ramone to come get me." At her nod, I return to my office to call Ramone.

Packing up my laptop, business papers, and other essentials, I then walk into Ethan's office to let him know. I pace while I wait for Ethan to get off the phone, knowing it is a woman by the smooth casualness of his tone, and his whole-hearted laughter.

"Ok, thanks, Georgie. Bye." Ethan looks at Xander as he hangs up. "What's up?"

"I've just had a call from Greece. Nikolas has had a heart attack and they need me to come over. So, I'm just letting you know I have rearranged my schedule and will be flying out as soon as possible."

"Damn, that's no good about Nikolas. Are you okay?" Ethan stands and comes around his desk, gripping me on the shoulder.

"Hmm. Yes, thanks." I appreciate Ethan's support and give him a taut smile as I nod. "Just distracted with juggling things here and what I might be walking into there." My father and I have always had a rocky relationship, which Ethan knows, but Nikolas is still my father, and I am still feeling caught off-guard by how the news has affected me. "I'll let Mom and Jonathon know what is happening, but you might need to entertain them while they are visiting. I'm happy for them to stay at my place for as long as they want."

"Well, you know I will cover whatever I can for you here. And if you need to talk, just call me." Ethan adds, "Mom was talking about a family dinner, but she'll understand that it will have to be just Louisa and I now. I'll touch base with them about it and keep them entertained, don't worry."

"Ok, thanks, bro. I appreciate that. Really. What was Georgina calling you about?" I feel my features flick from warm sincerity to frowning irritation as I shoot a glare at my brother. I haven't missed the familiarity in Ethan's tone when talking to Georgina, and even though I know they are good friends, for some reason, I am annoyed by it.

"Just updating me on the project, which is advancing well," Ethan responds openly, seemingly pleased, although I am not sure if that is because of the progress or because he had spoken with Georgina. Ethan has always seemed to have a soft spot for her.

"You didn't mock her about last night, did you? Like you did with me?" My voice is a sharp bite; irritation, and a flash of protectiveness toward her evident in my look as I glare at him.

"Would I do that?" Ethan asks, tongue in cheek. He continues in a more serious tone. "No, I wouldn't do that to her. You, on the other hand, big brother, I revel in taunting."

"Good, because if you hurt her in any way, I will knock you off your feet," I shoot back, surprising us both with my over-the-top comment, as if I am staking a claim on Georgina. *Whoa, where did that come from?* Unclenching the fists I hadn't realized were clenched at my sides, I consider that I must be losing it. Ethan's quizzical expression clarifies the strangeness of my behavior and comments.

"Ha, got ya." My flippant comeback falls flat, as Ethan stares intently at me as if he can't believe his ears. *Well, that would be right,* I muse. I have never staked a claim on a woman before, either implied or outright, so no wonder Ethan is looking at me like I have had a personality change or lost my mind.

Making a fast exit out of the office, I add, "I'll ring you when I get there. Oh, and can you get Cynthia from Media to do something tasteful about last night?"

CHAPTER 14 –
Gina

I HANG UP THE phone after talking with Ethan and stare at it, contemplating how the two brothers can be so different. After Xander's cold dismissal last night, I am still smarting, chiding myself for falling for his charm and believing that he had more substance than his playboy image.

Ethan, on the other hand, seems a genuinely caring person. We often laughingly tease each other, as well as have serious discussions about the project. Our friendly banter gives me an insight into the man, and I feel that he respects and genuinely cares for me. He has been careful not to cross boundaries from business to personal, which I appreciate, and he is firmly in my friend zone, which I told him not long after we met. Like my brothers, I know if I need help or advice, Ethan would happily oblige. I am fond of Ethan, but Xander is the one who makes me feel alive and who makes my heart sing. Even after last night. And if nothing more eventuates between Xander and I, he has left an indelible mark on my heart.

As good a friend as Ethan is, however, I am adamant I will not discuss Xander with him. Not only will that make it

difficult for Ethan, but I don't want him to know what an idiot I have been to fall under Xander's spell. That would be too embarrassing.

Xander.

Still humming from his expert lovemaking, my body tingles, and my stomach flips at the thought of him. *What should I do about him? Should I text him? And say what? Thanks for the great sex. Shame it's not going to happen again. Huh, not likely. What would texting him achieve anyway?* He wouldn't respond to my messages because he had made it clear that sex was all it was going to be until he got bored with me. Besides, I am not the sort of person to create conflict. So, I decide to put it behind me, and only have contact with him when it is necessary for business.

Nodding, happy with my 'do nothing' course of action, I busy myself to go on-site and finish some plantings with Jamie. Hard, manual work always takes my mind off my problems and should ease my restlessness.

CHAPTER 15 – Gina

One month later, I sigh, releasing the physical tensions of the past week and a bit as I soak in the bath. I have pushed myself physically, digging and planting more than usual, and as the warmth and bath salts seep into my sore and tired body, I feel much more relaxed. For once, I have the house to myself. Soft music is playing in the background, and my head rests against the back of the tub as my eyes drift closed. I haven't felt this good since I had been with Xander.

Flinging my eyes open, I shake my head to rid my thoughts of him. Too late. My inner core is already pulsing in memory of my star-spangled orgasms with him. My eyes shut as I moan, and like a movie reel in my head, flashes of him pounding into my pussy, his cock twitching in my mouth, and him pinching my nipples hard makes my pussy throb, as if he is here tormenting me. My body seems to be starving for him and I have battled against this hunger for days, weeks, only for it to invade my dreams and my quiet moments. Like now.

KERRIE MAXON

Damn the man. Why couldn't I lust after Ethan, or Mark, instead of the cold-hearted Xander? But neither of them lit the inferno within me like Xander. And probably no one ever would. *Geez, I hope that isn't the case*, I muse dismally, because I don't want to be pining my life away for such an undeserving, emotionless prick like him. I haven't heard a word from him since he'd dropped me home a month ago and, even though Ethan had explained about Xander's dad and that he was called away, my head went on believing him unworthy, while my core still ached for him.

I need to get him out of my system. Once and for all. My hands skim my breasts, pinching and scraping my sensitive nipples. As I moan, my hands slip down over my body, skimming around my inner thighs, teasing myself, before I reach down to my pussy. While one hand opens my outer lips, I use a finger on my other hand, and slip it through my slick, silky slit, landing on my swollen nub.

I imagine it is Xander's tongue pressing against my center, and groan, my legs spread wide, knees bent and feet resting sole to sole. Again and again, I slide my finger through my folds, pressing and circling on my clit, occasionally slipping a finger from my other hand inside myself, feeling my walls tighten. The memory of how Xander's tongue had worked me drove my hands, simulating the intense pleasure with my fingers circling and thrusting, my hips bucking against them until I grunt and shudder with the rush of release, clamping around my finger. My hands remain still against my sex, enjoying the deep spasming, as I suck in several deep breaths to calm myself.

Returning to normality and surprised by the force of my orgasm, I realize the water has cooled and step out of the

BUILT FOR SIN

bath to dry myself. Chuckling wryly at the amount of water splashed on the floor, I quickly mop it up with my towel.

As I lay in bed not long after, I reflect on my orgasm, which had been one of my most powerful self-induced climaxes, thanks to Xander. *He may not be suitable as relationship material, but he certainly was an amazing lover.* And fantasy land is where he would stay as far as I am concerned. At least that way he can't hurt me.

***

Looking forward to a much-needed catch-up with my girls, I saunter into Hayden's restaurant the next night. Feeling happy and relaxed, I am surprised to see that I am the last to arrive. Normally Simone is the tardy one, and as she wasn't home that afternoon, I assumed she was working tonight. Our work schedules often had us passing each other, with the occasional sounds from Simone's room late at night, the only indication she had been home at all. So, I am surprised to see Simone has made it after all.

We greet each other with kisses and hugs and they continue their conversation while I settle myself at the table.

"Have you ordered yet?" I ask when there is a lull in the conversation.

"No, we were waiting for you to get here. How come you are late?" Tash, my mother hen, prods nosily.

"I was just finishing up a few things at the office."

The last couple of weeks have been consumed with over-seeing the hotel development project and planning stages for my upcoming display at the gardening show. My company has been selected from hundreds of applications, so I need to ensure that it is the best I can produce. My concept plans had been accepted months ago, but I had amended them to include some smaller-scale elements from the hotel project, like a water wall. Even though it is still a few months away before I need to start physical work, I want to ensure nothing is left to chance.

Xander is almost a figment of my imagination. I haven't heard anything from him, and Ethan hasn't updated me on his movements at all. Despite my intention to put him out of my mind, I am reminded of him and our passionate night together every time I visit the hotel site. I had seen his name recently on the site office's sign-in sheet and knew he was around, but fortunately hadn't run into him. I still feel disgruntled at the callous way he has ghosted me, but it is my pride that hurt, not my heart. I can live with that. *Lesson learned*, I remind myself.

Over dinner and drinks, I catch up on gossip as I hadn't been able to attend our last catchup.

"Oh, I've been meaning to ask you, Georgie. Whatever happened with that gorgeous alpha male after we all went dancing a while back?" Simone queries interestedly. All the girls lean in to listen.

"Well, I'm not sure what the others have already told you, but after you left the club, he dropped me home, came inside and saw Hayden, then left because he thought he was my boyfriend."

"And? Nothing more after that? He was so hot for you," Simone blurts.

Before I can respond, Tash pipes up with, "Oh, yes. They went out to dinner. At the Casino."

Tight-lipped, I glare at Tash. Gauging by the other girls' avid looks, they already know. And they are keen for more information. I love Tash, but the girl doesn't know how to keep her mouth shut sometimes. I don't want to get into an analysis of my non-existent relationship with Xander with the girls, because it is too embarrassing and still stings.

"Yes, we did. And it was a superb dinner. The food was first class as you would expect," I admit, in a non-committal manner.

"Well, did you get laid?" Simone, who is always straight to the point, and never minces her words, asks, obviously excited for whatever juicy tidbit she can gather.

I have no intention of answering that question, so deflect, "Wasn't much point in getting involved when he said that he gets bored easily." *Well, it was almost the truth, and nearly meant the same thing.*

Taking advantage of their deflated looks, I turn to Emily and enquire, "What about you, Em? Has anything progressed between you and Ethan?"

Emily blushes and shakes her head, then questions, "You talk to him regularly about work. Has he said anything to you?" As I shake my head, Emily continues, her eyes downcast, "We had emailed and texted a few times and we went out for dinner once as well. But things have stalled a bit lately."

Geez, what is it with these brothers? They toy with women's hearts and emotions, playing then leaving them cold, the condescending thought flits through my head.

"Oh Em, I'm sorry," we chorus, then someone changes the subject to more neutral ground, and we continue to chat and giggle over more drinks.

Suddenly, our laughter is broken by Allie's hushed, "Oh no." She is staring at the restaurant entrance, and then she continues, "Xander is just walking in with a stunning blonde woman." Our heads swing around; our eyes glaringly cold as we watch. My stomach lurches at the sight of him. I feel like I have been stabbed in the heart as pain swamps me. So I quickly turn away from the sight of him with his hand resting on the woman's back, hoping he wouldn't see me. My glance, however, tells me that he looks just as stunning as always; his tall, dark, rugged good looks drawing the attention of everyone in the restaurant, as usual.

The woman by his side is indeed beautiful. Her tall, tanned, trim figure is accentuated by her short form-fitting dress, which also highlights her long shapely legs. As she sashays alongside Xander, she seems vaguely familiar. *Maybe she is a model. Well, that would explain why he never contacted me again.* He has moved on to more glamorous conquests.

As my eyes stare blankly at the table, I feel my friends watching me. Plastering on a fake smile, I look at them, hoping they believe I am fine. But they know me well enough to know I'm not.

The mood for the night had been ruined by his appearance, despite me trying to put a positive spin on it so, not long after, we decide to leave.

Seeing that he is seated at the far wall of the restaurant, facing the door where he would easily see us as we walk out to leave, I straighten my spine, marching out as if engrossed in conversation with Allie but I feel the moment his eyes land on my back.

CHAPTER 16 –
Gina

I AM BUSY WORKING in my office when I overhear Tash telling someone several times on the phone that I am unavailable. Puzzled, because I certainly hadn't given Tash any instruction that I am not to be interrupted, it is unlike Tash to be so insistent. So, when she is finally off the phone, I quiz her about the caller.

"No one you need to talk to at the moment." Tash is in full mother-hen mode, and my alarm bells clang as I watch Tash turn to her computer screen, putting an end to the conversation.

"Let me decide that, Tash. Now, who was on the phone?" I insist sternly.

"Tsk. Oh, all right then," Tash huffs. "It was Xander."

"Xander?" I am perplexed. *Why was he calling now after so long? Probably because he saw me last night.* Then another thought hits me. "How many other times has he called, and you've told him I was unavailable when I haven't been?"

"Just today. I swear," Tash responds sulkily.

"Why?" I ask, confused because this behavior is so unlike Tash.

"Well, after seeing how upset you were last night, I thought you needed some space from him. I was just looking out for you," Tash replies, as if affronted.

I sigh, exasperated. "I love that you look out for me, Tash, but I'm a big girl and can fight my own battles, particularly where Xander is concerned. Please, don't do that again."

"Okay," Tash mumbles and nods as I stride back into my office, shaking my head. The girl has a huge heart and unswerving loyalty, but both sometimes blind her logic and reasoning. This is one of those times, apparently, when she'd taken it upon herself to protect me from any more hurt and discomfort at Xander's hands without knowing all the details.

Spinning on my heels, I pace into the foyer and hug Tash, knowing I would protect her in the same way.

"I'm going for a walk to get a coffee. Do you want one?" I ask lightly, intending to give both of us some space. As Tash shakes her head, I stride out the door. I need some fresh air, hoping it will clear the confusion in my head over why Xander was calling. Maybe Ethan is away and Xander has some business questions. *Yes, that would be it,* I resolve as I arrive at the coffee shop. *Maybe I should get Tash a sweet treat,* I ponder, then decide to get coffee and cakes for the whole team.

Carefully juggling six coffees and my bag of treats, I stroll back to the office, enjoying the mid-afternoon sunshine. Today is a day I would love to be working outdoors; warm, clear, and with a slight breeze, but I have too much paperwork to tend to right now.

My head and mood are lighter as I approach the office and, carefully pressing the handle with my elbow and using my bottom to push open the door, I backed into the office, gleefully announcing, "Afternoon tea is here." My hand shakes as I turn and see Xander sitting in the foyer. Fortunately, I only spill a small amount of coffee into the cardboard tray, and not over myself.

"Xander," I acknowledge, nodding in his direction, quickly putting my professional mask firmly in place. Handing the coffee and cakes to Tash, I ask her to share them with the team, as I grab my cup.

"Can I get you a coffee too, Xander?"

"No thank you, Georgina." He has been watching me close-ly, with his eyes narrowed. His manner is deceptively casual as he lounges in the upright foyer chair, one long leg crossed over the other at the ankle, and his hands clasped in his lap.

"To what do I owe this honor?" I ask coolly, as I walk past him and stand at the doorway to my office, extending my hand, inviting him into the office, then shut the door behind us. I take the opportunity to steal a glimpse of his tight backside in his well-cut, light gray trousers before he sits down again.

"How have you been, Georgina?" I feel his eyes as they sweep up and down my body as I walk past and put the desk between us. His ocean blue eyes hold mine while I sit.

"Quite well, thank you." My response is a cool, polite smile, determined not to let him see any emotion from me. "But I am sure you didn't come here to enquire after my health." Raising my eyebrows, I indicate I am waiting for a reply.

The corner of his mouth quirks up, and with a slight tilt of his head, he briefly drops his eyes. They have softened a little when they return to meet mine.

"I saw you leave the restaurant last night," he states. His voice has a huskier tone to it, but I know him well enough to know this is a strategic ploy.

"Oh, really? I didn't see you there," I counter in a polite non-committal way.

His eyebrows quirk upward as if challenging my statement. I remain silent, my facial expression politely enquiring where he is going with his comment.

"I was reminded how remiss my lack of contact over the last month has been and felt I owed you a long overdue explanation." His eyes bore into me, seeking some sort of reaction, but I hold onto my indifferent mask with everything I have.

Nodding my head slightly, I give the appearance that I am slightly surprised. "No explanation necessary, Xander. It is what it is."

His eyes flash and his lips draw together in a tight line. *Is he annoyed because I'm not gushing over his apology or lack thereof? Or is he annoyed because I appear that our tryst means nothing to me?* I can feel my anger rising and battle to stay calm and professional.

"My father had a heart attack, and I was called back to Greece to attend to his business affairs while he was in the hospital." Xander's voice and expression have turned cold. "His recovery took longer than I expected."

My tone is indifferent as I respond, "I'm sorry to hear that your father was ill, Xander, but I'm pleased he has recovered." Then, the memory of the beautiful woman he was with last night and the hurt I felt at the sight return unexpectedly. My voice hardens while my eyes scorn him with ice. "Thank you for telling me. Now, is there anything else? I have a very busy afternoon ahead."

Xander's eyes flash fire, and his nostrils flare at my disdain. He stands; anger evident in the rigid way he holds his body and the scowl on his face and tightened jaw. Nodding his head, he turns and strides out of my office as if he needs to get away before he tears shreds off me. I flinch when the outer door slams as he leaves the building.

Exhaling deeply, I slump in my chair and gulp my forgotten coffee. I am a mass of conflicting emotions. Proud that I could stand firm against a master manipulator like Xander; relieved that I hadn't gushed all over him when he mentioned his father's illness; pleased that I gave him the impression that our tryst was a distant memory as far as I was concerned. But I am also angry. Angry that it is only seeing me last night that has stoked his guilty conscience when I haven't crossed his mind enough in the last month for him to contact me. A simple text from Greece would have been all that was needed. Angry that he thought all he had to do was explain about his father and I would jump all over him and into his bed. Disgusted also that he had probably been working out ways to get back into my pants while he was with the blonde bombshell last night.

I jump out of my chair and pace my office, my agitated thoughts spinning in my head as I rant. "How dare he? Bastard! Grrr. Scumbag!"

When Tash pokes her head around the office door, asking "Are you okay? What was that all about?" I am startled out of my mumblings.

Propping myself on the edge of my desk to face Tash, I run my fingers through my loose hair in frustration. Most of my anger has been expended with my pacing, so now I just feel flat and confused, which colors my tone.

"Xander said that he saw us leave the restaurant last night, and he was reminded that he hadn't contacted me since our date and felt that he owed me an explanation. I told him it wasn't necessary, but he told me anyway. His father in Greece had had a heart attack, and his recovery took longer than expected."

"Seriously? He remembered while he was with another woman that he should explain to you, after all this time, why he hadn't contacted you," Tash fumed. "Was he angling to get you into bed?" Tash is beside me now, irate on my behalf.

"Exactly! That is the impression I got, too." A spark of anger inflects my voice. "Tell me that I am not misreading the situation, or that there is another explanation," the rational side of me searches for options, trying to balance out my emotional reaction.

"Nope. Can't think of any. Even taking his words at face value, why would he feel obliged to explain now?" Tash seems just as confused. "What did you say to him to make him storm out like that?"

"I thanked him for telling me, said that I was sorry to hear about his dad, and if there was nothing else, I had a busy afternoon."

Having just taken a sip of coffee, Tash nearly spurts it out. Her mouth falls open in surprise and a bark of laughter escapes. "What? You just dismissed Xander Drakos from your office? The tycoon, Xander Drakos?" she questions, astounded and in awe. "Wow. No wonder he is pissed off." After a pause, she continues, "Well done you, but I hope he doesn't hold it against you."

A look of worry crosses my face as potential ramifications are added to my turbulent thoughts.

CHAPTER 17 – Gina

"HELLO, ROBERT. HOW ARE you?" My cheerful voice when I answer my phone reflects the friendly relationship we have established during our regular meetings.

After exchanging pleasantries, Robert continues apologetically, "Unfortunately, I have just had an urgent meeting scheduled over our meeting tomorrow. I could have sent you an email, but it seemed faster to call you and see if you are available same time Friday instead?"

Checking my calendar, and confirming that the new time will be okay, I make a mental note to take an earlier lunch that day.

"Good, I'll send a meeting request straight away. Oh, and could you bring a report of your budget versus actuals and a progress report with completion timelines? I apologize for the short notice," Robert continues in a matter-of-fact tone.

"Ok, I'll pull that together for you, but we did discuss that last month with Ethan," I query the need to replicate the information.

"Yes, I know, but I need a written report for progress payment acquittal."

"Sure. Not a problem, Robert. I'll see you Friday." My forehead furrows as I hang up the phone, reflecting on how unusual his request is.

After talking on the phone in the scorching heat for nearly twenty minutes while I walk to my next meeting in my long-sleeved jacket and matching trousers, I am relieved to be in the cool air conditioning. Perspiration beads on my forehead and upper lip. My underarms feel moist, and a trickle runs down my back. I pause in the foyer to dab at my forehead and lip and quickly spray myself with deodorant, before catching the elevator to Robert's floor.

"Ms Colby. Good to see you again. Mr. Mitchell is in the conference room. Go straight in."

"Thanks, Anne-Marie." I smile warmly at the receptionist before making my way slowly down the corridor, subtly blowing air over my face to try to cool it. I am a bit early but would rather be in the air conditioning than wait outside.

Robert shakes my hand, and seeing my face flushed with heat, offers me a glass of cold water, which I gratefully accept. Dropping my tote bag on the desk, I take off my jacket then I sit, letting some of the cooling air drench over me while I chat to Robert. I have just taken the last mouthful of water when, unexpectedly, Xander walks into the room. I gulp at the sight of him, all six foot four of gorgeous manliness, causing me to cough and splutter. He smirks at my reaction. *The rat.* However, I quickly recover my composure.

"Xander, so nice to see you," I say it with what I hope is a natural smile, but with no warmth in my voice or eyes, wanting him to wonder if I am being sincere or sarcastic. His eyes glint and a corner of his mouth quirks up as if fully aware of my intended tone before he resumes his usual stern business demeanor.

"You too, Georgina." He looks away as he deposits his satchel on a chair, then peels off his jacket and rolls up his cuffs, exposing his muscular, tanned forearms.

His movements, and the way his crisp white shirt hugs his body, captivates me. My mouth goes dry as I remember those forearms wrapped around me and that firm body pressed against mine. My body stirs at the vivid memory, so my jaw clenches and I cast my eyes to the papers in front of me, trying to push those visions from my mind and focus on the job at hand.

Why am I still remembering him naked against me after all this time? I silently rage at myself, struggling to adopt my normally calm business facade.

Xander sits opposite me, and looks cool and sharp, while I feel hot and flustered in his presence. He gets straight down to business.

"I just want to touch base with you both about progress on the hotel development, as Ethan is away. I have reviewed your reports but have some questions." Xander pauses, seemingly in his most authoritative CEO element, before turning his gaze to Robert.

"Can you outline why the lobby and Porte Cochere areas have fallen behind their timeline?"

Oh, it's going to be one of THOSE meetings, is it? Xander's demeanor puts us both on notice and, taking heed of the warning shot, I run through my projects, trying to determine if there is anything that Xander is likely to grill me about while I listen to Robert and Xander discussing contingencies.

"Thanks, Robert. Let's proceed with those slight amendments. Georgina, I notice that you are over budget in a couple of areas. Can you explain that to me, please?" He scrutinizes me closely, trying to gauge my reaction. However, my mental review and confidence in my figures and report information have calmed me, so I respond coolly, maintaining eye contact with him throughout my explanation.

"Firstly, you can see the over-run in Stage One, which was unexpected. It was the result of sewer lines impacting the proposed plantings, which resulted in the relocation of that garden bed two meters north and a delay of one week. Both you and Ethan were made aware of the situation at the time." I pause as Xander nods in acknowledgment. *Am I mistaken, or did Xander's eyes flash fire before quickly being masked, as he remembered the site visit where I had explained this situation to him, which also resulted in our very heated initial embrace?* I feel heat creeping up my neck as I also remember that moment. Taking a deep breath, I continue.

"The overrun in Stage Two stems from the issues Robert has just been discussing with you, which have a flow-on effect on my work. I can't start landscaping around the Porte Cochere until Robert's team has finished their plumbing work because I need to piggyback off that plumbing groundwork for the sprinkler systems. Robert and I have discussed this, and I have been able to bring the planting timeline for Stage One forward while waiting for Robert's team to finish their work. Also, the nature of the excavation work Robert's team must undertake impacts the area I need to work. Again, I need to wait until they clear the site so I can rehabilitate and plant it out. We are working closely together to create synergies and maximize efficiencies so we can come in on time."

Xander flicks through some papers to the site layout map. "Is this where you mean?"

"Yes. You can see that this area must be dug up for the underground plumbing, which means the adjacent area is a no-go zone till that is complete." I reach across the table and point to the specified areas, without realizing that I have revealed some cleavage. Xander inhales deeply at the glimpse of the rounded tops of my breasts, then looks at Robert as he speaks, as if nothing has happened.

Quickly, I sit back down; my face is now flushed in embarrassment. Not because Xander has seen my cleavage. No, he has seen far more of me. I am embarrassed that he could possibly think I deliberately flaunted myself to him.

"I am doing what I can to get that area started as soon as possible, Xander. My foreman tells me it should be started by the end of next week," Robert replies, unaware of the frisson that had passed between Xander and myself.

Xander nods thoughtfully. "Okay. Please let me know as soon as possible if there are any changes to any aspect of the work. I need the project finished on time or before, if possible."

Robert and I nod in agreement.

Xander piles his papers away in his satchel, and his glance passes from Robert to me. "Thank you both. You are doing a great job and I am very impressed with what I have seen so far. Ethan will be back next week, and I will be staying up to date with your progress." He stands and asks Robert a couple of questions while he rolls down his cuffs and puts on his jacket. Xander the businessman is equally as jaw-droppingly awesome as Xander the lover, and I can't get enough of seeing him in his alpha male splendor. Trying hard to not drool and gush over him, I stand and turn to put on my jacket before I make a fool of myself.

The extra layer of clothing is like donning a suit of armor. I feel shielded from the X-factor that Xander seems to be dripping with. Standing tall and composed, I shake hands with both men as I say goodbye. However, as my hand clasps Xander's I catch a whiff of his enticing earthy cologne, and the Xander effect up close and personal makes my body go into meltdown; my breathing shortens, my body heats and thrums, and I feel flustered and prickly. *So much for him not affecting me.* Mocking myself, I quickly make my escape while he lingers to talk to Robert.

Before I get too far down the corridor, Xander has caught up with me. *Damn*.

"Running away again, Georgina?" his tone mocks, smirking as he comes alongside me, adjusting his stride to match mine, with no apparent sign of his earlier broken ankle.

"Not at all, Xander. People to see, places to be. You know how it is." Replying flippantly, I hope he will leave the conversation at that as we step into the elevator.

"I'd like to be added to your list of people to see," he replies softly, his eyes narrowing slightly as he watches my reaction.

His double meaning is clear, so I turn my head toward him, raise an eyebrow, batter my eyelashes, and smile flirtatiously. "But I've just seen you, Xander. Don't you remember?" I mock.

"Touché, Georgina. How could I forget?" His eyes twinkle as his mouth curves into a smile. He moves his free hand behind me, ever so softly touching my back, as he guides me ahead of him and we make our way through the building exit. In his typically chivalrous manner, he circles behind me to place himself between me and the curb as we walk down the street.

"Seriously, I would like to see you again." His voice is soft but firm.

I stop and turn to face him, tilting my head to the side in surprise as my brow creases. His statement is more of a politely veiled order than an invitation as if he expects me to jump at the chance to be with him again. Schooling my features into a shuttered expression, I take a calming breath before responding.

"I'm flattered, Xander. I really am, but I can't see the point. You get bored easily, remember?"

"For God's sake, Georgina, I'm not talking about a long-term relationship." He growls and then leans in close, his breath warm against my ear as he holds my elbow. "I'm talking about a casual affair. I need to get this insatiable desire for you under control, and the only way I can do that is to fuck your brains out again."

He pauses, running his hands through his hair before taking a breath, as if he has revealed too much information. His tone changes and becomes more moderate, like he is making a convincing argument. "I see the same desire in you, Georgina. Think of it as a mutually beneficial 'friends-with-benefits' situation, like the one you had before." He smiles cajolingly, his thumb gliding over my covered forearm, while his face has an expectant look.

My face flushes, and I blink several times, frowning, trying to make sense of his confession and his suggestion as I stare at him. I am tempted to slap him but I am also excited at the thought of getting naked with him again. But I know he will tire of me quickly, and I will get hurt. The heat of the day and his proximity are playing havoc with my reasoning. My eyes note his relentless, darkened gaze studying the conflicting expressions that cross my face. I step out of his grasp and take a deep breath.

"I'll have to think about that, Xander. I'll get back to you," and I promptly scurry away to my parked van a few streets away. As I maneuver out of the city, my thoughts are ping-ponging around in my head, driving me crazy.

Could I keep my emotions out of a sexual relationship with Xander? I had been able to with Mark, but there was no real substance to our friendship other than sex, and surprisingly I realize I haven't given Mark another thought since we parted ways. Xander is different, though. Not only does he make me burn just being in the same room with him, but he is an amazing lover. He brings out the best in me as well, turning me on with a simple look, making me adventurous and playful. He is like a drug; I have had a taste and want more.

I also know myself well enough to know that if I go down that road, I will get hurt. I already like Xander a lot, which is why my heart felt injured after our last time together. I admire his sharp mind, his business acumen and integrity, and the caring side of him I've had a brief glimpse of that only a few got to see. I enjoy our banter and his honesty. His divine body and film star good looks are the icing on the cake. *Get a grip, Gina. You sound like you are already smitten.*

Deep in thought, I huff as I trudge back into the foyer of my office, waving to Tash, who is on the phone. Peeling off my jacket as I walk through to my desk, I throw it over the back of my chair and deposit my tote bag, then walk through to the kitchenette and grab a water out of the refrigerator. Returning to my office, I plop into my chair, gazing into space as I sip at my cool water.

"Tash, have you got a minute?" I call out when I realize she is off the phone.

"Sure. What's up?" Tash enquires as she comes in and stands in front of my desk.

Nodding to the chair for her to sit, I begin, "Just wondering if I can run something by you?"

"Of course. Go for it." A look of excitement crosses her face as she waits expectantly for me to continue.

Sighing heavily, my forehead puckers as I continue to look out the window. "I don't know what to do, Tash." I hesitate. Turning to look directly at her, and taking another deep breath, I quietly continue, "Xander was at the meeting, and he looked so good. Afterward, he asked to see me again, and when I tried to brush him off, he said he needed to, quote, get his insatiable desire for me under control by fucking my brains out, unquote. And that he was proposing friends-with-benefits casual sex."

"Whoa! Whoa! Oh my. What did you say?" Tash's eyes are wide and excited. Her mouth curves into a wide smile as she bounces in her chair.

"I told him I'd think about it and get back to him." I groan at how lame and pathetic that sounds. Surely, I could've come up with a far better sassy remark. Only my brain had temporarily blanked out.

"You what?" Tash is just as astonished as me. "Why didn't you say yes? You know it's what you want."

"I know. I didn't want to seem too easy, and I don't want to get hurt. You know me, my emotions always get involved." I exhale, deflated. "But I desperately need to get him out of my system too, and I can't see any other way to do that. Despite not seeing him for several weeks, I still have the hots for him."

"Well then, there's your answer. What have you got to lose?" Tash pauses, choosing her words carefully. "I know you're afraid of getting hurt again, but even the man you once loved hurt you. It will be casual sex with Xander, and you will be going into it with your expectations managed. You know what they say... nothing ventured, nothing gained." Tash seems pleased as if she is a wise sage dispensing valuable information, then she continues, "And if you do get hurt, you'll bounce back. You always do, Georgie, because you're resilient. It can't be any worse than your breakup with Murray. When the time comes for it to be over, you or Xander, being the people you are, will end it swiftly and decisively. No stringing you on for months like Murray did."

Although I had come to this conclusion myself, I needed to hear it from my friend, as reassurance.

My lips tighten resolutely, and I nod to myself as I walk around the desk to hug Tash. "Thank you," I say softly.

As Tash walks out, she throws over her shoulder, "When are you going to tell him?"

"I might let him sweat it out for a bit," I chuckle, feeling a bit mischievous now I had made my decision and I ponder on the timing and wording of my reply.

***

Uncertainty continues to plague me during the night as I debate whether I should or shouldn't get involved in a casual fling with Xander. Fed up with my dilly-dallying, I fire off a text to Xander over breakfast.

Gina: Offer accepted, Big Boy.

CHAPTER 18 – Gina

MY PHONE VIBRATES AND beeps in my pocket, indicating I have a message. I have been sweating on a response from Xander all day. It appears that he was making me wait, maybe as payback for my slow response to him yesterday. My heart races as I read the short text.

Xander: Tomorrow night, ok? I'll pick you up at 7 pm.

What am I to make of that? It is impersonal and uninformative, but then, when I consider the arrangement I had had with Mark, the texts were much the same. Short and to-the-point confirmation of rendezvous time. So, I respond in the same manner.

Gina: Sounds great. Pick up from my place?

Xander: Yes. Looking forward to it.

Gina: Me too. See you then.

I close my phone but continue to stare at it. Excitement and nervousness are building in my stomach, which I can't deal with right now, so I force myself to focus on work.

I am helping Jamie plant out some of the larger garden beds and mark out the area near the Porte Cochere, where we would have to excavate later. My wide-brimmed straw hat provides some relief from the burning sun, and I take the opportunity to rehydrate while I have stopped digging. Jamie joins me on a short break before I climb onto the tray of the truck to unload the mature plants, passing them to Jamie, who places them in their positions.

Once the truck is unloaded, I hop off, groaning, and stretch backward with hands on my hips to knock out the kinks in my back from bending for so long. I have the eerie sensation that someone is watching me. Glancing around, I realize it isn't Jamie, as he is on his hands and knees, facing away from me in an adjacent garden bed. There doesn't seem to be anyone else around, but as I cast my glance further afield, I spot Xander down near the site office, facing toward me, but talking to the foreman. I can't see his eyes because he is too far away and wearing sunglasses, but he looks damn fine in his business suit, as he always does.

I drink in the sight of him as a fluttering, empty feeling fills my stomach. My heart pounds, and I tingle all over as anticipation of his proximity bubbles inside me, making me wonder how someone could affect me so much from so far away. He is dangerous to my well-being, and I decide there and then that I will have to ensure that my heart is locked away, out of his reach.

With one last stretch, I turn my back on him, acting as if I haven't seen him, and continue with my work, promising myself that a hot soak in the bath will be in order tonight.

The next night, I finish work early and race back to my flat to prepare for my night with Xander. After a quick shower, where I shave everything that needs attention, I lather myself in a subtly scented body lotion. I have spent all day imagining what will happen and daydreaming about getting my hands on Xander's beautiful body again. My anticipation is peaking, to the point that I am questioning my choice of clothes, and whether either of us would live up to our expectations a second time around. *Will he still be as desperately crazy for me as he was last time? You wouldn't be meeting him tonight if he didn't feel a driving hunger for you,* I chide myself.

Xander hasn't provided me with much information on his plans for the night, so I play it safe by dressing in a black, knee-length fitted dress with matching stilettos. I have been conflicted as to how far to go with my lingerie. Should I stick with a matching bra and panties, or go with something more elaborate? Opting for elaborate, I want to see how wild I can drive him; I have chosen sheer, silky, black stockings and suspender belt, with a matching bra and G-string panties. My makeup is done, and my hair is pulled off my face in a ponytail that hangs down my back. A red jacket and gold drop earrings add the finishing touches to my outfit. I am pleased with my appearance as I give myself a cursory glance in the mirror before grabbing my clutch bag and heading downstairs just before 7 pm.

I wait by the window, my heart pounding, smoothing my hair and resisting the urge to check my makeup again. I check my watch every minute until I hear a car pull up outside. Glancing out the window, I spot Xander's car and hastily make my way to the front door, flinging it open with a big, inviting smile on my face.

At the sight of Xander's driver Ramone on my doorstep, I try to hide my deflated excitement and school my features into a polite smile instead.

Ramone is also very courteous as he speaks, his look apologetic.

"Good evening, Miss Colby."

"Hello, Ramone. How are you?"

"Mr. Drakos apologizes that he can't collect you himself, and asks that you accompany me back to his apartment."

"Certainly. Thank you." I close the door behind me, hiding my disappointment as Ramone moves ahead to open the rear car door for me. I slide in gracefully, taking care to keep my dress low on my knees so my thigh-high stockings aren't exposed. Ramone swiftly closes the door and returns to the driver's seat.

"We won't be long. Is there anything I can get you?" He turns in his seat to ask, clarifying, "I have alcohol and water onboard if you need."

"No, thank you." He turns around and pulls away from the curb.

BUILT FOR SIN

Ramone is silent during the ride, so doubts about my sanity overwhelm me. *What do I know about Xander? Is being picked up like this going to be a regular occurrence?*

I had imagined Xander being blown away by my appearance when I opened the door to him. So, seeing Ramone has been anti-climactic. This feels sleazy, like I am a courtesan on her way to meet a client. Maybe this is the way rich, powerful men conduct their casual affairs. After all, it isn't as if this is a date. *Stop letting your emotions get involved and treat the situation for what it is. Great sex with a god-like lover for as long as it lasts.*

Pulling up outside a fancy modern apartment building in the CBD, Xander strides out of the lobby and opens the car door for me. Wearing casual loafers and dressed in smart navy trousers that look like they could be part of a suit, and a blue short-sleeved cotton shirt with the top three buttons undone, which hangs over his trousers, Xander looks casual, comfortable and sexy as sin.

Holding my hand as I step out, his eyes widen, and pupils dilate when he catches a glimpse of my stockinged legs. He runs his eyes over me, drinking me in. I recognize that look. It says he wants me undressed as soon as possible. It also fires my lust, pooling deep in my lower belly, whilst I tingle at the touch of his hand. His reaction at the sight of me is everything I have hoped for and makes up for my earlier disappointment. Excitement at the promise of the best sex of my life bubbles to the surface, and I give him a wide, beaming grin.

"Thank you, Ramone." His eyes haven't left me as he dismisses his driver. "Georgina. Come this way." His voice is a husky growl, and he places a hand in the small of my back as he escorts me into the lobby and introduces me to the doorman, whom I politely acknowledge.

Xander escorts me further down the lobby to a private elevator for the penthouse. Once the doors close and he has swiped his card to access his floor, he grabs me, turning me to face him, and pulls me against his strong, powerful body. I feel the hardness of his erection as I give him a knowing smile. My lips part slightly as his delicious lips hover over mine.

"You look amazing," he breathes. The elevator dings, so he drops his arm to hold my hand and leads me into his apartment. I gasp at the size of the open plan hall and living area, which have a modern minimalist feel, but it is warm and inviting decorated in soft beiges and creams, with colorful artworks breaking up the space.

Xander steps further into the large room. "Would you like a drink or something to eat?"

"What are you having?" I follow him to a cabinet where he is pouring himself a neat scotch, which he holds up to show me. "I'll just have iced water, please. Are we eating?"

"The only thing I want to eat right now is you, Georgina," he growls as he stalks toward me like a predator. My body zings and suddenly my empty stomach because I'd missed dinner didn't seem to matter anymore. He hands me the drink and his eyes roam up and down my body while he circles slowly around me, making me feel like I am his next meal.

"I'm sorry I couldn't collect you myself, but a late overseas call came in that I couldn't ignore. Sending Ramone for you also gave me time to get changed." His tone has reverted to a hospitable host, but his eyes darken as he watches my tongue run around my lips, licking away residual water from my drink.

"Okay," was all I manage to utter as he snatches the glass out of my hand, depositing it on a nearby coffee table, his eyes never leaving mine. His other arm wraps tightly around me, pulling me roughly against his eager body while his mouth crashes onto mine, hungrily devouring it. My hands rake up and down his back as our tongues snake and intertwine. My body throbs, and I become desperate to feel more of him. Slipping my hands under his loose shirt, my hands continue roaming, and I trace my fingers over his muscles, mapping the contours of his body from memory. Groaning, he releases his hands long enough to remove my jacket, letting it drop at my feet, while our mouths stay locked together.

Xander breaks the kiss, then places his forehead gently against mine as he inhales a deep breath.

"Georgina, you drive me wild, and if we keep going like that, I will blow right here in my trousers." His voice is soft as he tries to harness his hunger for me, to slow things down and draw out as much pleasure as he can. I love the way he touches me; how I ignite in his arms and feel heat and moisture radiate between my legs. Only he seems to be able to get me aroused and wet so quickly. Placing both hands on his cheeks, I look directly into his sultry, hungry eyes as I give a small chuckle.

"Well, we had better do something about that, hadn't we?" I intend to show him how much I enjoy his touch and everything he does to me. My hands move down his ripped stomach to his belt. I revel in watching his pupils dilate as I undo the buckle, then the button on his trousers. Slowly, I inch the zip down as I groan with need. My warm hand slips inside his trousers and cups his cock over the soft cotton of his underwear, causing his head to tip back as he hisses loudly. Sliding my hands under to cup and gently squeeze his balls, I grin as he growls. Then I slide my hand up his shaft and run my thumb over the head of his erect dick, feeling the dampness of precum on his underwear.

He grabs my hand and removes it, mumbling something under his breath. He toes off his shoes hurriedly as he pulls me down a hallway into his bedroom, kicking his trousers off as he goes.

Vaguely I notice the dark-blue themed room, but my attention is drawn to the neatly made king-size bed with a navy blue patterned throw and crisp white sheets and pillows.

He stands me near the end of the bed, his hands moving possessively down my sides and then over my breasts. I know he can feel my pebbled nipples, even through the bra and dress fabric. I inhale sharply as he pinches my nipples. Turning me so I face away from him, he rubs his hard cock against the crack in my butt cheeks, while his hands cover and squeeze my ample breasts, his mouth dropping to kiss my neck. Moaning, I squirm, grinding my ass against him. My body is clamoring for him, needing him inside me. Heat bathes my body, and my legs grow shaky as a pulsing desire shoots through me with his every touch.

"I'm dying to see what is under here," he whispers before he takes a step backward and slowly undoes the long zip that runs down the back of my dress. His breath hitches when he spots the black silky fabric of a suspender belt around my waist, then the top of the G-string.

"Oh fuck," he groans, quickly pushing the dress off my shoulders and guiding it down past my waist, till it falls to the floor. "Oh fuck," he groans again on a long sigh, mesmerized. His hands run over the taut, rounded globes of my ass, squeezing them as I step out of my dress, then glide down my thighs, over the suspender straps to the top of my silky stockings. His hands retrace their path, back to my shoulders.

Slowly, he turns me and holds me, still at arm's length, while his hungry, scorching eyes rake over me, relishing the full impact of my sexy body covered in seductive lingerie.

"Oh, my God, Gina. You are gorgeous." His big hands skim my body, tweaking my nipples again and then sliding over my hips. One arm wraps around me, his hand landing in the curve of my back, holding me still while the other traces the wide fabric of my G-string over my flat lower belly and between my legs. We both moan as his finger slips into my drenched slit.

Frantically, I unbutton his shirt then tug down his trunk-style underwear. He steps out of them before removing his hand from my folds and moves quickly to a bedside table to grab a condom, throwing off his shirt on the way. I salivate, peering at his taut butt as he moves. Ripping the foil packet open with his mouth as he returns, he spins me around and bends me face down over the bed.

Resting my body on my forearms, I turn my head to watch him, engrossed in the look of him in this primal heat. He is glorious, all alpha male, claiming what he wants. And what he wants is me. Desperately. And I am thrilled that I am able to drive him to frantic need because he has the same effect on me.

My body trembles with anticipation of what he will do with me. Quickly he sheaths his cock, then shifts his focus to my ass, raised in the air and ripe for the taking.

His large hands knead my firm butt cheeks, then slip down the back of my thighs, tracing the line of the suspenders again. I squirm as his hands run up the inside of my thighs, as he spreads my legs wide open before pulling my G-string to the side.

"Holy fuck, Gina, you are so wet," he growls, his thumb sliding effortlessly through my slick slit. Groaning at his touch, I push back against his hand.

"I need you, Xander," I pant, desperate to have him inside me. My body is an inferno, and he is the only one who can extinguish this burning need.

In one deft move, he guides his huge swollen cock to my opening, teasing the tip at the entrance before slowly edging in, stretching me as he goes.

"Ahh," I exhale, relishing his thickness and length wrapped in my pussy. Reminded of how big he is, I realize I have desperately missed this burning stretch. He pulls out slowly, then drives in again, pausing when he is balls deep to savor the feel of my intense heat. I buck back against him, needing more, although I'm not sure what *more* he could give me.

He plunges in and out of me, setting a blistering rhythm, each stroke rubbing on my G-spot, flooding me with ecstasy. With both hands on my hips, he pulls me back against him with force, getting in as deep as he can. The sound of skin slapping against skin and muttered sounds of our pleasure drives each of us into a frenzy. There is no coherent thought, only the ferocious need for release.

Leaning over me, gripping my breasts, his index fingers and thumbs pinch my nipples and squeeze them with each thrust. Arching my body, clenching the bedclothes, I exhale a keening wail as my body explodes in a thundering climax. My vision blanks as I convulse uncontrollably around him.

"Oh fuck, Gina. Fuuck," he groans in my ear, stilling himself inside me as his orgasm erupts. With another softer thrust, he collapses onto me and then rolls us, so we are both laying on our sides. He stays inside me, delighting in my spasming on his shaft, and we both gasp for air.

After a few minutes, when our senses begin returning to normal, Xander gets up to dispose of the condom. I am still floating in the aftermath of my shattering orgasm, trying to regroup my scattered self as I listen to my pounding heart. Slowly I become aware of Xander standing in the doorway and turn my head to see him admiring the sight of me sprawled on my back, arms flung out to my sides, mouth agape and body covered in a dewy sheen.

He moves toward me with the stealth and purpose of a lion stalking its prey and my eyes open wide as he straddles me, leaning down to kiss me softly on the lips, before propping himself above me to peer into my glazed eyes.

"You look delicious, Little One. Did I hurt you?" he queries softly, his eyes searching mine in concern.

Shaking my head, I give him a sated grin and place my hands on his cheeks, bringing his head down for another kiss.

"You can do that to me anytime you like, Big Boy," I chuckle.

"I intend to have you in many ways, Georgina," he purrs. "Come, you must be starving." Standing, he drags me off the bed, his hungry eyes roaming over me, promising more delights.

"Why don't you go and clean up and I will wait here for you," he suggests, nodding toward the ensuite. "There's a robe on the back of the door, if you would like it."

Nodding, I pad softly to the bathroom and don the large white fluffy robe after I freshen up, returning to the bedroom to see Xander has put on a black satin robe as well.

He leads me by the hand to the kitchen and I perch on a stool at the island counter, taking in the sparkling marble benchtops and modern white cabinetry. The kitchen is huge, classy, and fit for someone who does a lot of entertaining. I wonder about that, as he pads around, grabbing out some glasses.

"I wasn't too sure what you like, so ordered a few dishes for you to choose from," he says as he gets them out of the large refrigerator and places them in front of me. I am touched by his thoughtfulness, but not totally surprised, as he is well known for his attention to detail.

"You didn't need to go to so much trouble, Xander," I remark gratefully, amazed at the ten different dishes of varying cuisines he'd obviously ordered fresh to be delivered for tonight.

"No trouble. Whatever we don't eat tonight, I will finish during the next few days."

"I might have the lasagna if that's okay. Let me give you a hand."

"No problem at all. Stay there, I've got this."

True to his word, our food is quickly heated in the microwave and smells delicious. My tummy rumbles loudly as he places my dinner on a dish in front of me, then serves up his roast beef and vegetables.

"You certainly know your way around a kitchen, Xander. Do you do a lot of entertaining?" I query as I cut up my meal.

"Occasionally I will entertain business associates here, but I usually get a caterer in for those. My mother was very insistent that her children should be able to fend for themselves with all the domestic duties, so I can cook a few dishes when needed. Mostly I don't have time, so prefer to order good food like this and reheat. What about you? Can you cook?" he asks after a few mouthfuls.

"Yes, I can, and I've learned some great tips and tricks from Hayden over the years. He's a chef and has his own restaurant. Mostly I just have something quick and nourishing or leftovers that Hayden brings home. It's a bit difficult to get too elaborate in a share house though, because everyone usually wants to eat at different times, and often they will each want something different as well... and I hate cooking for just myself. It seems so wasteful."

"I hadn't considered that," he comments before having a long drink of water.

We continue chatting over our meal, and then Xander clears the dishes before leading me back to the bedroom. After removing his robe, he pulls back the bed sheets while I take off my robe, letting it drop next to his on the floor, and stand next to him.

Peering into my eyes, he brushes some loose strands of hair away from my face, then holds my face gently between his hands and kisses me softly, teasing me. As the kiss ends, he drops his hands to my waist and wraps his strong arms around me, holding me against him, allowing me to hear his steady heartbeat as my face rests against his chest, loving this moment of intimacy with him.

His deep voice rumbles when he speaks. "As much as I adore what you are wearing, Georgina, I need more access to your exquisite assets." He moves quickly and my bra drops to the floor, as does my G-string then he gently pushes me onto the bed, wearing just my stockings and suspender belt.

"Climb in," he instructs, then follows me. While I lay on my back, he is on his side, head propped on his hand, watching my changing expressions as he fondles my breasts and nipples with the other hand. "Mmm, I love your breasts," he drawls. "I'm obsessed with them, the way they jiggle and move, and how reactive they are to my touch."

I reciprocate by trailing my fingernails over his hip, lower back, and butt cheek. Our unhurried teasing becomes heated after a while as lust engulfs each of us like a tornado again. I writhe under Xander's attention, and his erection grows stiff against my leg.

After reaching behind me to grab another condom from the side table, he lay on his back to put it on. Quickly, I straddle him, gripping his shaft, and guiding it into my entrance. We both gasp as I slide slowly down, pausing before lifting myself again.

It feels so right having him inside me, like I am whole when we are joined. The intensity of my thoughts alarms me, but I push it aside to revisit later. Now I am just going to enjoy the moment. I ride him, at first slowly, while he fondles and squeezes my breasts and nipples, making me whimper and moan from his touch. Then he seems to lose control and his dominating side takes over as he grabs my hips and places his feet flat on the mattress, driving into me harder, huffing and moaning with each stroke. Shrieking, I reposition my feet on the mattress for stability and my hands are on his chest to brace myself as we pound against each other. The sounds of our bodies slapping together join with our moans and cries to create an erotic chorus, primal in its harmony.

Riding the wave of pleasure and at the point of no return, Xander flips me onto my back, lifting my legs over his shoulders so he can plunge deeper. I shatter around him, digging my nails into his hips as my back arches. My inner muscles clench hard as I fall headfirst into the vortex of oblivion. Xander thrusts again and, gripping my thighs and clenching his buttocks, lets out a roar as his cock spills into the condom.

His body is covered in a sheen of perspiration, and his neck flushes as he stills and inhales deeply. He releases my legs from his shoulders, letting my torso drop to the bed, then collapses next to me, resting his hand on my belly. I gasp for breath, then moisten my dry mouth.

"Wow. Wow," was all I can utter when I find my voice again, stretching out the words, my voice husky. Unable to move, my body is so relaxed and limp from the whirlwind of arousal and orgasm that has wreaked havoc on me.

Xander turns his head toward me, gazing at my flushed afterglow with a satisfied grin. Reaching out a hand to cup his cheek, the slight roughness of his stubble grazes my palm. We lay in silence, each lost in our thoughts until Xander stands, and casts an appreciative glance over my sex-sated body, skimming his hand down my front.

"You look so deliciously inviting that I could take you again right now, but it will have to wait a while, Little One."

Salivating, my eyes are transfixed on his tight butt cheeks and thighs as they flex when he walks to the ensuite. He is gorgeous; his beautifully sculpted body, endowed in all the right places, with wide shoulders and narrow hips, would and does draw lustful glances from most women and envy from most men. I can't deny that his skill and prowess in bed are the best I've ever had, and I don't know how I will find anyone after this who can take me to the same dizzying heights as Xander has. My wayward thoughts are interrupted by the sound of running water as Xander returns.

"Give me your hands, Georgina."

As I comply, he pulls me gently to my feet, then scoops me up in his strong arms.

"I can walk, Xander," I laughingly grumble, surprised by his strength as he carries me into the bathroom.

"I know, but I just have this urge to carry you." He has a mischievous glint in his eyes as he slides me slowly down his body, depositing me next to the long, deep bath. He kneels in front of me, his tongue lapping at my over sensitive nipples, while his hands open my legs. His hands caress my legs as he unclips my stockings and slides them down, his tongue following on the inside of my thigh as he removes the silky, sheer nylons. Wrapping his hands over my hips, he buries his face in my crotch, his tongue dancing over my sensitive clit, causing my body to twitch as I bury my fingers in his hair, pulling his mouth harder against me and tilting my hips toward him. He chuckles at my response to his insatiable teasing and I feel it vibrate on my sensitive nub.

"Ahh. Cheeky devil. Two can play at that game, you know," he challenges.

Xander pulls his head back to look up at me and, waggling his eyebrows with a devilish glint in his eyes, he winks suggestively at me. He is the definition of mesmerizing; a macho, self-assured alpha going after what he wants. He is intoxicating and addictive, and I already know I'd never be able to get enough of him.

Standing, Xander quickly unclips my suspender belt, tossing it to the other side of the room, and steps into the bath, holding my hand as I step over the edge into the deliciously warm water. He sinks his body into the warm depths, pulling me down between his thighs. Tilting my head back, I rest it against Xander's shoulder, lazing in the calming, warm water.

He nuzzles my neck and ear and I sigh, physically spent and emotionally content for the moment. I will deal with the fall-out later. For now, I just want to make the most of my time with this intoxicating man. Like my body, my mind stills as I drift into a dreamy haze.

Xander's hands, slick with soap I hadn't noticed him pouring, begin roaming over my body, massaging my breasts, snapping me out of my drowsiness. Slowly, his hand finds my mound, resting against it while a finger slips between my folds, pressing on my pleasure point as he nips the soft skin where my neck and shoulder join. I jerk at his touch and moan as his finger slides further down into my entrance.

"Are you sore, Little One?" His soft voice against my ear asks hypnotically.

"Mm, a bit, but in a good way. What about you?" I snake my hand around behind me to grasp Xander's cock, running my thumb over the crown. He nips my neck and presses on my clit again, and I retaliate with a gentle tug and squeeze on his shaft.

"Mm. A bit tender, but nothing lasting," he murmurs.

His hand splays across my stomach while he plunges his finger inside me again, and he mutters, "Tell me if you want to stop."

"I will, but I don't want you to. That feels sooo good." I exhale a long breath, widening my legs, twisting my wrist as I work his cock some more.

Spent from our torrid sex, but needing to fondle each other, we continue touching and playing till the water cools. The earlier demanding urgency of lust has quietened to a slow burning arousal when Xander helps me out of the bath, handing me a towel. We quickly dry ourselves and then he leads me back to bed, where we lay facing each other, stroking, kissing, and touching till our arousal demands its release again.

I crave the feel of him in my mouth, to run my tongue up the underside of his shaft, to taste his salty precum, to feel him swell as he nears his release. Pushing his hips flat on the bed, I position myself between his spread thighs, sliding my mouth over his head, listening to his moans as I lavish his slit with my tongue, groaning as he spills more precum.

"Oh fuuuck. I need you to sit on my face," Xander groans, grabbing my legs, and dragging me over him into a sixty-nine position. His hands hold me open, a thumb against my clit, while his tongue plunges deep into me. I tease his balls while swallowing him deep into my mouth, letting him hit the back of my throat as I hollow my cheeks. Our movements blend into a synchronized rhythm, muffled grunts and moans building with the intensity of the storm within us.

I shriek in a rapturous explosive release that makes me see stars. A deep rumbling roar escapes from Xander as he lifts his hips, his cum rocketing out of him violently. Swallowing what I can of his warm salty fluid, I lick the rest off his cock.

Spent, I roll off and collapse next to him. We gulp in air, neither able to move, where we stay motionless, gradually drifting off into a light sleep.

Waking with a start as Xander moves off the bed, I am disoriented, and realize as I look around that I am still naked on top of the covers. The bedside clock shows it is well past midnight, and as this is just casual sex, I assume I should leave and go home.

Smoothing out my hair as I stand, my body exhausted and tender from our exertions, I gather my clothing from around the apartment and enter the bathroom as Xander is leaving it.

He stops, arms folded, staring angrily as I collect the last of my lingerie.

"What are you doing, Georgina?"

"I know we haven't discussed this arrangement, Xander, but I assume your definition of casual sex means no actual sleeping together. So, I am heading home." I start to dress, leaving my suspender belt and stockings off, intending on shoving them in my handbag when I finally remember where I'd left it.

"You don't have to do that. You're welcome to stay."

Sensing his need for control, I decide to try to explain my reasoning for leaving. Placing my hand on his arm, I peer up at him, trying to melt his icy glare.

"Thank you for a truly amazing night. I would love to stay, but we both know there is still a lot we have to learn about each other before either of us feels comfortable staying the night. And I don't know how we do that and still maintain a 'casual sex' relationship." I pause, casting my eyes over his stern expression, trying to gauge his thoughts. There is a softening in his eyes; they are now cool instead of glacial. And his expression is now frowning and thoughtful instead of angry. "So, I am just trying to give us both some space to get used to the newness of us. We can work out the rest as we go."

I stand on tiptoe and kiss him lightly on the lips, but he doesn't respond. Rolling my eyes, I turn to check I have all my belongings. "Besides, I need to sleep after you exhausted me," I tell him, hoping to make him smile. "And I don't think you or I would get any sleep if I stayed."

Unsmiling, he nods his head, walking past me into his large walk-in wardrobe and emerges wearing jeans and a casual long-line leather jacket over a crisp white t-shirt. I assume he has dressed to escort me to the lobby, but then think he is a bit overdressed for that. I also assume he will say goodbye to me at his apartment door or the elevator. Not that I have thought much about our goodbye.

"Are you ready to go?" he asks coolly.

Blinking in confusion, I mutter, "Er, yes," and then follow him as he collects his phone and keys and holds the front door open for me. He is silent as we walk to the elevator and stands apart from me, without touching, as if reminding me this is a casual thing. It is so contradictory to the intense, orgasm-filled evening we have shared that I wonder if I'll get whiplash from his ever-changing moods. His distance pisses me off because, despite my wanting to leave, I feel like I am being marched off the premises.

"Xander, I can find my own way out. You don't need to come down."

He turns and glares at me as the elevator pings. "I am driving you home, Georgina." His voice matches the hardness of his gaze and, as he sees I am about to protest, he barks, "It is not open for discussion."

He strides out into the underground garage. What can I say to that? Nothing, but I can silently comply. So, I follow him to a sleek, metallic blue Maserati sportscar, step inside, running my hand over the smooth beige leather of the seat and admire the sophisticated clean lines of the dashboard then buckle up as the engine roars and Xander speeds out of the garage.

CHAPTER 19 – Gina

THE BEEPING OF MY phone mid-morning interrupts me from some complicated design calculations.

> **Xander: Morning Georgina. Today would have started much nicer with you in my bed, but I agree that it's probably a bit soon for sleepovers. Thank you for being the voice of reason. Hope you are well rested Little One. Talk soon. X**

I read and re-read the message, thinking I had misunderstood. But I realize as I read that I feel chuffed at the minor victory of winning an argument with Xander. I don't fool myself into thinking that it will be a common occurrence, though. Still, I had argued my point and given him time to digest it, as I often do with my brothers, so that appears the best way to get through to Xander as well. *I must remember that.*

What to reply, though? Should I thank him again for a great night? Should I wait for him to arrange the next? There is no question in my mind that I want to see him again, but does he feel the same way? His message had said 'Talk soon', so he must want to have more to do with me. *You're an independent woman Gina, you can ask him out*, I chide. *Why, though, am I so daunted by the thought of arranging some time with Xander? Is it fear of rejection?*

Snapping myself out of my head-spinning internal reverie, I pick up my phone to respond to his message, typing quickly and sending it before I can second-guess myself. My body craves more of him, despite being well-satisfied last night. He is like a drug. The more I have of him, the more I want, and I can feel my pussy throbbing in anticipation.

> **Gina:** Morning, Xander. Thank you again for a great night. Would you like a repeat this Friday night? Dinner and 'dessert' at my place?

> **Xander:** **I'm starving and can't wait till Friday. Any chance of sooner, so I don't die of starvation?**

Xander's immediate reply made me chuckle. I am thrilled that he wants to see me again so soon, but don't want to seem too eager. But I am desperate to have sex with him again and getting hornier by the minute at the thought.

Gina: I have a meeting with Ethan this afternoon. If you like, I could swing by your office and hand deliver to you some delicacies to tide you over.

Xander: Perfect. See you then.

He adds an emoji smiley face with its tongue hanging out, making me chuckle again.

After that, I make a few phone calls and settle back into work to prepare for my meetings.

By the time I am ready to leave, my libido is in overdrive and my panties feel damp from my thoughts of Xander, so I make a quick stop at my apartment to change them. *Should I go without underwear altogether?* I am tempted, but as I have a lot of sitting to do before meeting Xander, I think better of it, as I don't want any staining on my skirt during the meeting with Ethan. I have never been so uninhibited with other men. *Xander brings out a wicked side of me that I hadn't realized existed.*

I am on edge throughout my meeting with Ethan, which drags on because he seems to just want to chat. I make my excuses as soon as I can and walk quickly to Xander's office. No sooner has his PA announced me than his door swings open. He looks so delicious in his gray-fitted trousers and crisp white shirt as he stands in the doorway giving me the once-over. His eyes light with fire, and he licks his lips in anticipation.

"Georgina, thanks for fitting me in at such short notice." His careful word choice is meant for his PA's ears, but the double meaning behind his words is not lost on me, and my eyebrows rise cheekily.

"Glad I can be of assistance." My lips quirk while my eyes eat him up as I walk past him and stop just inside the door. He quickly shuts it behind us, locking it as we turn to face each other. I hand him a small white cardboard box, which he glances at and gives me a quizzical look.

"Some delicacies for you." I keep a straight face as I utter my tongue-in-cheek words, then smile as he lifts the lid, throws his head back, and roars in laughter at the selection of sweet artisan petit fours inside.

"Nicely played, Ms Colby." His voice is smoky and his eyes darken as he places his arm around my shoulders and leads me to a large chesterfield lounge. "Have a seat. Would you like a coffee?"

"Only if you are having one." I am feeling nervous, not sure how to proceed. Then Xander sits next to me, turning slightly to face me, his knees touching mine, stoking the heat inside me. He shakes his head slightly, gazing into my eyes, and plays with a tendril of hair as it hangs over my shoulder.

"No coffee," he murmurs, his mouth hovering over mine. "I want to sample some of your delicacies, Georgina." He tenderly cups my jaw as his soft lips caress mine.

Overcome with desire, which gushes through me at his touch, I wrap my arms over his shoulders, one hand pressing against his scalp, my fingers running through his thick, soft, dark hair. My lips open willingly to his touch, craving more of him.

His lips crush mine, his desperation evident as he pushes his tongue between my seam, twirling it around, exploring my mouth while he holds me tightly against him. He slides his hand from my jaw, skimming down my arched neck to my perky breast, well defined in my fitted blouse, then squeezes, and presses it against his palm.

I moan and move a hand to unbutton his shirt, slipping underneath and circling one firm nipple before skimming to the other and doing the same again. He presses his lips harder against mine, moving both hands to frantically undo my blouse buttons. As our lips grind against each other, Xander lifts me, so I straddle him, opening me wide before he skims his hands up my skirt, pushing it up as high as he can. His hand roams over my damp panties, pulling them to one side and slipping a finger beneath and groaning at my wetness, easily sliding over my clit and into my opening.

I squirm, wanting him to feel the same urgency I do. The steel of his erection juts against my thigh, so I buck against it at the same tempo as his probing finger. I fumble undoing his belt buckle and zip in my position, then slip my hand between the folds of material, pulling his rigid shaft from its confinement. My thumb swipes across the head, smearing the pre-cum collected there, making his hips twitch.

Suddenly Xander breaks our kiss and, as he gulps for air, grabs my hips, and lifts me to a standing position. I give him a puzzled look when he stands as well. My lips curl into a smile as I watch him reach into his pocket before dropping his trousers and underpants and quickly rolling on a condom.

Frantically, I drop my panties and hitch up my skirt again while I wait for him. Xander sits, positioning himself near the edge of the seat, lounging backward and spreading his legs wide, exposing himself to my hungry gaze before dragging me toward him. My knees fall to the lounge cushions and he guides me down, so I sink onto his shaft until he is buried deep within me. Tilting my head back, my eyes shut as I exhale a long sigh of contentment that turns into a moan. Having Xander inside me like this is euphoric.

I rise and drop again, increasing the pace with every downward stroke, while Xander suckles and nips my bouncing breasts. We buck against each other, desperate for release, moaning with pleasure, until I still and throw my head back, emitting a stifled cry as my internal muscles clamp around his length. Xander buries his face in my breasts and gives another deep thrust before he explodes within me as well.

"Fuuuck, Gina." His voice is raspy and dry as I tighten my walls, milking every last drop of cum from him before he falls backward, and I collapse on top of him. "That was fucking mind-blowing," he murmurs against my throat, inhaling deeply.

"Mmmm, it sure was." My brain is in too much of a fog for any smart repartee. I am enjoying leaning on him, savoring the mixture of his sandalwood scent with sex, and the mouthwatering sight of his toned fit torso covered in a light sheen of sweat.

After a few moments of silence, while we collect our breath, he gently eases me off his lap. Standing on shaky legs, I watch as he moves toward the small ensuite hidden behind a wall panel where he disposes of the condom and cleans himself up with a flannel. On his return, he points to the bathroom.

"There is a fresh flannel in there for you as well. Take your time."

I quickly pick up my panties and walk to the bathroom, locking the door behind me.

When I return to the office, I am pleased that no one will be able to tell what we'd just been up to as my hair is smoothed out and everything is in the right place. Xander is also fully redressed and, other than a light flush over his neck, looks like nothing has happened. I notice him casting his sultry eyes over me like he wants to go again, so I throw him a beaming smile, stretch up, and kiss him lightly on the cheek.

"Thank you for the afternoon delights, Xander. I really should get going, and I expect you still have a busy afternoon ahead."

He nods regretfully, acknowledging that work beckons. "Thank you, Little One. Your delicacies are extraordinary, and I can't get enough of them," he murmurs as we walk to the door.

Xander pauses, dipping his head, resting his brow against mine. "I'll call you later." Warm lips brush feather-soft across my forehead, then he opens the door. With my sex thrumming from its intense workout, I nod and smile, then stride out like I always do, with a confident stance and a subtle swing to my hips.

Deep in thought as I lay in bed, I reflect on the elation I had felt this afternoon, trying to understand why I felt on such a high. *Is it the endorphins from great sex making my body and brain zing?* If that is the case, then, surely, I would have come down from my orgasm high by now. That buzz hadn't lasted like this with other partners. But, hours later, I still feel happy and carefree and have even found myself dancing around the apartment, which is unheard of.

Even the fact that Xander hasn't called me like he said he would doesn't dampen my spirits. It has to be the endorphins, and an internet search confirms that the post-sex good vibes can last up to forty-eight hours. *Xander is good for me. Who would have thought?* I chuckle at my temporary insanity, but know myself well enough to realize there is more to my feelings for him than sexual euphoria. Quickly, I remind myself of Xander's low boredom threshold and warn myself not to get emotionally involved.

My mind projects images of him sitting half naked on the lounge this afternoon, in all his glory with a beautiful, sinful look in his smoldering eyes. Distracted by the buzzing of my phone, I glance down to see a message from Xander, as if my thoughts have reached him.

Xander: Are you awake?

Gina: Yes. Just.

My phone rings, his name on the screen.

"Hi." He speaks softly, his tone warm and sensual.

"Hi, yourself." My body melts at the sound of his voice. "What are you up to?"

"Just getting ready to turn in for the night. What about you?"

"I'm already in bed."

"Mmm." His tone indicates he is picturing me in his bed. "Alone I hope." The quip has a stern edge, revealing shades of Mr. Scowly Face, who is never very far away.

"Of course, Xander. Otherwise, I wouldn't be on the phone with you," I scoff.

"Good." He ignores my retort and hesitates, as if choosing his words carefully, before he continues. "Today was amazing, gorgeous. Thank you."

"I should be thanking you. I have been floating on a cloud since I left your office." My voice is soft and dreamy.

He chuckles. "Me too. I want to see if we can meet up tomorrow night?" Smooth, velvety, and enticing like high-quality chocolate and just as delectable.

"I'd love to Xander, but I already have something arranged that I can't get out of." I hesitate when he is silent. "What about Friday night instead?"

"Yeah, that will probably work. I'll text you the details," he answers, a touch of disappointment in his voice. "Good night, Little One."

"Good night, Xander." I drift off to sleep wondering how many pet names that man will use with me and why I like it as much as I do.

***

"Tash, what are you doing tonight?" I ask mid-morning, poking my head around the door.

"I've got Peter's family coming over for dinner. Why?" Tash shuffles papers as she replies, and I remember that

Tash doesn't see much of her in-laws, so her husband Peter wouldn't be too happy if she missed the get together.

"Damn. Murray is in town and has been badgering me to meet up with him, 'for old-time's sake'. I've been putting him off for days now. I was hoping for some backup in case things got messy." I sigh.

"Wait. What?" Tash is now cross, her attention focused on me, and I blush under the scrutiny. "You are meeting up with that scumbag? Why? After he cheated on you and broke your heart, then married the boss's daughter and moved overseas? Why, Georgie?"

"Mainly to shut him up and get him off my back. Believe me, I have no interest in him otherwise, and intend to tell him never to contact me again. I've told him I only have an hour to spare, just so I have an escape option," I retort, annoyed with myself for allowing the whining, conniving tyrant, Murray, to manipulate me into agreeing to meet him. I am fully aware of his bullying tactics and intend to shut him down so I can cut ties with him for good this time.

"Seeing him is not a good idea, Georgie. Are Hayden or Jack able to be your backup?"

"No, they are both busy. And before you ask, Simone is away, and Allie and Emily already have plans and Kurt is working." I sigh heavily again. "If I put him off, he will just keep pestering me."

At Tash's continued look of concern, I add, "I'll be fine, Tash. I'm a much stronger and more assertive person now than I was three years ago and have stood toe to toe with more powerful men than Murray could ever be. We're meeting at the bar of Hayden's restaurant, so at least I will have some familiar faces around me, and Tony, the maître d', won't stand for any nonsense."

"True." Tash seems pleased that I had thought this out, but her brow is still furrowed with worry. "Just call me as soon as you can afterward. I need to know that you are safe from that creep."

"I'll be fine, Tash. Really." My words are just as much for my benefit as they are for my concerned friend. Although I know I can handle myself, I don't trust Murray's motives for wanting to see me.

CHAPTER 20 - Gina

LATER THAT EVENING, I stand outside, a few doors up from the restaurant, while I draw in a deep breath and gather my wits, steeling myself for my meeting with Murray.

I had convinced myself for a while after we broke up that I still loved him, but in hindsight, I realize our parting was for the best. What we had was more about being in love with the idea of being in love rather than a deep, enduring love for each other. Yes, we had cared about each other, but then he cheated on me.

Murray is very money-oriented, and he would walk over people, even those he cares about, to climb the ladder of success and get what he wants. It still pisses me off to think about the promotion he got after he had taken credit for work I had done. It didn't take me long to find out about it, given that we both worked for the same company. I still feel bitter about being used and that I was too gullible to recognize the signs.

Now, standing here, I feel curious about whether Murray has aged in the last three years since I have seen him, or if he has changed with married life and my need to find out sent my feet moving toward the door of the restaurant.

Plastering a neutral expression on my face, I push the door open and step inside. Smiling, I greet Tony and look toward the bar where I recognize Murray instantly.

Murray's eyes light with a lecherous glint at the sight of me as he stands and leans in to kiss me on the cheek. I step back and extend my hand instead, making Murray momentarily sneer before replacing it with an emotionless stare. Returning my handshake, while the other hand grasps my wrist, he holds onto my wrist for a heartbeat too long, trying to remind me who was in control.

I have seen that sneer and handshake many times when he thought himself superior to whoever was unfortunate enough to be standing in front of him. *He hasn't changed at all,* I consider, my bitterness rising as I seat myself next to him at the bar.

Murray looks a bit heavier than I remember and he has some graying at the temples, but his narrow, beady eyes still hold a look of superior smugness. Loathing rises in me; with him for his hateful mannerisms and personality, and with my kind heartedness expecting that he had changed.

"Georgie, you look great. It's so good to see you," he drawls, his eyes roaming over me as if remembering my nakedness, which makes my skin crawl. Turning to the barman, he orders me a glass of wine—also a throwback to our time together—and another beer for himself.

"No, I'll just have a soda water, please," I counter, smiling at the barman, who nods in acknowledgment.

"You look quite the successful businessman, Murray. How is life treating you?" My tone is cool, my expression polite and impassive, and my body language confident and friendly, just like I am meeting a prospective client.

"I'm now the Head of Projects and Development and have two hundred and fifty people working under me," he boasts pompously, although I am not impressed.

The barman returns with my drink. I pay and thank him and suck on the straw, welcoming the icy coolness.

"My father-in-law is set to retire next year, and I am in line for his position. We have a twenty-thousand square foot home by the water, and all the trappings," he continues to crow, unaware of how indifferent I am.

"Hmm, impressive. You have done well for yourself." My tone is laced with sarcasm, which he doesn't pick up on. "Still married, I see." I glance at the diamond-studded wedding band he wears and press my lips together as my eyes return to coolly observe him.

"Now, now Georgie. No need to be jealous," he taunts.

My eyebrows rise as I glare at him icily. "Why would I be jealous, Murray? You have the life you wanted, and so do I." I take another sip of my water before challenging him. "What did you need to see me about so desperately?"

Murray stares into his drink, his expression subdued, the bluster restrained as if he is choosing his words carefully.

"I've been missing you lately and being in this city reminded me of so many good times with you that I just needed to see you," he divulges awkwardly as he leans in closer and tries again to hold my hand.

My eyes narrow, my brows crease together, and my lips purse slightly in annoyance as I snatch my hand away.

"Really? Missing me? Does that mean the gloss has dis-appeared from your marriage, Murray?" I goad, saccharine sweetly. He was always a fickle character, so I am not surprised that discontent has set in.

He nods, shoulders hunched as he holds his bottle in both hands, his expression downcast.

"Yes, she's turned into a harpy; continually nagging me and questioning my movements. She's complaining to her father about me, so my promotion could be in jeopardy." He spits the words and thumps his fist on the bar. *Payback's a bitch*, I think with contempt, surprised by his aggressive behavior.

"Is she questioning your movements because you've cheated on her?" My tone is icy.

"You think because I cheated on you, that I would cheat on her too?" he challenges, feigning insult.

I arch an eyebrow and give him a sideways glance. I see through his bluff and silently call him on it.

"Yeah, okay. I cheated on her," he confesses, his tone surly. "But she's boring and always nagging." He tries to justify his actions, but I'm not having any of it. "Being married to her is not like what you and I shared, Georgie. I just want to recapture that sense of fulfillment... that love we had." Murray stares brazenly into my eyes. "Can we try again, Georgie?" he pleads, reaching for my hand, and giving me his best puppy dog eyes look. I am speechless, incredulous, and disgusted, choking on the sip of water I have just taken, and quickly withdraw my hand from his for the second time.

"Definitely not," I fume. "Have you forgotten you are married? We have been there and done that, Murray, and I could never trust you again. Besides, I have moved on and don't have any feelings for you anymore." I stand, my body rigid and cold. "Goodbye, Murray. I don't ever want to hear from you again."

I stride toward the door, furious with him.

"Georgie, wait," Murray demands, as he grabs at my arm, which I shrug off, ignoring him.

I make it out the door before he grabs my arm again, his fingers biting into my flesh, fury emanating from him. My heart races and my stomach quivers with unease.

"Don't you walk away from me, bitch," he barks, standing menacingly in front of me, his face so close to mine I can smell his beer-laced breath. "I'm not finished with you yet."

I stand rigid; my hands tighten into fists and then loosen. Even though I feel a bit uneasy, I refuse to be intimidated by him. Where I may have once yielded to his bullying, his departure had taught me a valuable lesson; how to stand up for myself.

"I have nothing more to say to you, Murray. You have disrespected me in so many ways, we are done. Now go away and leave me alone." I spit, contempt dripping from my words. His face reddens and nostrils flare as I step sideways to walk around him, but he grabs my shoulders and forcefully drags me against him, crushing his lips against mine. I shove him violently, forcing him to stumble backward enough so I can remove myself from his reach.

"Murray, go now before I call the police." I enunciate the words slowly and forcefully. My cold eyes glare at him, reminding him how far over the mark he has stepped. His expression pales and he steps back, suddenly unable to meet my gaze, his hands pressing against his cheeks, shame cloaking him as he realizes his actions.

"Please, Georgie, give me another chance," he begs remorsefully.

I open my mouth to speak but am interrupted by another deeper male voice that I recognize instantly.

"No way in hell."

Shocked, my eyes fly to Xander, as do Murray's. Finding him standing tall, rigid, and ominous, as if he would like nothing better than for Murray to take a swing at him.

"You heard the lady. Get lost. And don't contact her again!" he thunders, his words resounding around us. My mouth falls open and my skin prickles while my racing heartbeat pounds in my ears. I can see a vein pulsing in Xander's neck. His jaw clenches, he grinds his teeth and flexes his fingers while he his cold hard eyes continue to impale Murray. I have not heard this level of anger or cold hatred in his tone before and am thankful it is not directed at me.

Murray grimaces, nods, and shoves his hands in his pockets. His cheeks are flushed, and he gives me an embarrassed look before staring down at the ground and walking away subdued.

I turn to glance at Xander, who is still standing rigidly, anger oozing from him.

"Thank you," I offer softly, appreciatively, relieved that his presence has de-escalated the volatile situation. I let out a huge sigh of relief. His eyes bore into mine and note my trembling hands and momentary slumping of my posture as tears well in my eyes, which I rapidly blink away.

"Come. I'll take you home." It is a command I am happy to accept, so I quickly follow him to his car. His eyes are steely and cold, his lips pressed tightly together.

"How much did you hear?" I ask as we pull away from the curb.

He starts to speak but huffs out a breath first, as if trying to control his rage. "I was sitting opposite the bar, so I heard most of the conversation." His words are clipped, and anger laces his tone. "I can't begin to think of what would have happened

214

to you if I hadn't been there," he barks. Thumping the steering wheel, he explodes. "For fuck's sake, Georgina, how could you put yourself in such danger? What were you thinking?"

"I didn't expect things to go the way they did," I lamented, feeling dazed, my thoughts jumbled.

"Obviously," he snorts before he shoots me a furious glare. "Who was he? And why did you meet up with him?"

I flinch and answer, my words spilling out fast in relief and emotional overload. "He is my ex-fiancé who pinched my designs and made out they were his, then dumped me two months before our wedding. He moved overseas after we separated and married his boss' daughter, the woman he had an affair with while we were together. I hadn't heard from him in years and suddenly he contacted me two weeks ago to say he would be in town and wanted to catch up. I kept putting him off because I had nothing to say to him, but he kept pestering me, so I relented for the sake of getting him off my back."

"I thought I had a backup plan," I concede, after taking a calming breath. "I told him I only had an hour to spare him, and I had planned on getting Tony to help if things went awry. I had also asked my friends to be there tonight, but they were all busy," I choked out.

He holds my gaze for a moment, as if gauging my credibility, before looking away again. I rest my head against the headrest, suddenly feeling weary and wrung out, and can feel my eyes welling.

"Did you sleep with him?" He spits the words out through gritted teeth and glares at me without blinking.

"What? God no!" I shriek and give him a look designed to peel his hide. "How and when am I supposed to have done

215

that when I only met him less than an hour ago, in a public place? How dare you think I would stoop so low. Having been cheated on, I never break the trust of someone I am involved with by cheating on them," I snarl. "Can you say the same, Xander?" I spit out the words, hurt and angry that he has such a low opinion of me. I would much rather Xander see my anger than my tears.

"I never cheat," he growls and thumps the steering wheel again. The car is filled with heated, angry silence for the remainder of the short trip to my apartment.

"Does he know where you live?" Xander coldly grills me as he pulls up to the curb.

"I don't believe so," I reply hesitantly, as I open the door to get out. "I wasn't living here when we were together."

"You should report him to the police, Georgina."

I scrutinize his features. There is still a note of anger in his voice, but I also recognize the concern in his tone. Then a flash of fear crosses my face as his words sink in. Murray was a loose cannon tonight, and who knows if and how his ego will exact payback.

Nodding wearily, deflated from my anger and the night's events, I thank him for bringing me home and get out of the car, deep in thought. I flinch when I feel a hand on my back as I unlock my front door and spin around with scared eyes until I realize it is Xander.

"Sorry," he apologizes, realizing he has startled me. "Is any-one home?" When I shake my head, he asks if he can come in and make sure it is safe.

I nod, commenting unsteadily, "Now you are scaring me."

Xander has a look around, stomping as he goes, and after a few questions, demands that I call Kurt, Hayden's boyfriend to come over. When he is satisfied that everything is in order, he insists that I lock up after him and he leaves. He hasn't even said goodbye. Just stormed out in a gray cloud of anger. *Mr. Scowly Face had left the building.*

Not long after, I am sitting in the kitchen with a cup of tea, reflecting on the evening, and wonder whether I could have handled things differently when I hear a rattling at the front door. Spooked by Xander's comments, I grab a large kitchen knife, then poke my head around the wall to see Kurt entering. He is ex-military and now works as a security guard. He is well built, but not over the top with muscle, but he is a big softie to those he cares about.

I drop the knife on the bench and run into his arms, relieved to have him here. At his concerned questioning, I tell him about the events of the evening, watching his emotions change from incredulous to outrage toward Murray and relief that I am safe. And he was also annoyed with Xander for not staying with me.

It takes me a long time to go to sleep, but I feel safe knowing I am not alone.

***

Tash gives me an inquisition the next morning and is livid that Murray has acted in such a vile manner, but thrilled that Xander had stepped in, but also annoyed that he hadn't stayed. She also agrees that notifying the police is necessary, regardless of whether Murray contacts me again or not. So, most of the morning is spent at the police station giving my statement.

I am exhausted after all the questions and, ironically, feel that I betrayed Murray, but I keep reminding myself of his anger and how he'd grabbed me. Still too raw from the situation, I vow to tell my family later because I know my brothers will want to hunt him down, and probably end up on the wrong side of the law as a result and I can't deal with that right now.

I flop into my office chair, slowly sipping a fresh coffee, and check my phone again for the umpteenth time. Still no messages from Xander. He is probably busy, maybe still angry with me, although I had done nothing wrong except misjudge Murray. Still, I thought he might have called or messaged to see how I am feeling today, even to nag me about going to the police.

I caustically remind myself that I am only his friend with benefits, and clearly, he has no emotional investment at all. I realize that I am probably more invested in Xander than I want to admit, and his lack of communication has hurt. *Am I beginning to fall in love with him?* Love is a big leap, but I feel that there is mutual respect and caring for each other. Xander has proven on several occasions that he wants to protect me, and I know I would do the same for him. But love? I am infatuated with him, I acknowledge, but realization dawns on me that what I feel is more than that.

I AM in love with Xander.

Oh. Damn the man, I fume, ranting that I don't need him or his unpredictable moods. I decide to let him contact me, and I will be unavailable if asked for another hook-up. Love or no love, I fume again, knowing that I will cave if the opportunity arises.

Just then, my phone pings with a message.

Xander: Are you ok? Did you go to the police?

Gina: I'm fine, thanks. And yes, I went to the police.

Xander: And?

Gina: And... report has been made, and I am sick of the questions about the whole saga.

Xander: Has he tried to contact you?

It irks me that he continues to interrogate me, ignoring my comment about how sick and tired I am of the whole saga.

Gina: I have blocked his number, so I don't know. I wouldn't answer even if he did.

Xander: Ok. Good.

There is no further response.

What the hell was that all about? He was checking to make sure I was okay, and that I have done what he suggested by going to the police. That I understood. But his terse abrupt texts feel like he is trying to relinquish any involvement he had had in the situation. *Is he wiping his hands of me?*

Fed up and still simmering from our argument last night, I put my phone in my bag. *Out of sight, out of mind.* This whole Murray and Xander situation has me on edge, and I can't sit still. I need some fresh air, so I gather my things together, telling Tash that I am going on a site-visit.

***

Walking around the hotel development site is just what I need. Fresh air, sunshine, and some manual labor in the garden always grounds me. I am pleased to see Jamie and, after explaining my dilemma, laugh at his good-natured ribbing about attracting the wrong type of men.

Our work on the site is nearly complete, so I scour the area for any problems or unfinished work that will need to be followed up on, then catch up with Jamie again to discuss our options. As we are working out a plan for future work on the Garden Show display, I spot Xander entering the site with a woman, whom I assume by their body language is a colleague. He is engrossed in their conversation as they enter the hotel, and I make sure to leave the site before he comes back out. I am not ready to face him yet.

Later that evening, Jamie texted me.

> **Jamie: Thanks very much, Georgie. I copped an ear bashing from Xander this afternoon interrogating me about how and where you were. He is very protective of you. He seemed quite annoyed that he had missed you, too. Looks like another male who has fallen under your spell. *smiley face emoji***

His last comment has me confused. Who is he referring to other than Xander? Is Xander under my spell? Not coming up with any plausible answer, I file that question away to ask Jamie about later.

Putting my phone on charge, I walk to the bathroom to run a bath and soak away the stress of the last few days.

CHAPTER 21 – Xander

I PACE LIKE A caged animal around my office. I have snapped at everyone today and haven't been able to calm myself, even though I know it is unfair to those around me. I can't get the sight of Georgina being accosted by her ex out of my mind and fume at her stupidity in allowing her big heart to overrule her common sense. I had wanted so badly to lay my fist in the guy's face and pummel him that I had struggled to keep my hands by my sides.

Fortunately, the idiot moved on quickly. What a low life! Married, cheating and looking for another conquest. I don't understand what Georgina saw in him, but am relieved that she has no obvious feelings for the man now.

"Hey." Ethan bravely pops his head into the office, after standing outside watching me pace.

"What do you want?" I bark, wanting to be left alone, but Ethan is unperturbed, walking in and seating himself on the chair across from my desk.

"What's going on with you, man? You've been a prick all day." His tone is firm and matter-of-fact but concerned while his eyes study me, glowering as I pace.

"Fuck off," I snap back, then huff out a breath guiltily and perch on the edge of my desk. I sit silently, gripping the edge tightly, inhaling deeply while I slowly decompress, inwardly grateful that I can discuss my fears with my brother. Ethan stares patiently, waiting for me to explain.

"Georgina met up with her ex-fiancé last night and he assaulted her," I grate.

"What the fuck? Is she okay? Who is he? Where is he? I want to beat his head in." My glance is steely and I hold up my hand at Ethan's shocked and angry expression, appreciating my brother's protective reaction at the thought of Georgina being hurt.

"She's fine." I huff, "Sorry for that lousy explanation, but I am still angry about it as well." At Ethan's nod, I continue tautly, "The asshole is married, and wanted to get it on with Georgina because his life is dreary, apparently." Ethan swears again and I continue, "She handled herself superbly, cut him dead, and told him to never contact her again. But being the scum that he is, he grabbed her and kissed her until she shoved him away. Luckily, I was in the restaurant and followed her outside. I stepped in to support her, but all I really wanted to do was smash his face in. He soon scurried away with his tail between his legs." I pause, watching as Ethan's expression flitters between relief, anger, and confusion.

"I'm pleased she is okay, but why did she meet up with the creep in the first place?" Ethan quizzes.

"I know, right?" I expel my frustration, then explain the situation. I go on to tell Ethan how furious I was with her on the drive home and still am, for putting herself in that situation and that I am glad she'd listened and contacted the police.

Ethan's brows draw together as he peers shrewdly at me and chooses his words carefully. "I understand your anger at Georgina being in a dangerous situation. I feel the same way about how things turned out. I'm playing devil's advocate here, so don't jump down my throat." Pausing momentarily, he then continues at my nod of acknowledgment.

"Georgina is a strong, capable woman who can match herself against most people, including her over-protective brothers. She had obviously weighed up the situation, which led her to arrange a backup plan, but also felt that she could handle the man she used to love by herself. She alone had to be the one to tell the creep that she wanted nothing more to do with him."

Ethan's words sink in, and I recognize the sense in his reasoning as I nod in agreement.

"You need to ask yourself Zee whether you're angry at Georgina because of the danger she inadvertently found herself in, or because you are jealous that she met up with a man she used to love?"

"What's with all this philosophical bullshit?" I demand, glaring at Ethan, who smiles wryly, knowing he has hit a nerve. "I don't love her. I just love to fuck her."

Ignoring my brash statement, Ethan continues, enjoying the opportunity to tease me.

"So, are you going to call her and explain you were so angry because you thought you were losing her to another man?" I know Ethan has raised the jealousy comment to gauge my reaction, which confirmed he is spot on, even though I won't admit it.

"Oh, fuck off. Go back to your office." my anger has subsided to mild irritation, and I am relieved to have discussed things with my brother, who, as always, has made some good points. Although Ethan has snatched the opportunity to taunt me, to be fair, I would have done the same thing in similar circumstances.

I call out, "Thanks," as Ethan goes back to his office gloating, but I remain perched on the edge of my desk while I contemplate his words. *Am I jealous?* I like Georgina. A lot. But love? No. Just like I would have for any of my lovers, I had been helping her out of a tough spot and felt protective of her. I acknowledge that I have a soft spot for her, or should I say, a hard spot. She certainly gets under my skin, stirring my blood, and creating a perpetual need to be inside her. But it was more than that. I also admire her drive and determination, her loyalty and confidence, and her sense of humor. I thought back to just yesterday when she was here in my office, with her delicacies, and my libido fires up again. I haven't been so constantly horny with my other lovers, so why is Georgina so different?

My phone rings, interrupting my introspection, so I walk around my desk and sit in my chair while I discuss the potential for a new project.

Later that evening, as I punish myself with a grueling workout on the treadmill, my thoughts return to Georgina, as they often do. That surprises me, because I usually don't give much thought to my lovers unless it is to arrange a liaison.

I don't want to know what they are thinking, how their day had been, or any other sort of mundane detail about their lives. With Georgina, I have gotten glimpses of her personal life, had met some of her family members and friends and seen her in her job, and it all has me craving to know more.

Is Ethan right in assuming I am jealous of her ex? Yes, he felt some animosity toward the lowlife and was at a loss to understand what Georgina had seen in him. *Jealous though?* My initial reaction when I had seen them in the restaurant together was that it was a business meeting, as I recognized Georgina's business persona she wore so well. But when her scumbag ex tried to hold her hand, I wanted to jump the shrubbery separating the dining area from the bar and punch him in the face. *How dare the creep make a move on my woman? My woman? Where had that come from?*

I had watched and proudly admired Georgina's strength and control as she held the guy off and froze him out with her words. Rage had filled me when the slimy married lowlife hit on her again, wanting to pick up where they had left off. The guy was so full of himself that he hadn't picked up on the fact that Georgina loathed him for expecting her to ignore her principles and have a pointless affair with him. That thought echoed in me for some reason.

I witnessed how insulted Georgina was and was pleased that she had walked away from the good-for-nothing, son of a bitch. Until he followed her and accosted her outside. I had been on my feet and out the door after them without thought, driven by my need to protect her. Then the detestable scumbag forcibly kissed her, and I thought I would explode with rage. It was only Georgina's threat to call the police that stopped me from belting the guy to a pulp, filtering a shred of reasoning through my fury. I recall my relief when he skulked away with his tail between his legs. The guy was punching above his weight with Georgina, and now at least he knew he didn't stand a chance with her anymore.

I had still been battling to control my fury when Georgina's eyes welled with tears and her body crumpled, relief on her face that I had been there. Her tears melted me and I know I had unfairly directed my anger at her for the situation because I had been genuinely scared for her safety. I told myself that I would have reacted the same for any woman in a similar situation. However, the roiling emotions driving my anger made me now realize that my reaction was more about my feelings for the remarkable woman that is Georgina.

I don't want to lose her or see her hurt in any way. And I want to fuck her for a long time to come. *Is that why I am thinking of her as my woman?*

Jumping to the sides of the treadmill, shocked at my revelation, my arms rest on the control panel, and my head slumps onto them while I inhale deeply, sweat dripping from me. I have been in a perpetual lust haze since meeting Georgina that doesn't seem to be going anywhere anytime soon. If anything, it is increasing the more we are intimate. And I know before long it will be aching to be inside her again. I need to see her, talk to her, and explain. I just need to be with her. *Man, you have it bad*, I scoff as I grab my towel, throw it around my neck, and go for a shower.

The hot water revives my tired body; my dick is back to its semi-hard state, and my balls are heavy and aching.

My head feels a lot clearer afterward as well. Lounging back on my large sofa, I dial Georgina while guzzling some water.

"Hi," she quickly answers, her voice neutral, as if she isn't sure whether she is happy to hear from me.

"Hi." My throat is dry and raspy from my exercise. "How are you?"

"I'm fine, thanks, Xander." She answers in a polite voice and breathes heavily, her tone flat and the words noncommittal.

"Are you home?"

When she finally speaks, her voice is hesitant, cool, and tempered. "Why?"

"Because I'd like to see you, Georgina. And I'd like to apologize to you." I speak in a husky consoling voice, a crease forming between my eyebrows as I wonder where the idea of an apology comes from. Then I hear male laughter in the background and am hit with a surge of rage. *Calm down, you idiot, it's probably her flat mates*, I reason, surprised by how quickly I've gone from calm to rage where she is concerned.

"Yes, I'm home. But so are Hayden and Kurt." Her voice is husky but subdued.

"Is it okay if I come over now?"

"Yes. Okay. I'll see you soon then."

I say goodbye and hang up, reasoning that her coolness and lack of enthusiasm to see me must have been because she was in earshot of her flat mates. But doubt niggles at me over my volatile reaction. Eager to have her in my arms, I race around collecting my wallet, phone, and keys before rushing into the lift and punching the button for the garage.

CHAPTER 22 - Gina

IN THE FIFTEEN MINUTES that it takes Xander to get to my place, I have changed out of my sweatpants into a pair of jeans and a t-shirt and have added a zip-up jacket, as the night is cool. I have also brushed my hair out and applied a light touch of neutral-colored lipstick. I had been watching television with Hayden and Kurt on a rare night when we are all home together, so they are surprised to see that I have changed outfits.

Hayden gives me a quizzical look and eyes me up and down, then asks, "Are you going out?"

"No, Xander is coming over," I answer, a bit nervous at how they both will react. Both had expressed their annoyance with him for getting angry the other night and not staying with me but had also appreciated him saving me from Murray. So, I hope they don't make a scene.

I jump to my feet to answer the door, as does Hayden. He turns to me and barks in a voice I have not heard him use before. "Sit. I'll get this." Stunned, I stand rooted to the spot as I watch Hayden pace to the door and fling it open.

He glares intimidatingly at Xander on the doorstep. *Oh, this doesn't look good,* I worry, as I realize that Kurt has also stood and looks ready to pounce. Xander looks unrelenting though and isn't daunted by Hayden's stance.

"Hayden," Xander nods, his eyes scrutinizing the face of the burly male blocking his entry. Both alpha males aren't backing down. If they were wolves, they would have been snarling and growling at each other, circling and staking their claim.

"Oh, for God's sake. Get over yourselves," I snap at them, exasperated by their macho posturing, as I walk to the door, followed by Kurt. I gently place a hand on Hayden's arm. "Hayden, let Xander in, please."

Hayden turns his glare to me but steps aside to let Xander enter. I realize I need to diffuse the male tension before it gets out of hand.

"Xander, this is Hayden and Kurt. Hayden, Kurt, remember that Xander saved me from a difficult situation last night."

Xander speaks, his voice firm with sincerity as he extends his hand to Kurt. "Yes, thank you, Kurt, for coming and staying with Georgina at such short notice. I appreciate you looking after her."

Kurt shook his hand begrudgingly, nodding in acknowledgment of Xander's thanks, then turns to me and smiles warmly as he says, "Anytime for you." I reach up on tip-toe to kiss him on the cheek.

Xander turns back to Hayden and extends his hand to him. "Hayden, I know you would have been here if you could, and I am thankful you are such a good friend and have Georgina's back at all times." Again, his voice was firm and sincere. Hayden huffs and tones down his intimidation level, then reluctantly shakes Xander's hand, his eyes locked on in warning as he said gruffly, "She's a very special lady."

"That she is." Xander nods, then turns his softening eyes to me and smiles warmly at me.

I watch the interchange between the men, trying to comprehend the hidden code that had passed between them, which brought them to a point of conciliation. The words themselves were innocuous enough, but there seemed to be an invisible message in the sentences they all agreed on. *Men are so bizarre*. I had seen the same situation occur with my brothers. One minute they were ready to throttle each other, the next they had reached a non-verbal mutual understanding.

I turn to Xander, shaking my head and blinking at the testosterone permeating the air. "Let's go to the kitchen and let the boys finish watching their movie."

He nods, then smiles at Hayden and Kurt as he comments, "Nice to meet you both," before following me to the kitchen. It isn't too far from the lounge room but enough distance to have a quiet conversation.

"Would you like a drink, Xander? Tea, coffee, Scotch?" I ask slowly, my eyes evading his. I am a bit nervous about having Xander in my apartment and unsure how to entertain him. Should I broach the looming subject of last night and his anger, or chat idly about work?

Xander moves close, facing me. His hands grasp my shoulders and his eyes focus intently on my face as I peer into the warmth of his beautiful eyes.

"Georgina, I'm sorry for being angry with you. I was surprised and annoyed seeing you with another man when I walked into the restaurant, then jealous when I realized you had had a relationship with him. Then I was infuriated with the way that scumbag manhandled you and I struggled to contain my rage over him." Pausing, he brushes some hair off my face. "I was also confounded at how you could have loved someone like that. I couldn't get my emotions under control." He takes a deep breath. "I know you are a strong woman and can look after yourself, but I was worried he would come after you, find you, hurt you. I'm so sorry I took it out on you. That is why I couldn't stay with you, because I knew I needed some distance between us to calm down."

Tears well in my eyes at his honest words. He wraps me in his arms and pulls me snugly against his warm, strong body, and rests his cheek against my head, while my arms extend cozily around his waist. We stood like that for a while, bodies pressed together, content with being in each other's arms.

"Thank you," I utter in a soft voice, tilting my head back to smile warmly at him. I place a hand on his cheek, the stubble brushing against my palm. My eyes drink in his warm liquid gaze. "I was very pleased you were there, actually," I confide quietly. "Because Murray's weird behavior had started to frighten me."

Xander turns his head, his lips gently kissing the palm of my hand, before moving to claim my luscious lips in a deep, sensual kiss. "I don't want to lose you, Georgina," he whispers against my lips when we stop for a breath.

"Ahem."

Startled, we both look toward Hayden and Kurt, who had come around the corner and are watching us with curious looks on their faces. I feel my cheeks flush slightly, and I pull out of Xander's arms.

"Sorry to interrupt, but I was just going to cook a late dinner. Would you like some, too?" Hayden asks. I know that Hayden is checking to make sure I am okay and love that he included Xander in the dinner invitation. He wouldn't have done that if he had concerns about the sort of man that Xander is.

"Have you eaten yet?" I ask Xander, who shakes his head but has a devilish twinkle in his eye, like he is thinking of a sexier meaning.

"I don't want to impose though," he adds, looking at Hayden.

"No problems at all. I usually cook more than enough, so there is something to reheat later." Hayden starts rattling around in the cupboards and refrigerator as Xander, Kurt, and I sit at the bench and watch. "Any food allergies or preferences I should know about?" Hayden queries, looking up at Xander as he begins chopping onion and carrots.

Xander shakes his head in response because he is mesmerized, his mouth hanging open as he watches Hayden's hands skillfully and precisely chop while looking elsewhere.

Kurt chuckles. "I was just as amazed the first time I watched Haydz cook. You wait till you taste it though. He can make scrambled eggs taste like a gourmet dish."

"Sounds impressive." Xander smiles warmly at Kurt, then turns to observe Hayden as he moves swiftly around the kitchen. "You run a restaurant, don't you Hayden? Don't you ever get sick of cooking?" Xander's expression shows genuine interest in the other man, his admiration evident.

"Yes, I do sometimes. Then I get Kurt to cook. Don't let him tell you otherwise, but he is a damn fine cook too."

"Are you a chef too, Kurt?" Xander queries, turning to examine the man mountain sitting next to him. Kurt is as tall as Hayden and Xander, broad-shouldered, and every inch of him is hard muscle. Xander seems to be imagining him in a tight commercial kitchen, obviously thinking it would be like an elephant in a china shop.

"Ha! No. I'm ex-military and now working in security. But cooking is a hobby that came about from trying to eat healthy and nutritious food while training. Haydz finessed my repertoire substantially." Kurt shoots Hayden a warm smile and a loving look, which Hayden reciprocates.

"Hayden has this unique ability to teach people about food by involving them in the preparation, cooking, and presentation of meals, just by asking 'can you stir this' or 'can you chop that', so you pick up bits and pieces and then suddenly you are turning out some decent meals," I explain while I poured each of us a drink. "Whenever we have our friends round, everyone is here in the kitchen doing something for the meal."

Jumping into the conversation, Hayden shares the philosophy which makes him a great chef. "I read a blog written by Flavia Scalzitti that rings so true for me. She wrote 'The preparation, eating, and sharing of food with others is what keeps us connected. Just as the kitchen is the heart of the home, the table is where we eat, talk, share, and connect. It's simple: food gets people talking and asking each other questions. It strengthens and nurtures relationships.' Look at us, for example, you don't know us, yet we are connecting."

Xander blinks a couple of times, ruminating on Hayden's words, before acknowledging with a sincere look. "You know, I never thought of it like that before. Thank you for opening my eyes."

Kurt slaps him on the back and chuckles. "That's the Hayden effect. It knocks you off kilter with simplistic reasoning."

He then gets some plates and cutlery as Hayden serves their meal.

"Mmm, this is amazing." Xander compliments. "Reminds me a lot of the stir fry from The Food Connection restaurant." The other three lift their heads and stare at him, smirking, while Xander looks from one to the other, bewildered by their looks.

"I should hope so," Hayden mocks.

"The Food Connection is Hayden's restaurant," I explain, laying a hand on Xander's arm to soothe any embarrassment he may have felt. If he did, he hid it well.

"Ahh. That explains it. I have always savored the food you create and go there regularly." His intelligent eyes shine with respect and admiration.

After a few moments' silence, each enjoying their meal, Kurt asks Xander, "Do you cook, Xander?"

Xander repeats what he had mentioned to me some time ago and then we chat for a while about all sorts of topics, and it appears the men are developing quite a bromance.

Xander and I help with clearing and stacking the dishwasher while the boys take care of the rest.

As I take Xander's hand, I mention, "Let me show you around," then lead him through a door in the large glass window wall into the darkened courtyard. There is enough light streaming from the kitchen to easily see our way around, and I show him how my offices connect via a doorway on the other side of the courtyard. Within the long narrow space, there are pockets of garden beds and plants as well as an outdoor bench where we sit. The clear, starry sky could be seen through the structural glass roof, and we also have a view through the apartment to the front door.

"They are genuinely great blokes. And very protective of you," Xander comments as we watch Hayden and Kurt pottering around the kitchen.

"Yes, they are amazing friends. I don't know what I would do without either of them." I smile warmly, gazing lovingly at the cute couple. "It's getting cold out here, so I'll show you around upstairs."

Xander admires the use of space and the airy feel of the three bedrooms and particularly likes the large bathroom and utility room that opens off the main bedroom at the front of the building.

"You and your father have done an amazing job of renovating and designing this old warehouse, Georgina. I don't think I have ever seen a warehouse conversion that accommodates so much. I am very impressed," he compliments as he stands in the middle of my bedroom, gazing into my large warm eyes and holding my hands gently.

"Thank you. It is my home and haven," I reply with pride, as I look around and then back to Xander.

Xander claims my soft pink lips before I can continue, his arms wrapping around me and pulling me against him. I bask in the warmth of his body against mine, his kiss igniting my passion as my arms fold across his back. My fingers draw circles against his back, relishing the feel of his taut muscles through the soft fabric of his shirt.

Xander breaks the kiss and rests his head against my forehead, inhaling my scent.

"I'm sorry I hurt you, Gina," he utters quietly.

"Thanks for apologizing, Xander. That means a lot to me." Tenderness and sincerity glow in my eyes as I look directly at him. My hand cups his cheek, and my thumb runs over his full bottom lip.

"Would you like to stay, Xander?"

"I'd like that very much, but I can't stay all night." His voice rumbles as he brushes a strand of hair from my face. His firm sensual lips capture mine, the kiss hot and demanding, stoking the simmering lust within us, and quickly becomes a scorching, tongue-thrusting fusion of mouths.

Our hands roam wildly, touching, teasing, and undressing, as passion consumes us. Falling onto the bed, clutching each other, Xander caresses my body with his lips and hands while I grip and stroke his rigid shaft. His hand dips between my hot, wet folds as his tongue copies the movement in my mouth. My hips buck, desperate for him. Xander presses against me, then stops suddenly as he hears a noise on the stairs, shushing me.

I giggle, then sing out, "Goodnight, boys," and flick a switch next to my bed to turn out the overhead light. My bedroom is illuminated by a streetlight shining through the upper window making the room feel cozy and seductive. I return my gaze to Xander, tweaking his nipple as he sheaths himself, and watch his pupils dilate and shine. He growls and nips my nipple before plunging his lips onto mine again.

Our lovemaking is torrid as his expert tongue explores every inch of my mouth and body. He drives his steely, hot rod into my sex, smothering my mouth with his as I groan in delight, softening the sound because of the nearby occupants.

Although quieter than usual, the sex is just as mind-blowing as previously, leaving me sated and content in the aftermath. Slumped on the bed, gasping for breath with Xander's arm flung over my belly, I feel a wave of tenderness wash over me as I gaze at the adorable man lying next to me. He opens his eyes and smiles, pleased to see me watching him.

Propping himself up on an elbow, his glistening blue eyes peer deeply into mine, while his index finger traces my swollen lower lip as he whispers, "I missed you."

I raise my hand to cup his cheek with my palm as I watch his face intently.

"Me too." I smile tenderly.

Kissing me lightly on the forehead, Xander gets up, moves to the bathroom, and when he returns, lies on his back, and pulls me in close to him, with my head resting on his shoulder. I throw a leg and arm over him as I snuggle in closer. I adore these times together when we were in harmony and content to just be in each other's arms. My heart swells more every time, and it feels like bursting right now. *Is this love?* It certainly feels different from what I'd felt for Murray.

"Do you still have feelings for Murray?" Xander asks quietly, interrupting my thoughts as if he has read my mind.

"Hell no," I exclaim vehemently, surprised that he would think that I did. "Any residual feelings of friendship or nicety I had for him were obliterated last night."

"Good." He sounds pleased.

I lift my head and give him a quizzical look, trying to decipher whether Xander is pleased because he wants me to have feelings for him, or because he is jealous of Murray.

"He is not worth your time or energy, that's all," he explains, watching me as I nod in agreement.

"What are you doing this weekend?" he asks, changing the subject as he strokes my hair.

"Not a lot. Why?"

"I am going to see the Grand Prix Motorcycle Racing on Phillip Island and thought you might like to come too. I know how you love your motorcycle." Xander offers the invitation casually, but I am flattered that he has thought to include me.

"Xander, I would love to. Thank you for asking me. When are we leaving?" I lean over and peck him on the lips, excitement bubbling within me at spending more time with him and the added bonus of seeing the racing live.

"I'll text you the details." He presses his lips firmly against mine, caressing my lips in a lush, lengthy kiss, while his strong arms embrace me.

"Mmm. So good," he murmurs sexily. "You make it so tempting to stay, Little One, but I have a flight in a few hours, so I will have to head home soon." He glances at the time on the bedside clock. "I'll leave now before we both fall asleep." After another long sensual kiss, he groans, rolls out of bed, and quickly dresses. I grab a robe and walk downstairs with him.

"Good night, Little One. I'll call you tomorrow." Then he leaves.

My body is craving him again after our hot, lustful kiss fest, so after locking up after him, I make myself a cup of chamomile tea, hoping it will help me sleep. I take it up to my room and sit on my bed, pondering my fledgling love for Xander, and whether his invitation means he is developing feelings for me too. Or whether it is just the bliss and contentment after great sex that makes me think I am in love with him. *Maybe the weekend away might provide more insight into my feelings.*

CHAPTER 23 - Gina

IT IS LATE FRIDAY afternoon and the business lounge at the airport is bustling with people moving around for the weekend. Wanting to avoid any traffic hold-ups, and knowing I have arrived earlier than needed, I look up from my tablet, only half interested in the e-book I am reading. I cast my eyes around the area again as I watch for Xander and sip on my chilled sparkling water. Most people in the lounge are on their laptops or devices or chatting with traveling companions. A couple of attractive-looking men have smiled at me as they sit nearby and keep glancing my way. One had even offered to buy me a drink, which I politely declined.

Xander sent me all the travel details, including the e-ticket, earlier in the week and because his week was crazy, said he would meet me at the airport. Although we had texted and had the occasional short phone conversation, I haven't seen him since last weekend when he came to my place and met the boys, so I am yearning to see him again.

Excitement bubbles within me. I am about to fulfill one of my long-held dreams of watching top-tier international and local motorcyclists race in a highly publicized Road Racing World Championship premier event on the only suitable course in the country. And I will be enjoying the full VIP Hospitality that Xander has purchased, which my brothers hadn't even taken advantage of when they attended several years ago. Xander has told me he has seen the event before in Italy, so he is keen to see the challenges posed to the riders by a different track.

I check my watch and look down the hall again, then review my web search on the race circuit and hospitality options, so I can discuss them with Xander later. My phone beeps with a message from Xander, telling me that he has arrived. My heart lurches as I spot him striding down the hall, watching me closely, with a sly grin on his face. *God, this man looks good in a business suit. And superb out of it.* He is model material and outshines all the other men. His magnetism is so potent that heads turn and crowds part around him wherever he goes. Licking my lips to stop the drool trying to escape, my eyes follow him as he approaches with a carry-on bag in tow.

I stand as he approaches, my eyes eating him up and my heart pounding in my chest. Xander stops in front of me, wraps one arm around me, and pulls me against him as his mouth drops to mine in a lingering kiss.

"Stop looking at me like that or I might have to take you here and now," Xander whispers against my lips as he pulls away and peers lustfully at me while I chuckle.

"Have you been waiting long?" His tone reverts to casual business, given our surroundings, and his arm rests along my shoulders.

"No, not really. I thought there might have been more traffic on the way, but it was relatively light." I mimic his tone and casualness.

Before he can get himself a drink, boarding for our flight is called. I gather up my tablet device and shove it into my shoulder bag before grabbing my carry-on bag and phone and moving with Xander toward our gate down the hall.

We find our seats on the plane, in Business Class, with Xander sitting next to the aisle so he can stretch out his legs. He orders us both a drink and we chat about our respective weeks. It isn't long before we are landing and disembarking. After finding the car hire desk, then the car, Xander drives to our accommodation, and because his secretary has arranged all the details, they are seamless. All he has to do is turn up and collect the keys.

Our accommodation is stunning. A top-floor apartment in a low-rise block by the beach with gorgeous ocean views, central to restaurants, shopping, and only a ten-minute drive to the race circuit.

While Xander changes out of his suit, I am standing on the wrap-around balcony admiring the scenery when he approaches me from behind. He pulls me tightly against him, wraps his arms around my waist, and slides my long braid aside to nuzzle my neck. I can feel his hardening bulge against my bottom and my tummy flip-flops in anticipation.

I sigh, appreciating the view and the delightfully familiar stirrings from his touch.

"Isn't this view amazing?" I ask huskily, tilting my neck to give him more access.

"Mmm. Smells deliciously fuckable as well." He murmurs behind my ear as one hand slides to fondle my breast, while the other roams to rest against my mound, pressing his fingers into the heat between my legs. I chuckle and grind my bottom against his bulge, which earns me a nip on the earlobe.

Turning in his arms, I wrap my arms around his neck, my smiling face turned up to him. His lips mesh with mine, his tongue hungrily probing my mouth and tangling with my soft tongue. Holding his head and his lips firmly against my mouth, I run my fingers through his neatly trimmed hair. His hands stroke my buttocks and back, occasionally dipping into the crevice between my cheeks. My panties pool with heat and moisture from his hot, ardent kisses. He has the most luscious lips, and my body reacts this way every time they touch me, and he instinctively applies just the right amount of pressure to set my body ablaze.

While he rubs his straining cock against me, we both moan with increasing delight, savoring the taste and feel of each other. Xander unlocks his lips from mine, inhales deeply, and peers into my questioning eyes before he rests his forehead against mine.

"I want so much to take you to bed right now, Little One, but I've barely eaten all day. I need to refuel, so I can cherish you properly. All night long."

"Mmm, you're forgiven then." I laugh, appreciating his explanation. "But I will hold you to being cherished all night long."

"Your wish is my command." His eyes light with fire as he mocks me with a slight bow and nod of his head, and I laugh at the irony of Xander obeying orders. I don't think it is possible. Not unless it suits him to, and even then, he would end up being the one issuing the orders. Just the thought of Xander obeying my commands in bed ramps up my libido.

"Let's go eat." Xander grabs my hand and tugs me inside the apartment, and stands in the open doorway while I grab my phone and bank card.

As it is such a beautiful, balmy evening, we decide to walk along the beachside promenade, discussing what type of food we feel like. We opt for something simple and quick, but tasty and healthy, and manage to find a beachside restaurant that meets our needs.

We eat and laugh and discuss the race, the beach, amongst other topics, then laugh some more, the promise of a lust-filled night ahead not far from our minds as hands sneakily slide up each other's leg, tantalizing and just stopping short of each other's sex.

Fortunately, we are in a darkened corner, at the rear of the restaurant, because I ask Xander if he would like a taste of my meal and when he nods, I surprise him by holding the piece out on my fork for him to take straight into his mouth. His eyes widen, then darken as he meets my teasing eyes. He holds my wrist, rubbing his thumb over my beating pulse, then gently bites the food off the fork.

"Mmm, delectable," he husks, his eyes never leaving mine.

Looking back to his plate, while I return to my meal, he slowly and carefully cuts a morsel of gravy-covered steak and then reciprocates by feeding me from his extended fork.

"Your turn."

Again, our eyes lock as I bite from his fork. I feel the gravy drip down my chin, but Xander gently swipes it away with his thumb, pressing it to his lips, then licking it clean with a stroking motion that imitates what he would do to me later. Dessert was a share plate of mixed fruits, which we again occasionally fed a piece or two to each other, licking or sucking the giver's fingers as we take each morsel.

By the end of the meal, my body is thrumming, and I can tell by the way Xander has to reposition his bulge a few times that he has been affected too.

The walk back to the apartment is leisurely, despite our urgent need for each other. Xander wraps his arm around my shoulder, tucking me close to his body, while my arm wraps around his toned waist. We pause by the beach for a while and silently watch the moonlit waves racing to the shore until the sea breeze becomes chilly.

As soon as the apartment door closes behind us, the need to be naked and against each other consumes us. Our lips lock, and we hastily undress each other, only pausing to remove our clothing, which we fling to the side as we make our way further inside the room.

Whilst running his hands over my bare breasts and thrusting his tongue into my mouth, Xander guides me to the sofa, backing me up to it so I can walk no further. His hands hurriedly move to my wet sex, growling deep in his throat at my slickness. I feel his erect cock twitch against my belly, eager to be consumed by my heat, and press myself against it. He pulls away from me, breathing heavily. Dilated, dark eyes, like the ocean outside our window, devour me. Then he spins me around, bends me over the back of the sofa, and spreads my legs wide with his feet. He quickly sheaths himself, then places one hand firmly on the small of my back and uses the other to guide himself to my pussy, circling in its moisture. I can feel his thick, hot cock as it slips slowly just inside, stretching me, before being retracted. My body floods with anticipation, but he pauses to wrap my plait around his hand, tugging my head backward. A husky moan escapes my arched throat as I wonder if he is acting out a fantasy. I don't feel concerned with his overt show of dominance because I know he will look after me, protect me and would be mortified if he hurt me. I also know if I ask him to stop, he will.

He plunges deep into me in one swift movement, stretching and filling me, then pauses and groans, reveling in my slick tightness. I love how his long, thick shaft inside me, particularly in those first few seconds, gives me a feeling of fulfillment, like I am home and exactly where I need to be.

He drives in deep again and again, like a ramrod, gripping my hip and pulling my hair, causing my body to arch from his touch, pushing and pulling me up and down his cock in a frantic rhythm until I explode. Xander stills momentarily, yelling out as I clench around him, then continues plunging into me. I see stars and gasp for breath, moaning with every exhale as the room closes in around me. All my senses become attuned to Xander; he is all I can feel and hear as I inhale his musky scent. He pushes into me full tilt, stills, and roars as his powerful orgasm devours him, buckling him at the knees. He collapses over me, bracing himself with his arms on the sofa back, gulping in deep breaths.

"I can't get enough of you, Gina. No matter how many times I have you, I still need more," Xander croons the soft words in my ear when he is finally able to speak. He stands, then helps me upright and lifts my listless body. My arms are wrapped around his neck, and I pepper his jaw with soft kisses as he carries me to the shower.

"You have the same effect on me, too, Xander. Your body calls to mine, and I can't stop it or deny the yearning." I kiss him tenderly as he slides me down his body, returning my kiss, holding me against him as my feet touch the floor.

We quickly wash, laughing as we discover each other's ticklish spots, and wash each other's sex before hopping out and toweling each other dry. Xander flicks my bottom with his towel, and I yelp as I race him to the bed, flinging the covers back over myself as I jump in.

"Vixen," Xander chuckles as he bounds over me, flops onto his bottom, then scrunches himself under the covers. He drags me against him, and we spoon till we fall asleep.

***

I stir from my slumber, only half awake, and swipe at whatever is brushing against my nose. It happens again just as I drift back to sleep. I swipe at it again, mumbling incoherently to herself. Then again. This time, I crack one eye open to see what the nuisance is. My eyes fly open wide, and I shoot upright at the sight of Xander, clothed and wearing a great big smile, sitting on my bed. *Wait, where am I? This isn't my room. Oh, that's right, we have gone away together for the weekend.* I blink a couple of times as coherency replaces the sleep-muddled fog in my brain.

"What are you laughing at?" I grumble at Xander as I rub my eyes.

"You make these cute little snuffly noises when you sleep," he chuckles again and kisses me on the nose.

"Come on. Up you get, sleepyhead. I'm starving. And we have a big day ahead."

"That would be your fault for exhausting me last night, Big Boy." I stretch languorously, reluctant to move, until Xander pinches my nipple hard. "Ouch. What was that for?"

"To get you moving, Little One. Come on, or we'll be late." His good-natured tone sounds excited as he jumps off the bed and grabs my hands, pulling me to my feet.

"Do you think you can be ready to leave in ten minutes?"

Now I am up, my brain is fully firing. Hastily, I grab some clothes, wash my face, brush my teeth, and apply some light makeup with good sun protection for the day ahead. A hat, sunglasses, and a jacket are shoved into a bag, and I am ready to go.

Even though it doesn't take long to drive to the track, it takes a while to get through the crowds to the entrance gates and find the VIP parking. From there, we catch a shuttle bus to the VIP hospitality marquee on top of the Pit Lane building.

The excitement of the event is tangible, the noise deafening, and the racing hasn't even started yet. This is practice day, and already the hospitality marquee is crowded. Making our way to the food banquet, we grab some hot croissants and order coffee before finding a bar table to eat at.

I take the opportunity to look around while I eat. I recognize some famous faces and am in awe, practically speechless, when one or two of them come over to say hello to Xander. There are also some stunning women, some of whom smile and wave at him, and others who are openly ogling him. Subtly, I shift my hand and lay it on his forearm, staking my claim, even though I know it is probably only short-term.

I turn to him, smiling, when we are alone again after he returns with a plate of fresh fruit for us.

"How many times have you been to this event, Xander? You seem to know a lot of people here."

"I have been a couple of times, either here or in other countries. Most of these people I have met at the same events, or at social events that I attend for business. It is a good opportunity to network and for a corporate presence, but mostly I come for the racing." He eats some fruit as he glances around the room, as if mixing with society's elite is an everyday thing for him. I suppose that it is commonplace to mix with these people when he is as rich and powerful as he is.

"Seems like a few prospective or former bed partners here as well, going by the female adulation," I tease, trying to keep the sudden stab of jealousy I feel out of my voice.

"Look around, Georgina. There are a lot of males eyeing you off as a delectable morsel as well." His voice hardens as he glares warningly at an overt ogler standing nearby, who appears incredibly inebriated for so early in the morning. Turning toward me, he lifts my chin with a finger, so I am peering into his darkened eyes. "You are my delectable morsel and I intend feasting on you later." He rubs his thumb over my bottom lip, then lowers his head and kisses me softly. I am not sure if he is staking his claim for the benefit of the watchers or if he just wants to kiss me. Either way, I kiss him back, totally under his spell.

He grabs my hand and leads me out of the marquee, down some stairs, and into Pit Lane, where we met a guide who escorts a small group along the straight to view the bikes lined up outside of garages, the riders and crew hard at work in preparation. Xander supplements the guide's talk by explaining to me some of the technical equipment and processes, enlightening me with his overall knowledge.

Lingering behind the rest of the group, we stand in front of one garage, where a few men in racing attire are milling near the garage door. Suddenly one tall, lanky, fair-haired, swarthy-skinned man comes striding out, waving his arm around and bellowing in what I think sounds like very fast Italian. Thinking that the man is telling us to move on, I am startled when, as I began to move towards our group, Xander lets out a loud, genuine laugh, grabs my hand, and speaks fluently back to him. My mouth falls open as I recognize the man as a famous world champion rider. I look in awe between the two men, who are now embraced in a man hug and slapping each other on the back. Xander introduces me, in English, to the confident Italian, who bypasses my extended hand and hugs me instead.

"It is a pleasure to meet you, Georgina. You must be very special to Xander for him to bring you here. You know, you can always come to me if he doesn't treat you right. I will show you how a beautiful woman like yourself should be treated."

Chuckling, I blush slightly, and decide to not read too much into his words. The man is obviously a charmer, but it seems that his words are meant more to rile Xander than to flatter me. A glance confirms that the taunt had hit its mark. His chin has lifted slightly, his smile has slipped, and his eyes have hardened.

"Huh, you should talk. You treat women well for a very short time. That's how you got the nickname Speed King, isn't it?" Xander retaliates, ribbing his friend like it was part of a game they play.

I take Xander's hand and squeeze it, reassuring him that I'm not swayed by the Italian's charm as I smile politely at the other man.

"Thank you, Luca, but please call me Georgie or Gina. And I can assure you that Xander treats me very well indeed." I smile warmly up at Xander before continuing to Luca, teasing him in return, "You are surrounded by beautiful women all wanting to be treated right. That must be exhausting for you. So why add another one to the mix?" Luca throws his head back in laughter and says something to Xander in Italian, who in turn laughs and replies, "Si. Si." His eyes light up as he turns to look at me and I smile warmly up at him.

Luca watches the interchange between Xander and I, then slaps Xander on the back, saying he has to get ready for the race, in his thick Italian accent. He gives us both a bear hug before heading back into the garage.

As we return to the group, one of the tour members mentions he has taken a photo of us with Luca and offers to send it to us if we want. Xander thanks him, asks for his name, and gives him the number for his phone, but doesn't look at the image when his phone pings a moment later. Xander explains when we are back in the hospitality marquee that he got the guy's name and phone number, in case he decides to go to the press after the event with the photos. I look shocked when he mentions it, but Xander just replies in a frustrated and disenchanted tone, "Believe me, it happens."

The rest of the day passes in a blur as we move between the hospitality area and Pit Roof Suites to watch each team's Qualifying Practice session, taking advantage of the high view of the Start/Finish Line from the Suites on Pit Lane. I jump for joy and Xander's fist pumps the air when Luca's time earns him pole position, a spot he has been in many times before but had been closely contested during this Qualifying Session.

We are about to leave the Circuit when Xander's phone pings. Reading the message, Xander asks, "Luca has invited us back to his team's garage if you would like to go?"

"I'd love to go for a little while, Xander, if you want to catch up with him. But I'd like to spend some quiet time afterward with you, too."

Xander wiggles his eyebrows as he gazes at me, with his hands firmly on my ass cheeks, pulling me against him. "Mmm, I'm getting hard just at the thought of some alone time with you, Little One."

I giggle and rub against him.

He wraps an arm around my shoulder, and turns me, walking us downstairs to Pit Lane, where we hover behind the barrier in front of the team garage until Luca spots us. Again, he welcomes us both in a bear hug and ushers us into the garage.

CHAPTER 24 – Gina

MY HEAD SWIVELS AS I take in the number of people and equipment in the small space and I am astounded at how clean it is. Computers and large screens surround the roller doors to display race, rider, and bike statistics. I notice that there are four motorcycles on stands, one each for Luca and his team rider, plus two spares. Large tool chests line the walls and I soon notice that a black partition adorned with sponsor logos splits the large garage space into working and storage areas.

A few chairs are scattered around, and there is a sofa against the back wall. The atmosphere is happy and relaxed; everyone seems to have a job to do, scurrying around in an orderly fashion, a bit like ants. The team staff and crew joke and laugh as they busily pack equipment away, preparing to lock the garage down for the night. However, they watch and wait as Luca chats with mechanics about minor modifications, ensuring everyone is relaxed and on track for the next day's race. Luca introduces Xander and me to the team manager, his fellow team rider, and a few key staff before he gives us a rundown of how the team syncs on a race day and answers my enthusiastic questions.

In the back corner of the work area, six stunning women, all dressed in casual, trendy clothes, sit chatting amongst themselves. Occasionally, one of the men will walk past and stop next to them. As Xander and I talk to Luca, a few of the girls exit behind the partition with some of the team members, so I assume they are girlfriends or wives.

As I look around with interest, I notice another stunningly beautiful woman has just joined the group and has her back to us. She is tall, lithe, and has long black hair caught up in a ponytail. Like the other women, her jeans look like they had been painted onto her perfect figure. I feel quite inadequate amongst such beauties, and as we move deeper into the workspace, Xander laughs at Luca's quip that his work is done for the day and now it is playtime.

The black-haired bombshell spins around as she hears his laughter, then advances on Xander like a lioness stalking its prey, her face beaming in pleasure.

"Xander. How lovely to see you, dahling," she purrs, her eyes never leaving his.

"Hello, Arana." Xander's initial surprise quickly turns into a cold, tight facial expression. His voice is clipped and his body rigid. She lays her hand on his upper arm possessively as she tries to kiss him on the lips, but Xander takes a small step backward to avoid her invasion. My jaw clenches as I scowl at the woman.

Arana's body is so close to Xander's that her huge breasts are almost rubbing against him. I stake my claim by stepping against Xander's side and holding his other hand, glaring steely eyed at the man-eater.

"Arana, this is Georgina." Xander's introduction is obviously wasted when the bitch looks me up and down, then ignores me like I am a piece of trash, turning her lustful gaze back to Xander.

"Piranha." I nod, deliberately mispronouncing her name with a fake smile, and flash a scowl of disapproval at the woman, who huffs and gives me a black, scathing look. Xander turns his face toward me, and I spot his lips twitching and eyes glinting with humor.

Fortunately, Luca interrupts us, with one arm wrapped around a blonde woman's waist, then sidles up to the black-haired bitchface and wraps an arm around her waist as well. He then kisses them both, turns to Xander and grins widely, then winks. The piranha turns to face Luca, places her hand on his cheek and French kisses him, before throwing Xander a sly look over her shoulder, as if to remind him of what he is missing.

Xander's lips tighten in annoyance as he says farewell, thanking Luca for the tour and wishing him good luck for the race tomorrow. I say a hasty goodbye as Xander takes my hand and we stride back to the Pit Lane area. I am very relieved to be away from that she-devil, sensing she is nothing but trouble. A glance at Xander reveals he is feeling the same. His facial expression is still tight, like he is deep in thought, but softer than it had been in Arana's presence. We walk to our car in strained silence, the Arana effect impacting us both.

All sorts of thoughts ran through my head. *If he dated someone as beautiful as Arana, what does he see in me?* Although the piranha's personality didn't match her stunning appearance, and she didn't seem to be a nice person, I still wonder if that standard of beauty is Xander's norm. I am an ordinary, moderately attractive woman, so why is he interested in me? I have never really been jealous of anyone before, so it is quite a shock to acknowledge that the blinding rage I experienced when Arana was coming onto Xander must have been jealousy. I had been ready to scratch the woman's eyes out, only stopped by my uncertainty about where I stand with Xander, and the scene it would create.

Xander let go of my hand to open my door for me and, once in the car himself, he turns to me as he put on his seatbelt and starts the engine.

"I'm sorry about that situation with Arana. I had no idea she would be here," he smiles placatingly.

"A jilted ex-lover, I assume?" My voice is cool, and an eyebrow is arched as I turn to him.

He nods.

"Were you together for long?"

Sighing heavily, Xander puts the car in gear and drives off, navigating to the snail-paced exit queue.

He breaths heavily again. "No, we were not together long, but long enough to find out she is cold and calculating... only after my status and money." His words are clipped when he replies, as if the subject is distasteful. After a pause, he glances at me. His eyes gleam and a low chuckle rumbles from his throat. "You had pegged her very well with your Piranha comment."

I return a half smile before asking, "So do you still have feelings for her?"

"Only of loathing and mistrust." Xander's instant response and solemn tone provides me with the answer I hope for.

"Good." I nod. "I don't like her narcissistic condescension." I still rankle at the way that woman looked down on me and every other woman, whether they had an interest in Xander or not. "Many others like her in your long line of exes?" I blurt, surprised that I had said that aloud but pleased to have it out in the open.

"A few. They latch on like an octopus and are very difficult to get rid of."

I watch him closely as he exits onto the main road and quickly takes off. His words shed an inkling of understanding as to how he has become the cold, wary, and reserved person he is. I had never considered this aspect of Xander's love life.

Seeing I am deep in thought he glances over at me. He rests his hand on my leg and smiles at me.

"What about the others who weren't octopuses? Do you still have feelings for any of them?"

"Geez. What's with the interrogation?" Xander snaps at me, fed up with my questions. His annoyed glance is met with my raised eyebrows and questioning stare that insists on an answer. Inhaling briefly, he continues in a matter-of-fact tone, as if finally understanding my need for clarification.

"Some I liked more than others, but none I could envisage a long-term relationship with. Mostly they filled a need." He pauses before continuing. "They are all fragments of my past that don't matter to me, Georgina, so don't overthink it. You are the only one that matters to me now."

His eyes soften as the sincerity of his words shine through, removing most of the angst I had felt about encountering one of his exes. But the niggling doubt about how long I will matter to him persists.

"Thank you for answering honestly, Xander," my tone is subdued as I silently consider his answers while admiring the landscape on our short silent drive to the accommodation. It dawns on me that I don't need to know the ins and outs of every one of his affairs. Then I remind myself of my initial rationale to enjoy my time with Xander while it lasts and, if an issue arises as a result, like meeting one of his exes again, I will deal with it.

I notice him glancing my way a few times but continue to stare out the window. After he parks and we get out, he pauses at the rear of the car, takes my hand and lightly touches my chin.

"Are you okay? You're very quiet." His voice is soft, and his gaze is warm and caring as he gives me a quick kiss on the lips.

"Yes, I'm fine." Looking directly into his warm, inviting eyes, I give him a crooked smile. "I'm trying to comprehend how you could be attracted to such a vile person when you have so much depth and sincerity. All I can come up with is the sex must have been amazing." I pause, dropping my eyes briefly, battling my feelings of inadequacy, before boldly stating, "I don't like sharing you, Xander."

His eyes flash with an emotion I can't decipher before it disappears, and he peers meaningfully at me, as he props himself on the car trunk, taking both my hands in his. My feet are positioned between his wide legs, only our lower legs and hands touching.

"You do not need to worry about the likes of Arana. Just so you know, she came onto me, and the initial intrigue soon wore off when her true traits seeped through the glamorous surface. The sex was cold and faked like the rest of her, which is why I ended it after two weeks. She made my skin crawl by that stage. Unfortunately, it took a bit longer to get rid of her," he replies.

Xander pulls me into him, wrapping me in his thick, warm, strong arms and I rest my head on his shoulder.

"There is no competition between you and Arana." He speaks softly, his breath ruffling my hair. "You have warmth, heart, and genuineness that I don't often see. You give your all to others, sometimes at a cost to yourself. You voice your opinion, but don't walk over others to promote yourself. You are a unique woman, Georgina."

My heart melts at his words. I hug him tightly in appreciation, kiss him briefly on the lips, then smile happily up at him with bright puppy dog eyes.

"Thank you, Xander. That means a lot to me."

"I don't know about you, Little One, but I need a shower after all the sun and bike fumes today. Let's chill for a while, then we can either go out for dinner or order in."

"Sounds like an excellent idea to me." Grinning, I walk beside him, admiring the beautiful sunset over the ocean. As I stand at our door, rummaging for our key, he stands behind me with both hands on my waist, pressing his groin against my buttocks and nuzzling my neck. I giggle and press back onto him while I unlock the door. Then, as soon as it is open, he pushes me forward into the apartment and flicks the door shut behind him.

His hands roam from my waist to my boobs as he nips at my neck and earlobe.

"Mmm. I've been wanting to do this all day," he whispers into my ear.

Spinning around in his arms, I press my body hard against him and feel his dick awaken and swell. I wrap my arms around his neck and kiss him firmly on his sensuous, soft lips, twisting my tongue with his as he opens his mouth. My fingers run through the short hair at the nape of his neck, making him shiver and groan. He breaks the kiss and grabs my hand, dragging me into the bathroom, where we undress each other in between kisses.

We stand, fondling, and kissing with rapidly increasing hunger until Xander stops, gasping for air. He steps away to turn on the water in the shower, sheathes himself, then pulls me into the shower cubicle with him. Gently, he brushes my wet hair back off my face with both hands, then holds my head while he resumes his onslaught of my mouth.

I trace my fingernails up and down his back and ass, feeling his muscles quiver beneath my touch. The cascading water doesn't slow the raging inferno within us, as Xander places his hands under my buttocks and lifts me. I wrap my arms and legs around him before he slowly lowers me onto his rigid, erect penis. Throwing my head back, I groan in rapture as he fills my hot, throbbing pussy. He thrusts into me, lengthening each stroke, watching as I stretch around him, then slamming into me with each thrust. Locking my ankles behind his waist, I grip his shoulders, hanging on to him as he presses me against the wall and thrusts like a piston. I push down on his upstrokes, taking him deeper inside of me, hitting my G-Spot as wild abandon overtakes us. As I moan and nip his neck, he bucks harder and his groans become louder, lost in the euphoria as he fucks me hard against the cool tile of the wall.

Rocketing to orgasm, my fingernails dig into his shoulders, my back arches, my head knocks against the wall when I fling it back, and I let out an explosive, high-pitched scream as my internal muscles clamp onto his bulging cock.

"Ahhh. Yeess. Oh fuuck," Xander moans loudly. He rams into me twice more before I feel his hot rod pulse and twitch inside me. "Gina," he roars with a long breath, his head falling to rest on the wall next to mine as he gasps for air, dropping his arms and gently lowering me to stand on wobbly legs as he leans against the wall.

I nestle against his body, gulping in air, his intoxicating sandalwood scent filling my lungs. I would know this man anywhere by his scent. Its subtle notes touch deep inside me, warming and comforting me, arousing me. I have smelled the fragrance on other men with little effect, but when it is mixed with Xander's unique essence, it is heady and powerful.

Grabbing the soap, lathering my hands and running them over Xander's chest and taut abdomen, I savor the sensation as I move lower, gently cupping his balls, and making him jump as his senses return to normal.

"Fuck, Gina. You make me blow so hard every time that my knees buckle, and my vision momentarily blacks out." Taking my hands and wrapping them around his waist, he kisses me on the forehead and utters, "You are incredible."

"I don't know whether you noticed, but I feel the same way about you, Xander," I admit, gazing adoringly at him. I watch his face redden slightly, and he gives me a goofy grin. I am unsure if he has blushed, or if the heat from the shower and sex has colored his face, but I suspect my admission has touched him deeply.

"Okay, out you get." Xander turns me to the shower door and taps me on the bottom after I wash my body and hair while he watches.

"Why can't I wash you some more?" I pout mockingly.

He laughs. "Because if you do, we won't get out of the shower at all. And I want to wash my hair and you can't reach," he teases and smacks me on the bum again, gently pushing me out the door.

I watch him avidly as I towel myself dry before wrapping myself in one of the white fluffy robes hanging on the bathroom door. Xander's movements are brisk and efficient, and he is stepping out of the cubicle by the time I start blow-drying my hair. After drying himself, and ruffling his hair dry with the towel, he leans on the bathroom counter, watching me twist and turn with the dryer and fluff out my hair.

"What would you like for dinner? Would you like to go out or stay in?"

"Let's stay in."

"Ok, I'll go see what is available for delivery while you finish up here." He gives me a quick tap on my behind as he moves past me.

It isn't long before I join Xander on the sofa, still swathed in the large bathrobe, and with my hair brushed and pulled back in a ponytail. He is dressed in some sweatpants and a t-shirt and is slouching on the sofa and scrolling through his phone.

My body is sensitive from the shower workout, but I knew it won't take much to get me fully aroused again. That is the power of Xander. I can never get enough of him, and my body is in a perpetual state of arousal, like an idling engine just waiting to be revved up again.

"We can have sushi, Chinese, or pizza," Xander comments, straightening himself as I sit next to him, seemingly unaware of my wayward thoughts.

"Hmm, I think I might go for Chinese. What about you?"

Xander settles on Chinese too and, after placing our order, we chill on the lounge watching the news until it arrives, then decide to eat on our balcony to watch the comings and goings on the beach and the beautiful sunset. The food is hot and tasty, and even though I had been grazing a lot during the day and am not very hungry, I still manage to eat most of it. We comment on surfers and passersby and general things, till the cool evening air forces us inside.

Returning to the sofa, we settle in to watch a movie. I am surprised that our tastes are similar, and we laugh at the same parts. His arm has dropped from my shoulder, and his hand now rests comfortably on my thigh, while my hand is on his. My heart swells at his deep rumbling laugh, and his relaxed expression when I glance over at him. I love this man with all my heart, particularly this softer, warmer side of him. I suspect he is only relaxed like this with his immediate family and then only rarely, so I treasure the moment.

Xander turns his head, smiling at me, his warm eyes flashing an 'I'm-in-heaven' look before he lifts his chin and kisses me on the forehead. He lifts his free hand to cup the side of my face, his thumb softly stroking along my cheekbone, while his playful lips caress my mouth with feather-light kisses, his tongue occasionally darting sneakily between my partly opened lips.

Sighing in delight, I run my fingers along his inner thigh, pausing tantalizingly close to his balls, then lifting one finger to gently tap his sac, relishing the way his body twitches and his breath huffs silently against my cheek. I continue running my hand up and down his thigh, slowly increasing its contact with his testicles on every upstroke, while his kisses to my mouth and neck grew stronger and more ardent. He French kisses me, moaning as I fondle his balls and run my fingers up his now fully erect shaft. Then I slip my fingers below the waistband of his sweatpants, circling his cock head.

Moisture seeps between my legs and I moan, wanting to taste him so desperately that I pull the elastic down and grip his hot, velvety rod firmly in my hand, spreading the pre-cum over his head with my thumb. He bucks, breaking our kiss, his dark, sultry eyes peering at my grin as I move to kneel between his thighs.

Throwing him another suggestive smile, my eyes tease and as I drag on his pants, he lifts his hips so they slide further down. Then I take him in my mouth. He groans huskily, his head flung back against the top of the sofa, and his hands splayed beside him. I lick and suck him like a delicious pop-sicle while I cup and squeeze his balls. I run my hand up and down his shaft while my mouth laps at his balls, then returns to his shaft. I love hearing him moaning and feeling him twitch in my mouth and my occasional furtive glance sees him lost in the sensation of my hand and mouth tormenting him, which goads me on, moving faster and with more pressure.

As I pause to shift position, he grips my face between his hands, his eyes scorching into mine as he sucks in a deep breath.

"Enough, Little One. Enough." The stern command rumbles from him. He stands, staring down at me, his proud erection almost slapping me in the face.

"What's wrong?" I search his face, my eyes widening at his serious expression.

Xander extends a hand to help me to my feet, his expression softening at my look of concern, then leads me to the bed and gives me a bewitching smile while he brushes my hair from my face.

"I was close to coming and needed to slow things down because I want to spend the night enjoying every inch of you, gorgeous."

I lift my eyebrows, stand on tiptoe, and nip his earlobe.

"You know I give as good as I get Xander, so I hope you have the stamina to keep up," I challenge mockingly as I open the bathrobe, letting it drop to the floor, then jump on the bed, legs spread wide.

Xander roars with laughter and quickly strips off and crawls up and over me.

"Challenge accepted," he murmurs before claiming my nipple in his mouth.

CHAPTER 25 - Xander

I LAY AWAKE, STARING at the ceiling as the light of dawn gradually creeps into the room, listening to Gina's soft, rhythmic breathing while she sleeps next to me with her hand resting on my abdomen. After our long, torrid lovemaking, I, like Gina, had quickly fallen asleep but had awoken about an hour before dawn, as I often do.

My whirling thoughts are consumed by the woman next to me. She is remarkable, and I am in awe of her.

I recollect with a smile the first time we met in the hospital and the many times since when she stood up to my crappy behavior. Her passion, both in and out of the work place is amazing. She is an adventurous lover and fires my lust with just a smile. Rarely have I found a woman who can match my amorous endurance or drive me wild the way she does, with such little effort. Her opinion of me matters and there are only a handful of people to whom I bestow that honor. She fills a previously unrecognized void inside me. As a result, I challenge himself to be a better person around her, whereas I have never felt that need with anyone else.

Bewildered by my turbulent thoughts and emotions, I turn my head to gaze at my beautiful Georgina, then shake my head slightly as my brow creases. *Is she mine?*

I knew for certain that Georgina could never and would never be possessed by someone. Nor do I want to own or possess her like a prize. However, she seems to enjoy being with me and I know without a shadow or a doubt that I want, and need, her beside me for the foreseeable future. I have only ever looked a week or two in advance with any of my other women, so the thought of a 'foreseeable future' with Georgina scares the daylights out of me. *How long is the foreseeable future? One month? Two? Longer? Would I get bored with her, like all the others? Can I stay exclusive to her for that length of time?* The thrill of the chase had been part of the attraction with my exes, and once that abated, I sought a new challenge. I know I care more for Georgina than I have with any others, but what happens after the sex became monotonous? I don't want to hurt her, but with my track record, I inevitably will. I wonder if I can return to the shallow façade that was my existence before meeting her.

Despite my wealth and status, I feel I am not good enough for her. I hadn't been worthy enough for my mother to stay with my father. My mother had gone on to create a new life and had other children with her new husband without thinking of bringing me home to live with her. Neither of my parents wanted me, which is why I ended up in boarding school, so why would an angel like Georgina want to stay with me? That hurtful childhood emotion had spontaneously reared its ugly head, and it suddenly dawns on me that it had been the driving force that made me the man I am today.

Never getting too close to people to avoid getting hurt as my mother had hurt me. Hurt others before I get hurt.

My stomach churns with anxiety. A sense of hollowness fills me at the thought of life without Georgina. I realize she is the tranquility in my chaotic life, and I look forward to chatting, texting, or seeing her every day. Our connection is deepening, and there is more I want to discover about Georgina. *But how long before I move on?*

Sneaking out of bed, I pace the length of the lounge. *Maybe I need a bit of distance to gain a better perspective.* I consider the thought for a moment, then circle back to my earlier thoughts of not wanting to hurt Gina. In business, I take time to consider a proposition, because regardless of how good it looks, there are usually obstacles that require careful deliberation over time. *Why can't I apply that to my personal life, too?* Hmm, not a bad idea.

No matter how I look at it all thoughts keep coming back to me stepping back a bit to determine if the main attraction with Georgina is sex or if Georgina is the complete package, and if I will still feel the enthralling pull toward her if I am not in contact with her.

Feeling wretched and dirty, trying not to wake Georgina, I creep into the shower, hoping the blast of hot water will make him feel better. My erratic, depressing thoughts continue to torment me, though. Hurting Georgina is inevitable, either now or in the future, and that concerns me. *Probably better to rip off the Bandaid than prolong things.* Unlike my exes, whom I hadn't thought about again till I ran into them at social events, I know that it will take a long time to get Georgina out of my system and that I will be hurting myself in the process. But I am strong and will cope. I feel I know Georgina well enough to know she will cope, too. After all, we haven't been spending time together for very long, so it is not as if she is in too deep yet. She had managed to eventually get over her fiancé of several years, with whom she had shared a stronger commitment than what Georgina and I have after a short time.

Having made my regretful decision, I try to decide when I should tell her. I promised her a weekend away, so can't very well put her on a plane today. I have also promised Luca that I will catch up after the race. Looks like I will have to endure today, gathering as many memories of her as I can, knowing I won't see her again afterward.

As I dress, I realize most of her work on the hotel development is complete, and as she mainly deals with Robert and Ethan, there is no real need for me to see her in a business capacity, either. That gloomy thought is like a punch in the gut and a heavy, somber feeling weighs on me.

I turn my troubled gaze toward Georgina, memorizing her beauty, smiling tenderly as she stirs in bed and rolls over. Opening her eyes, she sits up and blearily looks for me when she can't feel me next to her. Then, as her eyes focus, they crinkle and sparkle as a warm, soft smile lights her face. My heart lurches at the love I glimpse in that look, resolving my need to remove myself from her life before her feelings for me deepen. She deserves better than me, someone who can return that love wholeheartedly, who can cherish her and provide her with a family.

The thought of her creating a family with another man stirs my blood with jealousy and anger. As much as I force the thought away, knowing I have no right to feel these emotions when I am pushing her into a life without me, it sits in my gut like reflux, burning me. I have never considered a family of my own for fear of turning out like my father. Now, I mourn the loss of children in my future. *Oh hell, this is going to be a long day!*

I run my fingers through my hair, plaster a congenial expression on my face, and hope my smile looks sincere as I move with trepidation toward her.

"Good morning." As I sit on the edge of the bed and kiss her lightly on the lips, I restrain myself from the fervent tonguing I want to give her. She leans in for a more fulfilling good morning greeting, a look of surprise crossing her face when I stand and step away.

"Are you hungry? I thought we might go down to a café for breakfast, if that's okay. We need to be at the track before 9 am so we can get into the VIP Parking area again." My excuse sounds lame, even to me.

Georgina blinks rapidly a couple of times as if trying to make sense of my reaction. She glances at the bedside clock, which displays 7:00 am in big, bright numbers, looks back at me, then clambers out of bed naked.

"Okay." She steps forward and leans into me, wrapping her arms around my waist and tilting her face up to me, expecting me to thoroughly kiss her.

"Did you sleep well?" she coos, affection in her gaze and voice as she looks up at me.

"Not really. I've been up for a couple of hours." I breathe out a sigh, my words clipped, then kiss her on the forehead and move out of her embrace.

I can see she is confused and hurt by my cool manner, her mouth slightly open and her brows creased. She blushes and her eyes are downcast for a moment before she quickly turns away.

"I'll just have a quick shower then," she says, playing it cool and trying her best to avoid my eyes as she gathers up her clothes.

Feeling loathsome, my mouth twists grimly as I state clinically, "Okay, but we'll be going straight to the airport after leaving the track, so you will need to pack before we leave for breakfast."

Georgina turns her head. Her eyes dart to mine, then focus intently on my face, which I am trying hard to keep impassive. Her lips purse together, and anger sparks in her eyes before she masks her hurt. She strides to the bathroom, her back rigid and head held high. Georgina is an intelligent woman, so I know she will suspect the meaning behind my aloofness.

Yep, I am a bastard for hurting her, I castigate myself. I thump my fist on the nearby bedside table, rattling the lamp, before snatching my carry-on case and throwing my belongings into it and slamming the lid shut. I throw myself into a chair to wait for Georgina, but am too restless and irritated to sit, so I stomp to the balcony. The ocean glistens and sparkles in the bright, early morning sunshine, but not even the beautiful view or exhilarating fresh sea breeze can lighten my despondent mood.

I hear Georgina exit the bathroom and move around the apartment as she gathers her things, so I stay on the balcony, checking my phone several times, hoping for an urgent work message that would delay me entering the room again. I can't trust myself to not take her in my arms and apologize for hurting her. I have to stay firm in my decision, for her sake, no matter what it cost me. My vice-like grip on the balcony railing loosens as she speaks from the doorway.

"I'm ready to go, Xander."

I note, as I turn to walk inside, that her head is held high, her back straight, and her eyes cool and expressionless. I recognize that look. It is her business persona, donned like a shield of armor, to protect her and hide behind. Just like I hide behind my ruthless and cold-hearted business persona. I also recognize her resignation to get through the day as fast as she could.

Nodding as I pass her, I gather my case, lead the way to the car, and then drive the short distance to a café. The conversation is routine as we order and eat breakfast, and very little is said on the drive to the track.

We are greeted by the concierge in the hospitality area, as we had been the day before, and find some seating where we can watch the race. I am courteous and civil as I explain the planned schedule for the race, but it irritates me that she only responds with polite interest, rarely engaging in eye contact. I kick myself for robbing her of the enthusiasm for the race that she had displayed the previous day. I understand that she is freezing me out, but I don't like it, so head to the bar to get us some drinks and to give us both some space.

As I make my way back through the jostling crowd, trying not to spill our drinks, my irritation spikes to anger when I spot Georgina talking and laughing animatedly with a good-looking, fair-haired man. He is nearly as tall as me and well-built. His shirt fits snugly across his chest and biceps, and tattoos are evident on his tanned forearms. My jaw tightens as I grit my teeth and stride furiously toward them.

Handing Georgina her drink, her sparkling eyes and a wide, easy grin still light her face as she takes her glass, while I glare at the look that is meant for the other man. She barely glances at me, so I give the man a baleful stare, restraining my anger.

I am furious that Georgina has picked up some random bloke so quickly and flaunts the attractive stranger in front of me.

"Xander, this is Luke." Gina turns to me, her bright sparkly expression becoming deadpan, before turning smilingly back to Luke and continuing, "We have known each other for a long time, haven't we, Luke? What a coincidence running into each other here."

I extend my hand aloofly to Luke, who shakes it with genuine warmth and sincerity, which puzzles me. *Surely the man should be feeling a sense of competitiveness with me over Georgina?* Then I realize that Luke had displayed a flinch of confusion at Georgina's explanation of how they knew each other. *Odd, very odd. I wonder what that was about,* I muse to myself fleetingly.

"Great day for a race. Hope the weather stays as bright and sunny as this, but you never know on this island. Do you ride motorcycles, Xander?" Luke queries good-naturedly.

Replying that I do, we all continue the conversation for a short while. Georgina mentions to Luke that I have introduced her to my good friend Luca De Costi, and chuckles when he spits out his drink in surprise. Even I smile when Luke goes into fan-boy mode, repeating, "No way. No way."

It isn't long before Luke is called away by his mates, who are raucously getting into the spirit of the day as the riders take their positions on the tarmac below.

"He looks like a lot of fun," I comment, with an edge of sarcasm, but also a begrudging liking for the man, as I watch Luke get dragged into a huddle by his mates.

"Yes, he is, but also a very sincere, loyal, and genuine friend," Georgina responds, casting her eyes adoringly to the fair head rising above everyone else in his group.

I notice the affectionate look in Georgina's eyes. My teeth clench and a burning sensation rises in my chest as another stab of jealousy hits me, then I became angry at myself for my jealousy. I am not enjoying this rollercoaster ride of emotions at all.

CHAPTER 26 - Gina

I HAVE BEEN SEETHING all day. I have only felt anywhere near my normal, calm self when I was chatting with Luke in the hospitality area before Xander returned with our drinks. As a result of Xander's foul mood, I deliberately omitted that Luke is my eldest brother. *Stuff Xander.* He is ditching me, anyway, so has no right to know. He hasn't said as much, but I can read the signs from his emotional and physical withdrawal.

All day he has treated me like a business colleague that he has to entertain. He has engaged in innocuous conversation with me out of politeness and ensured I have food and drink, as a good host would. However, there is no touching, and his whole demeanor has borne an edge of sullenness, as if his time can be better spent elsewhere, rather than babysitting me. And he has flirted meaninglessly with many women who have given him the eye, as if I never meant a thing to him. As if his ditching me isn't hard enough, he seems to be deliberately rubbing salt into my wounds, and I fume. So, I have responded to his behavior with short, aloof replies to his occasional question, and by frequently moving to the railing to watch the race, trying in vain to ignore him.

His detachment and the thought of not having him in my life anymore hits me hard. I know it was bound to happen sooner or later, but I wonder why he hasn't waited until we were home. I expected him to be man enough to discuss it with me first, instead of icing me out, and it angers me.

Then, with a bolt of clarity, I realize how much I love him. That is why I am so angry with him, because I am hurting. Bad. It feels like my heart has been ripped out. He is often cantankerous, but underneath that prickly, authoritative facade he is a genuinely warm-hearted man; lovable, funny, intelligent, and caring. He doesn't even acknowledge to himself that side of his personality, so I can hardly expect him to step out of his normal modus operandi because of me, but I thought I had made an impact on him. If I am honest with myself, I had secretly hoped he would fall in love with me, but it appears the good times outweigh the challenges of self-discovery for him.

I have spent most of the day alternating between rationalizing his conduct, understanding he is in flight mode but refusing to admit it because he is scared of getting hurt, and seething over his careless, unthinking rejection of me, trying to shore up my aching heart so I can get through the rest of the day.

Thrilled that Luca has won, the post-race celebrations with Xander are just as difficult, with him leaving me to stand alone on many occasions while he chats with Luca and the mechanics. Unlike the previous day, when he had wanted me by his side when doing the same, he is distant, both physically and emotionally. So that I am not standing around like a lonely loser, I engage the other women in conversation, but am aware of Luca glancing over to me on several occasions. He must suspect that there is a rift between Xander and I, but doesn't approach me at all. It isn't long before Xander approaches, his best authoritative manner on display.

"Georgina. We need to get to the airport." His brusque tone sounds like an order and implies it has been me delaying our departure. *Oh, joy. Mr. Scowly Face has returned*, the sarcastic thought crosses my mind.

"Ready when you are Xander." My response is saccharine sweet, but my eyes shoot daggers at him.

After a short silent trip to the airport, we return the hire car and are walking silently to our boarding gate. I am about to step into the lounge area when Xander grabs my arm, halting me. I turn to face him, my eyebrows raised questioningly. It is the first time he has touched me all day.

"I have some business to attend to here in Melbourne to-morrow, Georgina, so I won't be flying home with you." His cool, distant voice and impersonal expression are laced with indifference, as if our time together has meant nothing to him.

"I see." Sparks of anger shoot from me as I spear him with a glare, my voice cold and controlled. "So, the good time is over. Was that part of the original plan, Xander?" I snort and note a small flinch in his determined gaze. In my heart, I already know the answer. He opens his mouth to respond, but I cut him off.

"Don't bother answering. It's immaterial," I spit, disgusted with him. My angry gaze slices his face as I continue to glare at him. There is a hard tightening of his jaw and his chin tilts proudly upward at my words and palpable disdain.

"Your fear of attachment will lead to a lonely, shallow existence, Xander. I need a man who can rise above his fears, not surrender to them without a fight. So, it's probably for the best." I spit the caustic words at him, my eyes darkening with pain as they flay him. My heart is thudding in my chest, but then cracks into pieces. His face is hard, his eyes bleak as he looks at me. Faint color stains his cheeks and an almost unnoticeable twitch in his lips tells me I have hit the mark. He studies my face for a long moment. His mouth opens as if he was about to speak, then closes it again wordlessly.

My throat tightens as tears threaten, but I refuse to let them fall as he stands resolute and silent. My heart might be in pieces, but I am determined to remain dignified, at least while he is watching. Stiffening my spine, I spin on my heels, march into the lounge area, and deliberately take a seat facing away from him, refusing to look over my shoulder to see if he is still there watching.

By the time I arrive home, my jaw aches from clenching it so tight, holding back my anger and hurt, and my head thumps with a splitting headache. Thankfully, everyone is out, so I trudge up the stairs into my bedroom, drop my luggage, and fling myself on the bed. Only then do I allow the tears to fall. I have no idea how to heal my broken heart, though.

CHAPTER 27 - Gina

IT HAS BEEN SIX weeks since I last saw Xander, and another chaotic day is over. I heave a sigh of relief as I wearily climb into the van and head home. Finally, the Garden Show display is finished and ready for the grand opening tomorrow. My team and I have worked day and night for the last week erecting structures, planting, paving, pruning, and decorating till I am satisfied with the look and feel of our Boutique Garden display. Only six finalists are allowed to showcase their design talents in a five-meter by five-meter outdoor space, so I am honored to be one of the selected few. I have been challenged on every level of the build and have needed to draw on all my skill and quick thinking to overcome some of the obstacles but am very happy with the result. I am up against some tough competition with amazing displays, but regardless of whether I win a prize or not, I am thrilled to be an entrant.

The hard work and long hours over the last few weeks have been cathartic in taking my mind off Xander. I haven't had time to think about him, but my heart still aches for him whenever memories creep in past my fortress-like defenses.

So, I always quickly push the hurt and sadness away before they consume me. As hard as it is to accept our breakup at the time as a good thing, I acknowledge I wouldn't have had the single-minded focus that I needed for this showcase otherwise.

Xander is incredible in every way, and his absence has left a huge hole within me. Despite the best efforts of my friends to cheer me up and fill the void, I feel like a piece of me is missing. *It would be a long time before I will feel whole again,* I reflect glumly as I climb into bed. Still, in the quiet times before sleep takes over, my mind conjures up things I should have said or done, but I argue with myself that ultimately, the outcome would have been the same. Xander is afraid of emotional attachment, so no matter how much love I give him, it's up to him to take the leap of faith.

The last long day of the Garden Show is dragging by. Every day has been the same, sitting around answering some questions from passers-by, handing out some information but mostly just sitting around filling in time. Finally, Jamie arrives to man the site so I can take a lunch break and move away from my display. I stroll around the other displays, making mental notes of innovations and style ideas on my way to the shady but bustling cafeteria area. I need some peace after keeping my game face on for five days, so take my food to a nearby secluded leafy nook by a large pond. The splashing sound from the pond's central fountain muffles the surrounding hubbub, and I can feel my equilibrium slowly returning in the leafy oasis as I eat. I shut my eyes, lean back in my chair, and inhale the cool, water-infused air, relishing the calming effect on my tense body. My mind begins planning the pack down of my display once section winners are announced later that afternoon. I know it will be a late night and a long day following, so I linger in the serenity for longer than I should have.

Checking my watch, I jump to my feet to race back to my display but quickly sit down again, startled, and take refuge behind the leaf screening when I spot Xander and Ethan at the cafeteria counter. *Damn, what are they doing here*? I do not want to see Xander. Just the sight of him stirs up all the buried emotions–love, anger, hurt–that I still feel. Quickly, I pull out my phone and text Jamie.

> **Gina:** Xander and Ethan are here. I suspect they will come by the display. I'm hiding because I don't want to see X. Let me know when the coast is clear.

Chastising myself for being a coward, I watch the men with furtive interest, then follow them from a distance as they wander around the show. I don't want to return to my display until I know they are out of the grounds entirely. Their presence could just be a coincidence, but, as I had discussed being an entrant with Xander, I feel I know him well enough to know he is here to see my work, as is Ethan. *Xander would delude himself though, that it is only out of professional interest*, I scoff.

They pause briefly at each of the displays, occasionally taking notes. As they approach my area, I deliberately pull further back, hiding behind a large potted, thick clump of bamboo with just my head poking around it to monitor their movements. Sure enough, they stop in front of my display, just as I had suspected, and when they can't spot me, Xander looks up and down the pathway as if searching for me. My head darts back behind the bamboo concealment and my heart thumps loudly against my chest. Pulling some of the leaves aside, I create a peephole and peer sneakily at the brothers as they walk around it while they chat with Jamie as if stalling for time, waiting for my return.

Eventually, they move off further down the path, and as soon as they are out of sight, I come out of hiding, watching the crowd ahead closely as I make my way slowly back to Jamie.

"Chicken," Jamie laughs as I enter the display.

"What did they say?" My voice is hushed, as if Xander can hear me.

"Just that they were here to gather ideas for future developments. And that they admire your work so much that they just wanted to see your latest creation. Oh, also to let you know Robert has entered your design for their hotel development into the Landscape Design Awards." Jamie's eyes glint with humor, despite his deadpan expression. "They also said they are disappointed that they missed you." Jamie pauses, his searching gaze conveying his concern over my unusual behavior. "Not like you to avoid a challenge, Gee. What happened to the spitfire I know and love?"

"You can laugh, you jerk," Retaliating, I good-naturedly punch him in the arm. "I panicked when I saw Xander, okay?" I huff. "Call me a coward if you like, but I'm not ready to face him yet."

Changing the subject, I query, "Did they comment on our display?"

"Yes," he nods, accepting that I don't want to discuss my reaction to Xander any further. "They both love the way you have melded contradictory elements together and commented on the peacefulness of the space. They also recognized your water wall and glass-encased water channel, said how well it works here as it does at the hotel." Jamie's pride-filled eyes gaze at me adoringly before he continues, "You have huge fans in those two, Georgie." I have known for a long time that Jamie is a huge fan of mine as well, and I adore him as much as he adores me. I think of him as a surrogate brother, but often suspect if he didn't have a wife and kids that he might make a move on me. I love him all the more for not breaking that boundary.

"Hmm," I reflect on his words, silently thrilled by Xander and Ethan's praise. "I can't take all the credit, Jamie. You are the one who does the hard labor bringing the designs to reality. The Award nomination is just as much for you as it is for me. It was very nice of Robert to nominate us."

We are interrupted by some questions from a passerby and I warily watch the crowd for the rest of the afternoon, hoping that Xander doesn't return. Toward the end of the event, I notice the Judging Committee circling the displays, and hear a hush descend on the area before a loud resounding applause sounds from behind my display.

I turn toward Jamie; my voice is husky and subdued, and my lips form a lopsided smile. "Well, it sounds like we didn't win."

He nods in resignation and suggests, "Well, there is always next year."

"Yes, I suppose. We'll see what benefits come out of this one before we consider it next year," I comment pragmatically as I begin packing away my laptop and other smaller items. Despite feeling deflated, I rationalize that the competition is excellent and that just being selected to display is accreditation enough.

When Jamie calls out my name, I turn and am surprised to see a group of people gathered in front of my display, some of whom are wearing badges stating 'Judge'. I throw a questioning glance at Jamie, who shrugs, just as baffled as I am.

"Hi. I'm Simon Dellacourt, Chief Judge for the Show," a tall thin man who appears to be in his late fifties introduces himself to Jamie, before continuing, "Are you George E Colby?"

Jamie shakes his head, extending his arm and pointing in my direction.

"I'm Georgie Colby, Mr. Dellacourt. How can I help you?" I extend my hand to him, automatically donning my professional demeanor, and give him a friendly smile.

"Well, congratulations, Ms Colby. All the major prizes have been awarded, and you were a very close contender for the People's Choice Award. However, we are so impressed with your work that, this year, we are awarding you the Highly Commended Award, which includes automatic entry into next year's event." He shakes my hand as Jamie hoots and fist-pumps the air. I stare at Mr. Dellacourt, my mouth gaping, and I blink a couple of times as his words sink in before a beaming smile lights up my face.

Mr. Dellacourt turns to one of the other judges who hands him a glass trophy from a trolley, then passes it on to me, while Jamie takes some photos.

"Thank you so much for the honor," I rejoice, my mind at a loss for any other words.

The group move away, and I turn, stunned, to Jamie, who gathers me in his arms, lifts me off my feet, and twirls me around. I wrap my arms around his neck and hug him, my hands still holding the trophy while I laugh.

"Holy shit!" he repeats triumphantly.

"Oh, my god. Oh, my god," I exclaim at the same time, elation running through me as Jamie returns me to my feet. "Highly Commended against this competition is amazing! Jamie, thank you, thank you, thank you." I stretch up and kiss him on the cheek, then laugh again and take his hand as I exclaim, "Quick, we have to take a photo in front of our sign."

We giggle as we take selfies with the trophy, photos of the trophy with our display in the background, and numerous photos of the different elements of our display. I quickly send a photo of us with our award to my brothers and team, then gasp, "Oh my god. I've got to call Mum and Dad," while Jamie calls his wife as well.

As we are breaking down the display, the thought of letting Xander know my good news crosses my mind. *Out of professional courtesy*, *of course*, I almost delude myself, then decide against the idea.

CHAPTER 28 – Gina

I AM AT MY grandparents' lakeside acreage outside of the city, sitting at a table under the shade of a tree, filling party favor bags and helping with preparations for Grandfather's birthday party. My mum has cajoled me into assisting with the setup and, as much as I grumble about it, I am pleased to have some distractions during a quietish period of work.

The happy occasion makes my heart yearn for happiness of my own though and, as they often do, my thoughts wander back to Xander, reviewing again if I could have done or said anything differently to avoid him ending things six months ago. Ultimately, I come back to the same answer. I went into the relationship knowing it would be for a short time, so have only myself to blame for falling in love with him. My heart aches for him, but he appeared unaffected by our split the last time I saw him.

Four and a half months have passed since the Garden Show, I reflect. Initially, it had been frantic as the publicity surrounding the award winners had resulted in numerous work inquiries, but that has quietened down a bit now, as have the marketing commitments. All the while, an emptiness has shadowed me, making me feel not quite whole.

I celebrated with mine and Jamie's teams by taking them out to dinner in recognition of all their hard work and had also given my team a day off. Surprisingly, Xander had sent a congratulatory text a few days after the awards, to which I had responded with a very short noncommittal, "Thank you very much." I couldn't bring myself to say anymore as I knew missing Xander was the cause of the void within me and accepted that this feeling was a part of my life now. Ethan had also texted to congratulate me, and I replied in a much warmer and friendlier fashion, but remained slightly distant. My family had also sent many messages of praise and vowed to celebrate properly at Grandfather's eightieth birthday party.

Thinking back to just after my award, I recall how my friends had arranged a rowdy celebration of my achievement at our favorite nightclub. And we had been laughing and dancing up a storm when Emily dragged me aside.

"Georgie, I'm so sorry. Ethan has just messaged to say he, Xander, and a few friends have just pulled up outside. Xander insisted on coming here tonight," she apologized. She and Ethan had been seeing a bit of each other at that point, so they must have discussed the outing.

"It's not a problem, Em. I am sure to run into Xander occasionally, so it's no big deal." I smiled brightly at my friend and patted her arm to allay her concerns. Emily seemed relieved and went back to the dance floor while I made my way to the bathrooms at the rear of the club. My stomach dropped at the thought of Xander being there, as memories of our good times flooded me, making my heart ache. At the time, I thought I had buried that hurt, but every time I heard Xander's name, the pain started all over again. *The further I could get away from the front door and bar, the better,* I had rationalized, so lingered for a while, checking my makeup and my phone.

When I had felt more in control of my emotions, I had surreptitiously made my way back to the dance area, casting fleeting glances around the room on the lookout for Xander.

I noticed Ethan dancing with Emily, and it wasn't until I was further into the room that I spotted Xander leaning casually against the bar, scanning the crowd. I stopped in my tracks to ogle him hungrily. He looked gorgeous in dark trousers and a casual, dark gray shirt and, as usual, drew the attention of those nearby. *Pull yourself together, Gina. He had made it very clear that he did not want you*, I condemned myself and lifted my head defiantly as I squeezed through the crowd to the table in a dark corner where Simone sat. *Why did he congratulate you then? And why is he here now?* I had puzzled, not able to find the answers.

"Xander's here," I told Simone. My voice had shaken just a little, betraying my true feelings.

"Where?" Simone quizzed, narrowing her eyes as if ready to do battle, as she looked around the room.

"Over against the bar. The far end." I replied, looking down at my hands. He might not want me, but I still desperately wanted him. His presence had unnerved me, and I remember thinking that I needed to get myself together before I made a fool of herself.

"I see him. Uh-oh, he's spotted you." Simone stood glaring at him, then vehemently stated, "I'm going to tear strips off him for hurting you the way he did!"

"No need, Sim. It is what it is, and it won't make any difference," I had pointed out, ever the realist. "What's he doing?"

My curiosity got the better of me as I quizzed my friend with a tinge of apprehension in my voice.

"Nothing. He's just standing there, watching you." Simone turned to look at me, concern in her eyes. "What are you going to do?"

By that stage, I was sick of feeling like a wimpy, cowering castoff. I stood, steeled my spine, and clenched my jaw. My eyes flickered with anger, mostly at myself, as I looked directly at Xander. I was *not* going to let him spoil my night.

"I'm going to ignore him," I expressed, emphasis in my tone as I turned back to Simone and winked, before striding back to the dance floor. Brave words, but could I carry them out when he consumed my body and mind?

And I had evaded him as best as I could. When Xander had made his way through the throng of gyrating dancing bodies toward me, I moved back to the table, so he 'danced' (if you could call his swaying movements dancing) for a while near my friends, although their reluctance to fraternize with him was obvious. And when he made his way to our table, I took the long way back to the dance floor. Occasionally, I looked up to see him propped against the bar again, chatting, apparently unwilling to pursue me further. So, I had shut him out of my mind and enjoyed dancing with my friends.

When I went back to the table to rest, Ethan was there, talking to my friends. He leaned in close.

"Georgie, I'm so sorry about you and Xander. He is such a jerk, and I tell him that every day. You were the best thing that ever happened to him."

"Thanks, Ethan. I suppose it was best that it happened early on rather than build expectations by stringing it out," I commented with rational stoicism.

Ethan's mouth twisted with empathy as he nodded, then patted me on the shoulder. Realizing there was nothing more he could say, he turned back to the group and rejoined their conversation.

Later on, I checked my phone and noticed a text from a few minutes beforehand.

Xander: Don't play games with the Gamemaster, Little One.

My startled eyes flew to the bar. He wasn't there. I scanned the room and spotted him on the dance floor, watching me while he danced with an inebriated blond woman who was falling all over him. His eyes bored into mine, and he gave me a cynical smile and nod of his head before he turned his attention back to the blond hanging off him.

I had said my farewells, grabbed a bottle of water from the bar, then found Simone and Tash to let them know I was heading home. Simone waved goodbye, then joined me and we caught a cab home, during which I sought Simone's advice.

"Sim, what do you think Xander's text meant? Do you think it's a threat of some sort, or that he illogically feels justified in asserting his authority? Or is he just being a snarky prick?"

"I don't know, sweety, but he's certainly a snarky prick. To me, it sounds like he doesn't want to let you go, even though he threw you away."

I had mulled over those words for a few days and, as I hadn't heard any more from Xander, I assumed he had just been spitefully toying with me and pushed him out of my mind.

I was unsuccessful in getting him out of my heart though, I mused, my thoughts returning to the present, a somber mood settling over me despite the happy occasion. Realizing the last of the bags are filled, I return to the large marquee where my mother is issuing tasks to everyone while supervising the delivery of the large floral arrangements, then the caterers.

Luke is hanging festoon lights around the garden, while my dad and Ryan help unload the hired outdoor lounges, seats, bar tables, stools, large game pieces, and lots of other paraphernalia. I assist them with positioning tables and chairs around the grounds while my grandmother is adding some finishing touches to the Boathouse where some guests will be staying. My other brothers and their families are coming later with the rest of the guests because it would have been too difficult getting things set up with their little kids running around.

I am stunned at how huge this birthday party for Grand-father is, and the next-level arrangements that are more like a military operation. I had assumed it would just be a family gathering, and even though my extended family is large in number, the guest list of over two hundred people surpassed my expectations.

"The joys of being single, hey Luke? Getting to help with the hard work, while the brothers with family saunter in for the fun part," I mock as I walk past my brother who is descending a ladder.

"Yeah, so much fun," he utters in droll irony, wiping his sweaty brow.

Chuckling, I express my delight as I cast my gaze over his labor of love. "You've done a great job with the lights. Come and I'll get you a cold drink."

As we sit slaking our thirst, I survey the grounds which have been turned into a wonderful oasis. The large white t-shaped marquee sits prominently on the lush green lawns that roll behind the large house to the lake, and are strewn with pockets of activities and furniture. The lake shimmers now with late afternoon sunshine, and the air is warm for this time of afternoon despite it being late summer. I inhale a restorative breath of the salty air and lean in to bump shoulders with Luke.

"It doesn't seem that long ago you were teaching me how to handle a catamaran on that lake," I reminisce wistfully.

Luke chuckles, peering at the lake with a smile as the memories come flooding back. "And Zack and Tyler took great delight in pushing you overboard time and again to make you a strong swimmer."

"Huh. Are you calling that tough love? I call it bullying," I tease, knowing that my brothers always have my back and their overbearing harassment had provided some valuable life lessons for me.

"And look at the resilient, outstanding person you are now, kiddo," Luke declares with a look of pride in his eyes.

Our parents join us for a brief respite from the mayhem, and we chat idly while we watch the caterers buzzing around stocking the bars and dressing the tables.

"Well, I'm going to get ready before our guests begin to arrive," my mother announces. "You better not be too long either, David, because you are one of the main reception hosts, and you will need to brief the security team, who should be arriving soon."

"Plenty of time, Laura. Plenty of time." Our dad, who loves to make out he is in charge, winks at Luke and I as Mom turns with raised eyebrows and shoots him a mockingly stern look, but her mouth curves into a smile. Luke and I laugh at Dad, who stares after his wife, smitten, as she strides toward the house, her well-shaped hips swaying slightly with each step. It is wonderful to see two strong people, who are so well-matched and still so much in love after all those years together, I reflect with a warm smile, although a touch wistfully, as my eyes flick between the two. *Hopefully, I will find someone to reciprocate the love I have to give, the way my parents had.*

"I'll do the same. Catch you both later." I hurry to catch up with Mom and put my arm around her waist, hoping to be just as much of a dynamo when I am her age. My mother is a consummate organizer, managing not only all the family and their social gatherings, but several charity organizations' fundraisers as well, and she does it tirelessly, and with a firm, loving hand. She is my role model, as are my father and grandparents.

"Another amazing effort, Mom. I love you." Warmth, pride, and love radiate from me as I kiss Mom on the cheek.

"Thank you, my darling. And I love you too, my beautiful girl." My mom's arm stretches around my shoulders and draws me in for a loving hug.

Deliberately delaying my departure for as long as possible, I exit the glass conservatory doors of the house and make my way, as gracefully as I can in high heels on the grass, toward the marquee. "Damn, I should have gone via the carpark, and used the carpeted path," I mumble aloud as my heel sinks, yet again, into the spongy turf. "Whose hair-brained idea was it to make the dress code formal?" I continue my solitary grumbling as I fight hard to not stop and take my shoes off, and veer toward the carpeted path. My long, sleeveless, A-Line evening dress looks quite demure with its wide shoulders and scalloped neckline fitting around my collarbone. The fitted bodice highlights my trim figure and ample breasts without being unbearably tight and uncomfortable and tapers to a cinched waistline, then billows to a flowing swathe that drapes over my hips and buttocks. The back, however, is open to the waist, with diamante-detailed crisscross straps, while the emerald-colored material drapes in a cowl at the dip at my waist, accentuating my toned tanned back. I fell in love with the dress when I saw it and couldn't resist it, but hope I am not overdressed. My long hair is pinned to one side and hangs over my shoulder, an easy, elegant style that complements my dress. I carry a shawl with me, knowing the breeze off the lake can often turn chilly, and a small clutch purse.

I recognize a few faces as I enter the side annex of the huge T-shaped marquee, stopping suddenly in the doorway, stunned by the magical atmosphere created by expertly styled floral arrangements, decorations and cleverly accentuated subdued lighting.

I look around in awe, thinking that this is so much better than it had appeared in daylight. Divided into specific usage areas, the annex forms one of the cross bars of the t-shape and bar tables, stools, and lounges are scattered around the entry for mingling. The top leg, on the left of where I stand, consists of a dance floor area with a DJ desk set up in one corner. Another side annex, opposite the entry, is the catering area, which is a flurry of activity. An open passageway separates the dance floor from the main dining part of the marquee on the right and forms the bottom longer leg of the t-shape.

I am surprised by how many people are already amassed inside, milling around, but then remember that some guests came on a chartered bus. I don't like crowds, so tonight is going to be a challenge for me. Bolstering myself, I gather a glass of champagne from a roaming waiter and saunter over to where my sisters-in-law are standing.

After our usual hugged greetings and brief catch-up about family and discussing the seating allocations, we stand watching the crowd. Grandmother and Grandfather are skillful hosts, mingling and laughing as they make their way around the room, I consider as I watch them adoringly. I spot my younger brothers opening a side panel on the back wall of the entry annex, so guests could spill out into the open lawn area if they desire, so I amble over to say hello.

"Well, hello," Zack croons charmingly as I approach, then his eyes widen in surprise, nearly popping out of his head, and his honeyed pick-up tone becomes embarrassed. "Gina? Is that really you?"

"Nah, can't be," Ryan teases, eying me from head to toe, and continues with a big, mocking grin. "Gina doesn't own a dress, let alone one as stunning as that."

"Idiots," I chuckle, tsk-ing at them and shaking my head. I feel awkward enough without their teasing.

"Whoa. You look amazing, Gee," Zack compliments me, pride beaming in his eyes.

"Yep. Seriously beddable." Ryan teases, waggling his eyebrows. I roll my eyes at him and hit him on the chest with the back of my hand before he continues, "Honestly. Every male in the room watched you sashay over here, wishing it was them you were coming to talk to."

I eye them suspiciously, trying to determine if they are taunting me, then I hug them lovingly when they nod with sincerity. "You both look damn fine too, in your fancy suits. Definitely chick magnets tonight," I mocked back, then watch their faces tinge with a blush. "Wipe that drool off your faces and go and enjoy the party," I chuckle, then turn and walk away.

"Whoa!"

"Jee-zus. That is some dress."

I laugh as I walk away. Their honest, and surprising, reactions to my backless dress boosts my confidence, and I mingle with more inner calm than I anticipated.

As I stand with Dad, chatting to one of his clients a short time later, a loud laugh catches my attention, sending shivers down my spine in recognition and scattering my thoughts.

Xander? My heart begins to race. *Surely not. Why would he be here?* I question, turning my head in the direction of the sound, searching the crowd without success.

"What do you think, Gina?" Dad asks, drawing my attention back to our conversation.

I smile politely and reply, "Oh, I'm sorry," then give my advice, drawing on the pieces of conversation I can recollect. Thankfully, an announcement is made for all guests to move to their allocated tables, so I excuse myself as soon as possible and escape to find my table.

You are imagining things, Gina, I grunt to myself, trying to pull myself together, and plaster a cordial expression on my face, holding back near the wall as the crowd slowly moves to the dining tables.

My face lights up when I see my cousin, Tori, and her partner Isaac, circling the same table as I am about to sit down.

We hadn't seen each other in a while, so we are both pleased to have an opportunity to catch up. Some of our parents' business colleagues are also at our table, so conversation flows readily until entrees come around. Tori and Isaac have been laughing with me about their recent backpacking trip around the country throughout the first course, and after the plates had been cleared Tori leans in close to me to speak quietly in my ear.

"There is a man on the other side of the room who has been watching your every move, Gina."

"Really? What does he look like?" I jest.

"Tall, dark, and very good-looking," she confides. "Quick, turn around and have a look while he's looking away." I turn my head nonchalantly as Tori continues, "Second table over on your left. Grey suit and black shirt."

As if he feels me searching for him, Xander's intense, sinful gaze locks with mine from across the room. *Oh god, he is still gorgeous*. Unwanted memories of our sexcapades bombard me, and my stomach lurches, my heart thumps in my chest, and I fight hard to not show any emotion despite the stirring in my neglected pussy and the blush that creeps over my skin. He nods to me and gives me a wary smile, his steely eyes boring into me, trying to gauge my reaction. I feel pinned to my seat and, donning my business persona, give him an almost imperceptible nod, pressing my lips together into a fleeting straight smile, then turn back to Tori. My instinct is to escape, but I battle it down and take a deep breath before revealing that Xander had been a recent fling.

"It looks to me like he wants to be more than a fling, Gina," Tori speculates.

Sighing, I state in a dry and bitter tone, "The man doesn't have long-term commitment in him, Tori. He runs from it at the first inkling of emotion."

"Hmm, maybe so," Tori murmurs as she scrutinizes Xander, "but he looks pretty emotionally committed to me."

"Huh, more likely an intense case of lust," I quip, and change the subject.

For the rest of the meal, I refuse to look toward Xander's table again. Occasionally, I catch sight of him in my peripheral vision as I chat with the people on my left. And I feel his eyes on me many times, my body hyper-aware of him as it always is whenever he is nearby. My pulse continues to race, my stomach flutters, and I feel edgy from his constant surveillance. I lose all enjoyment in my food but go through the motions of eating because I don't want Xander to see how much he still affects me.

Eventually, the last course is cleared, and I stand with the excuse of going to the bathroom, vowing to stay in touch with Tori. I need fresh air and some solitude. More than anything, I need to get away from Xander.

CHAPTER 29 – Gina

AFTER HIDING IN THE bathroom, lingering for a while, retouching my makeup, I wander around the lawn area, watching some of the guests playing with the giant outdoor games. The three glasses of wine I had over the evening have made me a little lightheaded and, as I grab some water from a nearby waiter and scull it, I reflect how puzzling it is that fresh air amplifies the impact of alcohol. The night is balmy; the sky studded with sparkling stars, and I inhale deeply the salt-tinged air blowing off the lake, trying to clear my head. Xander's proximity has caused a video montage of memories to run through my head, despite my best efforts to stop them.

My extended family have joined up in teams to compete against each other at the ring toss area and the boules and their raucous laughter and rivalry have gathered a small group of spectators in each area. I mingle and move between the groups, enjoying the merriment, and hoping to avoid Xander. I join my younger cousins at the beanbag toss and then saunter to join the short line of adults and kids for hopscotch.

Giggling in pleasure, enjoying the moment of carefree childishness as I hop barefoot, with my dress clutched at my knees, through my second round of hopscotch. Xander has been pushed to the back of her mind for now. Then, as I spin around to return to the starting square, I spot him standing off to the side of the few remaining participants. My eyes, sparkling with laughter, meet his dark, intent gaze that is focused on my face. I blush and my eyes drop for a moment, the smile slipping from my face as I finish the hopping game.

As I bend to collect my shoes and shawl, an announcement over the PA advises that my grandfather is about to cut his birthday cake. *Damn, I'll have to walk right past Xander to return to the marquee, so there is no way of avoiding him now.* His stunning blue eyes hold me captive as I walk toward him, his expression pensive as the corners of his mouth lift slightly.

"You look beautiful, Georgina," he says as he stares into my eyes. I note that his deep voice has a husky note, and his accent is more pronounced than usual.

I meet his gaze with indifference. "What are you doing here, Xander?" I challenge, letting out an exasperated sigh and stride away without waiting for a reply.

"Your grandfather invited me," he declares with just the right note of composure that made it sound as if his words have been well rehearsed.

Looking over my shoulder, I find him right beside me. *I should have realized he would catch up to me with his long legs*, I chide myself.

"Really? On such short acquaintance? I find that hard to believe." Scoffing coldly, I lift an accusing brow in his direction.

"Touché," he chuckles. After a brief pause, his expression serious, he queries, "Can we talk after the formalities are over?"

My eyes flash and narrow at him as I retort haughtily, "Unless it is business-oriented, we have nothing to discuss, Xander."

I flounce away and hurry inside the marquee, weaving through and stopping amid the crowd amassing around the cake, hoping to lose Xander in the process. Irritatingly, the crowd parts under his imposing demeanor, and he stands next to me, his firm, bulging upper arm touching my shoulder, sending my thoughts and senses into a tailspin.

Even though Grandfather's speech is relatively short, I feel hot and clammy, my vision tunneling, and my hearing muted as a claustrophobic edginess overcomes me. I only just manage to hold myself together by rocking from one foot to the other till the cake is cut, then with perspiration beading on my forehead and cheeks, I race out of the marquee, struggling for control so I don't push people out of my way as I pass.

I stand outside, bent over, gasping, inhaling the fresh air deep into my lungs, then I straighten and focus on breathing and calming myself. As my equilibrium restores to normal, I become aware of Xander next to me, his expression concerned, watching for my dilated pupils to return to normal.

I give him an embarrassed smile. "I'm okay," I state, aware that my cheeks have turned pink, and I still feel light-headed and nauseous.

Xander nods. He wraps my shawl around my shoulders, lifting my hair out from underneath, then leads me to a nearby cozy pocket of seats under a tree, where the festoon lighting provides ambiance but is dim enough for privacy as well.

Under normal circumstances, I wouldn't have gone with him, but I need to sit down for a while to give my body a chance to recalibrate. Xander sits next to me and turns sideways slightly, looking at me, his face unreadable as he puts his arm across the seat behind me.

"Tell me what just happened," he asks in a voice tinged with alarm.

I let out a heavy sigh. "I get claustrophobic in large, tight crowds." My voice is small and timid with humiliation and my eyes downcast, looking at my clenched hands, which are holding the ends of my shawl.

"Then why did you march straight into the middle of one?" Xander queries, perplexed, causing his tone to be sharper than he intends. My pained eyes fly to his, and he continues, his voice soft and beguiling, "I'm not criticizing, just trying to understand, Georgina." His hand brushes my hair from behind, smoothing it as it falls over my back. My skin heats with his touch, as it always does.

After another heavy sigh, I turn my gaze back to my hands and quietly, awkwardly state, "I was trying to lose you, and in turn lost myself. Stupid of me."

Xander places his big, warm hand over my clasped hands and runs his thumb softly over the back of them. "I'm sorry I made that situation so much worse for you. I had no idea you have panic attacks." He seems genuinely contrite, I conclude, as my eyes scan his. "Please forgive me, Georgina?" his voice and eyes plead. Nodding, I give him a small smile.

"Thank you. But you can't be held accountable for something you didn't know about, Xander, nor for my actions."

He sighs as if he has been holding his breath, expecting me to berate him. We sit in silence for a few moments, looking across the grounds toward the lake, then back again at each other. *Is he feeling as awkward as I am?* I ponder.

As I peer into his eyes, I realize that I am tired of running away from him. It has achieved nothing, so I decide on amicability. I determine that if my brother can be amicable with his ex after a ten-year marriage, I can certainly be amicable with Xander after a few weeks together.

"You mentioned earlier, Xander, that you wanted to talk. Now seems as good a time as any," I state calmly. "While I'm in a subdued mood," I add, mocking myself with a wry smile that quirks my lips.

His eyes hold mine and crease in the corners as he gives me a tentative smile, acknowledging my dig at myself. He blinks several times, as if evaluating the best way to approach what he has to say. He clenches his jaw tight, clears his throat, then lowers his head as his dark eyes look up at me. *Just like big puppy-dog eyes*, I muse.

"I want to apologize to you for hurting you and treating you so badly at the end of our weekend away. I had no right to be so cold and callous." His tone is matter-of-fact, serious yet humble.

"So why did you?" I challenge, with just a touch of sting in my words, despite trying for a reserved approach.

He reaches out to touch my face, then pulls back as if in remorse. "Because I was falling for you, Georgina, and it scared the shit out of me. My emotions were all over the place. I tried to convince myself that it was just sex, but then I got jealous of that bloke you were talking and laughing with, and I couldn't work out why." He pauses, then asked in a flat, deflated tone, "I noticed him here tonight. Are you two together?"

I blink at him in confusion. "What bloke? Luke?" At Xander's nod, my eyes pop open, and my lips press together as I struggle to stifle my laugh.

"Luke is my eldest brother, Xander." I take pity on him and place my hand on his cheek.

"Seriously?" Xander asks, then voices his thoughts as he recollects my words at the time. "That's why you said you had known him for a long time." I chuckle and nod when I realize the penny has dropped for him at that moment.

"Fuck! I wanted to throttle him when I saw him here tonight. Wait. How many brothers do you have again?"

I battle to keep a straight face. It is truly endearing to know that the god-like Xander Drakos is jealous and wants to battle the competition. So, with a snigger, I remind him, "I have four brothers, two older and two younger, all of whom are here tonight. Would you like me to introduce them to you?" I add coyly.

"Will they want to fight me for hurting you?" A look of uneasiness crosses his face.

"Most likely. They are very protective of me, just like you are with your sister." I stir the pot a bit more, knowing my brothers will certainly talk about fighting him, but it is all bluff and bluster.

"Crap, I'm dead meat then." I laugh at his consternation. He doesn't look worried, more daunted by the idea of taking on four burly opponents simultaneously.

After a moment, I inquire, "Go back a bit, Xander. You were saying that your emotions were all over the place. What happened after you dumped me at the airport?"

"Ouch. I deserve that." He winces slightly before tentatively taking my hand in his. Peering sincerely into my eyes, he continues, his voice soft and remorseful, "Initially, I felt bad for hurting you. When you called me out as being a commitment-phobe I felt like I had been hit by a sledgehammer and was angry at you, then at myself. As the days went by, and I couldn't get you out of my mind, my unusually sour mood only got worse. I realized I was missing you and that I was miserable without you, and I thought my internal turmoil was based on guilt for hurting you." He pauses, glancing at our clasped hands, and runs his thumb over the back of my hand. I can see his struggle admitting to scary feelings that are beyond his iron-like control and love him all the more for his sincerity.

He takes a deep breath and continues. "So, I went to the Garden Show hoping to see you, thinking that if I saw you again, it would make the never-ending ache inside of me go away, knowing you had gotten on with your life and were quite happy without me. When you weren't there, Jamie told me how well your life was going and how happy you were. I felt like I had been stabbed in the heart, and that I had lost you forever." He pauses and clears his throat. "Then when you won the award, I was so proud of you that I needed to congratulate you, but couldn't put into words how I felt, particularly in a text message. I was so excited to get your reply but felt the ice in your response and knew you wanted nothing to do with me." He chuckles sardonically. "That's when it hit me. I had thrown away the most important thing in my life because I hadn't felt worthy of your love and the future looked bleak without you. Nothing gave me enjoyment. I couldn't think straight, and I was just numb all over." His voice cracks, and he pauses, collecting his thoughts and bolstering his emotions.

My eyes well as I take in his heartfelt words. I feel honored that this proud, assertive, alpha male has bared his most vulnerable and fragile self to me. A side of himself that he would never have previously acknowledged. But if he is only telling me to unburden himself in the hope of returning to his normal status quo, I will be incredibly angry with him.

"After your persistent avoidance at the nightclub, I thought you were just being petulant and bitchy till it dawned on me that is not in your nature. Then I ran into your grandfather. Your name came up in conversation, and he invited me tonight. I accepted because I wanted the opportunity to tell you how I feel but wasn't prepared to acknowledge how much I had hurt you until your evasion tactics pushed you to the point of setting off a panic attack."

I scrutinize Xander's face, and I school my features into a neutrally composed mask before I respond.

"Why are you telling me this, Xander?" Cautiously, I ask, watching as his eyes fly to mine.

"Your words at the airport about fighting to rise above my fears have resonated within me every day. To use your words, I was trying to lose you but lost myself instead. Please forgive me, Georgina, for hurting you." Pausing, he beseeches, "I need you in my life."

"As what, Xander?" I retort, annoyed that he doesn't seem to care what I want or need. *Does he think he can waltz in here telling me how he feels and I will fall at his feet?* "A casual bedmate that you can walk away from whenever you feel like it? A business colleague that you only contact when you have a project you want me to work on? Someone to prop you up and make you feel good about yourself?" Pausing, I draw breath while my eyes throw sparks at him. Calming myself, I continue. "Have you ever considered what I might want, Xander?"

Xander blinks a few times and runs his hand through his hair. He looks like he is out of his depth, scrabbling to find an answer. Then his eyes lift to mine, their dark, stormy color holding me captive and emanating a sincerity and vulnerability I hadn't seen in him before. This is the raw Xander, with his shutters and masks removed. And it takes my breath away.

He grasps my hands in each of his. His voice is clear, as is his intent when he speaks. "Yes, I need you as my bedmate for however long you wish to be there, Georgina. Yes, I need you as a business colleague and advisor in every aspect of my life. Yes, I need to feel good about myself through the many ways I can cherish and honor you." Xander takes a deep breath, then continues, "I love you, Georgina, with all my heart, and I want to spend the rest of my life with you. Only you can make me feel whole. I hope you want the same, too, but if not, I hope you will consider life-long friendship, because I need you in my life, in whatever capacity you are comfortable with."

I can feel my eyes welling up with tears, and I rapidly blink them away as I look down at our joined hands. His heartfelt words douse the fire of my anger. Before I can speak, Xander adds in a hushed, anxious tone, "What is it you want, Georgina?"

"She's over here!"

Our quiet reverie is shattered by a raucous shout nearby. I spot my brother striding toward us. *Oh damn, not now, Luke*, I think, standing, frustrated by his interruption. Xander stands too, and turns toward the loud approaching voice, and I can feel his body tensing next to mine, ready to do battle to protect me.

"Are you okay, Gina?" Luke asks, although his volume has toned down somewhat as he approaches, looking concernedly between Xander and I.

"What's he doing here?" Luke bristles, his eyes narrowing and body tensing, as he recognizes Xander and glares daggers at him.

"I'm fine, Luke. Go back to the party. I don't need your help," I snap at him.

"Georgina had a panic attack, and we were just talking, Luke," Xander interjects. He extends his hand as a peacekeeping gesture, but it is ignored by Luke.

Luke and Xander stand glaring at each other, assessing the situation, when Gina's three other brothers run in to join them.

"Oh God," I groan. "The buffoon brigade is here," rebuking them, but they choose to ignore my comment.

"Who are you?" Tyler and Zack question suspiciously.

"What are you doing here?" Ryan queries protectively.

"Let me spell it out for you bunch of bozos. I. Do. Not. Need. Your. Help," I fume, my voice loud and dripping with acid. I struggle to calm myself, then soften my tone and assert, "Now go back to the party."

Four sets of eyes crawl over Xander who stands stoic and firm, unflinching under their scrutiny, before they flick to me, standing with my hands on my hips glaring at them like I am about to seriously injure them.

"I understand why you are angry with me," Xander jumps in to diffuse the tension, "but I have just pleaded with Georgina to forgive me for hurting her. And to let her know how much I love her and need her in my life."

"What did she say?" my brothers chorus, still on guard in case they need to run Xander off the premises. Although their eyes flash with respect for him manning up, apologizing, and admitting to his true feelings, their glares soften, with one or two nodding as they realize he seems to be doing the honorable thing.

"You frigging idiots interrupted before I could answer. Get out of here so I can talk to Xander," I spit, my furious tone making all their heads turn toward me, and my brothers' eyes round in wariness. They knew that scowling look on my face. It meant they have gone too far, and they are in big trouble if they hang around.

"Okayyy. We're going," they patronize me as they turn and walk off, bemoaning, "Sheesh, she's in a foul mood," as they go.

Luke hangs back for a moment and looks directly at Xander then nods amicably. "Good luck, man. Don't hurt her again, though." He glances at me and comments, "We're not far away if you need us." He then runs off and catches up with our brothers.

Xander watches the foursome as they near the marquee, but they stop and turn to keep an eye on us. Xander turns to me, noticing my body is held stiffly and I am exhaling loudly. "Are you okay, Little One?" When I nod, he hugs me tightly, and as he feels my body relax against his, he comments softly, "I am so in awe of you the way you talked those four down. Remind me not to mess with you."

I chuckle. "That comes from years of practice. They infuriate me the way they stick their noses into everything," I grumble. "You held yourself pretty well in the face of their aggression."

"Mm, I could empathize with them. I know how I feel when someone hurts you or Louisa. I just want to beat that person to a pulp."

I stand comfortably in his embrace and tilt my head back to peer adoringly into his dark, cautious eyes. My voice is soft and melodic as I confide, "In answer to your question, I wanted you to love me Xander, and now that you do, you are all I will ever need. I love you with all my heart..."

I don't get a chance to finish, as Xander's lips claim mine in a soft caress. His hands are on my cheeks, his thumbs gently stroking my cheekbones, his lips, and body pressing harder against me, as they are consumed by the rising heat. I can feel his love for me in that kiss and I reciprocate with everything I have, baring my heart and soul to him. Vaguely I hear a joyous whoop coming from the vicinity of where my brothers had been standing near the marquee.

In what seems no time at all, Xander breaks the spell by pulling away slightly and resting his forehead against mine. "I want to show you how much I love and cherish you, Georgina, but I can't do that here," he murmurs adoringly. "Let's go back to the party where I can hold you against me for the rest of the night."

"Sounds idyllic," I agree dreamily and saunter hand in hand with Xander across the moonlit expanse of lawn into the marquee.

Grandfather looks up as we enter, and my eyes meet his across the room. He gives me a small, knowing smile that holds pride, love, and happiness, then he nods his approval to me before resuming his hosting duties. My brothers also spot us and give us a thumbs up, still not game to come near me for the moment.

Xander is as good as his word and holds me against him for the remainder of the night. We dance and sit side by side but still with bodies touching or hands on the other's legs. I introduce Xander to my parents and Grandmother, as well as my brothers and their respective families.

"You hurt Gina again, mate, and you will have all of us to deal with." Tyler's face is serious, and his eyes hold Xander's in warning, as he voices what his brothers are thinking while shaking Xander's hand.

I groan and roll my eyes at him, while Xander nods and eyeballs Tyler, then comments, his tone respectful and sincere, "I wouldn't have it any other way."

I observe the look that passes between them, like some sort of bro-code, then Tyler gives a definite nod of affirmation before his expression lightens and he slaps Xander on the upper arm as if they were long-time friends, before moving away.

"What was that?" I scoff, perplexed, as I watch Tyler smooching up to his wife, then turn to Xander for clarification.

"Just blokes establishing boundaries over a mutually respected interest," he chuckles, then kisses me on the forehead. "I need some alone time with you, gorgeous. Let's get out of here," Xander whispers in my ear, and pulls me close, pressing me against the hard bulge in his pants.

"I know just the place," I chuckle adoringly as I lead him into the balmy night and toward the large main house, where I am staying the night.

CHAPTER 30 – Epilogue

Sitting on the deck of the tropical resort accommodation, in the still of the early morning, I watch as tiny ripples disturb the glass-like turquoise surface of the pool just beyond the deck, and the still quiet blue water of the outlying bay. My satiny robe is tied around my waist, my long hair is tussled and falls over my shoulders and my long smooth legs are stretched in front of me with ankles crossed as I recline on the outdoor sun bed.

My body is sore in all the right places from hours of love-making, and I feel sated and relaxed. Xander is still sleeping, exhausted from his athletic prowess and insatiable appetite of the previous evening, so I have quietly slipped out onto the deck to let him sleep.

I sip my juice, sigh at the serenity, and watch the wispy white clouds float across the pale blue sky and their mirrored reflections in the bay. *I am happier than I could ever have hoped for*, I smile dreamily. The last twelve months with Xander have been amazing, culminating in our large wedding two nights earlier at the hotel that had bought us together.

I look back on the events of the last year, which was hectic and has flown by. When Xander wasn't away on business, we had alternated between each other's places, spending a few nights at each, mainly because my business is based at my home. But as much as I love my apartment and friends, I particularly enjoyed the privacy that nights at Xander's apartment held. We could make as much noise as we liked without disturbing anyone or getting raised eyebrows from my flat mates the next morning. My libido was continuously aroused due to Xander's passionate hunger and there were times when quick lunchtime visits to his office resulted in me being bent over his desk or couch. Where he is concerned, I can never say no.

Like any new relationship, there had been stumbling blocks along the way, sometimes quite heated as we both stood our ground, but we had worked through them with honest communication, respect, and mutual admiration, as we will any future issues that arise. Eventually, we settled into a contented groove.

I smile to myself and twirl my engagement ring when I remember Xander's proposal. Robert's company had been nominated for an award for their architectural design on the hotel development, which meant Xander, Ethan, and myself sat at a table with Robert and some of his key staff at that very hotel. It was quite a prestigious international award, so the Black-Tie dress standard necessitated elaborate designer wear. I had chosen a long, slinky, shimmering, emerald-green, strappy dress with a long slit up one side for the occasion, and Xander wore his fitted black tuxedo. No matter how many times I see him in it, his stunning good looks and physique always take my breath away, and that night had been no exception.

I had barely been able to keep from undressing him and had run my hands over his strong thighs under the table, teasing him occasionally when my fingers rubbed against his crotch while he was talking to other people. My body fluttered, and I watched his nostrils flare with a sharp intake of breath, making me silently chuckle to myself knowing it was driving him wild, and that he was unable to do anything about it. The next time I moved my hand up his leg, he grabbed hold of it and placed it directly on his bulge, pressing my hand against it so I could feel the heat and rigid outline of his cock. I remember that he had been very aroused, and I was thrilled at the prospect of him pounding into me at the first opportunity.

Xander had returned my hand to my leg and, when the opportunity presented itself that both my hands were above the table and occupied, he slipped his hand under the slit in my dress and traced circles over my thigh, then dipped under my thong into my hot, wet crease. His shock invasion as I swallowed some wine had made me gasp, causing a coughing fit, which Xander found quite amusing if his wry smile was anything to go by. He extricated his hand and innocently patted me on the back as if he hadn't caused my discomfort.

Excitingly, Robert won the award, and Xander and Ethan joined his team on stage to collect it. On his return to the table, Xander grabbed my hand, insisting there was something outside he needed to show me, then escorted me to the elevator up to our room. Once inside the room and as the door shut, he hitched up my dress, then pressed me against the wall, holding me there with one hand on my chest while he unzipped his pants with the other and let them fall to the ground. He slid my thong aside and guided himself into my slick heat, then ravaged my mouth and wrapped my legs around his waist as he thrust into me.

We came in a frenzied rush, both breathing heavily. Temporarily sated, we both knew the carnal heat would be reignited later and we would enjoy the slow burn and loving caresses that we would lavish on each other.

After retreating to the bathroom to clean up, Xander led me out of the room and down to the foyer. Instead of turning into the ballroom corridor, he led me through some doors onto a balcony overlooking the beautiful garden that I had designed, which was lit with fairy lights and looked magical, with its large pond and fountain, the sound of the water as it gently splashed subduing the noise from the hotel. The garden and the cooling breeze were welcome against our heated bodies and felt like an oasis from the glitz and glamor of the awards. We stood silently next to each other, our bodies touching, while we leaned on the railing, watching the lights reflecting on the water like sparkling jewels.

Xander stood upright and took my hand in his, turning me to face him. He peered at my hands as he rubbed his thumbs over the back of them, as if deep in thought, then his adoring eyes met mine.

"Georgina." He paused. "My Little One." His big hand moved to brush against my cheek. "Every day, I am so very grateful that we met, and that you challenged me to be a better man. Every day I love you more and am saddened when I can't be with you. I want to be with you for the rest of my days." Xander searched in his jacket pocket and pulled out a small velvet box. Using both hands to open it, revealing a large, oval-cut diamond yellow-gold ring surrounded by glittering emeralds on two sides and smaller diamonds running down the band. His eyes softened and glowed with his love. "Will you marry me, Georgina?"

Without needing to think about my answer, I smiled adoringly up at him. "Yes, Xander. A million times, yes. It would be my greatest honor," I breathed huskily, tears welling in my eyes. Barely noticing the ring, I reached up and took his face in my hands, pulling his head down until our lips met in a long, loving kiss. He wrapped his arms around me tightly, like he was frightened of losing me.

"I love you so much, Gina. You fulfill me and I can't get enough of you," Xander whispered against my lips as he peered lovingly into my glistening eyes.

"I can't begin to describe how much I love you, Xander. I just know my life is not complete without you in it, and I never want to lose you. You are my everything." I took his lips again, sealing my words of love in an unspoken promise.

Xander stepped back, took my left hand, and then slid the ring onto my third finger. I was surprised that it fitted so well and said so.

Xander chuckled. "I tied some string around your finger while you were sleeping to make sure I had the right size."

"That was sneaky," I giggled. "The ring is exquisite and perfect, Xander. Thank you so much." My words were dreamy as I peered at the sparkling gems on my hand, wiggling my fingers to watch them twinkle and glitter.

He pulled me against him and rested his chin on my head, content just to have me in his arms. "I chose the emeralds because they remind me of your eyes that sparkle with your love for me when you look at me."

His softly uttered words caused my heart to swell with love at his thoughtfulness. *He may not always say the words 'I love you', but his actions screamed them, instead,* I considered as I hugged him tighter.

"Are you okay to head back inside now, my darling? Unfortunately, we do need to return to the ceremony," Xander apologized.

"As long as I am with you, Xander, I'm happy," I beamed.

Ethan eyed us on our return, raising his eyebrows when we approached the table with Xander's arm wrapped around me. "You took your sweet time, brother. You nearly missed the finale," he commented, disgruntledly.

"We've had our finale, Ethan," I beamed as I extended my hand for him to inspect the ring on my finger.

Ethan looked at the ring and a huge grin split his face. He drew me in for a congratulatory hug, then turned to Xander and shook his hand, pulling him in for a tight hug and a slap on the back as he said, "About time, bro. You couldn't have chosen anyone better for you."

Sipping my juice again, and resting my head against the sun lounge, I recollected the whirlwind of arrangements that came after that night. Six months to arrange a large wedding was a stretch, but with Xander's extravagant budget and my mum's superb organization skills and the assistance of Tash, Emily, and Ally, we pulled it off.

The venue had been the gardens and ballroom of the hotel that had bought us together, and where Xander had proposed. Xander and I arrived the night before, checking into a suite so the early morning preparations for the bride could get underway. Xander had left early in the morning, and not long after Simone, Emily and Tash arrived, along with the photographer, to ensure I was relaxed and perfect for my big day. My mom and dad arrived just as my hair was being finished to see me into my ivory-colored wedding dress. It was a deceptively simple tulle and jeweled lace ballgown style with sheer sleeves, a scalloped neckline, and a fitted bodice that flared from the hips into a softly draping tulle full skirt. The train was small, and the illusion back had a zipper and buttons that ran down over the buttocks. My long hair had been tucked into a soft, low bun at the nape of my neck and trimmed with flowers.

I had looked up at my parents to see them both with tears welling in their wide eyes, my mom's hand splaying over her heart as if trying to stop her swelling pride and love from escaping. My dad was speechless but managed to utter, "My baby girl," as he wiped his eyes, his voice breaking, and chin wiggling, trying to contain his tears of joy.

The garden ceremony was an intimate affair with family and close friends, Tash as my bridesmaid and Ethan as a groomsman. My stomach flip-flopped again as I remembered how the sight of Xander took my breath away as my father walked me down the path toward my soon-to-be husband. He had looked stunning in his dark gray suit and pristine white shirt, but it wasn't just the suit. It was his mesmerized look; a mix of awe, pride, and lust, but most of all, his adoration and love that I will remember forever. I had taken a deep breath and controlled my steps, so I didn't run straight into his arms.

The reception was glamorous and lavish, with two hundred friends, extended family, and business associates who were already partying when we arrived as husband and wife. The food and wine were sumptuous, and the ballroom was jaw-dropping with decorations and floral displays, quite different from the blank canvas when mum and I had originally made the arrangements.

Our wedding was also the first time I had met Xander's father and his wife, Mariella who had seemed familiar to me. Then I remembered seeing her as the blond bombshell in a restaurant with Xander all those months ago. Xander's two half-brothers were also in attendance, but kept pretty much to themselves throughout the festivities.

Xander's mum and Jonathan also attended, arriving a week before the wedding, this time staying with Ethan. At my suggestion, Xander talked at length to his mum during that time about how he had felt when she left his father. He found out that there were stipulations in their separation that meant she wasn't able to see Xander outside of school holidays and it cleared a good portion of his emotional baggage. Reflecting on the situation as a wealthy businessman himself, he could intellectualize why his father had made those stipulations, but the hurt young inner child still occasionally struggled with the feeling of abandonment.

Xander and I had barely left each other's side all evening and were itching for some alone time so, as soon as we possibly could after the formalities, had made our escape to Xander's apartment; my new home now.

I chuckle as I remember our reasoning for returning to Xander's apartment for the night instead of staying in the room I had booked in the hotel. I hadn't trusted my fun-loving brothers to not play a prank on us on our wedding night, so opted for the apartment where lots of building security would prevent any antics from interrupting our special night.

My hunch had been correct when Mom informed me the next afternoon that my brothers, in their drunken revelry, had barged into our hotel room, not knowing that our parents were using the room for the night instead. Needless to say, the boys have a lot of making amends ahead of them and won't live that situation down for a long while, if I can help it.

"What are you chuckling about, my love?" Xander wraps his arms around me and captures my lips with a long, loving good-morning kiss. His voice is still husky from sleep, his tall, supple naked body stirring the smoldering embers of craving in my belly, as he snuggles onto the sun lounge next to me, spooning against me, his ramrod stiff erection prodding between the top of my thighs, insisting on entry while warm hands slip under my robe to fondle my breast. "I missed you in our bed." He nuzzles my neck and my body turned to molten liquid.

"I was just laughing at my brothers' embarrassment when they walked in on Mom and Dad," I husk my explanation.

"Mmmm. All I can think about is my beautiful, deliciously sexy wife, and how many ways I can make her moan." His lips trail over my shoulder and up behind my ear as his hands stroke and caress my body, sliding my robe aside. I do moan and feel his smile against my jaw as he lifts my leg up over his, opening me up to him. I turn my head toward him, gasping into his mouth as Xander claims my mouth and plunges into my body. I love this man with every fiber of my being.

THE END

Keep Reading

Thank you so much for reading and your ongoing support.

Keep reading for an exclusive preview of the next two chapters of my next book

Built for Pleasure.

PREVIEW – Built for Pleasure

CHAPTER 1

It has been another busy night at the restaurant and my feet and legs hurt from all the table I have done. Only half hour before I finish and I know I will be flopping on the bed as soon as I get home.

"Hey Em, can you take table twelve's order, please? I am busting to go to the loo," Marguerite asks as she hurries past me in the direction of the toilets. In the early stages of pregnancy, she has been struggling to hold her bladder for a while now.

"Sure. No problem." The wait staff have designated areas and tables but can often assist in other areas when the need arises, like now. A quick look around my area assures me that my patrons are all ok for now but some are close to needing plates removed.

Grabbing my ordering device, I turn toward table twelve and notice an attractive well-dressed redhead seated there, facing me, with an equally smartly attired male opposite her, with his back toward me. Strolling over to them, I admire the breadth of the man's shoulders and how his expertly tailored suit jacket hugs his lean physique. His light brown hair is neatly trimmed around his neck and he wears an air of affluence. The woman's olive green linen sleeveless dress complements her coloring and beautifully accents her trim curvy figure. Another beautiful couple enjoying the high life. Sighing, I hope that I will be bought here on a date one day. But as I have no romantic interest in my life, I will have to stick with sampling the food in the kitchen.

As I come alongside their table, they can't take their eyes off each other. I smile, guessing where their night will end as they both seem hungry but not for food.

"Can I take your order?" I glance smilingly from the lady to the man. Ethan! Oh God, not him, not here.

"Emily? Hi, how are you?" My smile slips momentarily as Ethan recognizes me. He looks just as good as the last time I saw him, and I am reminded not only that I used to think of him as a friend , but that I have a job to do. I feel the awkwardness of this situation for each of us, so quickly put on my waitress smile again; courteous, impersonal and no time for idle chit-chat.

"I'm well thanks, Ethan. What would you like to order." I ask smilingly as I turn back to the stunning redhead, who seems annoyed at being interrupted, although Ethan seems pleased to see me. I take my time tapping in the order, asking the woman questions on accompaniments for her meal, trying to compose myself before I have to speak to Ethan again.

"Ethan, what would you like?"

I notice a glint in his eyes and a twitch in his lips as he holds eye contact with me. His cheekiness and fun sense of humor were some of the things I liked about him and that doesn't seem to have changed. However, flirting with me while on a date with another woman is not something I can condone. I tighten my smile and raise an eyebrow as I wait silently for his order.

"I'll have oysters to start please," as he grins and winks at his date, "and the eye fillet steak with mushroom sauce please Emily." I tap in his request, then glance between them again. "Will that be all?" They both nod so I throw a fake smile at them as I gather up the menus.

"Thank you. Your meals shouldn't be long. Enjoy your evening." Hastily I walk to the central counter to process their order.

Marguerite arrives back from the restroom just as I am finishing, and I give her a rundown on their selection.

"Oh, and if he asks anything about me, just tell him you don't know me very well," I add.

"What do you mean?" She probes, her beautiful features shaped in a quizzical expression. We have become good friends since I started working here three months ago. On several occasions, I have seen her deliberately thicken her faint French accent to pretend a language barrier, particularly when men are trying to come on to her. She is tall and shapely with lightly tanned coloring and long black hair and is very happily married.

"We dated a few times back home, just over a year ago. I thought we were really getting along well, then he stopped contacting me without any explanation. It was always very awkward after that because his brother married one of my best friends." After a pause, I chuckle. "I doubt he will but if he asks about me, just put on your beautiful French accent and pretend you don't understand."

"Okay." she giggles as an impish gleam lights her dark brown eyes. "I like your thinking."

We chuckle as we carry out table-clearing duties at either end of the restaurant. As much as I try not to, my glance returns to table twelve far too many times for my liking. Ethan. He has everything I ever wanted in a man. Compassion, good looks, intelligence, a great sense of humor, loyalty and generosity, and a caring heart. I thought I was falling for him, till he stopped answering my texts, and blocked my calls. Sadly, he mustn't have felt the same way about me. Which hurt. Particularly as he was the first man I dated, and trusted, after a messy breakup.

My gaze frequently returns to their table and the way tonight's date seems to be going, dinner was part of their foreplay. There had been lots of hand-touching, laughter, and foot knocking and flirting so it would be no surprise if bed is where they ended up tonight. Humph. He never did any of that with me on our dates, the annoying thought flits through my head. Funny that his date has similar coloring to me. I wonder if redheads are his type. Hmm. That might explain his initial interest in me a year ago, but I obviously didn't beguile him with flirtatious and smart repartee, like his date tonight. I realized a long time ago that I don't need a self assured, opinionated, and impatient prick like him in my life.

While Marguerite had served table twelve's meals, I continue to painstakingly wipe down the tables and busy myself in the kitchen, all the while reminding myself that I am a much stronger, more confident woman now than I was then. In the aftermath of my ex's emotional gameplaying and caring for a sickly mother, I didn't have a lot of liveliness, confidence or broad life experience during the short period Ethan and I dated. Thanks to my close supportive girl friends and some counselling I am more comfortable in my own skin, and am not afraid to assert myself when needed and am finally enjoying life.

I loiter in the kitchen waiting for another tables' meals and when they are ready I realize I have to walk past Ethan again. Groaning, but straightening my back, I sail straight past Ethan as if he is just another customer. I take the opportunity to straighten cutlery on tables as I pass him again, so I don't have to look at him. The crowd in the restaurant has thinned, so I spend more time wiping down tables as far away from Ethan as I can. Not that they needed it, but I couldn't stand hiding in the kitchen any longer, and it was just as difficult to be in the same room as him. I don't hate him, but I don't like him very much either. My friend Georgie doesn't talk about him much, because she knows how hurt I was at his rejection. I was pretty fragile back then, but in a way he did me a favor, because I wouldn't have felt the need to escape and explore the world, bolstering my self-esteem along the way. Having done as much as I possibly can in the front of house area, I head back into the kitchen.

Knowing my reluctance to go near Ethan's table, Marguerite clears their plates, then tallies up the bill when they decline dessert. No doubt eager to feast on each other's sweet treats in private.

Afterward Marguerite pulls me aside in the kitchen, just as eager to tell me what has transpired at Ethan's table, as I am to hear it.

"Emily, he is delicious. He said he thought you would come back with the food, then asked me to tell you that Gina and Xander say hi and they miss you." She chuckles. "He still seems interested in what you are up to."

"What makes you think that?" I feel my forehead scrunch in confusion, as I try to work out her reasoning. I am sure she is teasing me, but know she is trying to make me feel better about stumbling across someone who has hurt me.

"Oh, just the way he turned to look for you, but then re-membered the other girl across the table from him. He played it cool as if he knew you were working here all along."

Chuckling, I shake my head. "Oh come on Marguerite. That doesn't mean he is interested in me. Just that he is intrigued by how I could pop up on the other side of the world. You are such a romantic and your pregnancy hormones amplify it." I give her a hug as we both laugh at her teasing and, as my shift has ended, I say goodnight. Donning my coat and scarf, I call out goodnight to Johan, the chef and Marguerite's husband, before making my way out the back door as normal.

As it is ten o'clock at night, it is quite cold and I am pleased I have my thick warm coat with me. Pulling my hood up over my head, I tuck my hands into my pockets to make the brisk walk to my apartment. Despite it being late and cold, I am surprised as I turn the corner by the number of people still out and about. I haven't got used to how freezing or how busy London is yet. Although I miss the warmer climate of Sydney, I am very glad that I decided to take a twelve month working holiday in the Northern Hemisphere. A change of scenery is just what I had needed. I have only taken a few steps onto the main street when I have to step aside for a group of six or seven people rowdily walking past. When they have moved on, I spot Ethan at the curb with the redhead. They are facing each other, oblivious to their surroundings as he pulls her coat collar upright to shield her from the cold, then pulls her in for a kiss. I heave out a sigh and pull my scarf up over my nose and mouth and pull my hood further forward, then walk briskly past, huddling into my coat as I hold it tightly around me. I hope he doesn't recognize me but then I reason that there are also many people wearing overcoats similar to mine my anonymity is safe. Then I chide myself that Ethan is too pre-occupied to be aware of anything.

On the short walk home, I reflect on how fortunate I was to find this job with Marguerite and Johan on my arrival two months ago. My hospitality experience years ago while at Uni came in handy for this position. It has allowed me to save some funds to travel, although so far I have only been taking short trips in the outlying regions of the city. Some of the other restaurant staff are also backpackers, so I have had travel companions when venturing. In some regards, I have it a bit easier than most backpackers, because I am staying at a centrally located apartment owned by my friend Simone. As she is an airline flight attendant, she uses it as a base for her long international flight layovers. Realistically, Simone only uses the apartment for approximately two weeks a month, broken into stints of four or five days at a time.

Seeing Ethan tonight makes me revisit how tumultuous the last year and a bit has been, and how much I have evolved as a result. My heart has been battered, bruised, and shattered, and feels like it is encased in ice most days. But I have learned to survive through it all and am now a more resilient self-sufficient person. The loss of my mother hit hardest though and my already broken heart has struggled to recover since then. I still enjoy life and friends and am mostly happy, finding joy in the simple pleasures of life. But my heart yearns for someone to love, and to love me; to make me feel complete. One day I will find that person.

I let myself into to the apartment and shake off my maudlin thoughts like I shake off the cold. I have already eaten at the restaurant, and Simone is away, so I crank up the heating and hop into a hot shower. Sitting on the lounge with a cup of tea and the TV playing quietly in the background, I check my phone, and notice I have a message about some Nanny work in two days. Quickly I accept the job and then send a message to my friend Georgina, Ethan's sister-in-law.

> **Emily: Hi Georgie. You'll never guess who came into the restaurant tonight? Ethan! I didn't realize he was there until I served him and his very sexy date, so we were both surprised to see each other. How long has he been back in London?**

> **Georgie:** Wow. That must have been awkward. What did you do / say? He's been back in London full time for about four or five months now. Xander is going over next week, so I've asked him to check in with you.

I didn't expect an answer so fast but remembered it was early morning in Sydney and Georgie always started early.

338

Emily: Oh, great. I'd love to catch up with Xander. Ethan didn't say much. Couldn't really because his date seemed peeved that he recognized me. Other than take his order, I didn't have much to do with him, because I hid in the kitchen and at the other end of the restaurant. *smiley face emoji*.

Georgie: That's understandable. Gotta go, Lovely. I'll be in touch with details of Xander's itinerary. Take care of you. Xx

Emily: Will do Gorgeous.

Yawning, I hop up and pack a few things into a backpack in preparation for a day trip tomorrow with Rashida and Lorenzo to Windsor Castle, which we have been excitedly anticipating for the last week. A few hours at the castle is not enough to do it justice, but we try to see as many sights as possible on our days off, with the intention of going back to explore further if we find a place we particularly like.

My excitement for tomorrow's adventure is dampened though by buried emotions and memories that resurface which I know I need to assess before I will be able to sleep. The hurt and bitterness of Ethan's rejection still stings. I had considered him a friend, and really admired him, so his abandonment with no explanation after a good night kiss had further eroded my fragile self esteem. At the time I felt like I hadn't been a good enough kisser or potential lover for him to pursue me further, but soon realized I was better off without him. My new found self-respect (and some good solid advice from my gal pals) chided that, if he couldn't respect me by telling me he didn't want to see me anymore, then he didn't deserve me. Treating it as another life lesson, I had got on with the ups and downs of life.

I remembered Marguerite's comment tonight about Ethan seemingly still interested in me that I had laughingly brushed aside. Finding it hard to believe, I rationalize that it was just his curiosity that had been piqued, as it often was when you see an old school friend whom you haven't seen in years. A five minute conversation is all it takes to slake the curiosity for another decade.

How do I feel about Ethan after seeing him? The words of Gotye's song spring to mind ... "Someone that I used to know." Yes that felt right, and I assume that Ethan would not give me another thought, and if he did it would only be a passing comment to Georgie or Xander that he had seen me.

Feeling settled now, I amble off to bed, mentally checking off things I need to do in the morning before departing on our trip. Sleep eludes me for a while as I toss and turn, and my tired legs become restless as they often do after a busy night.

PREVIEW - Built for Pleasure

CHAPTER 2

Damn! My alarm didn't go off and now I have half an hour before I have to meet up with Rashida and Lorenzo. Frantically, I throw on some tights under my jeans for warmth and several layers of tops. The I put some bread in the toaster to cook while I rush around and throw my scarf and coat, hat, sunscreen and water bottle into my backpack, as well as the power bank for my phone. Grabbing, the toast, I munch on it as I run out, slamming the door behind me. I could probably catch a cab to our pick up spot, but decide to power walk instead, figuring it will most likely be faster than the cab. I message Rashida on the way, knowing that she will buy a coffee before the journey, and ask her to get me on as well. I very much need a heart starter today after my restless night.

I make it to the departure point just as the bus pulls up to the curb and welcome the coffee Rashida hands me. She is always early, like I usually am too, and raises a dark eyebrow at me.

"What time do you call this? You only just made it in time Emily." Her voice and expression are irritated, but I know she won't stay that way for long, because her good natured happy personality and zest for life usually returns quickly. She is an organizer, naturally neat, punctual, ordered and efficient. She is also very beautiful, intelligent and exotic.

"Yes, I know." I puff trying to catch my breath. "My alarm didn't go off. Thank you for the coffee. I'll buy you the next one." Her long black ponytail sways as she nods her head, then looks around for Lorenzo.

There are quite a few people waiting, but it doesn't take long before we pay and board the bus, each sitting in a double seat, so we can reserve one for Lorenzo, who comes bounding on behind us and flops next to Rashida in front of me.

"What time do you call this? You only just made it in time Lorenzo." I mimic Rashida, nudging her and we both laugh.

"You weren't at the hostel this morning, so I didn't think you would make it," Rashida added.

"Okay. Stop nagging me, both of you." His brow creases into a frown as he continues awkwardly, his Italian accent lilting, "I hooked up with someone, okay, and they were on the other side of town."

"Why does that not surprise me?" I shake my head, chuckling. Lorenzo is a good-looking man, fit, beautiful dark eyes and long lashes and dark curly hair that curls over his forehead and ears. He has this boy next door appearance when dressed casually like he is today, but when dressed in his black trousers and white shirt as a barman or waiter, with his hair slicked back off his face, he is stunning.

Soon after, the bus takes off and the driver introduces himself as the guide. He begins pointing out sights and points of interest as we make our way out of the city, our heads swiveling to take in as much as we can, absorbed in the history and beauty outside the windows.

Despite all the photos we had seen, the breathtaking splendor of the majestic stone castle sitting on the highest point in its vicinity is indescribable. The driver pulls over momentarily and all we could hear on the bus were exclamations of "Oh Wow," "Amazing," "Magnificent," as everyone jockeys for position to photograph the stunning view and lush green tree lined avenue.

Continuing further up the road and stopping at the drop off point, I am in awe and speechless as I alight from the bus. The weight of history surrounds and engulfs me as I twirl on the spot, not knowing where to look first, and I notice Lorenzo and Rashida slightly ahead of me, looking just as amazed.

This is what I came to the United Kingdom for. To experience the wonders of the past centuries, painstakingly preserved for future generations. I wanted this to be the trip of a lifetime, and so far, I have not been disappointed. I hadn't realized what a fascination I have with historic architecture until I came to this part of the world steeped in antiquity and tradition.

Enthralled and overjoyed, I run up to my wonderful friends and give them a hug. Standing between them, I crook both arms, resting my hands on my hips, and in an exaggerated posh English accent and ask, "Would m'lord and m'lady care to accompany me on a stroll to the Round Tower?" Lorenzo plays along and gives me a mock bow before hooking his arm through mine, while Rashida dips in a mock curtsy and hooks her arm through mine too. Laughingly we stroll up the slight incline to begin our exploration, along with a bevy of other tourists.

As we follow a guided tour around the interior of the castle, we take turns posing for photos in various rooms and taking selfies of the three of us. We stand in a huge vestibule, mouths gaping as we look up at the massive ornate vaulted ceiling. No matter how we try, we can't manage to get a photo of the three of us with the huge ceiling in the shot as well. Rashida and I are looking at her phone and laughing at some of the botched photos that will need to be deleted when Lorenzo stands behind us.

"I think you two beauties have some admirers," he whispers in our ears.

Then a tall good looking American man with dark hair and a close shaven beard, probably in his late twenties, approaches.

"Hi. Would you like me to take the photo of all of you?" he offers. We had noticed he and another fellow with sandy blond hair and a stubble shadow along his jaw, who seemed of similar age, tagging along with the guided tour as well, and at one point Rashida and I had glanced at each other, raised our eyebrows and gave a slight nod of our heads in admiration of the men, and their toned physiques.

"Yes of course. Thank you so much," I gush and hand my phone over to him. He takes the photo with Lorenzo between Rashida and I, then after a moment he hands my phone back to me. Sneakily he has put his phone number into my phone as well. I look up at him and cock an eyebrow.

"That was a bit forward of you Tom." He looks a bit sheepish but throws me a lopsided smile while Rashida looks over my shoulder to see what I am talking about.

"I couldn't pass up the opportunity to give my number to such a beautiful woman as yourself."

"Smooth. Very smooth Tom," I reply, my lips tight but curling up in the corners as I try to hold back a grin. I can feel my face heating with a blush and curse my pale freckled skin. Rashida giggles next to me and Lorenzo tuts as if in disgust at my reaction.

"This is my friend, Aaron." He points over his shoulder with his thumb and Aaron nods in acknowledgement.

"Hi. You guys don't sound English. Where are you from?" Aaron enquires as he looks to each of us in turn.

"I'm Emily, and I'm from Australia. This is Rashida and she is from Egypt, while Lorenzo here is from Italy." They both respond with a "Hi."

"What about you two? You both American?" I smile enquiringly, looking from one to the other.

Tom laughs, and Aaron groans "God, no," although he sounds like he has an American accent. At my look of confusion he clarifies, "Thankfully, I'm Canadian."

"Ahh, I've heard about your cross-border rivalry," I chuckle.

"Are you guys here on holiday or for work?" Lorenzo joins the conversation, and I am surprised that Rashida has remained quiet. I watch her as I listen to Tom, Aaron and Lorenzo converse about their holiday plans, and note that her eyes haven't left Aaron, but she lowers them shyly when he looks directly at her and smiles. Wow, the confident outgoing woman I know seems star struck and speechless. I never thought I would see the day that Rashida, a proficient conversationalist, would have nothing to say. I nudge her gently on the arm and tilt my chin toward the tour group who are disappearing out a distant archway.

"We're going to catch up with the tour group, if you want to join us," I offer, but suspect they would have come along regardless.

Tom and Aaron join us for the rest of the day, and Rashida opens up more as she feels more comfortable. We learn that they are also backpacking around but have only just started their holiday, so we are able to provide them with tips on places to visit, transportation and pitfalls. They are staying at a different hostel to Lorenzo and Rashida, but not far away from them. We explain that we have all picked up jobs to help fund our stay and travels, so don't have a lot of free time. Tom and Aaron's tour bus leaves earlier than ours so as we say goodbye, the men exchange phone numbers so we can catch up at another time.

So many sights! I am suffering from visual overload as we clamber back on the bus two hours later and flop into our seats. My phone battery died half way through the day from all the photos I have been taking, so I am pleased that I had the foresight to bring along my power bank to recharge it, as well as Lorenzo's phone. The ever pragmatic and organized Rashida purchased several books with superb photos from the souvenir shop, saying she was more likely to look through those than thousands of photos on her phone. We have laughed, frolicked and walked, rarely sitting down the entire time. No wonder my feet, legs and back ache. It is a much quieter trip back to the city as all the passengers have exhausted themselves exploring the magnificent stateliness of the Castle, with some, including me nodding off.

When the bus pulls back into the depot I groan as I stand and follow my friends out. Spotting a nearby café, we call in for some dinner. As backpackers, we tend to be careful with our money, so each of us orders different pasta options, the cheapest selection on the menu, and we share a bottle of wine.

"This pasta is not great. Much better at home." Lorenzo complains but still scoffs his meal, while Rashida and I roll our eyes. We hear this same complaint every time we have pasta, which is practically every other night.

"You are such a pasta snob Lorenzo," Rashida laughs.

"You will have to come to my home to experience authentic Italian pasta for yourselves. Then you will appreciate why I grumble about pasta over here." Lorenzo casts an impish glance at us as he forks another mouthful of the delicious Bolognese into his mouth, then looks around the room before dropping his gaze again to his plate.

"When we are in Italy, we will expect you to show us this authentic pasta and all the wonderful sights you tell us about, Lorenzo. How much longer before we can go to Italy?" I enquire enthusiastically, calculating that it will be at least another month before I can afford the train fares and spending money.

After a few mouthfuls Rashida pipes ups "Oh, don't forget about the cocktail party at the Art Gallery tomorrow night."

Lorenzo and I look at each other. "Yes, we know. It is very important that we don't let your boss down," we repeat Rashida's words that we have heard many times.

"The agency has it all sorted, so it will be fine," I comment, hoping to appease her anxiousness. "Do we have to treat you like one of your swanky VIP guests?" My comment is tongue in cheek and has the desired effect of making her smile.

"Of course. I'll be the most important person there," she mocks back, her nose tilted in the air and waving her hand in the air like royalty. We all laugh and enjoy the camaraderie while we finish our meal. Since meeting Rashida four months ago, there has always been an air of affluence about her so the fact that she often works in the art gallery doesn't surprise me. It seems to fit with her well educated personality. She will be hostess at tomorrow night's function and not waitressing as would normally be the case and I get the feeling she will enjoy hobnobbing with the gallery's wealthy clientele.

"Well, I have an early start in the morning for a Nanny job for a couple of hours, and I am bushed after all today's walking. Otherwise, I would ask you back to my place," I explain as I stand not long after. "Do you want to share an Uber?"

They both nod and stand as well. Knowing that my place is on the way to their hostel, Lorenzo hands over some cash and pulls out his phone to arrange the rideshare while Rashida and I pay for our meals, then we wait out front for the driver. Fortunately, we don't have long to wait, and the drive back to my apartment is quick.

Yawning as I walk into my apartment, I reflect how different my holiday would be if I hadn't met Rashida and Lorenzo in a Paris backpackers lodge when I first started my odyssey. I probably would have gone back home by now if it wasn't for them. We had soon become firm friends, seeing some of the highlights of Paris together, and when I mentioned my next stop was London they decided to join me. Not long after arriving we joined a temporary employment agency, picking up odd jobs to earn some travel money, which is also how I met Marguerite and Johan.

Simone is due in tomorrow, so I rush around tidying up before turning in for the night. My phone beeps as I am about to turn out the light, so I quickly pick up and read the message.

Lorenzo: Guess what? Tom and Aaron are staying at our hostel. Looks like you girls will get to see more of your cute American and Canadian *smiley face emoji*

As I drift off to sleep, I feel blessed to have met my wonderful friends, who are like siblings I never had, and wonder where things will lead with Tom.

About the Author

Kerrie Maxon has been a lover of romance novels since she was a teenager. She has thought about writing a book for many years, jotting down ideas in several notebooks and phone apps without really doing anything about it because life got in the way. However, after breaking an ankle while on holiday in 2022, she decided to make the most of her idle time by finally getting her ideas into some sort of cohesive outline. One chapter led to many and finally became a completed novel.

Now, Kerrie is a contemporary romance author living in the beautiful south coast of New South Wales with her husband and cat. Her family consists of two daughters and three step-kids, their spouses and seven grandchildren, all of whom keep her busy. Kerrie has worked in office administration all her working life, often proofreading others' works and reports, so words are her passion.

Thank you for reading Built For Sin. I hope you enjoyed Xander and Gina's story.

Keep an eye out for follow ups **Built for Pleasure** and **Built for Love**.

Stay up to date on upcoming books, visit Kerrie at:

www.kerriemaxonauthor.com.au
admin@kerriemaxonauthor.com
Facebook: Kerrie Maxon Author
Instagram: #kerriemaxonauthor
TikTok: @Kerrie_Maxon_Author